OTHER BOOKS BY ROBERT L. SKIDMORE:

The Satterfield Saga

    If Genes Could Talk

    Yankee Doodles in Black Hats

    Point of Rocks

    The Drums, the Fog, The Terrible Shadows of War

    Did You Lose Your Elephant?

    The Ball Breaker

    The Sorry World

Inspector Richard Thatcher

    The City of Lost Dreams

    Cluster of Spies

GREEN EYES, RED SKIES,
PALE ALES, WHITE SAILS

GREEN EYES, RED SKIES,
PALE ALES, WHITE SAILS

VOLUME III

THE SATTERFIELD SAGA

THE STORY GENES WOULD TELL IF THEY COULD ONLY TALK

Robert L. Skidmore

IndyPublish

GREEN EYES, RED SKIES, PALE ALES, WHITE SAILS

VOLUME THREE OF THE SATTERFIELD SAGA

Copyright © 2001 by Robert L. Skidmore

Published in the United States by IndyPublish.com
McLean, Virginia

ISBN 1-58827-004-1 paperback
ISBN 1-58827-013-0 hard cover
ISBN 1-58827-010-6 Gemstar e-book

Dedication

For Margaret and Tad,
to whom I owe everything good in my life.

ALEXANDRIA, VIRGINIA

FEBRUARY 1801

James Satterfield sat in his grandfather's chair and rocked quietly while he stared at the roaring fire with unseeing eyes. On his lap he held a polished mahogany case that he distractedly caressed with a thumb as he teetered and worried. Inside the beautiful case, two matched dueling pistols nestled in their rich, purple velvet nests.

The howl of the cold, western wind caught James' attention. He paused and glanced through the dull window at the gloom of the dark February morning. He checked his gold pocket watch.

Six forty-five.

Fifteen minutes before dawn on February 18th, 1801.

When James was young, he had not carried a watch. Exact time had meant nothing to him then, but now, in the sixty-seventh year of his life, he was very conscious of time. To his dismay, he frequently caught himself consulting his gold timepiece. He regretted having purchased the watch. Its mechanism marked the irrevocable passage of his life, second by persistent second. The creak of movement in the room over his head kept James from escaping into the diversionary contemplation of the inevitable creep of time. He rocked and fingered the smooth wood of the case.

The dueling pistols, which had originally meant so little to him, now ranked high among his most cherished possessions. His lifelong friend George Washington had presented them to James at the end of the war, symbols of appreciation for James' long service as Washington's chief of secret intelligence. At the time, James had wondered why Washington had given him dueling pistols. James had recognized that they were a matched set, expensive, and tooled by an expert craftsman, but he had been a civilian throughout the Revolution and had deliberately eschewed the use of weapons. Unlike his twin brother John, James had never taken a single human life. He had treasured two gifts from his brother, a crude Indian tomahawk and a hunting knife with the initials "JS" carved on the hilt, and he had displayed them prominently on his desk. The tomahawk and knife had personal significance to him; they were not symbols of a warlike nature, and James assumed Washington knew that when he had presented the pistols to James.

"These small tokens symbolize my appreciation for your long and selfless service to our fledgling country. Few know now or will ever know the extent of your contribution, but I do. You have my eternal appreciation and thanks."

Washington's words when he had presented James the pistols had moved both men to tears.

Now, James was an old man, and Washington was dead. Washington had died quietly on December 14th, 1799; and their mutual friend George Mason had succumbed seven years earlier. Their deaths marked the passage of a generation, the men of the Revolution. New footsteps now marched along the paths of responsibility. The government that Mason and Washington and James had fought to create now controlled their destinies. Tom Jefferson, now fifty-eight, no longer young, would take the oath of office of President of these United States in less than two weeks. "Young" Tom had drafted the Declaration of Independence, but he had not fought in the Revolution. In fact, he had not distinguished himself as Governor of Virginia during the war; many of his enemies accused him of cowardice for his flight before the invading English army; James did not know if this were true or not, but Jefferson symbolized the next generation who were taking over from the revolutionists.

The thought of Jefferson brought James back to his current predicament. Jefferson's election had provoked this morning's duel. Determined to be honest with himself, James corrected his thought. James' emotional reaction to the election had produced this rash consequence. He now recognized this simple fact. James did not object to Jefferson becoming president, eventually; Jefferson after all was an old political colleague and friend; the problem arose because James thought it was still too soon. Jefferson had some strange ideas that needed to mature, and the new government still required time to evolve before undergoing the kind of internal convolution that a man with Jefferson's views would stimulate.

"Old man," James' wife Vivian interrupted his reverie. "Sitting there stewing is not going to make the problem go away. Have you checked the pistols?"

"They're ready. I've checked them three times."

"Then come and have some toast and tea," Vivian ordered.

"I don't want any toast or tea."

"What do you want?"

"I want ... to sit here."

James did not know what else to say to Vivian. She undoubtedly knew what he was thinking. She always did. James assumed that almost fifty years of marriage had given her that insight. James was more worried about the duel than Vivian; that fact should not have surprised him, but it did. Vivian had always been the strong one in the marriage. She was an independent woman who had managed Eastwind, her family's plantation after her father died. She and James had had an unusual life marked by Vivian's absences during the planting and harvesting seasons, by James' four year sojourn with Washington during the war and by his subsequent devotion to politics and the *Herald*.

"Don't worry," Vivian reassured James. "They'll probably apologize and not fire a shot. That's the way most of these things turn out."

James nodded his head. He could not think of a thing to say that would not make Vivian worry more than she was despite her bravado.

"Grandparents are supposed to be past this kind of silliness," James finally observed.

"You don't expect Jason to be involved, do you?"

James recognized that Vivian was trying to provoke an old argument to distract him from his worry. Both knew that if their son Jason were involved, it would be in support of the other side.

The front door opened abruptly, and their grandson, Jason's son Buster, entered.

"Gramps, Vivian, good morning."

Vivian refused to be addressed as "Grandma" and insisted that her grandson use her first name as his father Jason did.

James grunted acknowledgment of Buster's arrival and studied his grandson intently as he did frequently. James had difficulty accepting the startling fact that Buster at twenty-five was the mirror image of James at the same age when he had married Vivian. Nobody could question that Buster carried the Satterfield genes; he had the sandy hair, handsome face with the straight nose and square chin, and stocky, muscular body on a six-foot frame. Buster had the large hands that had made the Satterfield males competent blacksmiths and the penetrating eyes that revealed an incisive intelligence. James had to admit to himself that Buster's clear, crystalline green eyes were those of James' identical twin brother John. James' eyes were a soft hazel; everyone commented on Buster's resemblance to James--"he's the very image of his grandfather," friends were prone to say—but James, Vivian and members of the Satterfield clan knew the difference; Buster was the image of his grand uncle John, his grandfather's twin, but few remained in Alexandria who were aware that John had ever existed. James knew the difference, however; the green eyes were a special Satterfield trait, the mark of a man with very distinctive qualities.

"It's not necessary for you to be there," Buster said.

"I know that," James grumbled, "but I intend to watch. I'm responsible."

"You sure are old man," Vivian interjected.

Buster studied his grandmother as she spoke. At age sixty-five, she was a phenomenon. From a distance, strangers stared at the attractive, mature woman. Most assumed her to be in her mid- forties, in the prime of her life. Only when they drew closer did they see the lines that led them to conclude they had been mistaken in their first impressions; she was a very striking fifty-five year old.

"Who would have thought a man of your age would have succumbed to such foolishness," Vivian continued.

Buster detected a note of pride in Vivian's accusations. Buster, like most who knew the older Satterfields, was intrigued by the feisty relationship between the two elders.

"Now, Vivian, that's not fair," Buster intervened. "I'm the publisher of the *Herald*, and I printed the article."

"But he wrote it," Vivian persisted.

"I did," James entered the discussion, "but the ideas were yours."

"I admit that, but I did not intend for you to put them on paper and for Buster to print them for all to read."

"The world will be a better place without Mr. Richard Hodges," James declared.

"I must go," Buster interjected. "The sun will be up in a few minutes."

"I don't understand why these affairs of honor can't be settled at a reasonable hour," James grumbled as he pushed himself from his chair.

"Maybe because they are against the law," Vivian said.

"Let's not get into all that," Buster said. "Dad lectured me for two hours last night on the legal aspects of dueling. And mother, she threw a tantrum."

"Were you at Eastwind last night?" Vivian asked.

Buster's mother and father, Jason and Lily now lived at Eastwind. Vivian a year ago had retired from her active life as plantation owner. Unable to bring herself to sell Eastwind, she had given her family homestead to Jason, her only son, in return for a firm promise to keep it an active farm for future Satterfield generations. With Vivian's approval, Lily had moved to Eastwind, and she and Jason had adopted the unusual life style that worked so well for James and Vivian. Lily loved Eastwind and supervised the large farm's overseers while Jason divided his time between Alexandria and Eastwind.

Jason was a businessman with manifold interests. He owned Alexandria's largest shipyard, its second biggest brewery, was a principal stockholder in the Northern Neck's only bank, and was a primary investor in Fairfax land. James frequently complained that Jason had but one interest, making money, but he was silently proud of his son's accomplishments despite their many disagreements on most other matters. Jason, to James' dismay, had no interest in newspapers, ideas, literature and history, things that along with his family constituted the core of James' existence. Jason particularly was disinterested in the *Herald*; as a consequence, when Vivian had bestowed Eastwind on their son Jason, James had assigned ownership of the newspaper to their grandson, Buster. The move had delighted both Buster and his father, Jason, who had always wondered what he would do with James' toy when he grew too old to manage it.

"Yes," Buster answered Vivian's question. "Dad told her about the duel, and mother insisted that I have my 'Last Supper' at Eastwind."

"That must have been an occasion," James observed wryly.

"Your name was mentioned frequently," Buster laughed. "Occasional reference was made to the allegation that you wrote the offending article."

"Offending article?"

"Intemperate was the word used most often."

"Your mother blamed James?" Vivian asked.

"No. She blamed my father, and he accused Gramps."

"Harrumph," James and Vivian growled together.

"We must go," Buster said, turning towards the door. "Do you really want to come?" He asked James.

"I'm your second."

"And what about you, Vivian?" Buster asked his grandmother.

"A duel is no fit place for a lady," Vivian smiled sweetly.

"Even though her ideas are responsible for it," James persisted as he walked slowly toward the door carrying his mahogany case.

"Aim well," Vivian called as her husband and grandson descended from the porch. "Are you interested in dinner?" She asked Buster.

"Thank you grandmother. I have other plans."

Vivian frowned at the boy's use of the word "grandmother."

She watched as the two men turned left on Union Street and proceeded north along the river towards the hill where Alexandria's hotheads traditionally fought their affairs of honor. She noticed the top edge of the sun peeking over the horizon. Except for James and Buster, the street was deserted. Vivian studied the Potomac, which crowded its banks several hundred yards away on the other side of the street. When Vivian had decided to move to town, James had vacated his town home next to the newspaper offices at 66 Royal Street and purchased the brick house facing the river. Most of the houses along Union Street were mansions owned by ship captains who considered Alexandria their homeport.

Vivian watched as James and Buster made their way northward. James walked with a limp and a slouch. Vivian worried about him. While he had no serious health complaints, he was beginning to show his age. His joints were giving him trouble, particularly his left hip. He had recently given up his morning walks. Vivian knew she should be worried about her grandson who was on his way to a silly duel, but she was untroubled. Like James, she knew what those hard, flashing, green eyes of Buster's meant. Buster was James' grandson, but he had the gene mix of James' twin, John. For that reason, Vivian felt sorry for Mr. Richard Hodges, Buster's challenger.

At the hill northeast of town, two men waited. Ritchie Hodges looked at his friend and companion and asked:

"Do you think he will show up?"

"I hope not," Thomas Cruikstaff, "Cruiky," replied.

Cruiky looked at his friend meaningfully.

"Are you sure you want to go through with this?"

"I don't have any choice," Ritchie replied. "He challenged my honor." Ritchie paced nervously as he spoke.

Cruiky laughed. "What honor?"

"Even thieves have honor," Ritchie declared.

Ritchie and Cruiky were of the same age, about five years older than Buster Satterfield. The two had disembarked from a coastal schooner in Alexandria about five years previously. They described themselves as investors with independent means interested in exploring Virginia land. At first, the local gentry had welcomed the arrival of new capital, but as time passed, the two had not pursued their alleged interest in purchasing western lands. They occupied themselves with cards and women at The Sign of the Pig and seemed to support themselves with their winnings. Neither Ritchie nor Cruiky had ever let slip the fact that their stake had been acquired at pistol point from a Philadelphia bank and that their arrival had been preceded by a successful race with a posse. They had abandoned their horses in Baltimore and taken the schooner to Alexandria. Ritchie and Cruiky over time had submerged themselves in Alexandria's growing group of ne'er-do-well playboys, most the landless second and third sons of planters and ex-planters. Ritchie over the years had earned a modest reputation for being the possessor of a hot temper and a fast gun, the symbol of a disreputable underclass that troubled Alexandria's aristocracy.

During the recent elections, Ritchie, on a bet, decided to contest a long-standing incumbent for a position on the town council. Ritchie's whimsy symbolized a change that had meaning far more significant than the wastrel's candidacy. Alexandria since its creation in July 1749, had been guided by the paternal hands of George Mason, George Washington, James Satterfield and their peers. During the 1790's, the winds of time swept away Mason and Washington and aged the survivors like James and his friends. A new generation of leaders took over a growing town, which was not only the commercial and political center of Fairfax County, but a part of the new federal enclave. In July 1790, the new Congress in New York responded to George Washington's urging and passed the law implementing Jefferson and Hamilton's political bargain (Jefferson got the enclave and Hamilton his national bank) and included Alexandria in the new Federal District on the banks of the Potomac.

The people of Fairfax County were not sad to see Alexandria depart. Many had long felt that politically the new city had grown too large for its rural britches. Alexandria with its blatant commercialism offended the conservative farming population. Many had sympathized with George Mason who broke with his neighbor and long time friend George Washington over the creation of a new constitution and federal government, Mason having decided the new country needed neither. Others resented being forced to travel all the way to Alexandria to attend the sessions of the general court; they wanted the Court House moved to a more central location. Social and cultural changes abounded. The separation of state and religion loosened political ties; the de-establishment of the Anglican Church as the official religion opened the way for many dissenting sects, increasing the number of small farmers in the foothills. During the 1790's, the plantations abandoned tobacco and shifted to wheat; the planters like the small farmers opened their own mills and shipped their flour through Alexandria, a dependence that contributed to the increasing divisions. The cultivators resented their continued reliance on the city middlemen and merchants whose profiteering on their labors they begrudged. As a consequence of all this agitation, the Fairfax gentry moved its Court House from Alexandria to the intersection of Little River Turnpike and Ox Road.

Vivian and James had watched and worried as their town and county changed. The candidacy and surprise election of Ritchie Hodges to the town council had proved too much. At Vivian's urging, James joined her in a series of articles for the *Herald* that chronicled the changes under the overstated headline "The Second Revolution." The series had been controversial, thus good journalism. The *Herald*, which had grown into a thrice-weekly publication, Tuesdays, Thursdays and Saturdays, under Buster's competent hand showed a decided increase in circulation. Since it was now competing with the Alexandria *Gazette* for the limited reading public, every gain was welcome. Buster, perpetuating James' editorial policy of independence, professing to support neither the Federalist Party nor the Republicans, claimed for the *Herald* the distinction of being the Voice of the People. In truth, it was James' voice that spoke through the newspaper's columns.

After chronicling the changes that had beset their town during the years since independence, they had focused on the upsetting political alterations. At Vivian's suggestion, James had used Ritchie Hodges as the symbol of the new politician. Under the headline "He's No George Washington, Or George Mason Either" James had castigated Ritchie. James' basic theme had been: "Is this what the Revolution Wrought?"

If the truth were told, James had allowed his literary indignation to stretch itself a mite too far, a failing that James in quiet moments would admit. Buster, however, had been delighted with the Ritchie article and had featured it on the front page next to the stories detailing Thomas Jefferson's victory in the House of Representatives. Buster had originally planned to accompany the Jefferson story with an editorial denouncing the political machinations that had led to the tie between Jefferson and Burr in the first place and to use the scandalous situation as a basis for calling for a new method for electing presidents, but James' article had such sensationalism and potential for local impact that he had shelved his editorial for another day.

James too late realized that he had allowed his depiction of Ritchie to exceed good taste, but Vivian's encouragement and Buster's approval had overcome his good judgment. The *Herald* had been on the streets only an hour before Ritchie had stormed into the newspaper offices at Number 66 Royal Street and had angrily confronted Buster. James, unfortunately, had not been present; he reprimanded himself with the thought that if he had been present he could have taken responsibility for the article, passing it off as an old man's eccentric views, and avoided the challenge. Instead, Buster, as publisher, assumed full responsibility, refused to accede to Ritchie's demand for an apology and a retraction, and accepted the invitation to settle the matter on the field of honor.

"There they are now," Cruiky observed, pointing at James and Buster as they trudged up the hill.

"I ought to shoot both of them now. I'm sure the old man is behind the whole thing," Ritchie declared. "What kind of shot is Buster?"

"How do I know? I've never seen him fire a weapon."

"He's a town kid isn't he?"

"Yeh. He was born in Alexandria. His father Jason is a big shot."

"I know that."

As they approached the waiting pair at the hilltop, James sneaked a glance at Buster. As he expected, Buster appeared totally unconcerned.

"Buster... ." James began.

"Gramps... ." Buster said at the same time. He had sensed his grandfather was about to speak, and he wanted to head him off. He did not want the old man to feel responsible no matter what happened.

"Yes?" James responded, relieved at the reprieve. He had been about to apologize to Buster for getting him into this mess.

"Tom Jefferson's your friend, right?"

"I've known him a long time. I don't agree with a lot of his ideas. Why?"

"Can you get us an invitation to his inaugural?"

"Why? You don't need an invitation. The swearing-in will take place in the Senate chamber, and the public is free to attend. I doubt that many will."

Buster laughed at his grandfather's sour tone. James had been no great admirer of John Adams, but he had supported him over the native Virginian, Jefferson. James believed that the dour New Englander had earned his chance for a second term. James admitted that Jefferson might make a passable president, but argued he had to wait his turn.

"I was hoping for a private interview. Our readers might like that."

"I'm sure it can be arranged."

Ritchie with growing apprehension watched the two Satterfields approach. He glared at Cruiky as if affixing blame for his predicament. Ritchie was a competent target shooter at close range, but he had never fought a duel before. Usually, he had been able to bluster and intimidate his victim into an apology. Buster had surprised Ritchie when he had calmly accepted Ritchie's challenge when first issued. Since then, he had not given Ritchie an opportunity to maneuver. Ritchie did not know if Buster was skilled with a pistol or not, but the young publisher's cool demeanor worried him.

"You're late," Ritchie accused.

Buster glanced coldly at Ritchie, then ignored him. Ritchie waited with his pistol in his sweating hand. While Buster calmly lifted his glistening target pistol from the shiny mahogany box held by the old man, Ritchie nervously wiped his palm on his pants leg. Buster did not even bother to check the pistol's load. He glanced at his grandfather, who nodded, then turned to face Ritchie.

"We stand back to back. Start walking on your second's command. After ten paces, turn and fire."

Ritchie expected Buster to discuss the duel, giving Ritchie the opportunity talk his way free. Instead, Buster confirmed the ground rules, turned his back to Ritchie and waited for Cruiky to speak. Ritchie looked anxiously at Cruiky, hoping for advice. Cruiky looked at Buster who waited.

"Give the word or I will," James ordered.

Ritchie turned and stood with his back to Buster. He wiped his sweating palm again on his pants leg then waited, nervously shifting his weight from one foot to the other.

Cruiky cleared his throat then shouted.

"Ready, set, go. One, two, three, four," Cruiky counted the paces. ".... eight, nine, ten!"

When Cruiky shouted ten, Buster and Ritchie, now twenty paces apart, whirled and fired simultaneously. Cruiky, who had never before witnessed a duel, jumped at the loud crack of the firing weapons. With wide eyes and open mouth he stared at his friend. The bullet's impact had knocked him backwards. Ritchie lay flat on his back staring skyward through lifeless eyes. His pistol still clutched in his hand lay at his side. Cruiky watched as a small puff of smoke floated briefly in the air over Ritchie's body before dissipating. Now shaken and fighting on panic, Cruiky turned to look at Buster. Since both weapons had fired simultaneously, Cruiky expected to see Buster also on the ground. Cruiky did not know what he would do with the two bodies; certainly, the old man who had served as Satterfield's second would not be able to help him.

To Cruiky's surprise, he found Buster still standing with his lowered pistol at his side. Before Cruiky could speak, Buster strode quickly to Ritchie's prone form, and Cruiky hurried to stand beside Buster. Both men studied Ritchie's lifeless eyes. Blood seeped from a small hole in the center of Ritchie's forehead. Cruiky leaned over and recoiled in disgust when he saw that the back of Ritchie's head had disintegrated into a mass of gray and white mucous mixed with the dark red blood. Cruiky turned and vomited.

Buster looked at Cruiky with disgust. Without a word, he approached his grandfather who waited to one side holding the open mahogany box. When James and Buster locked eyes, James noticed the flashing white specks in his grandson's cold emerald eyes. At that moment, James, who had always been able to sense his identical twin brother John's thoughts, shivered. He felt John's presence, but he knew that was not possible. John, who James had not seen for ten years, was healthy and alive at his mountain home deep in the western Alleghenies. Still, James felt a familiar presence. As he stared at his grandson, James saw the flashing specks subside. When Buster finally spoke, his eyes had returned to their normal clear green.

"Sorry, Gramps. We've lost a subscriber."

Buster placed the pistol in its nest in the mahogany box, closed the lid, snapped the brass latch, and then took the box from his grandfather.

"I'll clean and oil both pistols then return them to you tonight."

James, still struck by Buster's icy calm, could only nod. He knew that if he had just killed a man, he would be shaking with remorse and filled with questions about the morality of his actions. Buster acted as if he had just handed a cup of tea to a guest.

Buster tucked the wood case under his right arm and caught the sleeve of his grandfather's jacket behind the elbow as he guided him back down the hill. Behind them, Cruiky shouted:

"What am I supposed to do with Ritchie?"

Neither Satterfield answered.

"Aren't you going to help?" Cruiky asked plaintively as James and Buster descended the hill.

WASHINGTON, D.C.

MARCH 1801

A dark gray sky filled with threatening rain clouds hung over Alexandria on Wednesday, March 4th, as Buster guided the buggy carrying his grandfather and himself northward towards the ferry that would carry them across the Potomac to Washington. James shivered and drew his heavy woolen overcoat tighter to seal out the chill of the river breezes. James had always suffered from the damp river cold, but as he grew older he found it more difficult to get warm.

Buster noted his grandfather's gesture and hoped that James' insistence on accompanying Buster to Jefferson's inaugural did not result in pneumonia or some other life-threatening malady.

"At least it isn't raining," James grumbled.

"Maybe it will hold off," Buster tried to be optimistic.

James grunted an inaudible reply.

Buster held the reins lightly and let the team pick its way along the soft mud of the well-traveled track.

"Doesn't look like many Virginians are rushing to help Tom celebrate his victory," James observed.

"We're early. The swearing-in is scheduled for noon. It's only nine."

"I know that," James said irritably.

Buster turned his head away from his grandfather in an effort to shield his amused smile. The reaction within the Satterfield family to Tom Jefferson and the Republicans' victory had not been a harmonious one. Buster's father's reaction had been predictable; Jason made no secret of his Federalist and pro-Adams opinions. He denounced Tom Jefferson's "Frenchified" radical views at every opportunity. Vivian, Buster's grandmother, was equally outspoken in her defense of Jefferson and the Republicans. Buster suspected that his grandmother supported the Republicans because Jefferson and his two lieutenants, Madison and Monroe, were Virginians; the fact that Adams and the Federalist leadership were New

Englanders weighted heavily on Vivian's scales. James privately supported Adams while publicly he squatted on the rail of indecision seeing good in both men.

James considered Tom Jefferson a "political friend." Both men had graduated from William and Mary and had made their names in Virginia politics. James had known and worked with Jefferson for over thirty years. However, their relationship had never developed an intimacy; both were strong minded, and Jefferson was ten years younger, but they had supported and opposed each other on issues without personal animosity.

James also considered John Adams a "political friend;" they had worked closely during the early years of the Revolution when James had been Washington's liaison with the Congress and, Adams, even then one of the foremost political figures of the colonies, had headed the War Committee.

James liked both men as individuals but had some doubts about their personal quirks.

James thought Adams had spent too much time in England representing his fledgling government where Adams had acquired a respect for pomp and form that led his enemies to tar him with the accusation that he was pro-English and wanted to create an American monarchy replete with costumes and titles. Jefferson, on the other hand, had assimilated too much of the radicalism of the French Revolution. If forced to privately choose between the two, James would reluctantly side with Adams and the Federalists. He believed in the need for a strong national government with clearly defined powers. James felt that Jefferson's idea of an agrarian state with minimal government too utopian to be practical. Jefferson actually thought that standing armies were a threat and argued that the only defense the country needed was its loyal citizenry who could drop their pitchforks and take up their long rifles when challenged.

Buster privately agreed with his grandfather's appraisal of Adams and Jefferson. Publicly, James, as publisher of the Alexandria *Herald*, pretended to be non-partisan. He praised and criticized both political parties, reacting to the issue and not partisan politics.

"Do you think we can arrange a private meeting with Jefferson?" Buster asked.

James snorted his derision at the question. "If anyone should want one, and I'm not sure why anyone would."

"I thought I would follow up my report on the inauguration with a personal interview in which I would let Jefferson outline his plans for the future."

"Thinking of making the *Herald* into a Republican mouthpiece?"

"No. You know better than that."

Buster studied his grandfather who smiled as he stared straight ahead. The *Herald* was James' baby. He had created the paper and had made it the respected force it now was in Virginia politics. James had given the *Herald* to Buster, but he had not surrendered his right to monitor editorial policy. Buster had no intention of turning the *Herald* into a semi-official organ of the administration like the

National Intelligencer, the Washington stepchild of Peter Freneau's *National Gazette,* which had been established in Philadelphia by Madison and Monroe, at Jefferson's urging, to support the Republican Party. The *Gazette* had quickly discredited itself among objective journalists and readers by shifting from philosophical contemplation of republican philosophy to sensational attacks on Hamilton, the Federalists and the Washington administration. Since Jefferson was Secretary of State and a part of that administration, he kept his support of Freneau hidden, but one did not have to be a genius to discern that this hypocritical subterfuge was a part of Jefferson's political style. Neither James nor Buster could understand how a man like Jefferson could sincerely hold such high-minded philosophical beliefs while at the same time be such a vicious, political in-fighter.

Buster reined the team to a halt as they approached the ferry.

"We're in luck. The ferry is on this side of the river."

"It's not luck," James responded. "Nobody but us is interested in seeing history made."

Buster did not respond. He concentrated on following the ferryman's directions as he guided the team on to the boat.

"I wish they had built the bridge closer to Alexandria," Buster observed, referring to the Little Falls (later Chain) bridge that had been built further north four years earlier.

"That day will come," James observed, speaking loudly for the ferryman's benefit. "And then these river robbers will be out of business."

"And that will be the day," the ferryman laughed. "You can mark my words, Satterfield, this ferry will be here long after that bridge falls down. If the good lord had wanted us to have bridges, he would have built them."

"And what is the fee today?" James demanded.

"One dollar."

"One way?"

"Certainly."

"Robbery," James grumbled as he reached for his purse.

"If you don't like it. Walk across, if you can. Some of these Bible thumpers think they can walk on water. Never saw one yet that could. The rest of you can pay your dollar, just like old Tom Jefferson did."

"Did Tom take your ferry?" Buster asked, sensing local color for his news story.

"Sure did. Didn't expect him to use the bridge did you?"

Buster knew that Jefferson had spent the night several days previously in Alexandria, but neither he nor James had troubled to seek him out. They had not wanted to appear as sycophants to the president-elect.

The ferry landed on the Washington shore not far from where L'Enfant's plan called for Fourteenth Street to be built. The plan was one thing; Washington, D.C. in March 1801, was something else. The new federal city had been under construction for almost ten years, but it did not have much to show for the passage of time.

James looked around and studied the forested countryside. One track led eastward through a gap in the trees.

"I don't understand why Washington insisted that the commissioners build the federal city on this side of the river. He was President and appointed the three commissioners who approved the plans. If he had built the city on the Virginia side, it would have put him much closer to Mount Vernon and made life easier for most of us." Buster shook his head in disapproval. "He at least could have located it near Alexandria."

"He couldn't have done that," James replied.

"Why not?"

"He told me, and I agreed with him, that if he placed the capital on the Virginia shore that everyone would say he did so to increase the value of his lands."

"Didn't he buy land in Georgetown and the Federal District?"

"No law against wise investing."

James had meant what he said. He knew Washington had scrupulously walked the line between corruption and legal investing.

"They had trouble selling lots in the Federal District. Only sold thirty-five parcels the first day of the lottery in 1791. George had to buy land as a patriotic gesture showing his confidence in the project."

"Did you buy a lot?"

James smiled at his grandson's question. One day the boy would be in for a big surprise. James had decided to pass control of the Satterfield Legacy—the large investment in land that James and his two brothers had made with Braddock's gold that John had sequestered following Braddock's defeat—to his grandson to manage "for the benefit of the Satterfield family." James was not sure just what that phrase now meant; he and his brothers had been young and immature when they had vowed to invest the captured bounty in Virginia land for the benefit of future Satterfield generations. Thus far, the value of the land had depreciated, and the Satterfields had prospered. No one needed their ill-gotten gains.

James had personally purchased over ten thousand acres; some was tilled by tenant farmers but most lay fallow. Income barely paid for expenses. The same was true for the land Will had purchased for the family in Loudoun County; James did not know how John had fared with his purchases in the west; James assumed John had acquired even greater quantities of useless acreage with his share. In any case, James planned one day to brief Buster on his future responsibilities. He knew Buster would be surprised; he delayed, however, because he did not know how Buster's father, Jason, would take being passed over. James feared he would interpret it has a rebuke. In a way, it was. James worried about Jason's proclivity for taking gambles in his quest for wealth. Thus far, Jason had been lucky and was one of the wealthiest men in Fairfax County. James was not sure, however, how long Jason's luck would hold, and he did not want to place the family's future in Jason's freewheeling hands. James often wondered where

Jason had gotten his risk-taking propensies. None of the Satterfields were gamblers.

Buster guided the team eastwards.

"We still have two hours, Gramps. Where shall we go? I haven't been over here in three years."

"Me neither. I want to have a chance to pay my respects on John Adams while he's still in office, so let's go by the President's house. I understand that John moved in last October before it was finished."

"I hear that it's a palace."

"I suggest that you not use that word in front of Mr. Adams," James warned.

Buster laughed, recognizing that his grandfather referred to Adams' sensitivities to the charge he wanted to create an American monarchy.

James carefully navigated the rutted road leading to Pennsylvania Avenue, the broad boulevard that L'Enfant had envisioned connecting the "two pieces," the President's House and the Capitol. When the buggy reached the intersection of Pennsylvania Avenue and the ferry road, Buster paused and stared. Pennsylvania Avenue was not quite as grand as he had anticipated. In fact, it was little more than a strip of cleared land connecting the Capitol and the President's House. The "two pieces" stood about one and a half miles apart. The connecting strip was nothing more than a mud track that cut through forest and swamp with not a single structure breaking nature's harmony. Several workmen labored on a single stone walkway that followed the path that paralleled the cleared strip.

"The President and the Congressmen will have to step carefully if they want to keep their boots clean," James laughed.

Buster turned the buggy northward towards the President's House. Overhead, the late winter sun forced its way through the dark rain clouds. The river breeze subsided, and James could feel warmth in the sun's rays.

"I can feel spring in that sun," he observed, loosening his coat collar.

"It won't be long now, Gramps," Buster reassured. April was his favorite time of the year, and he looked forward to its arrival. Within three weeks the buds and early blossoms would appear.

"I understand why so many of the politicians are staying in Alexandria," Buster said as he carefully guided the horses around the stumps and boulders. "I'm not sure there is anyplace for them to live here."

"I hope they rectify that situation soon. It's almost impossible to find a chair at Gadsby's."

James referred to Gadsby's Tavern, Alexandria's most prominent ordinary, formerly known as the Bunch of Grapes. It was James' favorite gathering spot, and of late it had been filled with celebrating Congressmen seeking respite from the drudgery of their new federal city.

Buster halted the buggy in front of the President's House. Despite his predilections, he was impressed. The rectangular two story, sandstone building lacked a portico but its center entrance was flanked by two imposing Ionic columns. The sight was marred by the temporary wooden steps leading to the front door, but Buster could imagine how they would look when finished. The columns, like the sandstone, had been painted white. Unfortunately, the paint had already been streaked and faded by the harsh winter weather.

"It's grand enough," Buster observed.

"Abigail described it as a palace," James cackled.

Buster studied the unfinished grounds. Several unsightly workers' shacks were clustered to his right. Tree stumps and boulders testified to an initial attempt at clearing the grounds, which were surrounded by virgin forest. Buster was struck by the unfinished picture that the aspect presented.

"I don't think John Adams found his new home to be much like Boston or London," Buster said.

He had no real basis for comparison. Buster had never visited a major American city let alone London. With the exception of the two years he had spent in Williamsburg, while attending William and Mary College, Buster had never strayed more than twenty miles from Alexandria in his life.

"Nor Philadelphia and New York either," James answered.

Buster considered his grandfather an authority. James had visited and lived in and near the northern cities during his tenure as Washington's aide.

"Shall I drive up to the front door?" Buster indicated the mud path leading to the entrance to the President's home. No fence barred their way.

"If you don't want to walk through the mud, you'll have to. We can ask those workmen if John is home." James pointed at the workmen coming and going through the front door.

"You don't think he's here?"

"He could have spent the last night at one of the taverns. Abigail returned to Quincy two weeks ago, so John's camping out as a bachelor."

"I understand one of his son's died recently in New York."

"Yes," James replied succinctly, not wanting to discuss the sad subject. One of Adams' boys had turned into a wastrel who had drunk himself to death. "Go ahead to the door," he ordered.

Buster took one last look at the setting. The President's House appeared lonely. **With the exception of the workers' shacks and two undistinguished brick buildings on the right and left, the mansion had only trees for companions. To** the east on the corner of Fifteenth Street and Pennsylvania Avenue stood the home of the Treasury Department. On the west, the Departments of State, War and Navy shared a building.

Buster snapped the reins lightly and urged the team forward. He stopped near the temporary wooden steps that led to the open front door and helped his grandfather climb down from the buggy. Buster was not sure what to do next, but James seized the initiative and proceeded up the steps, following a workman through the open doorway.

"Shouldn't we knock or announce ourselves somehow?" Buster asked.

"Why should we? It's our house isn't it? We're citizens."

Buster followed his grandfather and the workman up the temporary stairs, pausing to wipe the mud off his shoes before entering. He noticed the trail of mud leading into the house indicating that the workmen had not bothered. On entering, he found himself standing in a large hall. He followed his grandfather as he searched through the various public rooms looking for Adams or at least a servant through whom they could announce their presence. Despite the fact that except for themselves and the workmen the building was deserted, Buster felt like an intruder. James marched down the hallway to his left, acting like he knew where he was going. They entered a large reception room that was empty except for a few pieces of furniture that Buster assumed belonged to the people and not the Adamses. Obviously, John and Abigail had already moved their personal possessions. As of noon when Jefferson took the oath, the President's House would belong to him. Buster wondered where Adams would spend the night and if he suffered a sense of loss. Looking about him, Buster decided that he felt sorrier for Jefferson than for Adams. Since Adams was the first occupant of the President's house, his conduct had set precedent. Buster wondered if the President's successors would all depart in such apparent haste.

James reversed his steps, paused to peek into the large oval dining room that was located opposite the front door, then continued into the west wing. The president's small office and the library cum cabinet room were both empty. James turned and smiled at his grandson.

"Look's like we're out of luck. The bird's flown the coop."

Before Buster could respond, a house servant dressed in immaculate white entered from the hallway. Buster assumed he had come from the second floor or the ground floor where the kitchens were presumably located.

"Gentlemen, may I help you?" The tall black man asked.

"We're looking for Mr. Adams," Buster declared.

"I'm sorry but he's not here," the dignified man answered with a smile.

"Where is he?" James demanded irritably, acting as if Adams' absence were a personal slight.

"He's left."

"He's left?" James said, making no attempt to hide his disbelief. "The ceremony is not until noon. You tell him that James Satterfield wants to see him."

"I'm sorry, sir. Mr. Adams has already left Washington."

"When?"

"Four o'clock this morning." The servant acted as if he considered this a normal practice.

"Four o'clock this morning," James repeated and stared at Buster.

"Yes sir. He stayed up last night signing those judicial appointments he left on his desk in his office. He instructed me to make sure they're delivered this morning before the swearing-in. Which is just what I am about. Now, if you will excuse me." The man turned and left James and Buster standing in the deserted dining room.

Buster wanted to ask about the last minute appointments, but the servant had departed without giving him a chance.

"What judicial appointments?" He asked James.

James shrugged to indicate his indifference.

"Look at that fireplace," he ordered, pointing at a large rough brick fireplace built into the room's outer wall. "That's a disgrace."

Buster looked where his grandfather was pointing. The hearth was obviously unfinished and contrasted with the elegance of the room with its fine molding and crystal chandelier. The ashes and the remains of logs indicated that the fireplace had been used.

"They all be like that," a workman crowded past them. "We're waitin' for the marble, but Mrs. Adams couldn't. She complained of the cold and kept fires burnin' in all thirteen. Imagine. A house with thirteen fireplaces all burnin'. No wonder she complained about the cost of wood." With those words, the workman disappeared through the doorway on the opposite side of the room.

"Let's go," James ordered and led the way back towards the front door.

He paused at the doorway and let two mud footed workmen carrying tools and planking enter.

"Where you going with that?" James demanded as if he belonged in the house.

"To the East Room," one of the workmen replied, staring at James curiously.

Buster wondered if the workman thought they were part of Jefferson's staff.

"What for?" James asked.

"To finish the windows. That's what for," the workman said contemptuously.

"Wait," James ordered as the man turned to depart. "Where is Tom Jefferson?"

"Don't you know?"

"If I did I wouldn't ask. Where is he?"

"Probably at his boarding house." With those words, the workman followed his companion.

James turned to Buster and smiled.

"Let's go."

"Where?"

"Conrad and McMunn's. "

James stomped through the open doorway.

Buster recognized the name. Conrad and McMunn's was one of the few boarding houses in the new capital that catered to the visiting politicians. Buster assumed that his grandfather had heard someplace that Jefferson was staying there. It was located about a mile from the President's House. Buster joined his grandfather in the buggy and carefully guided it back to Pennsylvania Avenue. He looked left in the direction of Georgetown. In the distance he could see the houses that had been build along the town's main thoroughfare. Buster assumed that the lot owners felt more comfortable building their new homes along the road that led to one of the Federal District's four existing villages. He noticed that the houses appeared to have been built in clusters and speculated that the owners had done so for protection. He had heard that the district had many robbers and brigands but no police.

Buster turned the buggy to the right and followed the rough tracks that led north and east. Here and there, they found clusters of houses, but most of the area was still untouched forest. The woodcutters had slashed their way through the trees clearing the designated major streets and avenues as called for by the plan, but little else had been accomplished.

"Gramps," Buster said. "Do you think there is a capital like this anyplace in the world?"

"I doubt it, son," James replied. "Certainly not in the civilized world. "

Buster recognized that his grandfather referred to Europe.

"We're the only new country that has to build its capital from scratch. It'll take some time."

"I wonder if building a new city here was a great idea after all. I doubt it ever will become something we can be proud of. The President's house is a disgrace." Buster looked at the surrounding forest to emphasize his point.

James nodded his head in agreement without replying.   The City of Washington had a long way to go to catch up with Philadelphia and New York, and this thought made him wonder where all the money would come from to construct the necessary buildings. The Republicans had already made it clear that they were going to reduce customs and taxes and at the same time eliminate any public debt. James did not know how Jefferson was going to do that.

WASHINGTON, D.C.

MARCH 4TH, 1801

Buster halted the buggy in front of Conrad and McMunn's boarding house and followed James inside. When the old man wanted to, he forgot his stiff joints and moved quickly, forcing Buster to rush. James opened the front door and entered without knocking. He paused in the hallway, spotted the public room on his right and entered. To his surprise, the room was almost deserted. He had expected to find it full of red-faced politicians talking excitedly about the day's ceremonies. James paused abruptly and stared at the parlor's only occupants. Buster, taken unawares by James sudden stop, bumped into him.

"Sorry, Gramps."

The scuffle and Buster's voice caused the two men seated near the blazing fireplace to look up from their preoccupations. The older man held a book, and the younger had been writing in a notepad.

"James," the older man said as he rose to his feet.

"Tom," James replied flatly.

Buster studied the man who he assumed to be the President Elect as he walked towards them with his right hand extended. He was not what James had expected. Jefferson was tall, slender, with sandy reddish hair that was fading into white. It was cropped a medium length, long enough to reach the open collar of his shabby shirt, but too short to be tied with a ribbon. Jefferson had a handsome face marked by a square jaw, medium length nose and clear, gray eyes topped by thick, unruly, white eyebrows. A line of wrinkles under his chin disclosed his age which Buster knew to be fifty-eight. He had the complexion of a man who spent much time out of doors and the body of one who still engaged in physical labor. Jefferson, despite his imposing physical presence, was informally clad. He wore a white shirt that was soft with age; Buster could see two worn threads dangling from the open collar. Baggy brown pants protruded from under the old robe and almost touched the worn slippers. The robe held Buster's attention; its faded material once had been decorated with a regular red and black square pattern; heavy wear had distorted its symmetry and destroyed the checkerboard regularity.

"I hope we are not interrupting," James apologized as the two men shook hands firmly.

"Not at all. Just catching up on my reading."

Jefferson held up the book he held in his left hand for James to see the title.

James squinted. He could see the letters but could not make out the words. He was having trouble with his middle vision of late. Jefferson noted James' difficulty.

"An interesting study of the tree and plant life of southern Europe. It just arrived with my latest order."

Buster had difficulty believing that a man waiting to be sworn in as the third president of the United States was sitting virtually alone in his parlor reading a book about trees.

"I'm doing a little research. We must do something with Pennsylvania Avenue to accent the connection between the two pieces as they call them."

Jefferson stared directly into Buster's eyes as he spoke. Buster had the feeling the man had read his thoughts and had consequently explained his choice of literature.

"You must be Buster," Jefferson said as he reached past James to clasp Buster's hand. "You're the image of your grandfather when he was your age."

Jefferson's response surprised James too. He had not seen or talked with the man for ten years. The professional politician's ability to match names and faces was a continual source of amazement.

"Your grandfather and I talked frequently about you in Richmond during our days together."

Once again Buster had the feeling that Jefferson was anticipating their thoughts.

"Will you join us for a cup of tea?"

Assuming their assent, Jefferson returned to his chair near the fire and indicated that James and Buster should sit nearby.

"We only wanted to stop by and wish you our best. We have no intention of taking up your time."

"Nonsense," Jefferson said. "May I introduce my secretary." Jefferson indicated the young man with the notepad who had risen. "Captain Meriwether Lewis. James and Buster Satterfield."

"Pleased to meet you sir," Lewis spoke politely as he offered his outstretched hand to James. "Mr. Jefferson has told me much about your exploits during your service with General Washington."

"An exaggeration, I'm sure," James blushed as he spoke.

"Don't be modest, James," Jefferson laughed his admonishment.

Lewis nodded as he shook Buster's hand, obviously more comfortable with a man his own age.

"I'll arrange for the tea," Lewis said and hurried from the room.

"Captain Lewis is a bright young man from Albemarle County for whom I predict an interesting future. He has agreed to take his quarters with me in the President's house, though I don't know how long I will be able to keep him. He aspires to make his name exploring the west."

James nodded. He had wondered how Jefferson, a widower, would find life in the spacious presidential mansion. Among his many problems would be obtaining a hostess to assist him with the arduous representational protocol that the European ambassadors expected the chief of state to follow. James assumed that one of Jefferson's two married daughters might move in to assist her father. Fortunately, the pompous Adams had not lived in Washington long enough to set any arduous precedents that mimicked the silliness surrounding the English traditions.

"We stopped by the President's House to pay our respects, but John had vacated the premises. Do you know where he is?" James asked.

"John's not there?" Jefferson appeared surprised.

"All his personal possessions appear to have been packed and moved. The place is a shambles with workmen scrambling in every room. The single servant we found said John stayed up late last night signing judicial appointments before retiring only to rise early and depart in darkness at four this morning." James felt like he had as a staff officer delivering unpleasant information to General Washington.

"Oh dear. I was afraid of this," Jefferson sighed. "John felt badly about the election. We were once close friends, you know. I visited John and Abigail in London; they showed me all the estates, and I had the time of my life. But politics has changed things. John, I fear, believes much of the propaganda about me put out by his Federalist newspapers."

Jefferson paused and smiled at Buster and James.

"As newspapermen, you understand that."

Again, Jefferson surprised Buster. He doubted that the *Herald* and its Northern Virginia subscription base had gained that much prominence.

"I met John on the street, if Pennsylvania Avenue can be called that, three weeks ago while we each were enjoying our respective promenades. There's not much to do in Washington. At the time, we didn't know how the election was going to turn out. John knew of course that the Federalists had lost, but our eccentric electoral system had placed me and Aaron Burr in a dead even tie and the House of Representatives could not make up their mind. To nobody's surprise, Aaron refused to withdraw despite the fact the party had run him for vice president, but I don't have to tell you two that. In any case, John, like me, was worried about the precedent that would be set if the Congress overturned the will of the voters and chose Burr to be president. To have politicians reverse the people's decision would be very bad indeed. John suggested, despite his own disappointment, that the country came first. John opined I could guarantee my election if I gave assurances that I would do three things: honor the public debt, maintain the navy, and not displace federal officers. This I did, and as a result the politicians worked out their compromise on the thirty-fifth ballot."

Jefferson paused and studied James and Buster.

"This of course is all off the record. Just talk between old friends."

"As you wish," James answered for himself and Buster. Jefferson had not changed. He was still the two faced politician that he had always been. His principles were important until they confronted practical politics.

"So John stayed up late signing appointments," Jefferson mused aloud. "He has been doing a lot of that lately, despite our informal agreement."

Buster realized that Jefferson was referring to his promise not to remove Federalist jobholders. Washington and Adams had staffed the bureaucracy with Federalists, and Jefferson, in order to edge out his own Vice President, Burr, had had to promise not to remove them. Not only was Jefferson faced with a government staffed by the opposition, he had to cope with a new round of last minute appointments. In February, Adams had had an opportunity for revenge. Chief Justice of the Supreme Court Oliver Ellsworth, a Federalist, had been forced to resign by illness. He did so promptly to give Adams the opportunity to appoint his successor for life. Jefferson undoubtedly thought a Virginia gentleman would have deferred the appointment for a month so the people's new choice could make the selection, but Adams with obvious glee had appointed John Marshall, a long time Jeffersonian enemy, to the job. Then, the outgoing Federalist controlled Congress had passed a Judiciary Act that reformed the judicial districts and created some twenty-three new judgeships. These, too, had been filled with Federalists. Jefferson had anticipated being able to name the last three new judges who would serve in the new Federal District, but James' report indicated that Adams had preempted this prerogative at the last minute before fleeing town and delivering the final insult, deliberate non-participation in the inaugural of the new president.

Buster bit his tongue to avoid laughing as he realized the import of what he and James had learned at the President's House.

Captain Meriwether Lewis rejoined the group in the parlor. He politely distributed the tea then sat silently beside James.

"Are you interested in a federal job, Buster?" Jefferson laughed. "If I had one left to offer that my predecessor had not filled, I would give it to a good Virginian." Jefferson shook his head in mock dismay.

"John pulled one over on you when he got you to promise not to change the Federalist officeholders," James observed with a straight face. "Are you going to keep your promise?"

Buster realized that if Jefferson answered yes, he would be placing his administration in the hands of the enemy.

"What else can a gentleman do?"

Both Buster and James realized that Jefferson had not answered the question.

"Did either of you hear what that damned Federalist Congress did to me as one of its last acts of meanness?"

Buster knew that the Federalist controlled Congress had adjourned sine die the day before.

"No," James answered for both of them.

"Captain Lewis just briefed me. Their vindictiveness angered me so much I had to try to calm myself with study of my trees."

"What did they do, Tom?" James asked, playing the game; he realized that Jefferson was toying with them. Tom Jefferson was too clever to really lose his temper.

"Well," Jefferson smiled as he began his story. "After my election, I asked President Adams if the President had a stable at his disposal. The President informed me that I would have no worries in that regard. He said the stables already have seven horses and two carriages that are the property of the United States Government, and they are available for the President's use. This is all well and good and would have been adequate for my needs. I have my favorite stallion for my own use; I will ride no other, but the petty Congressmen thought otherwise."

The story was beginning to strike Buster as funny, but since Jefferson appeared almost angry, he was so serious, Buster fought the urge to smile.

"The members of the legislative branch in their infinite wisdom decided that President Adams had purchased the seven horses and two carriages out of an appropriation allocated for furnishings for the President's house. The Congressmen criticized President Adams, and I am ashamed to admit that the Republicans were foremost in this effort. They passed a resolution calling for the President to sell the horses and carriages and to place the proceeds in the new President's furniture account. Now, what am I supposed to do? Buy a large sofa and have the staff carry me royally about town to official functions like an oriental potentate?"

James could not repress a smile at the image Jefferson's words brought to mind. Buster looked at Captain Lewis whose eyes caught his before turning downward to contemplate the carpet. Buster noticed the slight upturn at the corners of the secretary's lips.

"Do you need a ride to the Capitol?" James asked helpfully.

"No thank you. I'll walk," Jefferson declared seriously. Jefferson then looked at Buster and smiled.

"Young man if you wish to recount this sad story in your newspaper and suggest that the new Congress allocate funds to purchase appropriate horses and conveyances for the President's use, you may." Jefferson stared at Buster until he replied.

"Certainly, sir. I think that would be only proper," Buster said after a perceptible pause.

Buster despised his words. He felt as if he had just been used. Since he had his own request for Jefferson, he had no choice. As he considered the matter, he decided that with the proper laconic tone, the little incident might prove amusing to the *Herald*'s readership.

"Well, gentlemen, James, I appreciate your visit," Jefferson declared. "I have another commitment scheduled for noon, and I must prepare. Although I am considered a man of the people, I doubt they would appreciate my appearing in my robe and slippers."

"Very well, Tom," James said. "The next time we see you we will address you as Mr. President, if that's the proper protocol."

"I wouldn't worry about that, James," Jefferson said. "I think you will be seeing some changes in how we do things around here."

"That should prove interesting," James replied, not completely veiling his amusement at Jefferson's words. "I think my grandson might have a request for you. I assume it will not be the first or last you receive."

Jefferson paused long enough to convey his mild displeasure with James' words then turned to Buster with a smile.

"Since I don't have a job to offer you, and you would refuse it anyway, what can I do for you young man?"

"Well, Mr. President, an interview after you have been in office for a period would be most appreciated by the *Herald*'s readership."

"A very good suggestion," Jefferson said. "The *Herald* is not a Republican supporting newspaper, is it?"

"No sir. Fair and independent. Objective, I hope."

"Then a conversation we will have Mr. Editor. If you contact Captain Lewis when you believe the time is appropriate, we'll meet at the President's house. I'll give you the grand tour."

Buster caught himself before he replied he had had the grand tour already.

"That would be very kind of you, Mr. President," Buster said and nodded at Lewis to indicate he would be hearing from him.

Following these words, Jefferson excused himself. Buster and James shook hands with Captain Lewis and returned to their buggy.

"A very interesting man," Buster commented when the two were alone in the buggy and headed for the Capitol where the ceremonies would take place. "I think I have just been manipulated."

"By a master," James laughed. "But you got your interview."

"I wonder at what price."

At that point, a commotion in the distance interrupted their conversation and thoughts. The rattle of drums marking a martial pace and the wail of fifes playing a version of Yankee Doodle Dandy surprised them.

"The festivities are beginning," Buster observed after recognition struck him, "Pull to one side," James ordered. "Let's watch."

Buster did as he was ordered. When the marching formation came nearer, Buster recognized the uniforms of the Alexandria Militia Company. He had heard that they planned to participate in the inauguration of another of Virginia's native sons. He made a mental note to stress in his report for the *Herald* that the Alexandria boys were the first on the scene at Jefferson's boarding house. The martial music sent a shiver along Buster's spine. He glanced with embarrassment at his grandfather to see if he had noticed Buster's tremor of emotion. To his surprise, James appeared to be sharing the moment. The two watched silently as the ten rows of five men abreast marched past. A second military unit followed the Alexandrians. They had their fifers and drummers who played their own tune, oblivious to what preceded them.

"Who are they?" James asked.

"I don't recognize the uniforms," Buster answered before he saw the banner that proclaimed the unit to be the "Washington Artillery."

Buster glanced at his grandfather who nodded that he had seen the flag.

"They don't march as well as our boys," James observed.

James was not speaking out of loyalty. The Washington Artillery, dressed in a motley collection of uniforms, unlike the nattily clad Alexandria Infantry, walked rather than marched and chatted excitedly as they did so. Behind them, a group of spectators, mostly workers with a sprinkling of youth and Negroes, proudly and loudly participated in the demonstration.

"Tom will have an escort," James said, nodding to indicate that Buster should continue to the Capitol.

"Gramps," Buster said as he followed his grandfather's instructions. "If President Adams had to surrender his horses and carriages to the Congress, how do you suppose he left town this morning?"

James smiled at his grandson's question.

"Now you are thinking like a newsman. But leave poor John Adams in peace. Abigail is already worried about how they are going to live now. John has not gotten rich out of politics, like some we could name."

Buster nodded agreement but continued to ponder his question. He wondered if Adams had commanded a government coach to take him home to Quincy. Buster decided it would be justified if he had, as long as he sent the coach back to the federal city after it had performed its duty.

Buster and James arrived at the Capitol a half an hour before the ceremonies were to begin. The edifice, really half a capitol, was unfinished. The swearing-in was scheduled to take place in the Senate chamber. The wing housing the House of Representatives was still under construction. The Capitol, standing on a rise, was surrounded like the President's House by virgin forest.

James had no difficult finding a place to park the buggy. Fewer than a hundred citizens milled about the cleared field in front of the Capitol. Buster recognized several of the politicians who were working even this sparse crowd. He assumed that many of the spectators were newsmen, like himself, present to acquire first hand material for the stories they would send to their home states by the evening stages.

"It's a smaller crowd than I anticipated," Buster observed.

"What did you expect?" James snapped peevishly despite the fact that he shared his grandson's disappointment. "How many residents do you think Washington has now?"

"I thought maybe more would come from Georgetown and Alexandria, at least, to see the 'man of the people' sworn in." Buster ignored James' tone; he was accustomed to the curmudgeonly disposition.

"Alexandria and Georgetown did not elect Jefferson."

Buster nodded. He knew this to be the truth. The merchants of both cities had made no secret of their support for the Federalists and Adams. Virginia had cast its electoral ballots for Jefferson, but it had been the backcountry that did so.

The two wormed their way slowly through the crowd, speaking to those they recognized and ignoring the out of town journalists and the shabbily dressed workers who formed the mass of the assemblage. They climbed the stairs and entered the building. Inside, they found a like number of people, another one hundred at most. James contemplated the chairs arranged in front of a makeshift podium, recognized they would be reserved for the Members of Congress and distinguished guests, and wondered if he would have to stand for the ceremony. If so, he considered leaving. While James was contemplating his options, the two Satterfields were spotted by several members of the Virginia representation in Congress. James was well known to most Virginians as a consequence of his long service in the Burgesses. They were immediately invited to share the delegation's seats in the front row, solving James' problem.

They chatted with friends in the delegation during the time they had to wait for the arrival of the inaugural participants. The politicians occupied themselves with speculating about Jefferson's probable appointments to the Cabinet. James Madison for Secretary of State and Albert Gallatin for Secretary of Treasury were the names most frequently mentioned. No one had anything bad to say about Madison. His appointment was a given. Virginia's Madison was a neighbor, long time friend, and loyal lieutenant of Jefferson. Madison had made his own mark as one of the framers of the Constitution and as a power in the House of Representatives during Washington's presidency, but Gallatin was another matter. Albert Gallatin was a Republican leader in the House, but he was also a native Swiss who too many felt could not even speak correct English.

"Certainly Tom must recognize that he will have difficulty getting Gallatin, a Republican Hamilton, confirmed," a man on Buster's left sniffed.

"But he is one of the most able men available," another replied.

"He looks like a Frenchman," the first man protested. "Tom's got enough trouble with his alleged bias towards France now."

Before the second man could reply, the celebratory bark of a cannon being fired outside interrupted. The group of dignitaries assembled inside the chamber paused and listened. Raggedly, several shots followed.

"That has got to be the Washington Artillery," someone behind Buster and James laughed caustically. Buster smiled agreement but said nothing. They were seated among Jefferson's proudest admirers.

A few minutes later, Thomas Jefferson, surrounded by a group of fawning hangers-on, entered the chamber. As Buster watched, Jefferson, now dressed more appropriately in a black, wrinkled suit, worked his way towards the front row where several empty seats were reserved for the President Elect and his party. Jefferson smiled, shook hands, and exchanged pleasantries with friends as he made his way to his assigned place. He nodded at James and Buster as if he had not been talking with them a half-hour earlier.

"At least he changed his robe and slippers," James whispered. "He still doesn't look very presidential."

To Buster's surprise, Jefferson sat by himself in the center of the reserved area with empty chairs on each side of him. Jefferson had no family members with him to celebrate the occasion. Neither of widower Jefferson's two married daughters had been able to travel to Washington to participate.

"I understand he walked here alone from Conrad and McMunn's," someone sitting behind Buster whispered.

Buster wondered what had happened to Captain Lewis and the two militia companies.

"The legend making begins," James said softly.

"Looks like Daniel sitting alone in the lion's den," someone on the Federalist side of the aisle said in a loud voice that carried to the front.

Jefferson, who had obviously heard the remark, turned and smiled in the direction of the speaker.

Buster noticed an empty section of chairs at the front of the Federalist side of the room.

"I'll bet those had been reserved for John Adams," James, who had caught Buster's glance, declared.

The six empty chairs stood in the crowded room as a grim reminder of the absence of the man who would be President of the United States for a few short minutes more.

The man on Buster's left leaned over and whispered.

"Adams isn't the only one who is gracing the occasion with his absence. I understand that Ted Sedgewick left town early this morning."

Buster looked at his grandfather to see if he had heard this last piece of information. James nodded to indicate he had. Theodore Sedgwick of Massachusetts, Speaker of the House of Representatives, was an ardent Federalist. The absence of these two powerful men, Adams and Sedgwick, was not only an insult; it indicated that Jefferson could expect trouble from the opposition in the near future.

The Chief Justice of the Supreme Court, John Marshall, one of Adams' last minute appointments designed to insult and inhibit his successor, strode to the podium. Jefferson's long time enemy's demeanor made it clear that the ceremony, at least Marshall's part in it, was to be short if not sweet. He invited both the President Elect and the Vice President Elect, Aaron Burr, who had almost wrested the presidency from his running mate, to the podium.

"Poor Tom" the loquacious man on Buster's left whispered. "The high point of his life and he celebrates it with the two men he despises most in this life as his companions."

Buster admitted to himself that neither Marshall nor Burr looked happy.

After he tersely administered the oath to Jefferson and Burr, Marshall turned the podium over to the new President.

Jefferson smiled at the some two hundred witnesses to his ascension, then took a few sheets of paper from his coat pocket and smoothed them on the podium in front of him. Just as he had written the Declaration of Independence, Jefferson, a wordsmith of note, had drafted his own inaugural address. Buster hastily retrieved a few sheets of blank paper from his own pocket and prepared to take notes.

Jefferson began to speak in a soft voice. Despite the fact that he was sitting in the front row, Buster had to lean forward to hear the words. He knew that to those in the back Jefferson's immortal words would be inaudible.

Buster's companion leaned forward and whispered in his ear. "Don't worry about notes. Tom's a clever one. He gave an advance copy of his speech to Sam Smith at the *Intelligencer*. Sam'll have an edition for sale when you leave."

Buster frowned. He intuitively felt that Jefferson's open suborning of the objectivity of the press was not right. While Jefferson droned on, Buster's mind wandered. He wondered if he was compromising himself by seeking an interview with the manipulative president.

ALEXANDRIA, VIRGINIA

MARCH 4TH, 1801

Jason Satterfield, Buster's father, sat at his desk in his office located on the second floor front of the Union Street mansion on the Alexandria riverfront and tapped his foot to mark the seconds being ticked off by the gold watch that he held in his left hand.

"Ten seconds more and that French whore will be sworn in as President."

Skinny Potts, Jason's long time friend and business partner, looked up from his desk and stared at Jason.

Jason in disgust spun in his chair and peered out the window. In the foreground he could see his brewery, located on the riverside of Union Street, and next to it his three-slip boatyard. A vacant field separated the boatyard from his pier and his large entrepot warehouse. The three properties covered a full Alexandria city block of prime riverfront. The sight calmed him. He watched three workmen load kegs of "Pale Ale," Jason's product, in a long wagon. No doubt their industry could be attributed to the fact that the boss could see them from his office window directly across the street. Jason nodded with self-satisfaction at the industrious workmen, then he stared at the three empty slips. The irritation returned. He had to make a decision this morning. In one hour he would meet with the manager of his bank—Jason considered the Potomac Trust "his bank" even though he was only one of five co-equal investors—to inform him of his plans for the coming year.

The time had come for Jason to levy his financial requirements on the bank manager for the coming year. Jason had already delayed for two months; now, he had to decide what he was going to do, and he did not know. So much depended on what the mad revolutionist who was being sworn in as President at this very moment intended. Jason did not know if Jefferson would destroy the economy, dismantle the federal government, eliminate the army and navy; even worse, Jason did not know what was happening in Europe and how the new President would react.

The question was: when would the French and English start another war.

The English controlled the seas, and Napoleon wanted the land. Another war was inevitable. Both sides preyed on American shipping, impressing American seamen, and confiscating ships and cargoes; war would only intensify the violation of American "rights," and Jason did not know what Jefferson would do about all that. Would he join his beloved French in war on England? And what would all this mean for Jason and his small fleet of ships that sailed between Alexandria and the West Indies taking northern Virginia's wheat and flour to the island planters and returning with sugar and molasses to feed local sweet teeth and fuel breweries and distilleries. It was all intertwined, and Jason did not have enough information to properly design his plans. Jason was forty-four years old and did not know what that damned fifty-eight year old President was going to wrought with his so-called Second American Revolution.

"Don't worry, Jason. It will all fall into place. It always has. You haven't guessed wrong yet." Skinny tried to reassure his friend. That was one of his functions.

Jason glanced at Skinny and then returned his attention to the window. Across the river the indecent gash in the countryside that was the Federal District intruded. Jason studied the slate gray sky. To his disgust, at that moment, the leaden sky parted and the sun burst through enveloping the very spot where Jason calculated the ceremonies were taking place. Jason wondered if it were an omen.

Jason spun back to face his friend. "Skinny. Is Jefferson going to get us involved in a war or not?" The question was unfair, but Jason waited for Skinny's answer. Since his days as a newsman running the *Herald* while James was at war, Skinny had assiduously followed politics, and Jason relied on his perceptions.

Skinny studied Jason before replying.

"I don't know Jason. I don't think the decision is in his hands. His friend Napoleon and the damned English will decide that question. Me, I think Jefferson will dismantle the army. He might keep the navy; rumor has it that is what he promised Adams in return for the Federalist support that got him elected in the House. But if he does, he won't build any more ships. My friends tell me that Jefferson has a theory."

"He's got nothing but theories, but will he do something harmful?"

"He thinks that the only navy we need are gunships to defend the harbors. They're small and inexpensive and could have other uses."

"Manned by citizens like the militia I assume."

"Who knows? Probably."

"And what does that stupid law mean?"

Jason had reached the crux of the problem. The day before, March 3rd, the old Federalist controlled Congress in a busy last day had passed a catchall Maritime Act which among other things authorized the President to sell all navy vessels except for thirteen frigates, seven of which would be taken out of service. Skinny assumed the Congress had attempted to be both frugal and protective of the strength of the navy at the same time, an impossibility. Navies were expensive. Neither Jason nor Skinny anticipated that the good old days would return; by that they meant the period during the Revolution when Jason had gotten his start building privateers for the new country.

"The question again is how is Jefferson going to use it?" Skinny replied.

Jason shook his head in frustration. Skinny nervously rubbed the stump, all that remained of his left arm. He did that when he felt himself close to volunteering opinions on subjects he knew nothing about. While Jason stayed home and built ships at his father's small Alexandria boatyard, Skinny in a burst of patriotic enthusiasm had volunteered to fight for freedom in Washington's army. He lost an arm in the battle for Long Island.. He had then returned home and surprised everyone by becoming an effective manager of the *Herald* during the long four years that Jason's father, James, had served with Washington.

Skinny as a newspaperman had astonished even Jason, his best friend since school days. Skinny was the only man alive who knew that Jason had killed a man, a pirate who deserved it, during a struggle in a Martinique waterfront tavern. When James returned to take over his newspaper again, Skinny, who had few job options available because of his limited education and a missing left arm, joined Jason at the boatyard. Together, they had grown as Jason took chances and became a trader, brewer, banker and speculator. By being willing to wager everything on his last deal, whenever it came along, Jason had become one of the wealthiest men in northern Virginia. The more conservative Skinny went along and profited, but since he wagered less, he garnered less.

Today, Jason was on the threshold of making another one of those decisions, betting everything against the possibility of another major coup.

"Shit, Skinny. There's no sense worrying about what we don't know. I'm going to do it."

Skinny nodded. He had never doubted that Jason would decide to proceed with his latest scheme. Skinny would hedge his bet by not risking everything, but he would invest enough to hurt if Jason failed. He had enough confidence in Jason's judgment that he did not worry. He had known for a month, ever since Jason had visited Thomas Kemp's small boatyard at Fells Point near Baltimore, that Jason had another of those itches that would persist until he scratched it. Fortunately, from a monetary standpoint, or unfortunately because of the stress that they caused, Jason's itches were all consuming. This time he was convinced he had discovered the designer of the ship of the future, the Baltimore Schooner as Kemp labeled it.

Jason's decision to proceed with his latest plan indicated that he had decided that war was inevitable again despite the current peace on the continent and Jefferson's infamous indecisiveness. The Clipper, as Jason now described his dream, was Jason's modified version of Kemp's design. To Jason, it was the ideal ship for an America at war. The American privateers had made life difficult for the English during the Revolution, and Jason was convinced they would do so again in the next war. His Clipper, so named for its anticipated ability to clip over the waves, was designed for speed. Jason's philosophy was: "never engage a man-of-war when you can out-sail them," and that is what his vision could do.

The beautiful ship's secret was its sharp, copper lined hull designed for low drag combined with massive sail power generated by fore and aft sheets rigged with double square topsails draped from two rakish masts. The Clipper carried some two hundred tons in its one hundred and twenty-five by twenty-two-foot frame. Jason planned a flat deck mounted by a twelve-inch quarterdeck above a companionway leading to aft quarters. The trim lines limited cargo space to a ten foot high hold, but neither Jason nor Skinny considered that a problem. The Clipper would be a predator, not a cargo hauler, though it could do that also if speed was required to move selected, profit intensive cargo with stealth and maneuverability past English blockades. Jason was confident that there would not be a square-rigged frigate or ship-of-the-line on the high seas that could match the Clipper's speed. Combined with swiftness would be maneuverability; Jason intended that his Clipper would sail closer to the wind, be easier to handle, more responsive to command, carry less weight aloft and require fewer crew than any previous ship ever launched.

Best of all, the Clipper could be built in Alexandria at Jason's existing slips. Virginia white oak was strong enough, flexible and abundant. Jason's ship-wrights were experienced and had built smaller versions of Jason's dream. Jason had sailed on the "Gray Ghost" twenty-five years previously and owed his and Skinny's lives to the small schooner's ability to leave heavily armed square-rig-gers in its wake.

Jason had not made up his mind about armament. He planned to adapt the cannonry to each ship's assigned mission. He anticipated the Clipper could carry one or two long toms, twenty-four pounders used to flail plump merchantmen from a distance, and several swivels, large mouthed short range mortars that could pummel rigging and opposing crewmen. The hulls would be pierced with covered holes adequate to serve up to fourteen smaller cannon. Jason doubted that this much weaponry would be required. His tactics envisaged stealthy approaches followed by disabling shots from a distance, then quick closures, grappling and boarding. The Clipper would carry more crew than needed so that adequate manpower existed to form fighting squads of marines and officers and men for prize crews to sail victims to friendly ports. The Clipper that Jason planned would use its holds for supplies, quarters and weaponry. Space for pris-oners and cargo would be limited.

Just thinking about the Clipper excited both men. Despite Jason's feigned intellectual agony, Skinny knew the decision was inevitable.

Jason stood up and waved at Skinny as he hurried towards the door.

"Let's grab a sandwich and an ale."

Without a word, Skinny rose and hurried after his friend. They always grabbed a sandwich and an ale at the AleRoom. Both men had acquired James' preference for salty, country ham on thick slices of hot coarse bread coated with spicy English mustard.

Jason and Skinny crossed the street and entered the brewery door under the sign that bore a large depiction of a foaming mug of ale with the word "IceHouse" on top and "AleRoom" on the bottom.

Skinny had been skeptical when Jason had converted the front section of the brewery into a tavern and had decorated it in rustic fashion with a sawdust floor, plank walls, a rough hewn bar and hand made tables and chairs. Jason had crowded seating for fifty people into the available space. Food selection was limited to country ham sandwiches, which were stacked every noon on the bar. The main attraction was not the sandwiches, though they had many devotees. Last summer Jason had decided that one of the reasons people consumed less ale in the summer than they did in the winter was because the ale was served warm. He reasoned that if a way were found to cool the beer to the temperature it was served in winter—he had learned someplace that the ideal temperature for brewed drink was sixty-eight degrees—he would double his spring, summer and fall sales.

Normally Jason's Alexandria Brewery produced a light, pale ale that he sold under the simple brand name "Pale Ale." Last December, Jason sent each of his three schooners on an ice run to Boston where they loaded up with large chunks of local ice cut by New England ice houses. The schooners delivered the ice to Jason's Union Street dock. By the time the first shipload had arrived in January, Jason had had his workmen from the idle boatyard join with the men from the brewery in digging an immense pit in the floor of one of the storerooms located directly behind the designated "IceHouse AleRoom." When the pit was filled with the last load of ice, it was covered with straw and old canvas. Kegs of pale ale were then placed in what Jason had dubbed the "cool room."

To the amusement of the town's drinkers, Jason had personally nailed up the new sign and declared the IceHouse AleRoom officially open on one of the coldest days of the year. Buster had celebrated the occasion with an announcement in the *Herald* stressing that the IceHouse would feature "chilled ale." The brewery did not distinguish between the fermented stock it placed in the barrels marked IceHouse Ale and those designated Pale Ale. The brew was the same. Jason insisted, however, that the chilled IceHouse Ale be sold only in the AleRoom. Alexandria's other taverns and ordinaries would have to be content with Pale Ale until they consented to install their own cool rooms. Jason had also concluded that if he could build up demand for IceHouse Ale and force others to chill their beer, he could expand his business by selling them ice he carried in his schooners.

Despite the cold on the day of the AleRoom's opening, Jason and Skinny's friends had patronized the new establishment out of loyalty to the owners and to try the "new" ale. To their surprise, it tasted better than Jason's regular product, Pale Ale, and the Brown Ale of his competitor brewer, Brown's Brewery. Word of the quality of the new product quickly spread. For the past month one had difficulty finding a seat in the AleRoom anytime between its opening hour of eleven in the morning or its closing time twelve hours later.

Skinny and Jason anticipated that the demand for IceHouse Ale would increase over the summer months. They did not know how they would meet the demand. Already, Jason had relaxed his rules and allowed his pub men to sell IceHouse Ale by the bucketful on the premise that the townspeople would take their brew home and consume it immediately before it lost its chill and uniqueness. Jason planned to watch his business over the summer. Then, if the demand remained constant, he would open a second IceHouse AleRoom south of Market Square and stock it with ale from his brewery and ice hauled in his schooners. Opening a third outlet in the Federal District was also a possibility.

Skinny led the way into the dark and crowded room. Out of deference to the chilled ale, the room was without heat, but the customers did not seem to mind. Many waved and called to Skinny and Jason. Their comments were all positive. The only vacant table was a one located in the right front corner. Upturned chairs stacked with their seats face down on the table top signaled its reserved status. Skinny and Jason, exercising their ownership prerogatives, took their customary places at the table. A burly barkeep delivered two sandwiches and two mugs of IceHouse ale as soon as they were seated.

"How's business, Jake?" Jason asked. He could see for himself that it was booming, but the barkeep expected him to show a proprietary interest.

"Not bad," Jake smiled. "I just tapped our second keg of the day."

Jason made his obligatory glance at the bar. Two workers were busy replacing one of the two kegs. At Jason's suggestion, two holes had been cut between the AleRoom and the cool room. Stanchions were built in the cool room to hold the kegs, which were then fitted into the wall so that the front with the tap bungs protruded into the AleRoom. This way, the ale was kept chilled, and the barkeep could still draw his drafts. Jason was not sure the system made a difference, but the customers thought it did.

"When are you going to lay the keel?" Skinny asked, returning to the subject of Jason's decision.

Jason smiled at Skinny. The two had been friends and co-conspirators for so long that they were closer than brothers. Each could anticipate what the other was thinking.

"I'll arrange for the money this afternoon then head out to Occoquan tomorrow. There's a nice stand of virgin white oak that I want to check out."

Skinny nodded agreement. Jason always selected the timber for the keel and the masts himself. He had a superstitious belief that he could sense the spirit of the trees and influence the character of his boats by personally visiting the forest and choosing the all-important timbers.

The two friends ate their sandwiches and sipped their ale in silence.

"This salty ham makes a man need another mug," Skinny observed as he waved for a second round.

"That's the object," Jason confirmed.

"Have you seen Fat Eddy since we opened the AleRoom?" Skinny referred to Fat Eddy Brown, the owner of the competing brewery.

Fat Eddy had been a classmate of Jason and Skinny at Corney Goodenough's academy. Fat Eddy, even then, had been an overweight bully. The class outcast, Fat Eddy had had few friends. Several years older that the other students, Fat Eddy had dropped out of school and gone to work in his father's brewery, known not imaginatively as Brown's Brewery. Fat Eddy, who had replaced his father as the head of Brown's, produced a heavy black ale that he called Brown's Stout. Fat Eddy had been angry when Jason had opened his brewery to compete with Brown's—he felt with some merit that Alexandria was not big enough to support two breweries—and accused Jason of trying to drive him out of business.

"No, but I doubt that he's happy." Fat Eddy's state of mind was not a matter of great importance to Jason.

"We should keep an eye on him. I hear he's not dancing over the success of our IceHouse Ale."

"Who cares what Fat Eddy thinks."

"He can be dangerous when aroused."

"To whom? He can bring in his own ice and chill that slop he calls stout if he wants."

Skinny smiled at Jason's feigned indifference. He knew that Fat Eddy worried him and suspected that Jason had entered the brewery business to spite his old childhood antagonist. Fat Eddy and Jason had fought more than one backyard battle, and Jason had usually ended up on the losing end.

Brown's Stout was not a bad brew. Fat Eddy had a good German brewmaster he had inherited from his father. The old German had a knack for roasting his barley and adding his hops in a way that produced a good black ale. Skinny, like many others, preferred Jason's Pale Ale. It was higher in alcohol content, was more hoppy, had a slightly acrid flavor, and was highly carbonated. The secret, Jason's German brewer maintained, was in the ale yeast and harder water. Pale Ale was brewed in the water from two deep wells, which were now covered by the sheds of the brewery. Fat Eddy indifferently used Potomac River water even though he claimed to use crystal clear water from an underground spring located on his property. Skinny knew from personal inspection that Fat Eddy's spring would not produce ten barrels a day.

"Fat Eddy's not about to spend money on ice. He's more likely to hire somebody to burn down the AleRoom. That would be cheaper."

Jason studied Skinny thoughtfully. He knew that arson was not beneath Fat Eddy who did not take slights or competition lightly.

"Think we better hire a watchman?"

"I do. "

"Take care of it."

With those words, Jason drained his mug, rose and started for the door. "I'll go make Houghton's day."

Skinny watched his friend depart. He smiled to himself at the thought of Houghton's reaction when he heard the extent of Jason's plans. Warrenton Houghton was another classmate. A mild mannered man, the grown up version of a soft boy, Houghton was the second son of a moderately successful tobacco planter whose plantation on the lower Rappahannock had fallen on hard times. Soil exhaustion caused by repetitive planting of tobacco had taken its toll. Jason, who headed the group of five investors who had equally invested fifty thousand dollars to start the Alexandria First Trust Company, the growing town's first bank, had personally selected Houghton for the job. Houghton liked to talk as if the Alexandria First, as the banking company was known, was a community institution. In fact, Jason had organized the effort to obtain a pool of ready cash to fund his personal speculations.

Every year about this time, the five bank founders met individually with Houghton to inform him of their respective needs for cash for the year. Anything left over could be used for the First's ostensible community objectives--mortgages, business loans and the like. The First had grown in the ten years since its founding; Houghton now boasted that the First had capital reserves close to two million dollars. This sounded impressive to many, but the five directors knew that in reality Houghton had no more that two hundred and fifty thousand dollars available to invest before the founders made their demands.

"Good morning Warrenton," Jason greeted the First's manager in his cubbyhole office behind the main room of the banking company's building on Royal Street.

"Good morning Jason," Houghton replied. He was not about to call an old academy classmate "Mister," particularly not Jason whose family roots were buried in the soil of the Blue Ridge foothills of Loudoun County. He had to admit, however, that Jason intimidated him, so as a compromise he rose politely to welcome the bank director.

"I hear the AleRoom is a success. Congratulations."

Houghton knew that the bank had loaned Jason ten thousand dollars to remodel his warehouse front, ship ice and establish the IceHouse AleRoom. At least, ten thousand was the front money the bank had loaned Jason. Houghton did not know how much profit Jason had made from hiring his own schooners to haul the ice and using his brewery and boatyard workers to do the necessary labor. Jason continually juggled cash among his enterprises so that not even Houghton could track his activities with certainty.

After a minimum of obligatory small talk, Jason turned to the business at hand.

"I will need one hundred and fifty thousand dollars of the First's money for the coming year," Jason declared flatly.

Houghton, who had been expecting the usual estimate of ten to twenty thousand, collapsed back in his chair with a whoosh. He was not sure whether Jason was putting him on or not. Jason knew to the penny how much money Houghton had available for investment. At the last directors meeting the five owners had accepted Houghton's report that two hundred and fifty thousand dollars would be available for community loans during the coming year. If Jason took one hundred and fifty thousand, Houghton might as well shut the front door. The other directors could be expected to draw at least fifty to sixty thousand, and when they heard of Jason's demand they would probably inflate their own out of self protection, fearing for the First's solvency and garnering as much for themselves as they could.

Jason watched the color drain from the surprised Houghton's face. Jason had anticipated this reaction, but he had decided to do nothing to lessen the shock. Jason estimated that he would require at a minimum forty thousand dollars to build one Clipper to the specifications he required. He knew from experience that unforeseen costs always developed, and he did not intend to build his dream on the cheap, so he had budgeted for fifty thousand. On the way over to the First from the AleRoom, he had decided he might as well go the whole way. Therefore, he had demanded enough money to build three Clippers.

Most shipbuilders financed construction on this scale by selling shares in the enterprise; the average big ship had ten to a hundred shareowners by the time it slipped into the water. Lotteries were often used to finance construction because the costs were so high, but Jason had resolved that he and to a lesser extent Skinny would be the sole owners of the Clippers. He would not allow anyone else to be in a position to tell him what to do. Privateering was a risky business; costs were high, but so were profits. The privateers were nothing more than legal pirates; they lived by the gun. They operated without maritime insurance; losses were total, but then, the prizes went to the victor. Jason had studied the subject and knew that during the Revolution successful privateers operating in the Atlantic off the American coasts had averaged a prize capture every ten days. Immense fortunes had been made, and lost, but that was the game.

Jason knew his gamble was bigger than privateering. The government today did not issue letters of marque and reprisal. The country was at peace. The new president would do everything he could to avoid war. The latest word was that the Republicans intended to reduce the national debt by shrinking the army and navy. Jefferson's views on national security were odd: rowboats would defend the coast, and farmers with pitchforks would repel invaders. Jason did not believe Jefferson would be successful; the French and English had a compulsion to wage war; history proved that, and the United States would have a hard time remaining neutral. Jason was betting that war was imminent, that privateering would be Jefferson's only recourse after having destroyed Washington and Adams' pitiful efforts at creating a navy, and Jason's Clippers would become the scourge of the high seas. A nagging voice of uncertainty told him they would have to because the Clipper was designed as a predator; it was fast and elusive, but its holds were small; it would not pay its way as a cargo carrier. Jason shoved the doubt out of his mind and waited for Houghton's reaction.

"Did I hear you right, Jason? One hundred and fifty thousand dollars?" Houghton had mustered his courage.

"That's correct."

"But..."

"Don't say it. I know."

"But the others."

Jason responded by saying nothing. He had found intimidation better than argument. If he pleaded his case, he weakened his position.

"I might have to close the First's doors."

Jason remained silent.

"I only have two hundred and fifty thousand altogether for the year."

"The others will have to be reasonable."

Jason rose and headed for the door where he paused and looked back at the stricken bank manager.

"Set up my line of credit. I will begin drawing on it next week."

Jason knew that he would be confronted by a thunderstorm of protests from his co-investors, but he planned to ignore them. They would make a profit, as he would, when he repaid the loan.

If he lost, well, they would lose too, but if that happened his partners' reaction would be the least of his worries. Jason knew they could do nothing but protest then go along and do whatever they could to make Jason's endeavor a success. He knew, because he had worked with the lawyer in writing the trust's by-laws. He had deliberately incorporated a provision that contained a loophole that let each investor establish his own requirements. The wording was such that the others had assumed each would be able to draw on his own invested capital; they had not realized that one director could lay claim to virtually the entire resources of the bank, as Jason just had.

WASHINGTON, D.C.

JULY 5TH, 1801

Buster halted his horse on Pennsylvania Avenue in the lane leading to the front of the President's House. He wiped the sweat that streamed from his brow and cursed the July sun that fried everything it touched. Buster regretted the decision to accept the President's invitation to an informal private dinner; nobody in his right mind ventured out in the Potomac tidewater's noonday sun, but Buster knew he had had no choice. When he and James had broached the subject of a personal interview with President Elect Jefferson on the morning of his inaugural, Buster had anticipated meeting with the new officeholder within a week or two. He had written a short note to the President's secretary, Meriwether Lewis, formally requesting his appointment, and the non-response at first had not been troubling.

Jefferson in March had been preoccupied with forming his government. He selected James Madison and Albert Gallatin for the two key posts, State and Treasury, as anticipated. As for the rest of the cabinet, the best that could be said for them was that they appeared to be friendly, amiable men chosen for their loyalty to the President. The new Attorney General did not even live in Washington; he resided in Baltimore and visited his Washington office once or twice a month. Buster deduced from this that Jefferson intended to live up to his philosophical truism that declared the less government the better.

Jefferson's early cautious actions indicated that despite his promises he had learned from poor John Adams' experience. As a Federalist, Adams had inherited Washington's office holders, most of whom were loyal to Alexander Hamilton, not Adams. As a result, the portly New Englander had spent his four years in office hostage to a Cabinet controlled by a mortal enemy, Hamilton. Jefferson appeared determined not to let this happen to him, but he was circumscribed by his promise to Adams not to unload office holders for solely political reasons.

The problem was made more difficult because of the high expectations of his Republican supporters. They formed long lines at the door to the President's House, all seeking jobs, most as postmasters or customs officials. With his hands bound by his own promises and dictum—he had assured Adams he would not engage in a wholesale sacking of Federalist job holders, and he had ordered his Cabinet Secretaries to proceed slowly and not to remove officeholders for solely political reasons—Jefferson confronted a major problem. He also had had to cope with Adams' last minute vindictiveness—the appointment of judges for the Federal District.

Buster understood that an interview with the editor of a non-partisan, minor publication did not rank high on Jefferson's list of priorities, Virginian or not. None-the-less, Buster had been disappointed when Jefferson departed to spend the entire month of April at his beloved Monticello without responding to Buster's query. This simple discourtesy led Buster to conclude that the burdens of office could not be so great after all if Jefferson could bag them and depart for vacation after one short month in office, particularly since Madison and several of his key appointments had not yet assumed office or even visited Washington.

On May 20th, the pacific Jefferson demonstrated that he was not going to let a little thing like principle inhibit his conduct of foreign policy. He had long opposed the practice of previous administrations and other world powers who had paid a modest tribute to the piratical powers of the Barbary states in return for rights of passage in the Mediterranean. The choice was a simple one, pay tribute or dispatch warships; since others considered the game not worth the effort, they paid. Jefferson surprised Buster along with many supporters when he dispatched a squadron of four ships, virtually his entire seaworthy navy, under the command of Commodore Richard Dale who sailed in his flagship "Enterprise." Jefferson had been unaware when he deployed his power that the Bey of Tripoli one-week earlier had declared war on the United States in his colorful fashion. Unhappy with the American tribute which he had believed to be less than that paid to his neighbors, the Bey ordered that the flagpole at the American consulate be cut down. When Jefferson learned of this simple act, he had found himself facing a philosophical dilemma. As President he could deploy the Navy defensively, but he needed the Congress to fight a war.

Jefferson gathered together a bunch of letters and documents and sent them to Congress, pointing out that under his strict interpretation of the Constitution actions exceeding defense required the sanction of Congress. The opposition responded immediately. Alexander Hamilton argued in the New York press that if the United States were attacked approval of Congress was nugatory. The President must respond without splitting constitutional hairs.

Buster found Jefferson's position amusing; the pacifist who did not believe in a standing navy was criticized for having dispatched force and, then, for having asked for approval for having done so.

By June, Jason decided to forget the entire idea of an interview. Pride had kept him from sending a second note. Then, on the first of July he received his invitation.

Buster studied the President's house with approval. The new President was whipping it into shape. The workers' shacks had been torn down and no longer disfigured the attractive building's appearance. The yards had been cleaned of debris, and several gardeners appeared to be preparing the earth for grass and gardens. Given Jefferson's proclivities, this was to be expected. Noting that all of the rakers and diggers were African, Buster assumed that Jefferson had brought some of his slaves back to Washington with him from Monticello. Since Buster was accustomed to the presence of slaves, he was not offended. He had heard that Abigail Adams had been disturbed by the sight of African workers on her first visit to an area where slavery was practiced, but Buster, despite the fact that he opposed the institution, had adapted to it at Eastwind.

Buster urged his mount forward across the rough front yard and halted in front of the temporary steps that were still in place. An African servant rushed from the house and took the reins to Buster's horse.

"Massah Jefferson be in da back," he informed Buster, indicating that he was expected.

"Should I go through the house or around outside?" Buster was not sure whether the servant meant that Jefferson was behind the house or in a back room.

"Tru da house be fastah," the African replied.

Buster mounted the stairs and entered the entrance hall where with approval he noted the mud had been cleaned up, the wood floors polished, and covered with eastern carpets. Buster, unescorted, proceeded through the reception area and paused when he reached the central hall that ran the length of the house. It was littered with Jefferson's possessions, one of which snagged his attention, an odd appliance that had metal rods pointing in all directions.

"Dat be da massah's rack." The house servant said.

"The rack?"

"Yassah. For da massah's clothes."

Buster nodded his head, concealing a smile. Jefferson was well known for his propensity to acquire and invent gadgets.

"Follah me suh," the African instructed as he slipped past Buster and proceeded across the hallway into the large formal dining room.

Buster sidestepped stacks of papers and books, apparently part of Jefferson's extensive personal library, and followed the servant as instructed.

A beautiful, highly polished, cherrywood dining table, surrounded by twelve matching chairs, had been installed in the formal room. At the head of the table, obviously the President's place, a chair had been pulled back. Stacks of official papers were arrayed in a semicircle on the table facing the chair. In the center stood another odd machine. This one consisted of two connected rods that held a pen in each extended arm.

"Da massah's writin' machine," the servant said proudly.

Buster studied the odd contraption. He assumed that Jefferson used it to make copies of his letters and memoranda.

The African continued past the table and exited the house on the backside with Buster in tow. Several men, all black except for Jefferson, were gathered several hundred yards away. The President was dressed informally; he wore a white shirt, open at the collar, no cravat, and had his sleeves rolled up to his elbows. His sweat soaked hair was pressed against the sides of his head. Jefferson was gesticulating enthusiastically while talking in an inaudible voice. The servant escorted Buster to the group.

"Ahh, Mr. Satterfield, the publisher," Jefferson said wryly when he noticed Buster's approach.

"Mr. President," Buster replied stiffly. He silently remonstrated himself for suddenly feeling nervous.

"Please call me Tom. We abide by good Virginian informality here."

"Yes sir," Buster agreed. He could not bring himself to address the President as Tom. Besides, he suspected that Jefferson used his relaxed personal style and the fact they were both Virginians to establish a false rapport, and Buster did not like being manipulated.

"We are making plans for our gardens. We can't have the President's house looking like a sty."

Buster nodded agreement.

"First, we must install a fence to keep the roaming creatures out. Otherwise, they will destroy our efforts. I plan to completely surround the house. Do you agree?"

"Yes sir. I can see the improvements already."

Jefferson took Buster by the arm and led him through the grounds describing his plans for the gardens. Buster, who was unfamiliar with most of the Latin names that Jefferson used to describe the bushes and trees he intended to plant, listened politely. Finally, they returned to the house and entered a littered room on the right, which Jefferson had appropriated as his study. After the African served tea, Jefferson leaned back in his chair and commenced with the meeting.

"I apologize for the absence of Captain Lewis. He's busy delivering some letters for me. Otherwise, he would join us."

"Captain Lewis is your secretary?" Buster, who liked to begin with questions he already knew the answer to, commenced easily.

"Yes. My secretary and confidant. I write my own letters—I assume you saw my machine—and Captain Lewis delivers them. He also serves as my aide, but he is virtually family. We have partitioned the room on the left, the one called the East Room for obvious reasons, and Captain Lewis lives there. I understand that Mrs. Adams used to hang her laundry in there to dry." Jefferson smiled at the last statement.

Buster realized that the clever man was deliberately providing him with a colorful story to make his report more interesting.

"How do you like the President's House?"

"I assume you mean the facility and not the office." At Buster's nod, Jefferson continued. "It's rather large you know, and unfinished, much like Monticello."

Buster recognized that Jefferson referred to the frequently cited stories that Monticello was constantly being rebuilt by its owner, an accomplished self-taught architect.

"It has twenty-three rooms, far more than Captain Lewis and I require. But, you should know the roof leaks."

Buster wondered why he should know this mundane fact but waited for Jefferson to continue.

"We must do something about that, if Congress compassionately provides the money. I have also decided to do something about the house's appearance, break the lines and make it a little more imposing, as a public building of our country should be."

"What is that, sir?"

"I am now designing two grand porticoes, one for the front and one for the rear, to decorate the entrances." Jefferson indicated architect's sketches on his desk. "It will take me some time. I must do some research. They must be just right."

Buster laughed as he realized Jefferson wanted him to emphasize his plans and generate compassion for the roof and support for the remodeling.

"Have you solved the problem with Mr. Adams' carriages and horses?"

"Oh yes. I recently purchased with government funds, duly authorized I might add, a carriage and two teams. I will use them only for formal occasions. Otherwise, I have my own stallion for my personal use."

Jefferson was clearly an accomplished politician, accustomed to framing his answers in a self-serving manner. Graciously, Buster assumed that if he had been buffeted about by a hostile press the way Jefferson had he would be cautious too.

"Do you have any other plans for the national district?" Buster kept to the easier part of his agenda, saving the substantive questions for last after he broke through Jefferson's protective barriers if he could.

"Oh yes. I have established two priorities for my first year in office. We must complete construction of the Capitol; the representatives of the people need a home, and we must build a road."

"A road, sir?"

"Yes, sir. A good gravel road from the Rock Creek Bridge (at M Street) along Pennsylvania Avenue past the President's House all the way to the Capitol, some one and one half miles."

"This would connect Georgetown, then, with the President's House and the Capitol?"

"Exactly. A little something for everybody."

"Except for Alexandria."

"We must work on that." Jefferson replied unabashed.

"And your other plans?"

Jefferson paused before answering, apparently trying to decide if Buster was still referring to cosmetic matters or was approaching substantive issues.

"The poplars," Jefferson finally smiled.

"The poplars?" Buster was beginning to feel that he was being used as an echo board.

"Yes. Lombardy poplars. We must plant two rows along each side of Pennsylvania Avenue. They will give it a stately appearance."

"I am sure they will, sir," Buster said, deciding to move on to more important matters. He realized the subjects Jefferson had discussed would appeal to his readers who followed the construction across the river closely, but he wanted to reach political substance while he could. He decided to back into the subject by broaching the issue of protocol, which appeared to be developing into a controversial political matter. The French Ambassador and the English Charge had been quoted as disparaging Jefferson's efforts to establish a "republican" style of formality.

"I understand, sir, that you have substituted frequent dinners for twelve for more formal receptions."

"That's right. There are few good tables in our virgin town. I have hired a French Chef, and we invite friends in frequently."

"And you have proclaimed a new style, pele mele, I believe its called?"

Jefferson laughed as if Buster had told a joke.

"That's right, pele mele. It's the French word for pell mell. Everybody goes as they can, sit where they find a chair. No formal ranking of guests. Everybody including the host is equal. There's common courtesy of course. I have dropped the European rules of etiquette and entertain my guests as I do informally at Monticello. Have you heard someone objecting?"

"Only rumors, sir." Buster was a little sorry he had raised the silly subject.

"Good. I assume, Mr. Satterfield, that you have some questions of policy."

Buster recognized that Jefferson's more formal response was designed to convey irritation with the previous question.

"Yes sir. May I ask your plans for defense?"

"From whom? The Barbary pirates? That is being taken care of."

Buster detected testiness in Jefferson's tone but did not back off.

"No, sir. I mean your plans for the army and navy."

"I have made it perfectly clear that I do not think we need an army. Our citizens have proven they can defend their country when needed. A standing army is too expensive and poses a threat to the state."

"What do you mean by that?" Buster dropped the customary "Sir." He was determined not to let Jefferson intimidate him.

"When one commands military force, one is tempted to use it. History contains many examples of military officers turning on their own governments. We do not need that risk."

"Do you have any particular officers in mind?"

Jefferson glared at Buster.

"Are you sure the *Herald* is not a Federalist supporting newspaper?" Jefferson paused then continued before Buster could respond. "No, certainly not.

I only meant to say our potential enemies are far away, and we will have time to assemble an army if we ever need one. It is more important that we now address the public debt."

Buster decided to ignore Jefferson's attempt to change the subject. Everybody believed in economy in government and thought the government should balance its budget.

"Do you plan to reduce the size of the army?"

"My hands are tied at this point. Until Congress passes new laws, the army will remain as it is."

Buster realized that Jefferson had not answered his question but continued.

"And the navy?"

"I will enforce the law."

"And that is?"

"You should know that. Your family is in the shipbuilding business." Jefferson paused for this comment to register.

Buster did not know if Jefferson was threatening him and Jason's shipyard or not so remained quiet.

"The law passed during President Adams' administration authorizes me to sell all but thirteen frigates and to take all but six out of service. I am required to keep those six armed; three of these, along with one armed sloop, I sent to the Mediterranean on a mission."

"And the remaining four frigates?"

"Are more than we need," Jefferson replied testily. "I believe the navy's mission is defense. Smaller and less costly gunboats should be up to the task. In any case, if problems should arise with foreign powers, diplomacy and economic pressures not guns will provide the solution."

Buster did not point out the inconsistency in Jefferson's argument; he had already dispatched force to resolve the Barbary problem. The fact that Jefferson's simple philosophies did not mesh with his actions was an item Buster intended to stress for his readers, so he concluded it was not necessary to debate the subject with Jefferson now.

"I intend to reduce the manpower in the navy forthwith," Jefferson continued. Noting the dismay on Buster's face, Jefferson lectured him. "Young man, I don't think you realize the extent of our country's debt. We, every man-child of us, owe $83,000,000. I estimate if I make every cut I can, including reducing the expenses of your army and navy, it will take me sixteen years to eliminate it. I have only eight years." Jefferson paused. He had not intended to publicize his intent to remain in office for a second term. It was better politics to keep the public guessing.

Buster, thinking ahead to his next question, missed Jefferson's slip. Buster had intended to pursue also the subject of Adams' last minute judicial appointments—Jefferson had created a controversy by withdrawing the names of the twenty-three Federal District appointments that he claimed were invalid because they had not been delivered before the expiration of Adams' term—and

Jefferson's own selection of office holders.   Despite his commitment not to remove Federalists from office because of their political allegiances, Jefferson's Post Master General and Secretary of the Treasury had already began making inroads.   They were responding to the clamor of partisan Republicans who aspired to the lucrative postmaster positions and customs officer slots. However, given Jefferson's testiness, Buster decided not to raise these delicate issues.

He closed his notebook to signal that as far as he was concerned the formal aspects of the interview were completed. Jefferson smiled agreement and again assumed the role of relaxed host. Over dinner, a modest two-course affair, soup and Potomac catfish, Jefferson surprised Buster.

"Have you given any thought to my suggestion?" Jefferson asked.

"What was that, sir?"

"That the *Herald* adopt a more partisan role."

"That is not possible, sir," Buster replied quickly.

"I'm sorry to hear that," Jefferson said. "You will, I assume, remain objective. At least as objective as your grandfather and father let you."

"My grandfather is objective," Buster said quickly. "My father's views are his own and have no connection with the *Herald*."

"I understand that Jason is building a privateer. Since privateering is illegal, to what purpose will his raider be dedicated?"

"I cannot speak for my father," Buster replied coldly. "I am sure he will not break the law."

"And so am I," Jefferson said ambiguously. "I assume he anticipates war and that the government will issue letters of marque and reprisal?"

"I do not know what he anticipates, sir."

"If the subject should arise, you may assure your father that I will under no circumstances lead this country into war. I fear your father's speculation may take him into troubled financial waters."

"Can we ignore the impressment of our citizenry?" Buster referred to the continuing problem of French and English warships stopping American merchantmen on the high seas and seizing sailors to serve in their Navies.

"Impressment is a complicated problem that we must solve, diplomatically. The English who are the major transgressors have a certain amount of right on their side. Did you know that, young man?"

"What is that, sir?" Buster was irritated by Jefferson's habit of referring to him belittlingly as a "young man."

"I'm sure you know. Life in the English navy is difficult. Most of the sailors have been impressed into service in England. They don't opt for a life at sea voluntarily, and they jump ship at every opportunity. America, with its freedom and opportunities, is a magnet. Many of the escaping English seamen hire on our merchantmen. The pay is considerably better than that offered by the English Navy and certainly the conditions are much improved. The English claim they stop our ships merely to recover their own deserters."

"But they take our sailors too."

"That's the rub. Yes, they have difficulty distinguishing Americans from Englishmen. Our people don't carry papers around to establish their nationality, and it is easy to become an American citizen. We need as many citizens as we can gather to people our large country."

"Can we allow the British to violate our sovereignty?"

"Is it worth bloodshed to resolve?"

"To those poor American souls forced to serve on English ships it is."

"Well, this is not an argument you and I will resolve. I plan to leave it to Mr. Madison."

James Madison, Jefferson's Secretary of State, had only recently arrived in the capital to assume his duties. Since Jefferson had reduced the number of posts overseas to four, as part of his government economy effort, most assumed that Madison would not be over tasked by the pressure of supervising his department's seven employees. Most observers expected Madison to continue as Jefferson's confidant, adviser and political operative, a role that he had played effectively for many years.

"Would you object to meeting with Mr. Madison and briefing him on your interesting views?"

"I'm sure Mr. Madison does not need my advice," Buster replied. He wondered why Jefferson continued to flatter him. Certainly the twenty-five year old Buster and his small Northern Virginia newspaper could be of little use to the older, more experienced and certainly more influential politicians.

"I have taken the liberty of mentioning your name to Mr. Madison. He is looking forward to meeting you."

"I am flattered, Mr. President," Buster said. He recognized that Madison would be a useful contact. For the first time, he realized that the location of the capital across the river from Alexandria might prove to be a boon far beyond occasional feature stories. If Buster were able to acquire informed sources, his stories could prove to be of interest to other newspapers to the north and south. Buster resolved to make the report of this interview as insightful as he could.

As soon as the dinner ended, Jefferson called an end to the interview. Jefferson, a good host, stood in the doorway and watched as Buster recovered his horse and directed it toward the ferry. On the ride home, Buster decided to visit his father's office on the way to the newspaper at Number 66. He wanted to put the President's words on paper while they were fresh in his mind. At the same time, he knew that Jason would be most interested in several of Jefferson's comments. Not all of them would please Jason.

SHORT HILLS, VIRGINIA

SEPTEMBER 1802

Fifteen year old J.J. Satterfield chewed on the blade of a wheat stalk as he leaned against a gnarled sour gum tree and studied the cloudless, bright blue sky. He was hot and his tired muscles ached. As he watched, a marsh hawk circled the recently harvested wheat field to his left. J.J., short for John Junior, wondered why he had been so anxious to come east. He had been living with his Satterfield cousins in the Short Hills for two months, and he sorely missed his family and his mountains. He estimated that his dad, Eli, would have already finished his much smaller harvest with the help of his mother and brothers and sisters. Harvest time, he had learned, came earlier in the high mountains.

J.J. looked forward to his year of study at the Alexandria Academy, the reason he had been sent back east, but he had not expected the backbreaking labor of a Piedmont farm. He had been raised on the stories of his Grandpa John, who had been born in the very house J.J. now lived; Grandpa John's reminiscences made life in the Short Hills seem like fun; he talked about farm work, but he had not described anything like the straining labor with a hoe and sickle that J.J. was experiencing.

"That hawk has his eye on some kind of varmit," J.J.'s cousin Toddy broke J.J.'s reverie.

J.J. nodded wearily and motioned for Toddy to join him.

The two cousins were both Satterfields. Toddy's father Eric farmed the Satterfield homeplace with the assistance of two tenants and whatever family and temporary help he could dragoon. Toddy's grandfather, Will, the brother of J.J.'s grandfather John, now lived in the family home with his son Eric and his brood. J.J. who had grown up in the mountains with only his immediate family and grandparents as kin was still adjusting to the fact that a whole passel of Satterfields lived west of the Blue Ridge.

"Will they be much longer?" J.J. asked, nodding in the direction of the mill where he and Toddy had spent the morning unloading the Satterfield long wagon of its heavy burden of wheat sacks.

"Another two or three hours."

"And then what?"

"Then, we put the flour sacks back in the wagon and head for the barn."

"I hope they take their time," J.J. said.

He had become far more intimately acquainted with wheat than he had ever had with anything else in his life

J.J. had arrived in the Short Hills in early July. He had delayed in the mountains long enough to help his father Eli plow and plant the small mountaintop fields in wheat and corn. Unlike the Short Hills Satterfields, Eli cultivated only enough grain to feed his family and his animals. By contrast, the fields of the Short Hills Satterfields spread across the slopes of the Blue Ridge foothills; Toddy, with exasperation, explained that his father increased their acreage every year. The townspeople of Alexandria and the new Federal District had a growing appetite, and Eric Satterfield labored to sate it.

"Don't you ever get tired of that damned wheat?" J.J. asked.

Already, he missed the days he spent alone in the mountains with his rifle hunting for game.

"I don't know what's worse," Toddy agreed as he dropped beside J.J. and shared the shade of the gum tree. "Plowing and planting is hard, but so is hoeing and cutting and threshing. The worst is behind us for this year. Next week we take the flour to Alexandria, and then you and I are free."

"To sweat over the books."

J.J. tried to sound discouraged by the thought. In reality, he anxiously awaited the first day of formal schooling. He had read every book he could find for miles around in the mountains, many several times, and he had been taught his numbers by his grandfather John. J.J. had been warned that he would be behind the others in his class and would have to work to catch up, but he was ready. He hoped to learn enough in a year or two to gain admittance to William and Mary in Williamsburg. His grandfather's stories about his Uncle James and Governor Dinwiddie had kindled a dream. J.J. loved the mountains, but his books and grandfather John's stories had made him ambitious to acquire an education.

"Anything is better than this," Toddy said.

Toddy and J.J. had already discussed their aspirations. Toddy wanted to escape from the farm and become a sailor. His second cousin Jason in Alexandria built ships, and Toddy secretly planned to sail one day down the Potomac to the ocean and then to see the world. Only J.J. knew of this plan, and he did not share Toddy's aspirations; he wanted to explore the adventures of book learning.

"Want to take a dip?" Toddy asked.

"The mill creek?"

"There's a swimming hole downstream."

J.J. nodded agreement.

"Lead the way," he said as he struggled to his feet. I think every muscle aches."

"You're not used to the scythe."

"Pounding those damned kernels out of the shocks is worse."

"It's all bad."

Toddy led the way to a path that curled through the thick forest alongside the creek. J.J. looked back at the water buckets that turned slowly on their large wheel emptying their loads into the creek then turning to be refilled by the water cascading through the runway.

"It doesn't look deep enough to swim in," J.J. observed.

"Take what you can get. It's cool. About a quarter mile downstream there's a beaver dam and a hole big enough for dipping."

The path narrowed and J.J. was forced to drop behind and follow his cousin. The hot, tired boys walked silently, each lost in his own thoughts.

As they approached the swimming hole, Toddy turned to announce they had reached their objective. Before he could speak, a loud shriek interrupted him. He looked at J.J., then smiled, putting his forefinger to his lips signaling silence.

"This might prove more interesting than I thought," Toddy whispered.

"What do you mean?" J.J. asked.

He had been looking forward to a quiet, relaxing dip in the cool, mill water. The shriek indicated that others were there ahead of him, and he did not look forward to the bother of dealing with strangers. He had already found out that the local farm boys were suspicious of outsiders and immediately set to test them. J.J., a strong, husky young man with thick shoulders and developed muscles with considerable strength, had nothing against fighting, but he was too hot and tired today to bother. Just in case, he clenched and unclenched his large hands to loosen the muscles.

"Not that," Toddy whispered. He had noticed his cousin's reaction. He had already tested his cousin and had learned they were equally matched. That meant they were the two best fighters in the Short Hills. "Just follow me. Quietly."

"I can out quiet you in the woods any day," J.J. said.

He was not bragging, merely stating a simple fact. He had grown up in the mountains and had learned his skills from the best woodsmen in the area, his father and grandfather, particularly the latter who was famous as an Indian killer.

The boys listened for another shriek, and heard two voices talking and water splashing. Toddy crouched low and quietly made his way to the stream bank. As they approached, both boys dropped to the ground and slithered through the dense underbrush. The sounds came from their right, about twenty or thirty yards downstream. Toddy slowly parted the high grass in front of him and stared. J.J. followed his cousin's example and was shocked when he saw why his cousin was suddenly silent.

Two girls stood waist deep in the stream in the middle of a small pool. They were engaged in a water fight, splashing each other from a distance of about five feet apart. It was not a serious fight; one girl would splash, and the other would shriek. They appeared to be taking turns splashing and shrieking. The commotion was not what caught J.J.'s rapt attention. Both girls were naked. One stood with her back to the boys. The other faced them head on.

"It's the Gutradt girls, Debbie and Sarah," Toddy whispered.

J.J. was too busy staring to listen to his cousin. The girl facing him had coal black hair which was soaking wet and pasted to the sides of her pretty face. J.J. hardly noticed her bright eyes and pert upturned nose. He stared at her bobbing breasts. The size of apples, they sported erect pink nipples. Each time the girl moved, the apples bounced.

"My God. Look at that," Toddy whispered.

J.J. was too entranced to respond. As he watched, the girl whose back was towards him turned to splash her friend. J.J. caught a glimpse of one large sloping breast as she turned toward him, smacked her palm against the water and sent a shower at her companion who shrieked. The breast was even larger than the two that had stared at him. He had the feeling that the nipples were eyes and were studying him. He slid back into the weeds, embarrassed at the thought of being caught. He pulled on Toddy's pant leg to indicate they should leave.

"No way," Toddy said, refusing to move.

Despite his concern about being seen, J.J. inched back towards the bank. He felt a strong, warm sensation in his groin. Before long, the girls tired of their game and waded out of the water. J.J. stared at the taller girl whose back had been towards him. Her large, firm breasts bounced as she walked. J.J. studied her slender stomach, her trim but rounded buttocks and her long perfectly shaped legs. She leaned over as she approached the stack of clothes on the riverbank giving J.J. a look at her backside.

"Oh my God," he repeated Toddy's words.

The tall girl retrieved a white shirt and used it to dry her wet body. J.J. had lost awareness of the other girl and Toddy. Only he and the tall girl who was about his age were alone on the earth. After she rubbed her arms and her breasts, she spread her legs and wiped between them. J.J. noticed the rust colored hair where she wiped and raised his eyes momentarily to the girl's head. She had striking red hair that curled over her beautiful face. J.J. was close enough to see the sparkle in her green eyes and the freckles on her cheeks. He studied her body and saw that the freckles were everywhere. Suddenly, to his intense disappointment she slipped her arms into the sleeves of the shirt and pulled it on. As he watched, she buttoned the front. The shirt, apparently a hand-me-down from an older brother, covered her to the thighs. Disappointed, J.J. watched as she slipped on a pair of cotton panties then stepped into a shift and a faded, checkered skirt. Only then, did J.J. turn his attention to the second girl, the one with the raven hair. She too had dressed while his attention had been focused on the redhead. The smaller one tossed her jet-black hair backward to dry it.

"We better get back. Mom will need help with the dinner." The redhead, who spoke, had a husky catch in her voice.

The other girl took her arm and the two hurried back down the path.

J.J., still lying on his stomach took a few seconds to catch his breath, then he spoke to his cousin.

"Does this happen very often?"

"First time," Toddy smiled. "That was really something. I like the smaller one."

His words pleased J.J. because he had already selected the redhead as his own.

"Either would do," J.J. observed, trying to appear accustomed to such experiences. "Who's Gotrach?"

"The miller."

"The old German man?"

"Yes."

"Those are his daughters?"

"Yes. "

"Where did all that red hair come from? Do Germans have red hair?"

"How do I know. I like black myself."

The two cousins rolled over on their backs and studied the sky. They quietly explored their own thoughts for about ten minutes until Toddy took the initiative.

"Have you calmed down enough to take a dip?"

"If you think we're safe," J.J. replied.

"From what?"

"Rude peepers," J.J. laughed. "I wonder if they come here every day at this time."

"Don't know. I wonder if Dad will have more wheat that needs milled tomorrow."

"Maybe if we work hard... ."

Two weeks later J.J. and Toddy were installed in James and Vivian's Union Street mansion facing the Potomac River. The selection of the proper place for the two boys to live while they attended Alexandria Academy had been a subject of much family discussion. Jason and Lily worried that acquiring two fifteen year old boys as boarders would be too much strain for Vivian and James, and James, approaching his sixty-eighth year, had had his doubts. Buster had been willing to share his town house next to the *Herald*, and Jason had reluctantly offered to take them into his home, but both suggestions had been overruled out of hand by Vivian and Lily. Both doubted that Buster, who was only ten years older than the cousins, would provide the necessary adult supervision, and Jason, whose wife Lily spent most of her time at Eastwind, was too busy to track and care for them. Finally, all agreed that the only solution was to move them in with James and Vivian with the proviso that two additional servants from Eastwind be moved to the mansion to help with the extra work. Vivian, to tell the truth, was pleased with the solution; she looked forward to the excitement that the two young men would bring to her household.

To celebrate the occasion and to welcome the two young men to Alexandria, particularly J.J. who had never before been west of the mountains, Vivian scheduled a Wednesday afternoon party. Visiting a city, even one as small as Alexandria was a new experience for J.J., and his enthusiasm perked up everyone but James. As the boys bustled about the house helping Vivian prepare for the arrival of the others, James watched sourly. He enjoyed hearing J.J.'s stories of the western mountains, particularly those focused on James' twin brother John, J.J.'s grandfather. Unfortunately, most of J.J.'s recollections were about an old man, and this was not the John that existed in James' memory. Besides, the references to age irritated him. His body was old, not his mind. Inside, he felt the same as he always had.

"Gramps, is there anything we can get you?" Toddy asked.

Both boys at Vivian's suggestion called James "Gramps." He was not either one of them's grandfather; to be exact, he was their granduncle, but he did not object. Buster called him "Gramps" so he saw no harm in J.J. and Toddy doing the same. Vivian, of course, insisted on being called Vivian.

"What for?" James grumped. "If I want anything, I can get it for myself."

"Pay no attention to the grouchy, old man," Vivian interjected. "Let him sit there and read his book."

To spite Vivian, James stood up, dropped his book, which he had lost interest in anyway, and stomped through the open door to the porch. He liked to sit on the porch in the summer. From his outside rocker, he could see Jason's boatyard in the distance. The "Clipper," as everyone called Jason's new project, was taking shape. The hull was almost finished. Workmen could be seen cutting, shaping and installing the planking.

James could tell from the lines of the hull that the "Clipper" was going to be a magnificent creature. Everyone who saw it agreed, but James worried. He did not know how Jason would make his investment pay. The cargo hold was too small for long distance shipping, and Thomas Jefferson seemed to be holding to his promise to keep the country out of war. The "Clipper" would be a predator with nothing to hunt.

"Hi Gramps," Buster came up from behind as James rocked.

The sound of his grandson's voice brought a smile to James' face.

"How's the rocking?" Buster joked.

"About as much as I can handle these days."

As best as Buster could tell, his grandfather continued to overstate the ravages of time. He appeared to be in good health. No one really knew. James refused to consult a doctor; he did not trust them and did not believe they knew as much about the mysteries of the human body as they pretended. The very mention of one of the doctors' favorite treatments, bleeding, was enough to bring James' temperature to a boil.

"Are the boys about?"

"They're inside helping Vivian. We're waiting for your father and mother to make a grand arrival. As little as we see of them, one would think they lived in another country."

"Dad's busy. He's got his problems. We all do."

James caught the worried tone in Buster's voice.

"Did you get another one of those letters?"

Buster nodded affirmatively.

James shook his head in commiseration. He did not know what to say. During the past year, ever since his first interview with Jefferson, Buster with James' approval had grown more critical of the Jefferson administration in the *Herald*. He had particularly stressed the inconsistencies between the philosophies that the President professed and his actions. Word was out that Jefferson was negotiating to purchase Louisiana and a great portion of the southwest. James, like most Americans, agreed it was America's manifest destiny to expand into the unsettled western lands claimed by the French, English and Spanish, but he was not sure it would be necessary to buy it. The *Herald* had approved the project, but once again had questioned Jefferson's rationale.

James had written the most recent article asking how Jefferson who claimed to be a strict constructionist—i.e. one who believed the central government held only those powers delegated to it by the states in the constitution—could rationalize the assumption of the authority to expand the country. The position of the *Herald* had been cerebral, academic, but the reaction of Jefferson's supporters had a tinge of violence. Several weeks ago someone had begun writing anonymous letters threatening to burn down the *Herald* if it did not stop questioning Jefferson's actions.

"I got another note today. Stronger than the last one," Buster said as he sat on the steps.

"Let 'em burn Number 66 down," James referred to the address of the *Herald*. "We need a new building anyway."

"We can't risk losing the press and the type," Buster said. "We just bought this one last year. They cost an arm and a leg."

"I know, but we aren't going to be intimidated. It's just some harmless nut anyway."

"I'm not sure of that Gramps. It's a nut. That much is certain. But I'm not sure how harmless."

"Then what do we do?"

"We can hire a guard."

"Your father already has a guard at the brewery. I'm not sure he does much good. Go past there anytime of the night, and he's no where in sight, out back sleeping somewhere."

Buster nodded agreement.

"Besides. We can't hire guards for everything. People will think we Satterfields are afraid of our shadows."

"That's the way I think," Buster agreed. "We'll just tough it out, but I will keep a sharper watch on Number 66."

"Why is that?" J.J. asked, having come through the front door in time to catch Buster's last comment.

"Oh, we've been receiving crank letters at the paper," Buster dismissed the subject.

While the three Satterfields, J.J., Buster and James discussed various matters, particularly what J.J. could anticipate at Corney Goodenough's Alexandria Academy, Jason and Lily arrived.

"Mom, Dad," Buster greeted them.   .

After a round of pleasantries, Lily entered the house to assist Vivian who was supervising the preparation of the late dinner.

"The "Clipper" is shaping up," Buster observed.

The three generations of Satterfields, now joined by Toddy turned to study the trim lines of the ship's hull. Jason nodded proudly.

"When will she be finished Cousin Jason?" J.J. asked.

"Three or four months. We have to finish planking the hull, then the caulkers will go to work. After that the decks will be installed, the masts raised, the riggin' put on and the sails fitted. I hope to have her in the water by December."

"Wow," Toddy exclaimed. "Could we visit her sometime?" Toddy spoke for himself and J.J.

Jason noted the young men's enthusiasm.

"If you like, we might find something for the two of you to do at the yards in your spare time," Jason let himself get carried away with family sentiment.

"Hey, that would be super," J.J. accepted before anyone else had a chance to speak.

"We'll have to explore that subject," James frowned. "First, see how the school work progresses before we make any long term commitments. Important things first."

"Aw Gramps," J.J. and Toddy protested in unison.

"We'll see," James retreated.

"They can at least come down to the yard and look around tomorrow," Jason intervened.

He knew from his own experience that schoolwork was not an end all for every boy. His own schooling had terminated at age seventeen when he had rebelled against his father's desire that he follow in his footsteps and attend college at Williamsburg. Jason had instead gone to work in the boatyard, and he did not consider that he had turned out badly.

Before long, the male Satterfields were called inside to dinner. The evening passed quickly as they all sat around the table and sated themselves on the chicken, ham, potato salad and fresh vegetables from Eastwind. J.J. charmed the family with stories of his Grandfather John's exploits in Indian country. All listened wide-mouthed, including John's brother James. John was the family legend.

As dusk fell, Buster announced that he had work to do at the paper. James and Buster exchanged quick glances that the others did not notice. James realized that Buster was still worried about the threats and wanted to check on his press, particularly since Sunday afternoons were usually a busy time for the town's rougher elements. They spent the afternoons at the Pig or other disreputable ordinaries playing cards and drinking and then by dusk, grew bored, and sought other amusements.

"May we walk with you to the paper?" Toddy asked. "I for one need some exercise after all that food."

J.J. quickly seconded the request. Both boys had enjoyed the afternoon with the Alexandria Satterfields but were growing restless after several hours of adult company.

"Don't see why not," Buster agreed, looking at Vivian for approval.

She nodded affirmatively.

"But don't be late. Tomorrow is the first day of school."

Vivian recognized that her young guests would need a long leash. She doubted that they could get into much trouble in Alexandria. Most of the citizens knew the Satterfields and would keep a passive eye on the two unwary country youths.

Buster, accompanied by J.J. and Toddy, strolled down the dusty Union Street. Despite the breeze rolling off the river, heat spires still rose from the hard baked Virginia clay.

"The river's pretty," J.J. observed as they walked. Despite the fact that the Potomac had shrunk back from its banks, a phenomenon caused by the long, hot, dry summer, it was still at least a mile in breadth. "But I think it's much hotter here than in the mountains."

"Or the Short Hills," Toddy said.

"I'm sure it is," Buster agreed.

Buster strode briskly, anxiously to get back to Number 66. Dusk had given way to darkness, but a full moon was rising on the horizon, bathing the streets with it's soft, reflected light.

"A real harvest moon," Toddy said, repeating a phrase he had heard often at home.

"And I'm glad harvest is over for us," J.J. said. "Mountain boys were not made for farm work."

"And what are they made for?" Toddy asked, a little put down by his cousin's observation.

"Skinny dippin'," J.J. laughed and thought of the miller's red headed daughter.

Buster, puzzled by the remark, studied the two younger boys who were laughing as they shared their private joke. He decided to ignore it and walked faster as he turned up Cameron Street and headed for Market Square. They passed other Alexandrians out for a pleasant late evening stroll. Many spoke to Buster as they passed. To the boys' surprise he did not pause to chat and continued to walk quickly. J.J. wondered what the hurry was but said nothing. He hoped they might encounter the miller's daughters.

Buster turned east on Royal Street and led the way towards Number 66. He covered the several blocks to the newspaper office quickly. When he was several hundred yards away, he stopped suddenly and motioned for the boys to do likewise and remain quiet.

They watched Buster as he studied Number 66. Buster thought he had seen movement at the front door of the log cabin that housed the newspaper office. Buster did not know if his eyes were playing tricks on him or not; he recognized that his worry could have fired his imagination. He waited and peered into the darkness. Again, he saw movement. Two figures huddled near his door studying the latch. A sharp clang of metal against metal echoed through the night.

"What's that?" Toddy whispered.

"I see two men," J.J. whispered. His sharp hunter's eyes had been trained to penetrate the night's mysteries. "They have a hammer and chisel."

"Hey there," Buster shouted. As soon as he heard the challenge of his own voice, Buster regretted his impulse. If the men ran, he would never be able to identify them.

Buster ran towards Number 66. J.J. and Toddy immediately followed. In the darkness, the two muscular boys looked like large men.

The man nearest the door dropped his hammer and chisel, leaped off the porch and charged in the opposite direction away from the Satterfields. His companion followed. By the time Buster had drawn abreast of Number 66, the men had disappeared. Buster could hear the fading sound as their boots hit the hard ground in the distance. Buster paused in front of his building. J.J. and Toddy, excited by the sudden chase, paused and looked at their older cousin for instructions.

"Shall we chase them?" Toddy asked anxiously.

Buster thought quickly and decided. He did not want to confront the intruders with the two boys. Despite their surprised flight, they might be armed and fight back if cornered, and he was responsible for J.J. and Toddy.

"No," Buster said. "Let them go. Just ordinary burglars. They're gone now and no harm done."

The two boys exchanged disappointed glances and followed their cousin to the cabin porch.

"We might've caught them," Toddy protested.

"And then what?" Buster asked, dismissing the subject.

Buster studied the doorjamb while Toddy retrieved the dropped hammer and chisel. Buster fingered a large gouge near the latch.

"They were trying to break in," Toddy exclaimed. "Look at that."

"Fat chance," Buster laughed. "They would have had to chip away the entire door to get around that brace."

Several days before, after having received his fourth warning letter, Buster had installed thick crossbars across both the front and rear doors of the cabin. He had also sealed the two small windows on the outer wall with heavy planks. He entered and exited the cabin through a connecting door in the wall that separated the original cabin from the adjacent town house where Buster lived. Anyone familiar with the two buildings would have known that access could have been obtained by entering the adjacent house, but strangers would not. The two structures abutted a common wall like many Alexandria homes built on the small lots.

"What's this?" J.J. asked.

Buster turned to see his cousin leaning over and studying a large tin. He was reaching for the container when Buster shouted.

"Don't touch it."

J.J. pulled his hand back and waited for Toddy and Buster to join him.

"Boy that smells," Toddy observed. "What is it?"

Buster immediately recognized the acrid odor.

"It's acid. Strong acid."

"Do you think the burglars brought it?" J.J. asked.

"What for?" Toddy pitched in.

"I'm afraid they intended to pour it on my lead type and printing press," Buster observed thoughtfully.

The aborted break-in and acid made his crank letters appear all the more ominous. Someone intended to put the *Herald* out of business.

Buster led the boys into his adjacent town house. He lighted a lamp then inspected the newspaper office. Everything was untouched.

The three cousins returned to the kitchen of Buster's house and sat around the table and discussed the event. After about half an hour Buster decided to send the boys home.

"Tomorrow's a school day, boys," he suggested tactfully.

"Right," Toddy agreed.

"We better be going," J.J. said.

Both boys were anxious to return to the older Satterfields and relate the news of their exciting experience.

As they approached the front door, Buster paused.

"And boys," he said as his two younger cousins turned to listen. "Let's keep this little incident a secret amongst us. I don't want to worry the old folks."

Disappointment immediately etched both boys' faces, but they nodded agreement. As Buster watched, the two walked quickly back down Royal Street towards the square.

WASHINGTON, D.C.

APRIL 1803

After the incident with the aborted break-in, Buster toned down his criticism of the new administration. Not completely to his surprise, the crank letters stopped, and no new attempts to harm his press and type occurred, but the respite did not give him peace of mind. He began to worry that in his effort to maintain objectivity he had leaned too far in the other direction. He began to suspect that the devious Jefferson had neutralized him, a perceived critic. In any case, Buster ignored Jefferson's suggestion that he meet with Madison; in fact, he studiously kept his distance from all of Jefferson's office holders in an attempt to convey a stance of total political neutrality. Then, in late March, the unexpected happened and forced the *Herald* back into prominence as a Virginian critic of the President.

Buster was sitting in his Alexandria office putting the finishing touches on a light piece about the glory of spring in Alexandria when a pudgy, cheaply dressed, middle-aged man with a pig snout of a nose entered. The man deferentially carried his hat in hand.

"Sir, may I speak with Mr. Satterfield, the editor," the visitor spoke softly, acting as if he feared being overheard.

"You're speaking to him," Buster responded blithely.

Visitors wishing to place advertisements of items for sale were a common occurrence. Buster studied the man's cheap clothing and bet himself the man had a cow for sale. Either that or he wanted to disclaim any responsibilities for his wife's debts. He could not have been more wrong.

"May we speak privately, sir?" The man spoke politely. He looked meaningfully at the two freedmen who were setting type in the back of the room.

"You may speak freely here," Buster reassured the visitor.

"What I have to say is for your ears only. Is there someplace we can be alone?" The man insisted, a determined stubborn quality edged his voice.

Something told Buster to humor him. The man's demeanor carried dignity as well as humility. Buster escorted him next door to the sitting room of his town house.

"Now, sir. Please identify yourself. I don't speak confidentially with strangers," Buster insisted.

The man studied Buster carefully and then decided.

"First, let me say I am placing my life, my livelihood, my wife's and my dear children's future in your discretion," the man said dramatically.

Buster was not sure whether he faced another sad crank or not. A newspaper office seemed to attract those with perceived problems they could not resolve.

"You can be assured that I will honor your request for confidence," Buster reassured the man. "Please remember, however, that you are speaking with a newsman."

"Jacob Wagner," the stranger said. "I am Jacob Wagner. Having seen me, you will one day learn my name anyway, so I might as well tell you."

Buster nodded, encouraging the man to continue. He was still not sure whether he was dealing with a crackpot or not.

"I am Mr. Madison's clerk."

These words caught Buster's attention.

"Sir, I am at your service," Buster said, wondering just what Wagner's mission might be.

"I am here on my own volition, without permission. If Mr. Madison should learn of this visit, I would be fired forthwith."

Buster silently waited for him to continue. He regarded Wagner with suspicion but decided to hear him out.

"You wonder why I am here under these circumstances. I don't blame you. Let me tell you about myself. I am a holdover from Mr. Adam's administration, and my loyalties are to that honest and forthright man. I have tried to loyally serve Mr. Madison and Mr. Jefferson, but many things are happening that concern me."

"Please be cautious Mr. Wagner. Surely you know that the *Herald* follows an objective line, supporting neither party."

"Yes sir, that is why I am here. I have worries that I need share with someone who can warn the American people."

Buster smiled. "Please don't overestimate our humble importance."

"I must speak frankly. I do not approve of many of Mr. Jefferson's reckless actions including his most recent proposal, that of placing our frigates in dry dock at the Navy Yard where they will theoretically be preserved until needed."

"You are not alone in that attitude," Buster agreed, trying to encourage Wagner to explain. "I should say, however, that Mr. Jefferson's explanation to Congress that this act would enable him to reduce the size of the navy commensurate with the restrictions he is placing on the army's manpower is viewed by some as being only fair."

"Fairly said, but Mr. Jefferson did not admit that he is reducing our country's ability to defend itself at the very same time he is taking actions that might precipitate need for those very resources he is circumscribing."

"Yes?"

"At the very same time Mr. Madison on Mr. Jefferson's instructions is secretly pressuring Spain and France to abandon Louisiana and Florida."

"You would agree," Buster played the devil's advocate, "that Emperor Napoleon makes a dangerous neighbor for us in the west."

"One cannot threaten a mad dog with empty hands," Wagner said. "You are also aware that war in Europe between England and France looms."

Buster nodded. He knew that Mr. Jefferson had dispatched his cohort James Monroe to Paris to negotiate.

"Please read these documents and you will understand my concern," Wagner said, producing a sheath of documents from his coat pocket.

Buster took them. The very first, a report from the diplomatic mission in Paris, appeared genuine. It indicated that Jefferson was preparing to issue an ultimatum to Napoleon, sell Louisiana or the United States would enter the war on England's side. This struck Buster as a foolish and dangerous game to play.

"Mr. Jefferson and Mr. Madison think they can resolve the problems with diplomatic means and will not need the military; the military threat is just a bluff," Wagner said.

"What else could it be?" Buster asked.

Having gotten Buster's full attention, Wagner unburdened himself of his many concerns. The documents had been cleverly selected to support his arguments. By the time they parted, Wagner had convinced Buster of his sincerity, and Buster promised to protect Wagner while exposing Jefferson's duplicity. The documents substantiated Buster's suspicions that the Republicans were playing a dangerous game. Buster supported the acquisition of the Louisiana and Florida territories, but he did not believe the administration should put the country at risk by reducing the military at a time their secret diplomacy risked provoking war. He realized Jefferson wanted to fulfill his rhetoric which promised to reduce the military and thus the national debt while at the same time greatly enhance the size of the United States through negotiation, but he believed that Jefferson's game was too dangerous to allow it to continue unrevealed.

Buster's subsequent stories based on the documents shocked the Administration and gained the attention of other newspapers in the country. The public and the press were not the only ones to react. Two days after the story appeared in the *Herald*, Buster received an invitation cum summons to meet with Secretary Madison.

Buster reined his horse to a stop in front of the new brick building, a square, unimposing edifice adjacent to the President's House. He tied his mount to the single, wood stanchion, stepped around the lingering puddles from last night's spring shower, and mounted the steps. He did so reluctantly, wondering what he was doing here.

Buster entered the red brick building and paused in confusion. He stood in an empty central hallway. He knew that the Departments of State and War shared the building, but no signs indicated where the respective offices were located. Buster contemplated the stairwell that stood directly before him leading to the second floor, and he considered the closed doors that led off the two hallways that flanked the stairs.

"May I help you sir?" A young man who had emerged from a door on his right asked.

"Yes. Which is Secretary Madison's office?"

"Upstairs, first door on the right," the man replied before turning and hurrying officiously down the hallway.

Buster mounted the stairs, approached the door, knocked politely, and then entered. He found himself in an anteroom. A table sat in the center of the room. Behind it, Jacob Wagner, the self described clerk who had visited Buster in Alexandria, sat. Wagner smiled thinly then reformed his lips into a neutral purse.

"May I help you, sir?" Wagner asked, acting as if he had never seen Buster before.

"Yes. My name is Satterfield. I have an appointment with Secretary Madison."

Wagner checked a paper that lay on his deck, acting as if he had to verify Buster's words.

"Oh yes. Mr. Satterfield. We have you listed here for ten. You are right on time," he approved.

"Please follow me, sir." Wagner rose from his desk, turned to the door on his left, opened it, then stepped back for Buster to enter.

Buster briskly walked into the room expecting to be in Madison's office. Instead, he found himself in a diminutive chamber sparsely furnished with four armless chairs, a not effective attempt to make it appear as a sitting room.

"This is the diplomatic reception room," Wagner explained. "If you will be seated, I will inform Secretary Madison that you are here."

Buster selected a chair near the window and looked out. He could see workmen shoveling gravel on Mr. Jefferson's new road to Georgetown. He waited and waited. After forty-five minutes, Buster decided he was being deliberately insulted. He consulted his watch: ten forty-five. Secretary of State or no, Buster decided to leave.

At that moment, the door opened, and a small, wizened man dressed in black entered the room. He was most unimpressive, no more than five foot six inches tall and a slender one hundred and thirty pounds. Buster knew his exact age, fifty-two, but he looked much older. His skin had an unhealthy pallor. His thin white hair had receded high on his forehead and left his prominent, veined English nose unprotected. Buster decided the man looked like a mouse.

"Mr. Satterfield. I have not had the pleasure," he said tonelessly, his demeanor contradicting his words.

"Mr. Secretary," Buster duplicated Madison's inhospitable tone.

"Please be seated. Tea?"

"No, thank you."

"Then, to business." Madison studied Buster without attempting to conceal his hostility. "I believe you owe us an explanation."

"For what, sir?" Buster knew exactly what Madison intended. He wanted to know where the *Herald* had gotten the information it had printed about the administration's plans to acquire Louisiana.

"Where you acquired one of our secret documents."

"You admit it's yours?"

"Certainly, it is. You know that. Where did you get it?" Madison focused his hard gray eyes on Buster who returned the glare.

"That I cannot disclose."

"A thief's work," Madison said.

"Are you accusing me?"

"Certainly not, sir," Madison interrupted. "Not you, but the person who gave you those documents. Do you have more?"

"That I cannot say."

"Print them, and they will tell me who your source is," Madison warned.

"Are you denying the Constitution?"

"The First Amendment?"

"Yes. Freedom of the Press." Buster felt he had scored a point because Madison made no secret of his pride in having been one of the drafters of the Constitution.

Madison contemplatively studied Buster.

"I'm afraid you have me there," Madison finally laughed mirthlessly. "The Constitution gives you the freedom to print what you learn. My problem is to keep you from acquiring state secrets."

Madison rose, went to the door, and directed his clerk to serve two cups of tea. While they waited, Buster had the impression that Madison was trying to change the tone of the meeting. He had conveyed his displeasure, now he was going to try to charm him.

"I was disappointed when you did not contact me last year after your meeting with the President. He led me to believe that I could expect you."

"Yes, sir," Buster replied sincerely. "I intended no disrespect, but I thought I could best protect my newspaper's reputation for objectivity by remaining aloof from officeholders."

"Objectivity," Madison laughed softly to lessen the acid in his tone.

"Yes sir. You do have a reputation for suborning editors."

"For respecting those who share our views."

"To the extent of providing financial support."

"That's never been proved."

"Need it be?"

Madison laughed again and paused while his clerk served the tea.

"I see we are going to have a difficult time being friends," Madison observed after Wagner withdrew and shut the door behind him.

"Yes, but we do not have to be enemies."

"Will you continue to publish state secrets?"

"When they fairly come into my hands, and I conclude the people have a need to know, the right to know."

"Fair enough. But, be aware. There is no such thing as the people's right to know. Not in the Constitution."

Buster nodded his acquiescence to Madison's point.

"But when the people's security is threatened, a free press is morally obligated to warn them."

"Possibly. Let me explain. President Jefferson has three simple foreign policy objectives: to neutralize the Barbary states and obtain free passage for our commerce, to stop impressment of our seamen, and to fulfill our manifest destiny."

"All remarkable objectives."

"And domestically to eliminate the national debt, to reduce the size of government, and to guarantee our citizens the opportunity to exercise their natural rights without interference from government."

"Again, all are noteworthy goals. The rub comes when the effort to achieve one objective imperils another."

"Shrinking the military to save money is a risk when our foreign adventures tempt war," Madison summarized.

"Exactly. You should not make threats you cannot implement."

"But problems can be solved without the exercise of force. Reason, economic pressure and diplomacy will win the day."

"Maybe."

"We shall see, won't we?" Madison decided to terminate the debate.

"And possibly imperil the nation."

Madison shook his head indulgently.

"Mr. Satterfield. What are we going to do with you?"

Buster sipped his tea and then decided to confront Madison directly on his own concerns.

"Mr. Secretary. I have a problem I wish to raise with you."

Buster described in detail the crank letters he had received last fall and the attempt to break into his office. He noted the letters had stopped when his newspaper had muted its criticism of Republicanism. He had disagreed with the Federalists, and no threats had materialized.

"Can I now expect the letters will resume and another attempt will be made to destroy my press?"

Madison smiled thinly without answering Buster's questions. "Mr. Satterfield. You as an intelligent man know that when you publicly take a controversial position you are going to antagonize the partisans of that endeavor. There are hotheads in every political quarter, and one cannot control all of them."

"Mr. Jefferson has said that periodically a little blood letting is a good thing. It revitalizes the people. Does that apply to me?"

"Words out of context," Madison countered.

"Then what precisely are you saying?" Buster asked. He recognized the Madison was trying to intimidate him.

"I'm not saying the administration condones such actions. After all, our supporters have had their rights transgressed. I promise I will investigate and do everything in my power to discourage such activity."

"And?"

"And I hope the *Herald* will adhere rigorously to its objectivity."

After this exchange, it became apparent that neither man was prepared to relent and that neither felt like trading pleasantries. After a few minutes of silence, Madison thanked Buster for his time, and Buster curtly reciprocated.

When Buster departed Madison's office, he nodded to the portly clerk with the pig snout nose who failed to conceal his concern and quickly exited the building. The meeting disturbed Buster. He had acquired nothing that was newsworthy and had neither confirmed nor denied that the Republicans were behind the attempts to intimidate the *Herald*. Buster had no doubt that Jefferson and Madison were aware of the *Herald*'s criticism, but he could not prove they had issued the orders to harass him. He had difficulty explaining the why. Why would they bother? In the scheme of things, his small Alexandria paper was pale beer. He could not persuade himself that the two respected leaders were responsible for a nationwide campaign to control the press. The question nagged him on the ride home.

Three days later Buster joined Vivian, James and the two boys, J.J. and Toddy for a late supper. At least once a week he visited the older Satterfields. A strong sense of family responsibility drew him to them, but he also frankly enjoyed their company. Vivian and James each had unique intuitive insights, the product of long introspective lives that helped Buster formulate his opinions he expressed forthrightly in the *Herald*. He also found attractive the bright eagerness of the two boys as they searched for knowledge. Both boys were struggling with their studies at the Academy; they had to compensate for the lack of formal education with long hours of intensive self-study, and the evening meals were often their only respite from the drudgery of rote memorizing of endless streams of facts.

At the end of the meal, Buster described his meeting with Madison. All, young and old, were puzzled by its portent. James summarized the views of the table when he proclaimed:

"I cannot believe that Mr. Jefferson and Mr. Madison are responsible for the petty harassment of the *Herald*. Both men are patriots. They rank high among those responsible for earning for this country the liberty it has acquired. They are men of principle and would not stoop so low."

James had just finished speaking when his son Jason burst into the house.

"Mom, dad," he greeted Vivian and James, nodded to each of the younger Satterfields in turn, paced once around the table, then sat heavily in an empty chair at his mother's right hand.

She studied Jason with concern. His face was flushed, and he was slightly winded by the pace of his arrival. Buster easily recognized the signs. His father was highly agitated about something.

"Will you have something to eat?" Vivian asked, reaching for the bell to summon a house servant.

"No thank you mother," Jason replied.

"What's the trouble, son?" James asked.

Buster, J.J. and Toddy stared at Jason and waited. He had their full attention.

"Who is this guy Cruikstaff?" Jason blurted. "Do any of you know him?"

"Thomas Cruikstaff?" Buster asked, exchanging smiles with his grandfather. They both recalled "Cruiky" who had served as a second to Richard Hodges on the morning of the duel.

"That's him. They call him Cruiky. What do you know about him?" Jason demanded.

James and Buster relaxed. Both doubted that "Cruiky," a minor hustler, would be involved in anything of significance.

"We've met the gentleman," James interposed himself between his son and grandson. "What has Mr. Cruikstaff been up to?"

"He's become a royal pain in the ass, that's what," Buster declared. He glanced at his mother who ignored the crude language.

"That's Cruiky," Buster laughed.

J.J. and Toddy looked from one speaker to the next as they spoke, not understanding what was happening. J.J. glanced at Toddy who shrugged to indicate his incomprehension.

"Tell us what Cruiky has done," James directed.

Jason studied his father suspiciously then began to calm down. He poured himself a glass of water from a pitcher that set in the middle of the table.

"Mr. Cruikstaff is a new member of the town council," Jason began.

Alexandria had been managed paternally by a handful of town fathers since its inception, and the town council was the instrumentality they used to effect their control. Initially, George Washington and George Mason had been the preeminent leaders; since their deaths, a second generation of gentry had replaced the founders, and their participation had degenerated into friendly indifference. Several representatives of the town newcomers had crowded over the past few years onto the council.

"Tonight Mr. Cruikstaff attended his first meeting," Jason continued. "And it was a remarkable beginning indeed."

"Knowing of Cruiky, I find that hard to believe," Buster laughed, trying to calm down his father.

Jason did not pacify easily. He glared at his son.

"Let me continue."

Buster nodded his acquiescence.

"I announced my intention to open a second AleHouse, and this pipsqueak objected," Jason protested.

He paused and sipped his water. While he drank, he noted the smiles on the faces around the table. All had relaxed when they learned the cause of Jason's anger. He was simply piqued. The smiles made Jason recognize the shallowness of his ire, and he began to shed the tension. Finally, he too smiled.

"All right. So I didn't get my way, tonight, but this guy is bad news. What has he got against the Satterfields? I've never heard of him."

"He claims to be the local Republican Party leader," Buster observed, not quite answering his father's question.

"That makes sense. All the new people on the council supported him."

"Can they stop you from opening your AleHouse?" Vivian asked practically.

"Not really. I still control a majority on the council, but they did agree to study the issue. What is there to study?" Jason asked rhetorically. "They're talking about setting limits on the number of ordinaries that can be opened in Alexandria."

"Cruiky?" Buster laughed. "I would think Cruiky would support opening more."

"He's speaking for the Pig and some of the other ordinary proprietors. They're afraid of competition. The AleHouse at the brewery is already cutting into their business."

"Maybe Fat Eddy's behind it," Buster ventured, referring to the owner of Brown's Brewery, Jason's competitor who had been suffering since the introduction of the chilled ale.

"It's all tied together."

"When will they decide?" James asked.

"At the next meeting," Jason answered. "Now, tell me. Which one of you has had a run in with Mr. Cruikstaff?"

James and Buster again exchanged glances, and this time Jason noticed them.

"You two. I should have known."

Jason studied his son.

"Please explain."

"Cruiky is or I should say was a friend of Mr. Richard Hodges," Buster paused, hoping that he would not have to explain more.

Vivian at that point recognized the name Hodges and surmised the source of the difficulty. She coughed and hid her smile with her napkin as she patted her lips. Again, Toddy shrugged his puzzlement to J.J.

"And Hodges is? Wait a minute. Isn't he the guy... .? The duel. That explains it."

"Cruiky was Mr. Hodges' second," Buster explained.

"That you and your grandfather left standing on the hill with his dead friend."

"Well, yes," James agreed.

"A duel?" J.J. asked, unable to contain himself.

"Yes dear. A mild disagreement between your cousin Buster and Mr. Hodges. I fear your Gramps was responsible," Vivian observed with a smile.

"And the idea was yours," James responded defensively.

"Let's not open that old argument," Jason interrupted, to J.J.'s and Toddy's confusion. "At least I know why I have a problem with Cruiky. Now, I can handle it. I'll shoot the bastard. Right between the eyes. That's the way you do it? Isn't it?" Jason stared at Buster.

Buster shrugged and looked at James. James smiled back. J.J. and Toddy looked at each other, not knowing whether to take Jason seriously or not, and Vivian rang the servant bell to call for more tea.

"I hate tea," James said to no one in particular.

ALEXANDRIA, VIRGINIA

AUGUST 1803

Jason and Skinny sat in their office on the second floor of the old mansion across the street from the brewery and suffered from the heat. The windows on each side of the building were open wide, and a slight breeze from the river ruffled the lace curtains but did little to cool the room. Despite the August heat, Jason was relaxed. He had no problems.

"Things are going too good, Skinny," Jason addressed his partner and friend.

"Then you had better start worrying," Skinny observed. He tried to find some relief from the heat by fanning himself with a piece of paper from the company report he had been reading.

"Both of the new AleRooms are doing well. The chilled ale is the only brew selling in the Federal District or here."

Jason was pleased with himself. He had finally pushed his plans through the council and had opened his second AleRoom in Alexandria. Then, he had opened a third ordinary near the new Capitol across the river. It had proved to be an immediate success. The legislators had bigger thirsts than working men.

"I hear Fat Eddy is frothing at the mouth," Skinny observed.

"Let him. That brown ale of his is too heavy for the summer months."

"And too hot."

"I offered to sell him ice."

"He's too cheap to buy it."

"Too dumb. All he has to do is raise his prices a few pennies to pay for the chilling, just like we do."

"And too dumb," Skinny agreed.

Jason walked to the window and watched as several workers entered the AleRoom.

"The place is crowded already," he observed.

Skinny did not answer. None was expected.

Jason switched his attention to the boatyard.

"That is one beautiful ship," he congratulated himself.

He studied the "Clipper's" rakish lines. The hull and its decking had been completed, and the masts raised. As he watched, workmen carefully stretched the lines connecting the booms and yardarms. One workman near the top of the mainmast waved to him. Jason recognized J.J. and waved back.

"The boys are enjoying their summer," he observed as he turned back to face Skinny.

"They're lucky to have a cousin who owns a boatyard and is building the most beautiful ship in the world."

"And the fastest too."

"With the smallest hold," Skinny reminded.

"Don't worry. The French and English are back at war and will soon involve us no matter what Jefferson and his little Secretary of State want."

"They better," Skinny responded, referring to the French and English. "They'll probably catch the "Clipper" on her first trip out."

"No way," Jason replied. "Don't say it, not even in jest. When will the sails get here?"

"You know as well as me," Skinny replied. "They're promised for tomorrow."

"They better get here," Jason warned. Jason turned and headed for the door.

"Where are you going?"

Jason, who thought better on his feet, felt the need to walk. He had to consider where to send the "Clipper" on her first voyage and to decide whether to build another clipper or a smaller schooner as soon as the big ship was launched. He had had to compromise with his colleagues at the bank and promise to build his three clippers seriatim not simultaneously. Now, with war a possibility but not yet realized, he had to decide what to do: delay with the smaller schooner or run against the odds and continue with his initial plan.

"I'm going past the store then over to the warehouse."

Skinny nodded. Neither the store nor the warehouse, two more of their investments, needed Jason's attention. Jason was reaching for excuses. He needed to walk and think. Skinny hoped that for once Jason would take a conservative chance.

Jason and Skinny were not the only ones feeling the heat. At Brown's Brewery, Fat Eddy Brown was in misery. Fat Eddy sat behind his worktable in his cluttered office at the back of his brewery. The sour smell of the wort permeated the room. Fat Eddy's office was located by choice behind the fermenting room. Fat Eddy liked to be able to step to the door and check on the workmen and all his brewery's processes with a glance. Usually, he did so several times every hour, but today he had not moved from his chair.

The sweat cascaded down his brow, ran in rivulets across his porcine cheeks, and dripped from his many chins onto his massive belly. His shirt was soaked and stuck to his skin. Fat Eddy pushed himself out of the chair, pulled the seat of his pants that was adhering to his ample posterior away from the skin, then dropped back into his chair. The heat was oppressive, even in his dark, moist cubbyhole, but Fat Eddy was not troubled by it. He had more important things to worry him.

He had been studying the figures for three hours, and no matter how he turned them, they did not change. Business was off seventy-five percent. His main customers, the ordinaries that catered to the swells and the taverns that swilled the scum, complained. All of their patrons wanted chilled ale, and Fat Eddy had none to offer.

Tastes had changed. For generations Englishmen had drunk their warm brews winter and summer without complaint, then that wise guy Satterfield had to throw his money away on ice and chill his ale; now, nobody wanted the warm stuff in August. Fat Eddy wondered if he had made a mistake; Satterfield had offered to sell him ice, but Fat Eddy had not wanted to admit he had been wrong. He could have hired somebody else's schooner to bring him ice, but he had been too cheap. Now, he was rediscovering something he had always known. Brewing was a tough business. The margins were small; profits came from high consumption. Nobody would pay big prices for beer; it was a poor man's drink, and Fat Eddy had to do something.

"Hey, Crip," he barked.

"What?"

"Get in here."

His number one man had been in the fermenting room, probably tasting the brew. Fat Eddy knew that on most days he had to give the Crip his instructions before noon. After that, he would be too drunk to remember. Fat Eddy sometimes thought about firing the Crip, but he would be hard to replace, drunk or sober. As Fat Eddy waited, he listened for the sound of the Crip dragging his bum leg along the dirt. He had worked out a crab like shuffle that let him move his immense bulk as fast as a normal man.

The Crip, when he had been whole, before the stack of kegs had broken lose and rolled over his left leg crushing it, had been something to see. Six feet five inches tall, three hundred pounds, he could in those days lift a two hundred pound sack by himself, easily. He still had the strength in his hands and arms, but his damaged leg made it impossible for him to lift. Now, the Crip's leg matched his brain, both useless. Fat Eddy once called his lieutenant "Leach". He still did not know if "Leach" was a surname or a nickname, but it did not matter. Now, Fat Eddy called Leach, Crip, short for Cripple, and he did not seem to mind any more than Eddy cared whether he was called Fat Eddy or just plain Eddy. In fact the latter did not seem adequate for a man of his size.

"Yeah, Eddy. What?" Crip growled as he entered.

"We have to do it," Fat Eddy declared.

"When?" Crip knew exactly what Fat Eddy meant.

"Tonight."

"Two of the boys enough?"

"No more."

For what Fat Eddy and Crip had in mind, any more assistance would be a threat. Nobody could guarantee that the kind of bums he employed would be able to keep their mouths shut after a few bottles of ale.

"How many tins?"

Fat Eddy pretended to think. He had been planning this lesson for some time, and he knew exactly what he needed.

"Ten five gallon tins."

Crip laughed gruffly. He knew that Fat Eddy over the past several months had quietly accumulated five-gallon tins of lamp oil. Crip knew because they worried him. So much lamp oil posed a fire hazard.

J.J. carefully finished the last knot that lashed the gaff of the small, square topsail to the main mast and then controlled his slide to the deck. There, he found Toddy waiting for him. The two boys had spent the summer at Jason's boatyard working on the "Clipper." The beautiful ship was almost finished. Tomorrow, Jason planned to install the sails. When finished, the workers would knock the chocks, and the "Clipper" would slide into the Potomac current, ready for a test sail. If all went as planned, Jason, accompanied by a test crew and the boys, would sail the "Clipper" to the mouth of the Chesapeake. Timing was important to the boys, and J.J. and Toddy kept their fingers crossed. School would resume in four weeks. Any delay would cheat them out of their opportunity to participate in a great adventure.

"She's a beauty," Toddy exclaimed for the thousandth time, gently rubbing the thick, varnished mast that canted rakishly at an eighty-degree angle to the deck. The canted mast was one of Jason's innovations.

"She sure is," J.J. agreed, proud of his role as one of those allowed to work the topsail rigging.

Toddy, too, had worked the mainsail, but not with the enthusiasm displayed by J.J. To his dismay, Toddy had discovered a latent fear of heights and had to fight nausea and dizziness each time he ascended the tall masts. As a consequence, he frequently found tasks on deck that afforded him the excuse to avoid the frightening ordeal. He knew he would have to overcome this shortcoming if he were to achieve his dream, that of becoming a seaman and eventually commanding one of cousin Jason's schooners on a voyage to China. He was making progress, slowly, and he rationalized that if he faced his fear progressively, he would eventually master it.

J.J. understood his cousin's problem, and he did what he could to help him overcome it.

"Is she going to be ready?" Toddy asked, meaning ready for launch in time for the boys to participate in the shakedown cruise.

"Depends on the sail makers," J.J. replied, equally anxious.

As the boys talked, a long wagon stacked high with canvas arrived and pulled alongside the "Clipper" near the makeshift gangway that led from the dock to the ship. Jason, who personally participated in each key step of the "Clipper's" construction and preparation, sat on the wagon seat next to the driver for the sail maker. He had found the wagon waiting for him at his warehouse.

"Look, the sails," Toddy called excitedly.

The two boys walked to the rails. Last year, at fifteen, they would have run, unable to contain their enthusiasm. After a year at Corney's Academy, the two sixteen year olds masked their excitement from the workmen and strolled nonchalantly towards the gangplank.

"Give a hand, boys," Jason called.

J.J. and Toddy joined the yard workers who were gathering about the wagon.

"How did they get them so white?" Toddy asked.

Jason looked at the sail master's assistant inviting him to provide the answer.

"Trade secret," the old man responded, spitting a stream of tobacco juice onto the gravel of the river shore.

Jason frowned.

"Bleached it, I guess," Jason opined. "I told them I wanted the whitest sails ever made."

Jason turned and studied the bright white canvas and remembered his first boat, "The Gray Ghost," a schooner that he had painted the color of the water and sky on an overcast day. At the time, he had been about the same age as the boys were now, and in his youthful enthusiasm he had hoped to devise a color that would make his craft invisible on the horizon. The fact that he and Skinny were alive today was a testimonial to his success. A pursuing pirate bent on revenge had almost overtaken them.

Jason looked back at his excited second cousins, remembering what it was like to be young and on your first ship.

"All right men," Jason said. "Let's unload the wagon, and be careful. I don't want a spot on these sails."

Jason, like the boys, could visualize what the "Clipper" would look like that first time when the wind caught the sails and filled them, driving the trim hull through the water at a rate previously unseen. The thought of what he had created made him proud. While the boys and workers carefully carried the bulky canvas up the gangplank toward the waiting masts and spars, Jason walked to the bow of his ship. He glanced at his office across the street, saw Skinny standing in his window, and nodded. Then, he turned and looked down the street towards his parent's house. He saw James sitting in his rocker on the porch, studying the "Clipper." Jason waved, and his father waved back.

The arrival of the sails was such an exhilarating experience for the two boys, primarily because the event marked the readiness of the "Clipper" for launch, that they lingered at the shipyard long after the workers had departed. They proudly paced the deck and carefully polished away any smudges that they found defacing the bright varnish and brass. The hull, a shiny black, reflected the setting sun. Alexandrians, out for their evening promenade, paused to study the "Clipper's" sharp lines. J.J. and Toddy, aware that "their" ship was the talk of the town, preened, waving to their schoolmates as they inspected the ship that the *Herald* had described as the most beautiful vessel ever to touch the banks of the Potomac.

Finally, J.J. and Toddy with reluctance parted from their pride. While J.J. waited, Toddy closed the heavy padlock that bound the chain to the gates of the fence that surrounded the boatyard. Jason, taking no chances, had built the six-foot high plank fence from the wall of his adjacent brewery, along the elevated Union Street, back to the water, then along the shoreline to the warehouse. Gates gave access to the boatyard from the pier and at the waterline along the slip that held the "Clipper."

J.J. and Toddy were walking from the pier towards Union Street when a husky, feminine voice called to them.

Is that beautiful ship yours?"

J.J. looked up and was staggered. Standing at the point where the pier and Union Street met were the Gutradt girls. Although he had not seen them since that day over a year ago at the pool below their father's mill, and he had never spoken a word to either of them in his life, Debbie, the freckled redhead, had been a constant visitor to his dreams.

"Oh my God," J.J. said and turned to catch Toddy's arm. His gesture was unnecessary. Toddy, too, had seen them.

"Well, is it?" The redhead demanded.

"Yes. Well. No," J.J. stammered.

The redhead's laugh had the same throaty catch J.J. had noticed in her voice that day at the pond. She turned to her sister.

"Sar, I don't believe he knows."

"She belongs to our cousin, Jason, but we helped build her," Toddy spoke directly to the raven-haired girl with the turned up button nose.

"Can we see her?" The redhead asked.

"Look all you want," J.J. said, regretting the sharp tone that his nervousness had imparted to his words. He had wanted to sound friendly.

"Don't be snotty," the redhead admonished. "I meant will you let us walk on the deck like you were?"

"Sure," J.J. said.

"Can't," Toddy said.

"Which is it?" The dark haired girl named Sar asked.

J.J. turned to Toddy to protest, then realization struck him. They did not have a key to the padlock—only Jason did--and they had already locked the gate.

"I'm sorry. He's right," J.J. said. "Only Jason has the key, and we locked the gate."

"Tomorrow," Toddy improvised.

The redhead frowned. J.J. noticed her green eyes flash, saw the freckles move as she smiled, then looked away when he saw her watching him. He studied the ground, raised his eyes to see if she was still smiling, but his attention snagged on her striking body. He immediately remembered the breasts and bare buttocks and the flash of rust colored hair and blushed bright red.

"I believe we've embarrassed him, Sar," the redhead laughed. "Don't be scared. We don't bite."

The dark haired girl's responding laugh had a tinkle in it. Toddy stared first at her then at his cousin's bright red face.

"You come tomorrow, and we'll show you the 'Clipper,'" Toddy said.

"My name's Deb. Short for Debbie," the redhead said, offering her hand.

J.J. stared at the hand, took it, and was surprised at the strength in the long narrow fingers as they squeezed J.J.'s hand tightly.

"And I am Sar. Short for Sarah," the dark haired girl said.

"Gutradt," Toddy said. "Mr. Gutradt, the miller, is your father."

"And you are Toddy Satterfield from the Short Hills."

"We saw you at the mill last year," J.J. said, not meaning to be ambiguous.

"We know," Deb laughed, intending her ambiguity.

Again, J.J. blushed, and Toddy stared. The two girls looked back innocently.

"Well, what is your name?" Deb demanded of J.J.

"J.J. Satterfield," J.J. replied.

"Another one," Deb said. "Another Satterfield," she explained her comment. "What does J.J. mean?"

"John Junior. My grandfather's John Sr."

"Brothers?" Sar asked.

"Cousins," Toddy answered.

"I'm from the west," J.J. said.

"Come walk with us and explain," Debbie said, brazenly taking J.J. by the arm and pulling him towards Union Street.

Sarah grabbed Toddy's arm. Both boys were speechless. The girls turned east on Union Street and pulled the boys along the river. In the distance, J.J. saw Vivian standing on the porch, staring in their direction with a broad smile on her face.

"Let's go the other way," J.J. said, spinning Deb with him.

They had covered about thirty yards and were passing the front of the AleRoom when they encountered Skinny and Jason who had just emerged from inside. Both men broke into broad smiles.

"Evening J.J., Toddy, girls," Jason said.

"Jason, Skinny," J.J. and Toddy replied in unison.

The girls giggled.

Jason and Skinny watched as the two couples continued past them.

"Those boys might be in over their heads," Skinny observed.

"Got to learn to swim sometime," Jason laughed.

As soon as they had turned on Cameron Street and headed toward Market Square, Debbie squeezed J.J.'s arm.

"Junior. Tell me. That was your cousin Jason wasn't it?"

"Yes. "

"And he has the key to the lock?"

"Yes," J.J. said as he recalled with embarrassment their promise to show the "Clipper" to the girls. He had forgotten all about the "Clipper" that only moments before had been the center of his life.

"I forgot," he apologized. "I'll get the key... ." he began.

"Never mind," Debbie said. "Tomorrow will do nicely."

"Who cares about old boats anyway," Sarah who was walking behind, arm in arm with Toddy, said.

On Union Street, Jason and Skinny paused to greet Vivian and James.

"Did you see that?" Jason asked.

Vivian smiled.

"See what?" James, who had just joined Vivian on the porch, asked.

"Nothing dear," Vivian patted his arm. "I do believe tomorrow is going to be another scorcher," she said, pointing at the bright red sunset and changing the subject.

"Where are you two going?" James asked, disinterested in discussing the weather.

"We're going to drop by the new AleRoom and see how business is doing," Jason replied.

"And to have a chilled ale?" James asked.

"Come and join us," Skinny invited.

James looked at Vivian.

"Go ahead. Have one. Then come right back. I'll wait here."

At Brown's Brewery, Fat Eddy, his flunky Crip and two disreputable workers sat in Fat Eddy's office drinking Brown's Stout.

"Tastes like piss," Crip complained, spraying a stream of the excessively warm stout on the floor.

"You're a pig," Fat Eddy accused without disagreeing with Crip who sat with his game leg propped on the table in front of him.

"Don't know why you don't buy ice and chill this swill like Satterfield does," one of the ragged workers contributed.

"Costs too much," the second worker chipped in. "Eddy's too cheap. Maybe we should call him Cheap Eddy."

Fat Eddy glared at the three men in front of him. Only the fact that he needed their help kept him from savagely thrashing them or running them off.

"Bullshit," Fat Eddy declared and spit on the floor for emphasis.

Crip looked down and noticed that Fat Eddy had hit the shoe at the end of his good leg.

"If that had been my bum leg, we would've had it out," Crip threatened.

Fat Eddy looked with disgust at Crip. He knew it was only bravado for the benefit of the two workers. Crip was deathly afraid of him. To emphasize his contempt and to get their attention, Fat Eddy opened a desk drawer and took out a knife in a dirty leather sheath, a pistol with rust spots on the barrel, and several boxes of matches.

The others studied the items on the tabletop. Fat Eddy took the knife from its sheath; he ran a fat dirty thumb along the chipped blade, turned the knife in his hand and held it by the point, then hurled it across the room at the door. It missed Crip's nose by inches and buried its point deep into the door.

"Christ, Eddy," Crip complained. "You damned near took off my nose." Crip rubbed a grimy palm against the end of his nose to emphasize his point.

"Anymore talk and next time I won't miss it," Fat Eddy threatened.

Not one of the other three doubted his word, particularly Crip.

Fat Eddy pulled the pistol towards himself. He picked up three of the large boxes of matches and threw one at each of the three men. The two workers deftly caught theirs, but Crip fumbled his, and it tumbled to the floor where he left it. Eddy glared at him, and Crip, with a groan, pulled his game leg from the table and leaned over and picked up the matches. While he was leaning over, Fat Eddy stood, kicked at the chair legs, and tumbled Crip onto the floor.

"Next time, catch it," Fat Eddy ordered and settled his immense girth back into his chair which squeaked in protest.

"Christ Eddy," Crip complained, showing his limited vocabulary. "Take it easy. I din't mean anything."

"We're set for tonight?" Fat Eddy asked.

"All set," Crip replied. The other two grunted.

"The lamp oil?"

"I said all set din't I?"

"O.K. Be back here at midnight. Sober," Fat Eddy growled.

The two workers, relieved to be dismissed and worried about Fat Eddy's vicious mood, tossed their tin cups still partly filled with the warm brown stout into a wood box that Eddy kept in the corner for that purpose. The cups rattled when they struck others and spilled their contents onto the dirt floor. There, the grimy cups would remain until Eddy offered another visitor a gratuitous sample of his product.

After the two workers had departed, Fat Eddy glared at Crip.

"You, too. Beat it. Be back here at midnight."

"Christ, Eddy," Crip complained, but he did what he was told and hurried with his crab like hop from the room.

ALEXANDRIA

AUGUST 14TH, 1803

The night was hot, business light, and the single barkeep exhausted when at midnight he hustled the last drunk out the door and closed the AleRoom for the day. The full, bright orange moon floated high in the sky and illuminated the countryside with its soft glare except for the strip along the Potomac. There, Alexandria, captured by a thick jell of humidity, lay captive. The heavy air distorted the moon's glow into a translucent haze. The tired barkeep decided to postpone his custodial duties until the morning; he threw his dirty apron on the bar, extinguished the last lamp and made his way to the front door by the moon's refracted glow through the veins of the imperfect window located near the front door. His hand on the latch, he paused, and surveyed the room to make sure the last piece of tobacco had been extinguished; he knew too well that the building's dry planks and timber and sawdust floor constituted a fire hazard. Satisfied, he closed the door and stepped into Union Street. He paused long enough to kick Jason's hired guard into semi-wakefulness. The man slumped with his back against the front of the AleRoom, his feet extended into Union Street; his club lay alongside his right leg.

"Good night, barkeep," the guard feigned wakefulness.

The tired barkeep grunted. He knew that as soon as he rounded the corner the guard would disappear to the rear of the brewery where he had made a soft bed in the straw kept for the brewery teams. He wondered why Jason Satterfield bothered.

The barkeep, a conscientious man, had complained to Jason many times about the guard, but Jason had done nothing. The man, little more than a sleepy watchdog, had become a habit. The barkeep guessed that he was better than nothing.

An hour after the barkeep had departed and the guard had retreated to his straw nest, a thin cloud drifted slowly across the moon. There, it joined with the humidity and darkness to intensify the shadows masking the brewery. The streets of Alexandria were deserted; the residents tossed on their straw comforters in a fitful sleep disturbed by the intense heat and discomfort of the unhealthy night. Across the river in the Federal District, the town was half abandoned. The President, the Secretary of State, the bureaucrats and the politicians had all retreated from the unhealthy miasma of the Potomac swamps to the cooler mountain highlands. The fireflies slept, and the crickets listened, too tired to sing their happy songs. Only the mosquitoes seeking their nocturnal fillings buzzed.

The Brown Brewery wagon with wheels greased and horses hooves muted with cloth silently exited its warehouse. Crip slapped the reins softly, and the team turned eastward towards Union Street and the river. Fat Eddy sat on the bench beside Crip. The wagon wheels crunched in the gravel of the track, but the sound did not carry. Fat Eddy glanced back. The lamp oil sloshed in its tins, softly, the sound merging with the whispering roil of the Potomac current as it lapped on the shoreline. Fat Eddy checked to make sure the two workers followed. He was concerned about them.

They, along with Crip, had reported to Eddy's office on the stroke of midnight as he had instructed, but it was apparent that all three men had spent the evening building their courage with a steady flow of brew. Fat Eddy selfishly hoped it had been Brown's Stout. His sales figures were so low that every little bit would help. He knew it would have been in character for the three to have spited him for his outburst of temper by swilling the chilled ale of his competitor. The thought did not trouble him because he knew that it would be their last opportunity for a long time. From what Fat Eddy's sources had reported, the loss of the brewery and that damned ship would be a terminal blow to Satterfield. The man, like most speculators, lived on top of an inverted financial pyramid; if one block were withdrawn, the entire structure would tumble.

Fat Eddy anticipated the smile he would offer Satterfield when offering his condolences.

Fat Eddy halted in front of the AleRoom only long enough for Crip and his two helpers to unload the ten tins of lamp oil. They cursed softly when the sloshing liquid spilled and soaked their clothing. As soon as the tins had been aligned along the pier side of the building, Crip approached Fat Eddy for last minute instructions.

"Soak the walls, set your fires, then get out of here," Fat Eddy ordered.

"Right, boss."

"I'll take the wagon back to the brewery. When you're finished, send the others home and meet me at my office."

"Right, boss."

The Crip watched as Fat Eddy guided the wagon along Union Street towards Gibbon. Crip knew Eddy would return to the warehouse by the quickest route. If seen, he would have difficulty explaining what he was doing out in the middle of the night with his team's hooves wrapped. Crip paused briefly to wonder why

he always got the dirty jobs. Finally, he turned and found his two helpers waiting for instructions. They, like Crip, had not believed that Fat Eddy would follow
through on his threats. He had been blustering about burning Satterfield out for
months, and now they were about to do it.

"OK." Crip took command. "Soak the walls as high as you can splash the oil.
Be careful. Don't get any more on your clothes than you have to."

The helpers stared at the Crip in disgust.

"Save the front until last. And be quiet. There's a guard around here somewhere."

"What do we do if he shows up?" One of the helpers asked.

"Don't worry. I'll handle him." Crip fingered the old hunting knife that Fat
Eddy had insisted he carry in its sheath

"He's probably sleeping it off on the straw out back," the second worker
observed.

All knew the guard spent his evenings cadging ale from the barkeep.

The three men quickly emptied all the tins but one, saturating the sides of the
building. One offered to climb up on the roof, but the Crip vetoed the idea. He
carried the last tin to the front of the AleRoom and doused the wall and door. At
his signal, the two others stationed themselves along the pier. The Crip stood in
front near the door. He cautiously looked up and down Union Street and at the
houses located across the street from the brewery. Detecting no movement what-
soever, he quickly struck a match and threw it into the puddle of lamp oil that had
gathered at the threshold of the door. His two companions lighted their matches
and tossed them at the base of the building. The lamp oil exploded into flame
with a loud croomp. The Crip spun and ran west on Union Street followed by the
two workmen. The Crip, slowed by his game leg and odd gait, fell behind. At
Wolfe Street, some two blocks from the brewery, he paused to catch his breath.
Running was difficult for him. He looked back and was impressed.

The entire front and side of the AleRoom were in flames. The fire had already
crept to the roof and was moving upward toward the peak and back towards the
warehouse. The dry planks burned like kindling. Spires of oily black smoke rose
skyward. The fire cracked loudly, sure to arouse the neighbors soon, and the light
from the flames illuminated the street.

Crip turned up Wolfe Street and scuttled in the direction of Fat Eddy's brewery. He chuckled with pride as he moved; Satterfield was finished, and not a soul
had seen them. No doubt Satterfield would suspect Fat Eddy, but he could prove
nothing.

In the front upstairs bedroom of James and Vivian's mansion, about a block
from the brewery, J.J. and Toddy slept fitfully in the bed that they shared. J.J.'s
dream carried him back to that day at the millstream-swimming hole. He had just
pushed back the weeds and was preparing to peer at the staring breasts when a
nudge from Toddy shook him from his reverie.

"What's that?" Toddy asked.

J.J. sensed alarm in his cousin's raised voice. J.J. opened his eyes and saw the
flames reflected on the wall to his right.

"Is the house on fire?" He asked, sitting upright, suddenly frightened.

He looked around quickly. Except for the glowing wall, the room was dark. He sniffed, but he could smell nothing. Toddy jumped from the bed and ran to the window.

"It's outside. It looks like the AleRoom and brewery."

J.J. ran to the window to stand beside his cousin and peer outwards.

"Christ. It is the brewery. What about the "Clipper?" The brewery was located adjacent to the shipyard.

"It looks all right," Toddy observed. "But it's sure to go next."

"Let's go," J.J. shouted.

Both boys were in their underwear. They rushed to their clothes that lay in piles on the floor and quickly dressed. J.J. finished first and ran to the door.

"The brewery's on fire," he shouted.

The door to James and Vivian's room opened. James appeared tying the belt of his robe as he moved.

"What is it?" He asked. "Is the house on fire?"

Vivian, still in her nightdress, appeared behind him.

"It's the brewery," J.J. shouted as he rushed down the stairs followed by Toddy.

James saw the flames reflected in the front window of the boys' room and rushed forward. Vivian remained at his side.

"Be careful, boys. Don't go too close. Sound the alarm. Wake Jason and fetch the fire wagon."

She was not sure the excited boys had heard her instructions. After dressing Vivian and James hurried along Union Street towards the burning building.

The brewery was now totally enveloped. The flames were shooting what looked like hundreds of feet into the air. Clouds of black smoke rose above the rooftops and then were bent by the river breezes into a funnel that followed the river southwards. The windows on the mansions reflected the glare of the flames making it appear that fires were raging inside the courtly homes of the ship captains.

J.J. and Toddy shouted as they ran towards the brewery.

"Fire, Fire, pass the word."

Windows opened and neighbors looked out. After one glance, the men of the house, like James, turned and hurriedly dressed. Fire in Alexandria was a feared but not uncommon occurrence. Twenty-nine years previously the people of Alexandria under George Washington's leadership had organized their first fire company. Before marching off to war, Washington had spent four hundred dollars of his own money to purchase Alexandria's first fire engine. Now, old and well used, it was stored at the Rainbow Tavern in Sharpshin Alley. Already, the fire bell was ringing, sounding the alarm.

The streets quickly filled with people, anxious sightseers and concerned volunteers, all rushing towards Union Street. Within minutes, the men had the fire engine with its hoses and hand pump moving towards the conflagration.

"Look at those flames," one of the firemen shouted. He carried a canvas bucket with its rope handle looped over his arm, ready to form a bucket line to the river. "We don't stand a chance."

"We'll have to worry about protecting the houses. Forget the brewery," another called.

J.J. and Toddy stopped as close to the fire as they dared. They did not know what to do, so they stood and stared. Within seconds Jason and Skinny joined them.

"What started it?" J.J. asked.

Jason shrugged. He stared mesmerized by the sight of the towering flames. He saw everything he owned and had worked for all his life rising in arcing clouds of oily black smoke. Tears formed on his cheeks.

"I smell lamp oil," Skinny shouted suspiciously.

"Those empty tins weren't there last night," J.J.said, pointing at three five gallon tins canted against the pier.

"What about the 'Clipper?'" Toddy asked. He too was worried about his future.

"The 'Clipper?'" Jason repeated as he turned to look at his boatyard.

The flames had totally engulfed the brewery and warehouse, including the side facing the boatyard. Already flames were eating at the plank fence, ignited by the heat of the burning building some twenty yards away.

Jason, crestfallen, studied the yard between the "Clipper's" slip and the burning wall. Thirty yards littered with lumber, tar barrels, the debris of the carpenters and shipwrights.

"She doesn't stand a chance," Jason whispered, speaking mainly for himself.

Skinny stared and nodded.

"Minutes. That's all she has. Minutes."

Behind them, the firemen were placing ladders against the mansions, and men were scrambling upwards to the shake roofs. The bucket lines were forming, and already water was being passed to the climbing men.

"Douse them good. Don't let them embers get a chance to start," a man, apparently the fire captain, shouted authoritatively.

He turned to another and spoke:

"If the flames get into the houses, the whole town could go."

"We can save her," J.J. shouted and raced for the fence.

"Unlock the gate, Jason," he called back.

Jason and the others stared after the running J.J. Jason looked at Skinny.

"Let's give 'er a try," Skinny said and ran after J.J.

Toddy, without a word, followed. Jason finally broke from his lethargy and raced to the gate. He fumbled in his pants for the key, finally found it, shoved it into the padlock, turned and released the chain. J.J. pushed the gates wide and raced towards the chocks.

"Get on board," J.J. called to Toddy. "I'll break the chocks. Somebody help me."

Jason turned to Skinny.

"Get help. Form a brigade and we'll douse her decks. I'll help J.J. with the chocks."

The chocks were braces that held the trim schooner in her slip above the beach and the waterline. When launching a vessel, workmen released the chocks and let her slide into the water.

J.J. found an axe and began to pound on the rear chock. Jason raced to the other side, retrieved a mallet and began to hack away. The chocks were solid, designed to hold the two hundred and fifty-ton ship's weight, and resisted their efforts. J.J. repeatedly swung the axe with his woodsman's skill. His large hands clasped the axe handle and his thick shoulder muscles bunched before each swing. Gradually, the chock on his side began to crumble. Jason's mallet bounced ineffectively off the thick four by fours. He could not budge it.

"Over here," he called, and others eventually joined him with axes, bars, whatever implements they could find. Soon the sound of pounding punctuated the shouts of the rescuers.

Toddy had difficulty boarding the "Clipper." The gangplank from the pier was too close to the fire, and the heat denied access. He frantically raced to the port side of the ship and peered upward. Skinny joined him.

"Find a workman's ladder," Skinny shouted.

Both men searched desperately. Finally, Skinny turned and raced back through the gates to Union Street. He stopped a fireman running with a ladder towards one of the mansions. He was one of the yard's workmen.

"This way," Skinny ordered.

The man obeyed unquestioningly and followed Skinny towards the "Clipper." The flames from the burning brewery reflected in the shiny black paint of the ship's hull creating the illusion that it too was on fire. Skinny with dismay noted the glistening paint had begun to rise in large bubbles.

The workman and Toddy maneuvered the ladder into place near the stern, and the youth scampered upwards. Skinny grabbed the ladder and shouted to the workman.

"Get others. Form a brigade."

The man nodded and raced towards the gate. Skinny held the ladder in his strong right hand. His stump braced the rung in front of him. He watched as Toddy reached the ship's rail.

"It's hotter than hell up here, and the paint's blistering'," Toddy shouted. "But she's still all right."

He ran to the stern and called to J.J. and Jason.

"Hurry. We don't have much time."

Within minutes, a bucket line formed. Several men joined Toddy on the "Clipper's" deck. They passed the buckets from one to the other. Below, Skinny swung the buckets upward with his one good hand. Toddy stood at the apex of the line and dumped each bucket of water on the blistering paint where he thought it would do the most good. Whenever he noticed smoke rising from burst bubbles, indicating incipient fire, he rushed forward. Blisters formed on his face and the back of his hand, but he did not notice. Sweat streamed through the black grime and burned his eyes, but he grabbed the buckets, poured, then repeated his actions.

Suddenly, the roof of the brewery collapsed, sending a fountain of sparks skyward. The blast of heat drove Toddy and his line backwards. He was about to retreat, defeated, when he heard a crunch of wood, shouts of victory, and felt a sudden lurch. Slowly, the "Clipper" began to slide down the smoking wood rails towards the river. Two men at the top of the ladder clambered over the ship's railing and fell on the hot deck. Others grabbed them and helped them to their feet. At the base of the ladder, men jumped back, landing on top of each other. The three men who had been on the centermost rungs were caught in a twisting fall as the ladder slid along the moving ship. Two of their mates caught the side of the ladder and held it firm long enough for the men to jump backwards. One twisted his leg on landing and screamed.

At the stern, J.J. and Jason stepped back and watched wide-eyed and helpless.

"Keep away from the keel," Jason warned, pulling his cousin away from the sliding ship that had taken on its own life and seemed to be fleeing the holocaust.

As the men watched, the large ship entered the water stern first, sinking as it progressed. Within seconds, the bow passed them. The ship righted itself and then began to turn sidewise with the current.

"Get the wheel," Jason shouted to Toddy.

He had visions of the beautiful ship foundering on the rocks along the shore.

"She'll beach herself," one of the men shouted.

"All that for nothin'," another called.

"Not if I can help it," Toddy vowed.

"Quick. Man a long boat," Jason ordered.

He and J.J. raced for the shipyard's long boats that were beached on the lee side of the fire. J.J. and Jason reached the first one and began wrestle the heavy workboat into the river. Several of the workmen who had been in the bucket chain arrived to help. On board the ship, Toddy found himself at the ship's wheel. He quickly unlashed the leather straps that had held it tight. Hours earlier, Toddy had stood at the wheel and had imagined himself piloting the "Clipper" through high waves. He had never been on a floating ship before and certainly had never held the wheel underway.

He felt the ship's gentle movement. He stared upward at the rakish masts then watched as the wheel began to turn. He grabbed it to steady it. He had heard one of the workmen say that helmsmen turned the wheel the opposite way from which they wished to go, but he was confused. He was floating backwards on the current, stern first. He did not know which way to spin the wheel to turn the stern away from the threatening shore. In the near distance he could see other piers with ships tied to their docks. He imagined crashing into them. Uncertainty froze him into inaction.

In front of him he saw smoke rising from the bow.

"The sails," he called to one of the workmen who had helped with the buckets. "The sails are smoldering. Put them out."

"With what?" The man helplessly pointed at the empty buckets.

"Throw the burning ones overboard," Toddy ordered. He had taken command.

The workman surprised Toddy by obeying. He and his two mates rushed forward. Toddy turned his attention back to the wheel and tried to visualize the "Clipper's" rudder. If he were going forward, if he turned the wheel right, the rudder would pivot to the left and the ship would go left. But he was going backwards. He reasoned if he turned the wheel to his left, the rudder would pivot right. If so, it would catch the water and with the river current's pressure would pivot the ship gradually right. At least he hoped so. The other men on the ship were forward struggling with the smoking sail. He had no advice. He looked at the shore. It was no more than fifty feet away, and the ship was turning inward, stern first. He had to do something. He took a deep breath, grasped the wheel spokes with his blistered hands and painfully spun them to his left. The ship did not respond. The current continued to carry them towards the next pier. Toddy gripped the wheel in painful desperation and wondered why he had ever imagined himself standing heroically in this position.

Then, he felt a slight shudder. The rudder seemed to catch hold. Slowly, the stern began to turn away from the shore. Toddy relaxed slightly and looked back over the turning bow.

He saw two long boats in the water frantically chasing the drifting ship. To the left, the flames continued to leap, and the smoke rolled skyward. Toddy for the first time was conscious of the falling ash. It felt like hot snow.

He looked to his left and realized that the shoreline was coming closer. The stern was gradually pivoting towards the center of the river, but that was the problem. It was pivoting, forcing the bow towards the shore and the waiting pier. As he desperately watched, the men in the bow succeeded in dumping the sail overboard. They did not cheer, however; they began shouting and pointing towards the approaching shore. The "Clipper" was now floating downstream with its bow pointing inland and its stern across the river. The bow seemed ready to touch the shore. Toddy did not know how it was missing the protruding rocks.

He held the wheel as far left as he could and prayed that was the correct thing to do. The men in the bow turned from the sails and ran towards the stern where Toddy clutched the spokes.

"Do something," one of them shouted. "We're going to hit the pier."

"What?" Toddy pleaded.

"I don't know," the man shouted. "I'm a carpenter, not a sailor."

He turned to look at his fellow workmen. They all shook their heads. It was up to Toddy. He clung to his decision. He turned back and looked at the following long boats. He recognized Jason standing in the front of one while two men rowed. He was pointing ahead and shouting something, but Toddy could not hear him. If Jason was trying to tell him that the pier lay dead ahead, he knew that.

He sank to the deck but continued to clutch the wheel. He reasoned that if they hit, he would be safer on the deck. The men sat on the deck with their backs braced against the hull. They all stared white faced at Toddy.

The boat continued to turn.

When moments passed and they struck nothing, Toddy began to wonder what had happened. He stood up again and discovered that they were now turned with the bow partially downstream. On the port bow, the pier stood scant feet away. A white-faced fool stood waving the "Clipper" away. Toddy took a deep breath and relaxed until he realized he now had to decide what to do when he had the bow pointed down river. He would have to again turn the wheel to keep the bow pointed in the right direction for him to steer. He had two questions: which way should he turn the wheel, and did the "Clipper" have enough forward momentum to give him any semblance of control.

When the bow finally came about, Toddy took a chance and turned the wheel back in the opposite direction, stopping at what he hoped was the midway position. Before he could relax again and get his bearings, a man behind him began shouting. He looked back over the stern and saw that the first boat bearing Jason was approaching.

"Get a rope and throw it over so he can get aboard. I need help."

Toddy's tone was not pleading. He gave a simple order and uttered an obvious fact. To his relief, within minutes, Jason and another man, an experienced sailor, were on board. Jason, breathing heavily, patted Toddy on the back and relieved him at the wheel.

"Good work," he exulted.

Jason held the wheel lightly with both hands and made minor adjustments as he guided the "Clipper" as she floated in the current of the main channel. He instructed the sailor and the other men to drop anchor. Somehow, the sailor and his inexperienced crew succeeded and soon the "Clipper" again faced upriver held firmly in position by a bow anchor. Toddy sat on the deck with his back against the stern rail, too exhausted and drained to speak.

In Alexandria, James and Vivian sat on their porch swing and watched as the firemen and their neighbors stood in Union Street.

The houses had been saved, and the flames were gradually burning themselves out. Smoke continued to rise into the dark night sky, no longer illuminated by the brewery flames. Everything for a block on the riverside of Union Street had been destroyed by the conflagration. The AleRoom and brewery were gone. The struts of the three slips had been burned. Jason's empire had been delivered a severe body blow.

"Jason's in trouble," James observed.

"He's got his schooners, his store and warehouse and the two AleRooms," Vivian tried to think positively.

"But no brewery, no ale and no ice," James countered.

"But he's got the "Clipper.""

"Yes," James smiled. "He's got the "Clipper.""

"Thanks to the boys," Vivian gave credit where credit was due. She had watched the entire struggle from her porch.

"Jason can make it back. We'll help him," James spoke with resolve in his voice. The challenge appeared to strip years from his frame.

"If he needs it," Vivian always took the last word.

James and Vivian sat side by side, contemplated the wreckage, and waited for their family to return. The silence was broken only once by Vivian's question.

"What are you thinking so deeply about, James?"

"How the fire started."

"You mean who started it and where is the guard."

At Brown's brewery, Fat Eddy and the Crip sat in Eddy's office drinking warm Brown's Stout by the light of a single lantern set on low.

"What time is it?" Fat Eddy demanded.

"How do I know?" Crip answered, his voice slurred by the alcohol that stiffened his bravado.

Fat Eddy consulted his cheap, silvered watch with the worn yellow finger marks on the case.

"Two o'clock," he observed. "Or is it two bells for the sea going folk?"

"How do I know?" The Crip repeated himself as he refilled his tin cup from the keg on Fat Eddy's desk.

"A lot can happen in two hours. Did you know that?" Fat Eddy observed, punctuating his comment with a vicious chuckle that originated deep in his obese body.

"Sure can," Crip agreed. "Know something Eddy?"

"Yeh. What?"

Both men were drunk.

"That lamp oil sure smells good sometimes." Crip patted the damp spots on his pants. The oil tingled on his good leg underneath.

"You gotta get rid of those pants," Eddy ordered. "Evidence."

"Sure Eddy," Crip replied craftily. "You goin' to buy me a new pair?"

"Sure thing, Crip," Eddy replied, not meaning it. "Draw me another," he ordered, sliding his cup towards his companion.

The two men had been drinking steadily since their return. Their two companions had disappeared as ordered, and Fat Eddy had driven the team directly to his warehouse. In fact, the team, still harnessed, waited patiently at the back of the building. Occasionally, one of them snickered to signal their presence, but Fat Eddy and Crip ignored them. At first, both had been excited by the blaze and smoke that they could see engulfing the riverfront, signaling their success, then they had saluted their courage with the freshly tapped keg; they saluted, and saluted, until they had drunk themselves into near oblivion.

"A man just isn't given many nights like this," Eddy gloated.

On board the "Clipper" Jason and Toddy sat with J.J. and Skinny in the stern on the quarterdeck. The workmen were gathered about them. Skinny and J.J. had arrived in the second long boat. All were exhausted.

"Thank God she's still afloat," Skinny spoke to the dark sky.

Jason glanced at the full moon before replying.

"I say thank Toddy and J.J. and you boys," Jason graciously included the workmen who had assisted in saving his ship.

"I wonder how the fire started," Toddy, embarrassed by the praise, tried to change the subject.

"Yes," Jason mused. If the others could have seen his face, they would have noticed a dark cloud pass over and a sparkle appear in his green eyes. "I definitely smelled lamp oil," Skinny sensed his friend's mood.

"I did too," J.J. confirmed.

"Do you think someone deliberately set it?" One of the workmen asked.

Jason did not answer.

"Who would have done such a terrible thing?" Toddy asked.

Again, Jason did not respond. He and Skinny exchanged a knowing look.

"I wonder what happened to the watchman?" Toddy asked.

"I fear we may find out in the morning," Jason finally spoke.

He wearily drew himself erect and nodded at Skinny.

"Come on. We have work to do."

J.J. and Toddy, whose younger muscles recovered more quickly, immediately leaped to their feet.

"Can we come too?" Toddy asked.

Jason first looked grim-faced at Skinny then back at J.J. and Toddy. He studied each in turn before speaking.

"All right. You boys are both Satterfields and earned your manhood tonight. Let's go."

Jason and Skinny each thought briefly of the day Jason had stabbed and killed the pirate in Martinique.

Jason spoke briefly with the seaman and other workers. He promised to send a crew to tow the "Clipper" back to Alexandria in the morning. Then, followed by Skinny, J.J. and Toddy, he climbed over the stern and down the rope to the long boat. Jason sat in the bow, Skinny in the stern, and the two boys side by side as they rowed the boat back to the pier. Jason did not say a word on the return trip. He silently studied the dying flames that marked the destruction of his brewery and boatyard.

ALEXANDRIA, VIRGINIA

AUGUST 15TH, 1803

Following Jason's instructions, J.J. and Toddy beached the long boat on the Potomac shore south of Alexandria at a point opposite the anchored "Clipper." Jason then led Skinny and the boys in a brisk walk to his store, carefully keeping to the back streets, avoiding the diminished crowds returning home from the night's spectacular fire. On Union Street, James and Vivian watched the remaining few conscientious firemen dampening the embers. The voices lamenting the loss of Alexandria's chilled ale carried on the wind.

Jason carefully assured that the street was deserted before unlocking the thick pine door that protected his general store. The unlit street was dark; the other shops were forlorn and empty, and the neighborhood had returned to its slumber.

"We must work quickly," Jason cautioned. "We have only three hours to first light."

Jason led the way through the murky blackness. Toddy, who was not as familiar with the store layout as the others, bumped into a table filled with china, which rattled but fortunately did not tip over. Jason paused, looked back, but said nothing. He proceeded to the rear of the store, groped in the dark for a latch, then opened the door and entered the storeroom. Still wordless, he groped his way through the pitch black to the corner where his clerks stored the tins of lamp oil. He carefully handed two ten gallon tins each to J.J. and Toddy, one to Skinny who had only one hand, and took two for himself. After the others had exited the rear door of the storeroom, Jason sat his two tins in the dark alley and carefully reset the lock.

Carrying the tins by the metal handle set in the top, Jason led the way northwest away from the store. Walking quickly, barely conscious of the bite of the sharp edges of the metal handles as they cut into their palms, they covered the mile to Brown's Brewery in a little over ten minutes.

Overhead, the friendly orange moon glowed through the thinning clouds of humidity trapped smoke that hung above Alexandria. An occasional dog barked to protest their passage, but Jason's sweating group took little notice.

"What if there's a guard?" Toddy whispered to J.J. as they approached the Brewery.

"Shhh," Jason cautioned before J.J. could think of a response.

The outline of Fat Eddy's brewery loomed ahead. Fortunately, it had few neighbors. It was located in a low, swampy spot north of town where the land was unsuited for either cultivation or habitation.

Jason paused, set his tins on the ground and rubbed his hands to relieve the strain. The others did likewise.

"What's your plan?" Skinny asked, speaking for J.J. and Toddy as well as himself.

"We'll do exactly what he did. Douse the outer walls, stack any straw we can find against them, light the oil and take off."

"Do you have any matches?"

Jason laughed and pulled a box of wood matches that he had picked up at the store from his pocket. He carefully divided the matches among the four of them.

"What about the roof?" Skinny asked.

"What about it?"

"If we can get a tin or two up there, we could pour it along the peak and drench the whole building. It would go up immediately."

Jason turned and studied the series of connected sheds that housed the brewery. The roof consisted of overlapping boards.

"That's a good idea. The fire might not spread fast enough if we don't. I'll do the climbing."

"I could do it," J.J. volunteered.

Jason peered at his young cousin.

"No," he shook his head. "I'll do it."

Jason retrieved his two tins and turned towards the brewery.

"Silently now," he ordered.

Toddy, who had been about to whisper a question to J.J., thought better of it. He had been about to ask what they would do if Fat Eddy had a guard.

Jason halted his group at the right corner of the first building that served as Fat Eddy's warehouse. He set his tins quietly on the ground, motioned for the others to wait, and silently stalked the front doors where the brewery wagons entered. Both were closed and Jason quickly determined they had been bolted from the inside. He tried to peer through the crack where the doors joined, but he could see nothing but blackness. He placed his ear against the crack and listened. He thought he heard movement, waited, heard it again, and then dismissed it. A horse had snickered. He returned to where the others waited.

"Skinny, you and Toddy go around that way. Soak the front doors, then go on around and splash the sides. Stack anything that will burn against the building. J.J. and I will go this way. Work quickly and quietly. If I can, I will get up on the roof. J.J. can hand me one tin."

Skinny nodded, lifted his tin and led Toddy to his left. Jason and J.J. went right. Jason paused to splash oil on the wall of the building.

"Wait," he ordered when J.J. prepared to do the same. "Use the oil sparingly. We have to make sure we have enough for all the sheds. I will leave a trail to connect the oil spots."

Jason worked his way carefully along the side of the warehouse using one of his tins. At the point where the larger building joined the series of sheds, Jason paused. He motioned for J.J. to link his hands and provide a step for Jason to use to reach the roof of the smaller shed. J.J. did so, and Jason, with difficulty, clambered to the roof. During his struggle to get enough purchase to make his way over the eaves, he inadvertently kicked the side of the building. He paused, worried that the sound might have alerted a sleeping guard to his intrusion.

Inside, the sound roused Fat Eddy briefly from his deep, alcoholic slumber. He stared vacantly around him in the dark. The lamp had burned itself out. He listened. Crip snored across the room. Fat Eddy heard one of the horses complain. He remembered he had not unhitched them, thought about it, and then changed his mind. He leaned back in his chair and relapsed into his stupor.

On the roof, Jason leaned over and took the tin from J.J. He indicated that his cousin should work his way along the sheds with his oil. Jason carefully climbed the slanted roof to the peak. He carefully poured oil as he moved across the roofs to the rear. There, he found Skinny, J.J., and Toddy waiting for him. He carefully slid across the incline of the shed, handed the empty tin to J.J. and then jumped down.

"The rear shed door is open and there is straw and hay inside."

Jason followed J.J. around the end of the shed to the open door. Jason could distinguish the stack of straw.

He directed the others to spread armloads of the straw along the base of the building in the pools of oil.

Jason was returning for his second armload when he encountered J.J. coming out the door.

"There's a team in there," J.J. whispered.

Jason shrugged, but J.J. dropped his straw and grabbed Jason's arm.

"We can't leave them in there to suffer," he pleaded.

Jason studied his cousin and noted the firm determination in his straight back.

"All right." Jason, against his better judgment, relented. "See if you can get them out."

J.J. nodded, retrieved his straw, stacked it against the nearest shed then returned. By the time Jason had placed another armload of straw J.J. was back, without the horses.

"It's a team. Still tied to a wagon. There must be somebody still here."

Jason pushed past his cousin and entered the blackness. About twenty feet from the door, he saw movement. He cautiously approached the two horses. J.J. was right. The team was still hitched. He turned to J.J. and whispered.

"You unhitch that one, and I'll get this one."

J.J. hurried to the other side of the wagon and began working on the harness. Jason glanced toward the end of the shed and noticed the closed door. He worked quickly, frequently glancing at the room he knew contained Fat Eddy's office. He and J.J. finished at the same time.

"You lead the horses out of here. Quietly. Tell the others to get ready. We can't dally much longer."

J.J. led the snickering and relieved horses towards the door. Jason, to J.J.'s surprise, turned and hurried towards the closed door. He paused outside and listened. Somebody was inside sleeping. He could hear deep snoring. Jason turned and saw the rears of the horses clear the back doors. J.J. did not appear to have heard the snoring of the sleeping man. Jason carefully opened the door a crack. It groaned softly, but it did not disturb the sleeping forms. Jason stepped quietly into the room and leaned over the man in the chair. He recognized Crip, Fat Eddy's stooge. He smelled the odor of lamp oil and looked down. Crip's pants were marked by large circles of a substance that smelled like lamp oil.

Jason rested his hand on the table and leaned forward to identify the figure behind the table. He had no difficulty recognizing Fat Eddy's form. As he straightened, he slid his hand across the tabletop and encountered an object. He fingered it. He felt the familiar shape of a knife in a sheath. Jason smiled to himself. He picked up the knife, withdrew it from the sheath, then cautiously circled the table. He stood behind Fat Eddy, grabbed a handful of the man's greasy hair and jerked the head back. Fat Eddy's eyes popped open. Jason waited just long enough for the darting pupils to focus on his own face, saw the terror of recognition, then sawed the dull blade across Fat Eddy's throat. He shoved Fat Eddy's head forward and stepped carefully around the spurting blood, careful not to be splashed.

A sound in the doorway caught his attention. Jason looked up and saw J.J. watching.

The flowing blood and air bubbles streaming from Fat Eddy's throat made an odd gurgling sound. Crip stirred. Jason grabbed the keg off the desk in both hands and smashed it on the top of Crip's broad head. The keg shattered, drenching the Crip in foaming brown ale.

Jason brushed the sour liquid from the front of his soot stained shirt and paints and pushed past the silent J.J.

"Let's get out of here," Jason growled. "There's nothing alive in here."

Outside, Jason, less concerned about making a noise, deployed J.J. and Toddy along the far side of the brewery buildings and Skinny on the other.

"Light it now," he called to J.J. and Toddy, then ran to join Skinny.

Jason lighted the handful of straw he carried and ran along the building igniting the oil. The straw and oil exploded into flame and within seconds the walls of the brewery buildings were alight. Jason paused long enough to watch the flames spurt across the roof and imperil the entire structure. He turned and ran towards the river followed by his three companions. Jason knew the flames would soon draw the same crowds that had gathered to watch the AleRoom and his shipyard vanish. By avoiding the streets, he calculated they could return to Union Street undetected then join the firemen and sightseers as they streamed to investigate the fire at Brown's Brewery. As he ran, the thought struck him that Alexandria which a few hours ago had two breweries now had none. Jason immediately began to plan how to make the most of the situation. He estimated that within two weeks his German brewer could have green ale ready for sale using a makeshift process in a rented barn. Jason wondered if the fire had melted all the ice in the cool room. He speculated that the wet canvas and straw and melted water might have protected most of it.

Union Street was now deserted. James and Vivian, weary from having rocked most of the night, were about to abandon their vigil.

"They have the "Clipper" firmly anchored," James observed. "I guess Jason and the boys are planning on spending the night on board to protect her."

Vivian stared at the sparking coals, all that remained of the brewery.

"I guess you're right. There's no sense our sitting here all night. The excitement's over."

"Thank God," James sighed. He hated the thought that Fat Eddy and his brewery would emerge victorious.

"I wonder if Fat Eddy had anything to do with all this?" He asked.

"Wouldn't put it past him, but don't worry, he'll get his comeuppance. Would you like a sip of lemonade before we go back to bed?"

"Sounds good," James agreed. I'll help you make it."

A schooner had arrived the day before from the Indies with lemons in its cargo. Jason had thoughtfully delivered the first basket to his parents.

James and Vivian were in the kitchen making lemonade when running footsteps hit the back porch startling James so badly he almost dropped the lemon he was squeezing.

"Made it," Jason gasped as he opened the back door.

Vivian and James turned and watched as Jason, Skinny, and the boys entered the kitchen.

"Any more of that Vivian?" Jason asked.

James noted that all four of them were breathing heavily as if they had been running. James reached into the basket and retrieved several more lemons. He deftly began slicing them in half.

"Thought you boys were going to spend the night on the ship," James observed. He thought it best not to ask why they had been running down Union Street in the middle of the night.

"Made it from what?" Vivian demanded, suspiciously studying her son.

J.J. and Toddy edged past Jason and sat at the table opposite James, the lemons and the lamp.

James studied them. Both looked guilty. They were soaking wet with sweat, and their clothes, hands and faces were streaked with grime. He thought he detected the odor of lamp oil.

"Nothing, Vivian. We were just relieved to have made it back from the 'Clipper.' It's been a long and hard night."

Vivian, holding the pitcher, suspiciously studied her son. She shook her head in disapproval, making it perfectly clear she knew he was dissembling. She turned, put the small pitcher in the cupboard and retrieved the large one she used for family dinners.

"And you, Skinny, what do you have to say?" Vivian knew how to attack the weak point.

Skinny stared at Jason appealing for help.

The silence lengthened, and Skinny stirred nervously. Before anyone spoke again, the sound of a bell clanging in the distance penetrated the kitchen.

"I must say," Jason said with a smile. "That sounds like the fire bell again."

Vivian continued to study her son. She noted the spots on the front of his shirt.

"Are those blood spots?" She asked.

Jason looked down. J.J. and Toddy exchanged anxious glances. During the run back, J.J. and Toddy had outdistanced the older men, and J.J. had breathlessly confided what he had witnessed inside the brewery. Neither blamed their cousin for his actions, but both boys were worried they would be found out.

Vivian crossed the kitchen and fingered the spots.

"I do believe that is blood," she declared.

James looked at the front of Jason's shirt and then at the worried J.J. and Toddy. The tableau before him combined with the clanging fire bell told him all he needed to know.

"I must have cut myself, somehow," Jason said weakly. "It's nothing." He studied the scratches on his palms caused by the rough tin handles.

James exchanged a meaningful look with Vivian before speaking. His expression said: "Let it be."

"You go upstairs and get in my drawers and find yourself an old pair of pants and shirt to replace those. Best thing we can do with them is burn 'em." James spoke with an authority that he seldom exercised.

James slid the sliced lemons and juicer towards J.J. and Toddy.

"You boys squeeze these lemons, I'll fetch some water from the spring house, and we'll have ourselves a good drink. Then, we can amble along and see what the fire is all about." James nodded towards the back door where a large fire was illuminating the horizon to the east.

"Best bring along some notepaper," Vivian advised the boys.

"Buster'll want a story on tonight's happenings."

"Yes, Vivian," J.J. and Toddy spoke in unison. Neither doubted that the two older Satterfields had surmised exactly what had happened. For the first time that evening, the two boys thought of their cousin Buster. They realized he would be disappointed he had missed the evening's adventures. He was in Leesburg on *Herald* business.

Toddy jerked awake and tried to open his eyes. His eyelids were on fire; flames leaped upwards, and the heat seared his eyeballs. He knew he was finished; he clawed at the clenched eyelids with both hands, but they would not open. The acrid smell of his burning flesh was agonizing. He had never felt such pain. He opened his mouth to scream, but no sound came out, nothing but a thick cloud of oily, black smoke. He wondered how he could still be alive, how the flames could have started inside of himself.

"Toddy, Toddy, wake up."

Toddy heard J.J.'s voice calling him and felt his cousin's hand shaking his arm.

Toddy sobbed and mourned his burning eyes; then, he woke up. The sun was streaming through the open window. J.J. was staring at him, and Toddy caught the odor of burned wood that wafted on the river breeze. He stared uncomprehendingly at J.J. He could see. The flames had vanished.

"You were dreaming." J.J. said.

Toddy nodded. The dream had been so real; the fire seemed to have penetrated to his very depths. At that moment, Toddy doubted he would ever forget the fear he had felt.

"The sun and the smoke must have played on your senses," J.J. said.

"My eyeballs were on fire, and I couldn't put the flames out," Toddy explained.

"Some dream," J.J. dismissed the experience. "Get up. It's almost noon, and we have things to do. I want to see Fat Eddy's place and check on the "Clipper."

Toddy shook the sleep from his body. His hands were shaking from the realism of his nightmare.

"I'll wait downstairs," J.J. said. "Gramps and Vivian are at the *Herald* getting out a special edition."

Toddy checked his face in the mirror over the china bowl that served as the boys' wash basin. His face was still streaked with grime. He noticed the water droplets on the rough wood tabletop; J.J. had considerately refilled the water pitcher, but he had not wiped off the tabletop. The single cotton towel was soaking wet. Toddy realized he deserved second place; he was the one who had dawdled in bed while the family rallied to recover from the night's tragedy. He quickly scrubbed his face, arms and hands; he decided to leave the rest of his body until he was able to bathe in the river later in the day. He selected a clean shirt and trousers, dressed, and slid his sock less feet into his everyday shoes.

Downstairs, he gulped a glass of milk that set on the table and grabbed a crust of the home baked bread. He noticed the Africans in the back yard hanging laundry out to dry. He turned and walked to the front of the house. J.J. sat on the porch swing, waiting patiently.

"Look at that," J.J. said, pointing down Union Street.

Clusters of people were gathered in the street facing the destroyed brewery and shipyard. Several were pointing at the still smoking timbers.

"Christ," Toddy blurted. The devastation was worse than he had thought last night. Nothing remained of Cousin Jason's once promising businesses. "Poor Jason," Toddy commiserated.

"I wonder," J.J. said, his voice strangely passive. A fleeting image of Jason coldly sliding his knife across Fat Eddy's throat passed through J.J.'s mind. "Jason's already got workers cleaning up the debris."

Toddy looked again and realized J.J. was right. At least ten men that Toddy had assumed to be sightseers were stacking charred debris in one corner of the shipyard near the destroyed plank fence. It appeared that they were preparing to reignite whatever had survived the previous night.

"Let's go," J.J. said, jumping up from the swing and leading the way in the direction of Jason's office. "Let's stop by Jason's and see if we can do anything to cheer him up."

As the boys climbed the stairs to Jason and Skinny's office, they heard their cousin speaking in a loud voice. He appeared to be giving orders. At the top of the stairs, they stared through the open door. Jason sat at his table with Skinny standing at his right. Five men, one of whom the boys recognized to be the German brewer that Jason employed, stood before Jason. Their cousin had several stacks of dollars arrayed on the table before him.

"I don't care what it costs," Jason said as they entered. "Hire every cooper in Alexandria if you must, and buy all the sugar, hops, and yeast you can find. I want our ale fermenting by nightfall."

"Ach, Mr. Satterfield. But where shall we work. The brewery is kaput."

"I've rented Mace's barn on the Rolling Road," Jason replied. "The men are already there getting it cleaned up for you."

"But the water... ."

"Use Mace's well. He must have one. If not, haul water from the river."

"Jawohl, Mein Herr, but the conditions will not be sanitary."

"I don't give a shit," Jason erupted. "Just do what I say. I'll build a new brewery for you. It'll be ready in a month, bigger and more sanitary than that old dump. After you get the wort working, draw up your plans. Tell me what you want in the new building. It'll have to be a big one. We'll be the only brewery in town." Jason smiled as he uttered the last words.

"I don't think Jason needs our help," J.J. whispered to Toddy. "Let's go over to the paper and see if Vivian and Gramps want anything."

As the boys turned, Jason spotted them.

"J.J., Toddy. Good morning cousins." Jason turned to the men in front of him. "I want you guys to pass the word. These two are heroes. They single-handedly saved my ship."

The men turned and stared at Toddy and J.J.

"We're going to the *Herald* to help Vivian and Gramps," Toddy said, hoping to change the subject.

"Sure thing, boys, but be back here in an hour. Skinny and I are going out to the "Clipper" to sail her back. You might want to be on board for her first cruise." Jason paused, then smiled. "Well, her second cruise. Toddy took her on her maiden voyage last night."

The boys, embarrassed, turned and descended the stairs. Jason turned his attention back to the workmen.

At the *Herald*, Vivian and James were busy writing the story of last night's fires. The two black freedmen were cleaning the press and stacking paper getting ready to set the type and print the special two-page issue. All were hard at work when Buster arrived. He had come down the Leesburg Pike and had not seen either site of the previous night's excitement. He had tied his horse to the stanchion in front of his house when he noted the door to the newspaper wide open. Since he had not expected any one to be working on this, an off day, he curiously strolled over and entered. He was surprised to find his printers preparing for an edition and his grandparents busily writing at separate tables.

"Gramps, Vivian," he said. "What's up?"

"I'm writing the commentary, and your grandfather is editing his news stories," Vivian smiled sweetly. "Have a seat. we're almost done."

"What stories?" Buster asked, hurrying to James' table and peering over his shoulder.

"About the arsonist," Vivian replied.

"What arsonist?"

Buster stared in frustration at his grandmother. In her most aggravatingly grandmotherly manner, she was forcing him to beg for the story.

"The one who burned down the breweries last night and killed three people." Vivian paused. "James," she said peremptorily. "We had better call the villain the arsonist and murderer. That is more accurate."

"Dad's brewery? The AleRoom?"

Vivian nodded affirmatively and continued to write.

"Dad. Is dad all right?" Buster demanded.

"Yes dear," Vivian replied. "Jason is at his office making plans to rebuild his brewery and shipyard and to recover his boat."

"The shipyard too?"

"Yes, dear."

"And the "Clipper" was lost?" Buster sat in his chair dumbfounded.

"No, dear. The boys saved it. The ship is floating at anchor."

"And the Brown Brewery?"

"Destroyed," Vivian answered impatiently. "James," she said irritably. "You explain to the boy while I finish this inflammatory commentary. We cannot tolerate all this burning and murdering."

Buster looked at his grandfather who smiled patiently.

"Who was killed?" Buster asked.

"Murdered," Vivian corrected.

"Do you want to tell the story or do you want me to?" James asked.

"You do it dear," Vivian smiled and continued to write.

"Fat Eddy, Crip, and the watchman at the AleRoom," James explained.

"Fat Eddy was fried to a crisp. Not a thing was left but bones," Vivian added.

James slid the news stories towards Buster.

"Since it's your paper, you might wish to edit these."

Buster took the sheets of paper and read the headlines:

"FLAMES CONSUME ALEXANDRIA BREWERIES; THREE DEATHS."

"Are you sure you don't want to say: "FAT EDDY SIZZLES?"

"No dear," Vivian replied. "That would not be tasteful."

At that point, Toddy and J.J. appeared in the doorway. Buster waved and continued to read. Vivian smiled and returned her attention to her pen. James nodded his head.

"If you don't need us, we thought we would take the girls and go out and look at Brown's Brewery," J.J. said.

At the mention of the word "girls" Vivian stopped writing and leaned to her left to peer out the door. She saw the attractive Gotradt girls waiting out front.

"As soon as I finish this commentary, if your cousin will stop asking questions, I will return home and fix some lemonade and cookies. Please ask your friends to join us when you return."

"Yes, Vivian," J.J. replied.

Vivian smiled when she saw J.J. frown when he turned to join Toddy and the girls.

"I hope there is nothing unpleasant left lying about out there," Vivian said to nobody in particular.

ALEXANDRIA, THE POTOMAC,
THE CHESAPEAKE

OCTOBER 1803

The first streaks of dawn had crept over the horizon when J.J. leaned out of the window and raised his spit-dampened forefinger to test the wind.

"How's it look?" Toddy asked anxiously.

Toddy felt the nerves deep in his abdomen stir. He studied the cotton curtains. He was sure one of them had moved. He poked J.J. in the back, hoping to prod an answer.

"Well, I... I, I just can't tell," J.J. responded. "I think so, but I'm not sure."

"Let me see," Toddy nudged J.J. aside.

He licked his finger and held it out the window.

"I think it's from the northeast."

"Great, me too," J.J. agreed.

Without another word, both boys dressed, grabbed already packed, identical cloth bags by their drawstrings, and quietly descended the stairs, careful not to waken James and Vivian who slept in the room across the hall.

They had been waiting for this moment since they had learned that Jason planned his first test cruise on the Chesapeake as soon as the wind was right. Jason wanted perfect conditions; he was confident the "Clipper" would perform admirably, but he wanted to take no chances. High tide and a steady, moderate breeze from the northeast were his minimum requirements. As a reward for their performance on the night of the fire, J.J. and Toddy had been given permission to participate in the "Clipper's" maiden journey.

"Wouldn't you know it, a Saturday," Toddy observed, referring to the fact that the wind would turn on a non-school day.

All week long, they had anxiously risen before dawn and checked the wind, and for seven days it had blown gently from the southeast, as it was wont to do. Alexandria weather in the autumn spawned in the warm tropical seas to the south and crept northward, barely hesitating as it explored the broad, inviting expanses of the Chesapeake Bay and its mothering rivers. Wind from the north-east was a rarity.

The boys hurried past the new slip where Jason had repaired the "Clipper's" superficial damage. Debris from the fire still littered the area, but Jason's boat-yard was back in business. One new slip had been completed. The pier had been rebuilt, and the boys could see the rakish ship bouncing on the river current, wait-ing impatiently for them. Already, seamen were in the rigging, checking the hal-yards and rope pulleys. "Clipper's" sails were reefed, but the Stars and Stripes gently wafted in the breeze.

"The wind's blowing down river," J.J. confirmed. He was anxious to assume his position as the topmast lookout.

Jason had refused to let J.J. work the rigging on this his first cruise; in its stead, in recognition of his skill aloft, he had been appointed lookout. Toddy had been assigned as Jason's midshipman, an honorific title indicating he would serve as the owner's dog boy, available to carry messages and perform errands on demand. Happy to be invited to share the first cruise, neither boy worried about his assigned duties.

"The crew's already on board," Toddy said with concern creeping into his voice.

Neither boy wanted to risk being left behind.

"Morning boys," Jason greeted them as he crossed the street. He carried a seaman's duffel bag. He was accompanied by the ever present Skinny who had traveled with Jason on his first sea journey on the "Ghost" almost thirty years ago.

"Morning Jason," J.J. and Toddy replied. "Skinny."

"Boys," Skinny said. "Ready to sail? Wind looks right."

The two older men and the two boys walked quickly along the pier and mounted the narrow gangplank. Members of the crew acknowledged their pres-ence with a wave or a curt "Morning Boss" addressed to Jason. Jason had per-sonally selected the thirty crew members for the "Clipper's" first sail. He had no difficulty acquiring Alexandria's best. Many of the local schooners were cau-tiously feeling out the first days of the resumed French and English war. Already, warships of both nations lurked along America's coast waiting for the opportu-nity to seize neutral shipping as a penalty for "trading with the enemy." The English had never flagged in their abuse of American shipping, impressing American sailors, but with war renewed they were seizing vessels and confiscat-ing cargoes as well, and the French, not to be outdone, emulated their traditional foe. Alexandria owners had already lost three vessels, and most Virginia ships had surrendered crewmembers to the predators. Jason's fleet schooners plying the West Indian trade had been lucky, but no one doubted that inevitable destiny waited.

Many of Jason's fellow owners thought he was foolish to sail his new vessel in these uncertain times; several had counseled him to wait, to first learn where the hostile powers concentrated before risking his fortune. All suspected that the large mouth of the Chesapeake was too enticing for the Halifax based English fleet to ignore; the French with their fewer vessels worked out of the West Indies islands, but the English men-of-war were everywhere.

Jason had been determined to sail as soon as the fire repairs had been completed. He wanted to introduce the "Clipper" to the high seas before the gales of winter struck. His one concession had been to limit the cruise to the Chesapeake. British warships had entered the bay, but most lurked in the Atlantic where they could prey on the coastal cargo carriers.

Captain Moses Wallace, Jason's most experienced schooner captain, had been selected to command "Clipper." The dour Marylander, a native of Baltimore, had been at sea for twenty years, the last five working for Jason. On this first cruise, Wallace would sail the ship, but Jason as owner would have his say much like an admiral who placed his flag on the vessel of a subordinate captain.

Captain Moses met Jason and his group at the top of the gangplank.

"Welcome aboard, Jason."

"How's it look?"

"Everything's shipshape. Wind's right; crew's on board, and the "Clipper's" anxious to get underway."

"Then do so," Jason ordered.

J.J. handed his bag to Toddy and scampered aloft to his lookout position high on the main mast. Toddy, who ventured aloft only when he had to, watched enviously. Jason and Skinny also offered their bags to Toddy.

"Put them in the main cabin aft," Wallace instructed.

Jason and Skinny accompanied the captain on a quick tour of the ship. The sailors, having noticed the owner's arrival, had taken their assigned places without being commanded to do so; all were anxious to earn a permanent place as crew on the new ship. She looked like she would live up to her owner's assertion that she would be the fastest bottom on the sea. With war on the horizon, she would earn ample prize rewards for the lucky crew. The men manning the ropes that tied the "Clipper" to land watched alertly as Jason, Skinny and the Captain strolled past.

"Standby to cast off," the Captain ordered.

"How many crew are on board?" Jason asked, all business. He recalled his first cruise with Skinny and two others, marveling at how naive and undermanned they had been.

"All thirty that we contracted for," Wallace replied.

Jason nodded. Thirty men were more than were needed to sail "Clipper," but he wanted an experienced crew on hand from the beginning. He was determined that nothing would go wrong on the first test. When the "Clipper" took to the high seas as a privateer, he would triple that number. She would need gun crews, prize crews, marines for boarding parties, all in addition to the sail crew. These initial thirty, or as many of them as proved out, would become "Clipper's" parent crew. They would be responsible for the ship. Jason wanted them to be the best that ever sailed. If the "Clipper" were to outsail and outwit the hostile men-of-war of England, the sailing master of the world, her captain and crew would have to be the best America had to offer. Jason did not intend to lose a single man to English impressment gangs.

Within minutes, the three men had circled the ship and gathered on the quarterdeck. Toddy joined them there and waited alertly, ready to implement Jason's orders. He knew that the ship's master, Captain Wallace, would command while under sail, thus Toddy's participation would be limited, but since he hoped one day to captain one of his cousin's ships himself, Toddy was prepared to watch and learn.

Captain Wallace looked at Jason, who nodded. Wallace turned to his first officer.

"All hands to duty stations. Prepare ship to get underway."

"Aye aye, sir," the young officer responded with alacrity.

Toddy visualized himself standing there one day. He would finish his formal schooling at the academy in June. Jason had already promised to place him on board one of the schooners to learn his selected profession. Toddy hoped he could start as a junior officer, not cabin boy, but he would take what was offered. One day he would sail aboard his own fine ship, something as grand as the "Clipper," all the way to the Spice Islands. The West Indies were not for him.

"Bosun, pipe the hands aloft," the young officer ordered an older seaman who stood nearby with a whistle that dangled from a string around his neck.

The seaman blew several shrill blasts on his whistle.

"Prepare to cast off," Captain Wallace ordered.

Toddy listened as the orders echoed through the ship.

"Ahoy there, on the pier. Withdraw the gangplank."

Toddy walked to the port rail and watched as shoremen pulled away the plank that linked the ship to the land.

"The breeze's light, but we'll get underway using only the jib and mainsail, partially furled," Captain Wallace informed Jason.

Jason nodded. "Then what?"

"I suggest we take her out into the current, come about and tack back and forth a few times going upstream. If anything goes wrong, we can drift back to port."

"The helm's yours, Captain. You sail her. I'm along for the ride. I suggest you not worry about anything going wrong."

The Captain smiled as Jason spoke.

"Very well, sir. If you will excuse me."

The jib and half-unfurled mainsail flapped in the light breeze. The Captain walked to the port deck, and Toddy stepped back. The Captain had precedence, and crew and passengers were expected to respect his privacy. The Captain noted the withdrawn gangplank and the crewmen standing near the bow and stern lines.

"Cast off and get her underway," he ordered the lieutenant.

While the young officer relayed the orders, the Captain spoke to the helmsman. Toddy closely watched the young man who stood before the wheel. He remembered the fear he had felt when he himself had stood in that very spot the night of the fire. Jason noted Toddy's stern visage and smiled, knowing what his young cousin was thinking.

"Take her into the current. When she is firmly underway, we'll bring her about and try our first tack upstream. On my command," he cautioned.

On shore, early morning passers-by paused to watch. James and Vivian sat side by side on the swing on their front porch.

"She's underway," James reported, unable to hide the tremor of excitement that had crept into his voice.

"I can see that," Vivian replied. "She only has two little sails up."

"The Captain's a cautious man. He wants to see how she behaves."

"If Jason were captain, she would be under full sail already. That would be something to see."

"Be patient," James advised. He had long suspected that Jason's impulsiveness came from Vivian's Randolph ancestors.

As James and Vivian watched, "Clipper" came about and turned upstream. Every several hundred yards, the Captain brought her about, exercising the crew and testing his vessel. After a half an hour, he unfurled the mainsail. By the end of an hour, the "Clipper" was about a mile upstream. Suddenly, the Captain unfurled the foresail and turned to run before the wind down river. The rakish ship's speed increased. When she passed Alexandria, she remained in midstream. She had all her sails deployed except her two square topsails. The bowsprit remained withdrawn. Jason had designed the bowsprit without figurehead so that it could be extended when needed to increase the breadth of the jib. He had tried to provide the trim, low hull with as much sail power as he could squeeze on to her.

The racing clipper raised a wedge of water as it cut through the river. The black hull, the greenish bow wave and the bleached white sails made one of the prettiest pictures James had ever seen. The Stars and Stripes waving against the rising morning sun and its cloudless blue skies brought a teardrop to James' eyes. He surreptitiously wiped it away before Vivian saw it.

"That is the most beautiful sight I have ever seen," James declared.

"I do believe I see J.J. waving," Vivian replied.

James noted she had a catch in her voice. He studied the mast just below the fluttering flag. He saw a figure standing in the crow's nest waving and waving.

"I'm sure it's J.J.," James said, although he was unable with certainty to identify his brother's grandson. He considered J.J. a grandson not a grandnephew. James figured he could call the boy what he wanted; they both had sprung from the same Satterfield seed.

After the "Clipper" got underway, Jason left the quarterdeck to Captain Wallace and his crew. He paced from bow to stern with Toddy at his side, studying the masts, the rigging, checking to make sure the anchor was properly seated in its place. He leaned over the rail and contemplated the bow wave. Silently, he ignored the crew as they nervously performed their duties. Overhead, the taut sail rippled. Jason placed a hand on the angled main mast, feeling the vibration.

Many had argued that eighty degrees was too sharp an angle, but Jason could detect no problems. He had wanted angled masts for his windward tacks, reasoning that the lessened resistance would let the ship sail tighter. Even an added degree would mean important distance in a race with a more powerful frigate.

The "Clipper" indeed skipped over the waves. The tide was full and the water salty. Jason anxiously awaited the moment when the Captain would unfurl more sail. He wanted the sensation of his ship under full power. He paused briefly and closed his eyes, trying to sense how the ship would react under gale winds.

Satisfied, he descended the steps to the hold. He carefully examined the hull.

"Any sign of water? He asked the crewmen who were likewise checking the caulking.

"Nary a drop," a bosun replied.

"A real beautiful ship," a younger seaman said obsequiously, attempting to ingratiate himself with the owner.

Toddy hid his smile. He did not blame the young man. He would flatter Jason himself if that would earn him a place on the crew.

Jason nodded. In the hold the slapping noise the water made as it resisted the "Clipper's" passage was much louder. It was a soothing sound befitting the smooth copper plated hull's slide through the water. Jason knew the ship would not always be so light. Barnacles would eventually encrust the plating and have to be scrapped off, and the ship rode high because it had only the pig iron ballast for weight. Later, several tons of heavy iron cannon would be installed. Jason had already ordered a long Tom twenty- four pounder, two heavy swivels, little more than big mouthed mortars to be used for raking rigging and killing crewmen, and fourteen nine pounders for close work. The "Clipper's" armament would be tailored for each cruise, more or less depending upon what was expected.

Jason's schooner captains were on his orders developing a network of paid informants in the ports of the West Indies where they called. Information was important to a privateer. If they could learn sailing dates in advance and obtain copies of cargo manifests, they could select their prey and not waste days and weeks and costly gunpowder and balls. Time would be money, and Jason wanted to average a prize every ten days for the "Clipper." At that rate, within a year he could have four clippers on the seas, and after that, it would depend on how long the French and English carried on their silly vendetta. Jason hoped for a long war.

The first day Captain Wallace slowly worked his way into the Bay. He frequently reversed direction, tacking and running, raising and lowering sails, testing his vessel and exercising and training his crew in as many ways as his experience and imagination could devise. He was pleased that the light breeze held steady. When they got lower in the Bay, they could test themselves against the stronger winds, preparing for the day when they would challenge the ocean with its northeasternlys and southwesternlys.

The first night they anchored near the mouth of the Potomac not far from the Chesapeake Bay. The second day they sailed in the broad tidal waters of the Bay, tacking between the Maryland shore and Virginia. Jason had originally planned to return on the tide up the Potomac, but the "Clipper" had performed so flawlessly that he decided to test her on the ocean itself. Captain Wallace, a more cautious man, recommended against pushing their luck. He admitted that the "Clipper" appeared seaworthy—a few halyards and pulleys needed replaced, and one of the smaller, square rigged topsails was outsized, an error that Jason intended to discuss with the sail maker—but one never knew. Ships had minds of their own and frequently flaws appeared at unforgiving moments.

"The "Clipper" is seaworthy," Jason declared adamantly. "And we will take her to sea on the morrow."

J.J. and Toddy, who sat in the main cabin listening to the discussion, smiled broadly and exchanged enthusiastic nods. Both, sunburned and windblown from their first two days on the water, now felt ready to challenge the Atlantic Ocean. Neither had suffered a pang of the seasickness that they had heard so much about and had concluded they both had mariners' sea legs.

"At the least," Captain Wallace persisted, "let's put in at Norfolk and learn the latest on the English."

Jason, pleased that his captain had relented, agreed.

"We'll anchor off Norfolk tomorrow night and go in and collect the latest word. Then, if the coast is clear, we'll give the Atlantic a try. I want to see how the 'Clipper' handles the swells and real wind."

Captain Wallace nodded agreement, but he did not appear convinced. He, too, knew that his employer had a tendency to play the long chance when wiser men waited.

Jason again recalled his first voyage in the "Ghost." He and Skinny had sailed all the way to Martinique; the brush with the pirates had been a near one, and Jason admitted they had been foolish in their youth, but this was different. He only planned to test his new ship on the high seas.

The next night they anchored on the lee side of the peninsula that protruded to mark the point where the James River joined the Bay and the ocean. The crew lowered the long boat from the stern, and Jason, Skinny, and Captain Wallace, with four strong crewmen as rowers, proceeded ashore. Both J.J. and Toddy were disappointed to be left on board ship—they wanted to see Norfolk—but Jason and the Captain treated them like the rest of the crew. They did not intend to lose a single man to the temptations of the waterfront despite the fact they had been on the water for only two days.

When the long boat returned, Jason was smiling, Skinny expressionless, and Captain Wallace frowning. Jason confided that English sails had not been seen off Norfolk for three days. Captain Wallace pointed out one last time that the harbor had been filled with American ships waiting for the maritime situation to resolve itself. Jason, however, as owner had the last word.

"The 'Clipper' will sail on the ebb tide."

J.J. and Toddy thought their cousin sounded terribly nautical. They were impressed. Until now, they had always considered Jason a businessman not a sailor. Just before turning in—the boys slept on hammocks in the crew's compartment where all shared the common space—they asked Skinny where Jason had acquired his maritime experience.

"He's sailed to Martinique, that's all," Skinny sourly remembered their first trip.

"How many times?" Toddy asked.

"Several," Skinny replied. "Jason got his start running powder through the English blockades. He sold it at high prices to General Washington who was glad to get it and paid for the "Ghost.""

The boys, impressed, retreated to their hammocks.

The next morning the bosun aroused the crew at daybreak.

"Mr. Satterfield's anxious to find the ocean," the bosun explained.

After a breakfast of hard biscuits and lukewarm tea, J.J. climbed to his lookout station. He wore a heavy wool sweater. The wind from the ocean was gusty and the sky overcast.

"All the better," Jason exulted when Toddy pointed to the gathering storm clouds to the east. "We'll see how the lady likes weather."

The "Clipper" required an hour to clear the harbor. As soon as they passed the Bay entrance and entered the deep water, the Captain sent the hands aloft to set all sail. For the first time, the "Clipper" had her fore and main sails, the jib and the two topsails unfurled at the same time. Jason even directed that the bowsprit be extended to give his ship her maximum sail power.

The wind was what Jason told Toddy the mariners called "brisk." The "Clipper" hummed through the water at a rate faster than Toddy had ever traveled in his life. The swells were high and rolling directly into the bow. The "Clipper's" sharp prow cut through them sending a shower of spray high into the sails. The moisture seemed to harden them and propel the ship even faster.

"Want to try your hand on the wheel?" Jason asked Toddy.

"Yes sir," Toddy replied. He studied the helmsman who stood with both legs spread wide and hands clenched on the wheel spokes.

Jason looked at Captain Wallace who nodded his approval. He was busy at the rail studying the horizon with his glass.

Toddy approached the wheel and stood next to the sailor. The man approvingly noted Toddy's muscular body.

"There's a fair amount of pull," he whispered. "Get a tight hold."

The helmsman stepped one leg back and moved his head to indicate Toddy should grasp the wheel with his left hand when the sailor removed his. Toddy did so and was surprised by the pressure. The ship wanted to pull to the port. They were on a northeasterly tack.

"OK, take her," the helmsman said and stepped back.

The wheel started to turn and Toddy lost his grip. It spun two times before the helmsman grabbed the spokes and held it from the side until Toddy was able to grip it with both hands. The wheel fought him, but he braced his legs and let his muscles relax.

"Now bring it back a point," the helmsman ordered.

Toddy looked at the man who was staring upwards. Toddy realized he was watching the sails that had begun to flap along the forward edge.

"Ease 'er back until the edges firm."

To Toddy's surprise the "Clipper" responded. The flapping stopped, and the ship heeled slightly. He was exhilarated. He was controlling the ship.

Toddy manned the helm for the next three hours under the old sailor's close supervision. Finally at noon, he surrendered the wheel when the helmsman's replacement appeared.

"I think he's a natural sailor," the man observed.

Toddy was not sure the man spoke the truth or was merely trying to flatter Jason. Jason, who was a natural sailor, nodded agreement.

During the afternoon, Toddy watched as Jason and Captain Wallace put the "Clipper" through her trials. Jason had the ship turned northeast. The swells increased in size, rolling thirty or forty feet in the air. The "Clipper" now caught them on the starboard bow at an angle that made the ship corkscrew and twist down the back of the waves. The helmsman now cursed and worked the wheel. The wind increased in strength and whistled through the stays, but the "Clipper" charged forward.

Toddy listened as the Captain discussed their ship's reactions.

"She holds tighter to the wind than any ship I ever sailed," Captain Wallace enthused. "And that includes any war sloop I ever handled."

"She reminds me of a schooner I once owned; she's faster and quicker, though." Jason was thinking of the "Ghost" whose speed had saved his and Skinny's lives.

A sudden squall swept over the ship, and the masts groaned. Captain Wallace looked skyward. Toddy studied his face and was relieved to note he did not appear worried.

"Those canted masts are doing their job. Can't tell if they help. They certainly don't slow her down."

"Do you think taller masts and double topsails would make her faster?"

"Might," Captain Wallace replied cautiously. He did not want to be the one to recommend to the owner the replacement of brand new masts in order to get a few more knots of speed.

"I'll remember that when we break one and have to replace it. If you're on board and I'm not and you're in another port, get a mast long enough to hold double topsails."

"Are you sure? Do you think the extra speed is worth the expense?"

Jason contemplated the stern features of his captain and wondered if he were the right man for the "Clipper." The man did not seem to realize that the "Clipper" was a predator not a merchant ship. Speed, every single extra knot, was essential.

"I think I better replace your cousin," Captain Wallace observed. He had noted Jason's scrutiny and had divined his thoughts. He nervously changed the subject.

Toddy leaned back to stare up the main mast at J.J. He was surprised at the motion. As the ship rose and fell as it cut through the waves, the mast swung back and forth to a remarkable degree. On the deck, Toddy was conscious of the motion but was learning to compensate, but J.J. in his little nest high up on the swinging pole appeared to be having difficulty. As Toddy watched, J.J. leaned to the leeward, one hand grasping a halyard, and vomited.

"He's been there long enough for the first day," Jason agreed. Captain Wallace turned to his first officer, the young lieutenant.

"Bring 'im down," he ordered.

"I sent up a replacement an hour ago, but he did not want to come down," the young officer replied, afraid of being criticized for having made a mistake.

"It's all right. Just send up a replacement and tell him I want to talk with him about the ship," Jason suggested tactfully.

Toddy rotated his head, stretched his neck muscles, and realized how tired he was. He looked at the sun and estimated it was no later than three in the afternoon. He watched as a sailor scampered up the mast. He joined J.J. in the crow's nest. The two exchanged a few words, then J.J. lowered himself over the edge of his small platform and slowly descended. Toddy made his way across the rolling deck to wait at the base of the mast for his cousin. J.J. carefully lowered himself to about five feet from the desk then dropped with a thud, landing on his feet. He turned and looked white faced at Toddy. Then, his cheeks puffed full, and he raced to the rail. While Toddy waited, J.J. vomited. Finally, when his stomach could contain no more, he heaved several times without result, then turned and staggered to rejoin Toddy.

"I don't think I've ever been so sick," J.J., who had initially taken to the heights with ease, said.

"Want me to help you below?" Toddy asked. Heights bothered him, but he had adapted to the rolling without difficulty. Noting J.J.'s agonized, pale face, he felt guilty.

"Thanks, but I better stay on deck. The wind might help, and I need to be near the rail." J.J. slumped to the deck and leaned against the mast.

"Stay in the center of the ship, if you can," Toddy counseled. "There's less motion. If you need anything, call me. I will be on the quarterdeck."

Toddy returned to the wheel.

"A little seasick, but he'll be all right."

Neither the captain nor Jason laughed. Both had suffered the sea malady and knew from experience it was not something to use for hazing novices.

"The mast in these seas will swing thirty feet. I should have done something sooner." The Captain peered compassionately at J.J. who had returned to the rail.

THE ATLANTIC

OCTOBER 1803

J.J., embarrassed by his performance the previous day, was back in his nest as dawn broke. The strong wind from the northeast pelted his lofty perch with cold droplets, and they felt good on his drawn face and still clammy skin. He breathed deeply, and the harsh, salty sea air burned his lungs, but despite his misery his queasy stomach was not fighting him, not like yesterday when he had retreated in shame from his post. J.J. had learned one thing from the episode. He was a scholar not a sailor. J.J. gladly surrendered the angry seas to his cousin Toddy.

J.J. had awaked early. The closeness of the crew cabin with the snoring men and the foul air made him crave the fresh sea winds. Before first light, he slipped from his hammock, retrieved his boots and silently made his way through the dark past his sleeping cousin. Toddy had been exhausted, complaining of sore muscles from his two stints at the wheel, so J.J. let him sleep despite the fact he wanted to discuss the previous day's fiasco and what it had taught him.

On deck, the skeleton watch that had sailed the ship during the long night wearily nodded at the owner's kin. Not one appeared to have given a second thought to J.J.'s nauseous display; he hoped it had been because they too had suffered similarly. The lookout was slumped and sleeping on the floor of his perch when J.J. appeared. After expressing his surprise at his early relief, the sailor eagerly descended the mast and hurried towards his waiting hammock.

J.J. turned towards the rising sun and let the wind blow through his matted hair. As he watched, the sun's leading edge turned the ocean waters in the east a fiery red. As he studied the phenomenon, something caught J.J.'s attention at the far extreme tip of the horizon. It was nothing but a black speck in the darkness beyond the rising sun's reach. J.J. blinked his eyes, and the spot vanished only to reappear when he blinked a second time.

The incident reminded J.J. that he was aloft for a purpose, not simply to watch the sunrise and to enjoy the refreshing winds. He retrieved the long glass from the floor of his nest and conscientiously scanned all three hundred and sixty degrees of ocean. Except for the "Clipper," the rising sun and the speck, the flat expanse of water was empty. J.J. focused the glass on the speck, but it made little difference other than to make it appear larger. Finally, J.J. relaxed and watched the ship stir to life below him. Toddy appeared on deck, paused near the passageway that led down to the cabins, and stretched.

J.J. smiled as his cousin winced at the soreness and turned his attention back to the sun. It had climbed higher in the sky, vanquishing the gray and obscuring the stars. J.J. looked again at the speck and was surprised to see a flash of white. He raised the glass, focused it, and was shocked when a miniature ship under full sail leaped into his vision.

"Sail Ho. Sail Ho," J.J. shouted.

Toddy seemed to be the only one to hear him and not well. He pointed at his ears and raised his hands to indicate he could not understand.

"Sail Ho. Sail Ho," J.J. screamed as loud as he could and pointed in the direction of the speck.

Toddy waved his hand in acknowledgment and rushed to the quarterdeck where he reported to Captain Wallace who had just emerged from below for his first inspection of the morning.

From his perch J.J. watched as Toddy repeated his words, "Sail Ho," and pointed towards J.J. When J.J. had the Captain's attention, he pointed in the direction of the speck and shouted:

"A sail, Captain. To the northeast. I can make her out."

The Captain turned and looked in the direction that J.J. pointed. He raised his glass but failed to discern the sail. He looked back at J.J. and raised his hands to indicate he saw nothing.

J.J. raised his glass again and studied the ship. It was a square-rigger under full sail. She apparently had not sighted the "Clipper" because she was sailing due west.

J.J. was surprised to hear a clatter below him. He looked over the side of his nest to discover the Captain scrambling up the mast.

"Where?" The Captain gasped when he joined J.J. in the crow's nest.

"Northeast, Captain. A square-rigger under full sail. She looks big."

Captain Wallace grabbed J.J.'s glass and aimed it where J.J. pointed. He silently studied the horizon. Finally, he lowered the glass and patted J.J. on the back.

"Good work, boy. Sharp eyes. It's an English man-of-war. Fifty guns or more."

Without another word, the Captain descended the mast as quickly as he had climbed. He rushed to the quarterdeck and barked orders to his first officer.

Within seconds the bosun was piping the crew to duty stations. J.J. could not hear the pipe's summons but he saw the man's cheeks puff. Soon the crew was scrambling across the deck, some hopping to pull on their boots as they ran. J.J. turned his attention back to the frigate. It had apparently spotted the "Clipper" because it was turning southwest. The two ships were now headed straight towards each other. J.J. estimated they had about a mile of ocean between them. As he watched, the frigate grew larger and larger until he could make out her huge sails.

Suddenly, the "Clipper" began to turn through the wind. J.J. grasped the mast and hung on. The sails fluttered as they lost their purchase briefly before snapping taut. The helmsman seized the spinning wheel and clutched it tight as the rudder turned the fleet ship until it was running before the wind. Sailors scrambled past J.J. and quickly unfurled the square-rigged topsails.

On deck, Jason appeared.

"What's happening, Captain?" He demanded.

"A man-of-war. She's spotted us and is in pursuit."

"Great," Jason shouted. "Now we can show her our heels. See how much faster we are."

Captain Wallace stared at the owner with surprise etched on his face. He could not believe that Jason actually welcomed being pursued by a hostile man-of-war that had the canonry to demolish his ship with one broadside. Compared to the double decked frigate, the "Clipper's" armament, if they had it on board, was a mere pittance.

Captain Wallace returned his attention to his ship. He ordered a slight course adjustment, turning to the southwest. The "Clipper" responded, fairly leaping over the waves as she ran with sails full.

"Deploy the spinnaker, Captain," Jason suggested. He had waited as long as his diminished patience permitted before speaking.

"But Mr. Satterfield. We have not tested her. If the spinnaker fouls, the frigate will be on us in minutes."

Jason studied the Captain and decided. The man was too cautious to command the "Clipper." He would be replaced as soon as they docked in Alexandria. Wallace could return to his tame West Indies schooner, and Jason would find himself a real privateer, a New Englander if necessary. Jason had long harbored the suspicion that the hard, close-mouthed northerners were better seamen. They seemed more willing to make the hard decisions.

"This is as good a time as any to test her," Jason spoke softly, not wishing to belittle his Captain in front of his crew. The man was a good sailor; he just was not a fighting captain.

"Very good sir. The decision is on your shoulders."

Jason nodded and watched as his Captain gave the orders which sent crewmen rushing to the front of the ship. Within minutes they had wrestled the large, balloon like spinnaker on deck and had attached her to the halyards. Two seamen hoisted the large sail up the foremast. Aloft, J.J. watched. Even though he had seen the huge sail unfurl, he was surprised by the large pop that resulted when the brisk wind filled it. The sudden increase in power forced the bow down briefly; the "Clipper" shuddered, then charged across the waves.

J.J. turned back to the pursuing frigate. He saw a puff of black smoke rise from her bow and heard the distant clap of a large gun being fired. He recognized that the frigate was probing the range with one of her long Toms, twenty-four pounders, that she carried on her bow for distant intimidation. J.J. saw the ball land several hundred yards to their stern. The frigate fired a second time, and the shot landed even further behind them.

The "Clipper" was showing the English her heels.

"She's as fast as you say, Mr. Satterfield." Captain Wallace tried to make up for lost face, but at the same time he was genuinely amazed at the slim, rakish ship's speed. He indeed had never sailed on such a craft.

Jason, accompanied by Toddy and Skinny, walked to the rear of the quarter-deck, leaving Captain Wallace with his command near the helmsman.

"Jason," Skinny said. "I think we need a more adventurous captain."

"Wallace's all right, but he doesn't have a privateer's instincts. He's exactly what we need for the cargo carriers."

"But not for the 'Clipper.'"

Toddy listened but said nothing. He had been thrilled by the appearance of the frigate, which was now slipping back on the horizon, but he was disappointed. He realized he would not have a chance at the wheel today.

"Jason," Toddy said. "With your permission I want to go to the bow and watch the sailors handle the sails."

"Go aloft if you want," Jason agreed.

Toddy looked upward with apprehension but nodded agreement. He knew that he would have to conquer his fear of heights if he wished to become a seaman. He had watched Captain Wallace climb up to confer with J.J.

For the next two hours, Toddy cautiously worked the high rigging. At first, the experience had been frightening. He had no difficulty climbing and moving along the spars and braces, but each time he looked down his legs trembled. He enjoyed the wind in his face and hair and tolerated the occasional rope burns. Before long the sailors begrudgingly accepted the lubber in their midst—it was hard to ignore the lad's eagerness, and they gave him small chores to do.

Once, when Toddy paused near J.J.'s nest, his cousin whispered encouragement.

"You're doin' it Toddy. You're doin' real good."

"I don't know if I will ever get used to looking down," Toddy said, forcing himself to study the figures on the quarterdeck to make his point.

"Don't think about it," J.J. cautioned. "After a while, it's just like walking on Union Street." J.J. spoke with the experience of three days aloft.

"Stay alert in the loft, lookout," the first officer called. "And you sailor," the officer shouted at Toddy. "Clear the pulley on the topsail."

Toddy looked upward and noticed a sail point caught in the topmost pulley. He swallowed hard and climbed up the mast past J.J. and his loft.

"Maybe I should be a lookout first," Toddy said.

"Go to it cousin," J.J. encouraged.

J.J. turned and studied the distant frigate with his glass. The warship with bulldog persistence tracked the "Clipper" despite the fact that it was rapidly falling behind. J.J., noting the Captain watching him, turned to sweep the horizon. He saw nothing to the west and expected to see nothing to the south. Except for the frigate and the "Clipper" the ocean had been empty all morning, just as it had been for the entire time since they had left the safe waters of the Chesapeake.

J.J. conscientiously studied the southern horizon and was turning to the east when a speck caught his attention. After his experience with the frigate, he knew what a speck meant. In fact two small specks appeared.

"Sail Ho," he shouted. "Sail Ho." He did not know how to announce two ships.

"How do I say two ships," J.J. called up to Toddy who now clung to the mast about ten feet over his head, trying to disentangle a loop in the new rope that was blocking the pulley.

"Just say it," Toddy called back, more concerned with his own problem.

"Two sails to the south," J.J. shouted as loud as he could.

He listened as the sailors working the topsail below him echoed his call. He saw the Captain rush to the port rail and fix his glass on the horizon.

"Looks like another frigate and maybe a war sloop," Captain Wallace observed. "They're trying to box us in. Maybe we blundered into a trap." He accusingly stared at Jason who said nothing in reply.

Jason appraised the "Clipper's" wake. His ship was caught between the frigate to the northeast and the two ships to the southwest. He studied the clouds and the sails, then turned to the Captain.

"What do you suggest?"

The Captain looked at the spinnaker. It was beginning to flap. He had been watching it for the past fifteen minutes and had been about to order it to be furled. The wind was shifting from the northeast to the north. He studied the owner, and then he made the decision. He was the captain and would sail his vessel.

"Take in the spinnaker," the Captain ordered without consulting Jason.

The Captain was listening to his orders being relayed and watching the crew rushing to fulfill them and did not notice the broad smile that spread across Jason's face. As soon as the spinnaker was down and four men were busy folding it to take below, the Captain turned back to his first officer.

"The wind's shifting. Bring her to the starboard to a northeasterly tack. We'll see how close to the wind she goes."

The captain studied the sun, which was almost directly overhead.

"And give me a sighting. I want to know where the Bay is. We may have to hit it running."

Jason approved of the Captain's decisions but said nothing. The new course would take them away from the sloop and frigate approaching from the south, but if the pursuing frigate detected their new tack and turned with them it might have an angle for intercept. The Captain, lost in his own thoughts, was fully aware of the possibility. He looked aloft at the lookout and wondered if he should send up a more experienced seaman. He turned to Jason, noted that the owner was walking toward the port stern, and made up his own mind. The boy had done all right so far. He had sharp eyesight and seemed to be alert. He had spotted all three pursuers. Besides, the Captain reasoned, if the owner were worried, he could suggest changing the novice.

The Captain joined the helmsman at the wheel. He studied the taut sails, ordered the seaman to bring her a little tighter into the wind, backed off slightly at the first ripple along the sail edge and then stepped back, satisfied that the "Clipper" was tacking as near the wind as physically possible. The boat heeled a good thirty degrees but skimmed through the water. He looked to his stern, but he could not make out the sloop and frigate. He spoke to his first officer who shouted to J.J. aloft.

"Lookout. What is the position of the sails on our stern?"

J.J. obediently studied the southern horizon, but the specks had disappeared.

"Over the horizon," he called down.

The Captain, satisfied with his tack, ordered the first officer to bring the men down from aloft.

"She's sailing nicely. Bring the men down and give them a rest. We might be running into some bad weather." Captain Wallace for the first time indicated the dark storm clouds in the northeast."

"Aye, Aye, Sir," the first officer replied.

As soon as he had repeated the Captain's orders, the latter spoke again.

"And tell the lookout to keep track of the frigate on our northeast. We're going to track close to her."

The first officer looked at the Captain in frustration. He had not yet had an opportunity to take his sighting and the old man kept issuing new orders. He reasoned any good lookout would know his duty, then he realized that J.J. was aloft. The first officer wondered why they did not send a seasoned hand aloft. He was about to suggest it, then changed his mind as the owner returned to the quarterdeck.

"What's your opinion, Captain?" Jason asked.

Since the owner had just returned from the starboard side where he had been watching the frigate, the Captain assumed the owner referred to their pursuer.

"Might be close enough for them to try their long guns, but I figure that weather ahead will work on our behalf."

Jason had reached the same decision. He would stay on the northwesterly tack until the frigate got close enough on their starboard to try its long guns or until the approaching squalls hit, or both, then come about and tack away from the frigate and disappear in the rain clouds.

Toddy was glad to reach the stability of the deck and at the same time disappointed at leaving the rigging; he had overcome some of his fear and had wanted to keep at it until he had conquered all. He did not join Jason and Skinny on the quarterdeck; he decided his place was with the sail crew. He quietly sat with his back against the rail and listened to them talk about the "Clipper" and how she was showing her heels to the English. An older crewman who had deserted from an English ship began telling tales about life aboard a man-of-war. If what he said were true, Toddy concluded, it was no wonder that English seamen deserted at first opportunity. According to the tar, few English sailors were volunteers; all were victims of impressment who had one day been innocently walking the streets when they were seized by gangs of toughs armed with clubs and led by officers. The toughs clubbed them into submission, took their belts, then forced them to march with one hand holding up their trousers to the gathering points. Life on board an English ship was hell for the seamen; rotten food, hard labor and the discipline of the cat-o-nine tails. All bosuns were sadists, and officers were uncaring nobs.

Aloft, J.J., alone, had a problem. He had learned the previous day that the lookout's loft had no chamber pot. After intense suffering, he had seized a moment when the crew and the quarterdeck watch had been otherwise occupied and had stood on the rail and pissed. He had been unable to relieve himself in the nest, not wanting to foul the confined area for himself and others. He wondered if this predicament was where the phrase "don't foul your nest" had originated. The first time he had made the mistake of pissing into the wind and had ended up soaking the front of his pants and shirt. It had dried quickly, but J.J. had had an uncomfortable feeling all day. He learned to stand on the rail while holding the mast and to aim down wind on the clear side of the sail. He doubted the sail master would approve of his marking the sail with his urine. The morning's pursuit had kept the Captain on the quarterdeck and while there he frequently peered aloft at his lookout expecting regular reports. J.J. did not want to be seen proudly standing on the rail and pissing downwind. He did not want the Captain to think that any of the spray that fell on the quarterdeck came from him, though he realized it was a physical impossibility.

Finally, J.J. could stand the strain no longer. Without looking downward, he mounted the rail and surrendered himself to the relief that the streaming spray engendered.

"Lookout," J.J. heard the Captain shouting. "When you finish playing with yourself, give me a report."

J.J. flushed red but was unable to stop. Since he had embarrassed himself, he was determined to ensure that the incident did not repeat itself. He squeezed out the last drop, then dropped back into his nest. He quickly retrieved his glass and studied the horizon. To the northeast, the frigate had grown larger as the courses of the two ships converged. To the southwest, the horizon was clear. J.J. shouted his report, estimating that the frigate would be in firing distance in thirty minutes. Jason, no expert on naval arms, based his guess on the frigate's first ball.

Below, Captain Wallace accepted the lookout's report. He paused to wonder how the boy had reached his conclusion about the length of time before the frigate fired but decided to accept it. He was determined not to send up another seaman to relieve him unless the owner suggested it. The "Clipper" was a

Satterfield boat and for all the Captain knew J.J. might one day inherit it. He did not want to give the youth motivation for a grudge.

J.J. looked down and noticed Jason and Skinny studying the ocean to the west. J.J. turned and discovered that the storm clouds had moved closer. The wind was shifting again. The sky was dark and in the distance lines of lighting cracked the sky. J.J. wondered what it would be like to be in the nest during a thunderstorm. He did not like the thought of lightning bolts streaking about his head. Then, he recalled how the mast had swayed during the storm and how sick he had gotten. For the first time that day, he felt a sinking sensation in his stomach and an acid taste gnawing deep in his throat.

At three in the afternoon, a seaman on the Captain's orders clambered up the mast to relieve J.J. He pointed out the frigate under full sail on his starboard and the angry squalls that were whipping the seas dead ahead.

"I'll give you fifteen minutes and then you'll be soaked," J.J. observed.

"It won't be the first time," the seaman replied stoically. "And I think you'll find it rains down below as well as up here."

"With lightning swirling about your head?"

"Anything that strikes up here will hit the deck too."

J.J. shrugged, bid the seaman good luck and quickly descended to join Toddy who waited at the base of the mast.

"Going to take a walk topside?" J.J. asked.

"In that?" Toddy pointed towards the dark front.

On the bridge, Captain Wallace made his decision after studying the frigate. Another few hundred yards and they would be in range of its long guns. The red and blue of the English flag had been raised, an indication that the frigate's captain was preparing for action.

"Bring her about," Captain Wallace ordered.

Skinny, who stood about ten yards to the Captain's rear, looked at Jason. Jason, who would have waited a few minutes longer in order to reach the masking arms of the storm, nodded his reluctant approval.

The "Clipper" heeled as the helmsman spun the wheel. The large booms of the foresail and the mainsail snapped viciously, missing the heads of the crouched seamen by inches. The jib flapped, then filled with wind. The square topsails twisted with the change of direction then popped as an angry gust smashed into the canvas. The sound of a distant cannon echoed across the quarterdeck. All eyes turned and anxiously watched the water.

"There, astern," J.J. saw the first splash.

About fifty yards to the stern on line with the tack the "Clipper" had been following water shot into the air. Toddy was surprised to see the big iron ball bounce along the surface.

"Christ, that's close," he exclaimed, realizing for the first time that the pursuers intended them harm. Up until then, it had felt like a race, a game.

The first skirts of the front hit the "Clipper" and enveloped it in driving rain and mist.

"Hold 'er steady," Captain Wallace encouraged the helmsman who was fighting the wheel that was trying to wrench out of his control.

"Got 'er Cap," the old seaman answered. "She want's to run."

A sudden gust hit the sails and bent the straining ship over. Toddy and J.J. exchanged worried glances, wondering if the lean would carry them into the water. Captain Wallace stepped to the helmsman's side and helped hold the wheel steady. The Captain studied the straining sails.

"She's flying," Skinny called to no one in particular.

Indeed, the taut sails seemed to be lifting the trim ship out of the water. Overhead, the Virginia white pine masts bent but held.

J.J. strained to see the sailor in the topmast, but the driving rain obscured his vision. He studied the leaning mast and thanked the heavens that he was on the deck and not aloft facing the storm's wrath alone.

The boys, soaking wet, stayed on deck with Jason, Skinny and most of the crew for the two hours it required "Clipper" to break through the storm. One minute they were careening through the waves with no visibility and the next they were free under blue skies and white clouds with a brisk wind in the sails and a moderate swell under the hull. As the boys stood in the stern staring at the black mass behind them, a clap of thunder signaled a nearby strike.

"A final warning, I think," Captain Wallace observed.

"Hold her steady as she goes," the Captain instructed the helmsman. "We should sight land before sunset."

The boys stood in the stern feeling like tested mariners and let the wind dry their clothes as they watched for their pursuer. To their disappointment, the frigate never reappeared. The sun was setting when the "Clipper" crossed the mouth of the Bay and turned northward to anchor in the lee of the Maryland shore.

"Will the frigate follow us into the Bay?" Toddy asked Jason.

He laughed.

"Not into American territorial waters." Jason paused then added thoughtfully. "Not unless he knows what Jefferson has done to our navy." The question made Jason realize that the English undoubtedly knew and that it was a matter of time before even the Bay would be threatened by enemy men-of-war. Jason, like his father James, had lived through the Revolution and could not think of the English as anything but "the enemy."

WASHINGTON, D.C.

DECEMBER 2ND, 1803

Buster, an inadvertent early arriver, though by no means the first, paid his respects to the President then tried to make himself inconspicuous by huddling in the corner of the reception room and talking with the only other observable person present who approximated his own age, Meriwether Lewis, the President's secretary.

"Tell me, Meriwether, why does the President invite me to these affairs?"

Buster was genuinely puzzled. After the series of threatening letters had ceased following the abortive break-in at the *Herald*'s office, and despite Buster's critical reports, an apparent armistice period had continued until early autumn when Buster without forewarning was invited to a general reception at the President's House, now being referred to by some as the White House in deference to the shocking white paint that decorated the building's exterior. Nothing of note had developed at the first reception; President Jefferson had received him formally, and Secretary of State Madison had chatted with him briefly. Otherwise, Buster had been generally ignored.

A second invitation of little note had followed in early November and then had appeared the request to dine with the President on December 2nd. Buster suspected that his protagonists had switched from threat to courtship, but he could not bring himself to refuse an invitation from the President of the United States. He attended out of respect for the office not for the man.

Lewis shrugged noncommittally and tangentially changed the subject.

"The new English Minister and his wife will be among the guests tonight."

Buster studied the bland young man's face and wondered if somehow he had answered the question. Was the President lumping his enemies together? Certainly Minister Merry as representative of England could be considered hostile. Buster was about to ask Lewis that blunt question, a prerogative of his status as a newspaperman, when the secretary continued.

"The Minister presented his credentials last week."

Buster did not consider the revelation news. He, like everyone else in the Federal District, had heard of the contretemps. Merry, an unimposing middle-aged man that most considered fairly typical of his class and profession, was the son of a London wine merchant. Rumor had it that Merry had spent most of his unimpressive diplomatic career in Spain before being appointed as His Majesty's chief representative to Washington, the capital of the upstart former colonials that most good Englishmen still considered to be recalcitrant subjects. The Washington *Dispatch*, the Federalist equivalent of the Republican *Intelligencer*, had subsequently reported that the President had "Behaved in an insulting fashion" towards Minister Merry. Buster discounted most of what the *Dispatch* reported—it was a scandal sheet that printed the most disgusting trivia—but Buster had suspected its Merry article had a kernel of truth buried amongst the sensational verbiage. The *Dispatch's* editor was close to the English embassy; some suggested he was on their payroll.

According to the *Dispatch*, Merry, adhering to proper diplomatic protocol, had appeared in full uniform complete with ribbons and a tricornered hat. President Jefferson had informally received him wearing baggy trousers, an open necked shirt frayed at the edges, a baggy sweater and the final insult of all, worn slippers. Merry had concluded that a diplomatic insult was intended and refused to accept Madison's subsequent explanation that this was the "republican style."

"Do you think Minister Merry will appear in full dress uniform?" Buster asked.

His question brought a smile to Lewis' lips. He shook his forefinger chidingly at Buster and said:

"You shan't catch me like that."

"I'm told that Mrs. Merry is a rather large, masculine woman, typical of her breed," Buster continued.

"I couldn't say. I've never met her," Lewis said. "They claim she's quite the talker."

"Is that unusual?"

"For a new bride?"

"Oh?"

"Yes. A very, very rich widow."

"Good for Minister Merry," Buster said sarcastically. "Who are the other guests?

"One you will find interesting."

Lewis' words piqued Buster's interest. He hoped they implied a young lady of his own age. As a bachelor, he had come alone, fully aware this would create a problem for the hostess, whoever Jefferson might have selected for the occasion. Of late the Jolly Dolly, Madison's plump but vivacious wife, had efficiently played the role.

"And that might be?"

"Minister Pinchot," Lewis replied with a straight face.

Buster could not restrain his laugh.

"The French ambassador? Bonaparte's representative? At the same table with his mortal enemy?"

Lewis nodded affirmatively.

"Minister Merry will never recover," Buster asserted.

"And of course Minister Yrujo of Spain, making it a proper diplomatic affair."

"It won't work," Buster declared. "Is Jefferson deliberately slighting Merry?"

"Who would you have preferred? Madam Bonaparte?"

Lewis' words again made Buster chuckle, as Lewis intended. He referred to Betsy Bonaparte, the beautiful, former Betsy Patterson of Baltimore who had recently wed Napoleon's nineteen-year-old brother Jerome. Betsy, daughter of a wealthy merchant and niece of Senator Samuel Smith, was a recent social sensation. Jefferson had hosted a reception honoring young Bonaparte and his new bride that was heralded as the event of his administration. Betsy had appeared clad, or unclad depending on the source, in a stunning sacrenet and white crepe dress that left her arms and most if not all of her sensational bosom uncovered. Since the thin crepe had displayed the remainder of her remarkable figure in translucent splendor, servants and passersby had gathered at the windows and doors to view the virtually naked Goddess.

"Now that would be a diplomatic slight of my choosing," Buster replied seriously. "Were you here?"

Lewis nodded affirmatively.

"Was Betsy au natural as described?"

Buster found Lewis' condescending smile infuriating. Before he could speak, Lewis excused himself, having detected a crooked finger summons from his master.

"Mr. Satterfield?" A lilting feminine voice addressed him. "May I share your corner?"

Buster turned. Lewis' abrupt departure had left him wondering what to do next. While the two young men had chatted, the room had gradually filled. An attractive young lady with full red lips stretched into a broad smile and penetrating blue eyes stood beside him. For a few seconds, Buster was speechless. He frankly stared. The striking brunette could almost look him directly in the eyes. He later learned that she was six inches shorter than his six feet, but the high heels compensated and made her appear taller. She wore a shiny white satin dress that exposed bare shoulders and displayed pointed breasts. After staring down the front of her dress and noting she did not wear a strategically placed handkerchief, a failing also attributed to the charming Dolly Madison, he blushed and looked at the floor, noting in passage that a thin veil like net covered the tight dress from waist to floor.

"Well, may I?"

Buster realized he had not answered her initial question. He raised his eyes and opened his mouth to speak, only to be stopped by the amused expression that danced around her eyes and lips.

"Don't I meet with your approval? Did I smear my rouge?"

Buster noticed the color on her cheeks, another daring innovation. He realized he had never seen the striking stranger before and wondered how she knew his name.

"What question should I answer first?" Buster finally regained some of his composure. "Is your name Betsy?" He asked.

The girl laughed and slapped him lightly on the shoulder with her closed fan.

"Touché. No, I am not the infamous Madame Napoleon though I appreciate being told there is a resemblance. Try the first one."

"First what?"

"Question. May I share your corner?"

"Only if you tell me your name."

"Do you always hide in the corners at these affairs?"

"Only when invited." Buster was embarrassed by the inadequacy of his response. Gay repartee was not his forte. He usually asked the questions.

"My name is Buster Satterfield."

"I know. Buster," she pretended to consider the word. "What a quaint name."

"I know. My grandmother's sense of humor."

"What on earth did she mean?"

"I don't know. No one ever explained. Buster sounds natural to me. It's the only thing anyone's ever called me."

"Buster late than never," the girl laughed.

"I don't understand what you mean."

"Your grandmother would, I bet. We may have the same curious sense of humor. Was she a southerner?"

"Vivian?"

"Is she your grandmother?"

"Yes, but everyone calls her Vivian."

"Then that's who I mean. Was she?"

"What?"

"A southerner."

Buster paused to consider the question. He had never thought of it before. The family always referred to itself as Virginian. He had never thought of the Satterfields in terms of northern and southern.

"She's a Virginian. A Randolph."

"I thought so."

"And now that you know all about me, what's your name?"

"Nancy."

"Nancy what? Are you always so difficult?"

Nancy laughed and waved her fan, still closed, twice in front of her face. Buster had trouble guessing what the abrupt motion meant. It looked like a challenge.

"Nancy Furman, sir."

Buster immediately recognized the name. Nancy Furman was the daughter of Senator Rodney Furman of North Carolina. Senator Furman was an ardent Jeffersonian; in fact he had been reputed to be responsible for managing the Republican victory in North Carolina where the electoral votes had split, eight to four. It was said Furman delivered the four crucial winning votes himself. Senator Furman had been widowed for several years, and his daughter Nancy served as his hostess on those rare occasions he entertained. Nancy had been described to Buster as a headstrong but beautiful young woman.

"Senator Furman's wife?" Buster, determined not to be bested, asked.

Nancy smiled sweetly and changed the subject.

"I have been assigned by Dolly to entertain you," she said ambiguously.

"I thought pele mele was the social rule in the President's House."

Pele mele, pell mell, were Jefferson's code words for the new etiquette designed to place the republican stamp on the infant democracy's social world. Many suggested that Jefferson was trying to create the illusion of a second revolution in style and informality which he hoped would replace what he considered to be attempts by his two predecessors to ape the formality of the English aristocracy and court.

"We shall see," Nancy smiled and nodded her head in the direction of the doorway.

Buster turned and saw two formally clad Europeans pause and survey the room attempting to locate their host. The man was dressed formally in black with a fluffy brocaded shirt and a large white bow at his neck. The woman, taller than her husband, wore a green taffeta dress with straight lines that concealed her big boned features. She had a horsy face, typical of English women, marked by a large aquiline nose. Both wore stern expressions. Buster had the impression they were inspecting the room looking for deviations from acceptable protocol.

"The Merrys?" Buster asked.

"In person," Buster's companion replied.

As they watched, Meriwether Lewis hurried forward to greet them. Buster could not hear what was said, but after Lewis spoke, Minister Merry nodded and was escorted with Mrs. Merry on his arm to the back of the room where President Jefferson was talking animatedly with Secretary Madison and several others from his Cabinet, apparently oblivious to his distinguished guests' arrival. At another time, Buster assumed, the Merrys would be the guests of honor. Buster deduced from their demeanor that the Merrys were commanding such treatment now.

"Is this planned?" Buster asked.

"Are you an opposition newspaper publisher?" Nancy countered.

"Mr. President," Lewis stood behind his superior and spoke in a formal tone.

Jefferson turned, ignored the Merrys, and waited politely for his secretary to continue.

"May I present Minister and Madam Merry," Lewis said formally.

Merry nodded coldly, acknowledging Lewis' words. Mrs. Merry duplicated her husband's movement.

"Welcome to my humble home," Jefferson said. His soft voice was courteous not sardonic, as best as Buster could tell.

"Now enter Dolly," Nancy whispered.

Almost as if in response to command, Dolly Madison appeared at Jefferson's elbow.

"I believe you are acquainted with Mrs. Madison, or should I say Madam Secretary," Jefferson said.

"Dolly will do," the smiling hostess said.

Minister Merry smiled thinly. Mrs. Merry frowned.

"Tom," Dolly turned to the President, surprising both guests with her use of their host's first name. "May I introduce the Merrys to your guests?"

"Please do," the President smiled.

Noting the looks of disapproval on the Merrys' faces, he explained.

"We are informal in this house. I find it appropriate to the customs of our republican nation. I say "republican" in lower case to distinguish it from the party of the same name."

"I see, Mr. President," Minister Merry spoke for the first time.

"Please come this way," Dolly said, wedging her ample figure between the scowling Merrys.

Jefferson turned back to his male entourage.

"I do believe the Minister just peered down the front of Dolly's gown," Nancy whispered to Buster, holding her spread fan before her face to mask her lips.

Surprised, Buster turned, looked down at his companion's innocent face, then, unable to help himself found himself staring at her cleavage.

"Oh dear. Et tu," Nancy said in mock shock, placing her white-gloved hand over the crevice where Buster peered.

Buster flushed and did not know what to say. He noticed the formidable Dolly and the Merrys heading towards his corner.

"Oh no," he exclaimed sincerely, not wanting to force small talk with the austere Englishman.

"Not to worry," Nancy stepped forward. "I will protect you."

As Buster watched, Nancy adroitly joined the approaching threesome several steps from Buster's lair.

"I just relayed your instructions," Nancy surprisingly reported to Dolly, giving Buster and the Merrys the impression that she had just conveyed the hostess' commands to him.

Dolly smiled at Nancy, not having any idea what the impulsive girl was talking about, and introduced the Merrys.

"Oh. Senator Furman's daughter," Minister Merry caught the implication of Dolly's introduction. "We are so much looking forward to meeting your father."

Buster turned and spotted a servant nearby bearing a silver tray filled with wineglasses. The ruby red liquid appeared quite inviting. Several of the guests had accepted the servant's offer indicated by a slight raising of the tray. Buster knew little about wine, content to imbibe his father's Pale Ale, but he was aware of Jefferson's reputation as a wine connoisseur. He tasted the ruby red liquid. He found it slightly acrid but not unpleasant. He knew it was not a harsh Madeira, the most popular wine found in local ordinaries, but he did not have any idea what Jefferson's choice was. He was about to ask the servant, in good republican style, but was interrupted by a hand on his shoulder.

Buster turned and founded the Mouse, as he had privately dubbed the Secretary of State, standing behind him.

"Welcome, Mr. Satterfield. We are so glad you could come." Madison stepped closer to Buster as he spoke.

Buster instinctively stepped back, not liking the little man's sour breath in his face as he spoke. Madison, for Buster, personified the "political animal," as his grandfather James disparaging referred to the professional politicians who formed the ranks of the emerging parties. Buster was about to ask the man why he acted as if the President's house belonged to him any more than it did to Buster or any other citizen, but the jangle of a bell interrupted him.

A handsome black servant stood at the entrance to the formal Dining Room. He nodded to President Jefferson, then stepped back into the room inviting the guests to enter.

All paused and stared at the common man's president who had introduced pele mele as his code of etiquette. No one appeared to know quite what it meant. Gossip said the President intended the rule to call for "every man and woman for himself." All were considered "equal," whatever that implied. Buster, inhibited by the strict social custom of deferring to the female sex, seniors in age, and supe-riors in rank held back, even though he stood near the dining room entrance. Vivian and Lilly's lessons in Virginian manners were not forgotten.

"Please, Mr. Satterfield," Madison encouraged Buster to go first with a nudge in the back.

Buster glared at the man's bony hand and retreated to the side. Nobody moved. Finally, the President turned to Dolly, who happened to be standing near-by, took her arm and gently led her into the formal room. The Spanish Minister followed by his wife pushed in after the President. Suddenly, with the path charted, everybody crowded behind. Buster noted that Minister and Mrs. Merry had been separated by the push and were carried with the rush. Buster, who had retreated to his corner, muttered under his breath.

"So that's pele mele. "

"Do you approve Mr. Satterfield?"

Buster turned and found Nancy Furman at his side. She smiled sweetly, as if all were in order, and took his arm.

"Will you escort me, please?" She asked.

Buster liked the warm feel of her hand on his arm but wondered if she ever stopped asking questions long enough for one to be answered.

Inside, chaos reigned.

The President stood behind his chair at the head of the table waiting for his guests to be seated. Buster concluded that pele mele did not discard all conventions. On his right, a smiling Dolly Madison cheerily watched the milling guests. Mrs. Yrujo, the wife of the Spanish minister, had acquired the chair on the President's left. Minister Yrujo sat beaming beside Dolly. Buster studied the table. Not a single place card was to be seen. The guests apparently acquired the chairs they conquered. The most efficient appeared to be members of Jefferson's Cabinet and their wives. James Madison had control of the chair opposite the President's. He seized a hapless Mrs. Merry by the arm and propelled her into the chair on his right. Minister Merry spotted the last vacant chair at the President's table, the one next to Mrs. Yrujo. As he moved towards it, a Congressman from Virginia shoved past and victoriously claimed it as his own.

"Excuse me sir," the Congressmen said to Merry, but he did not relinquish his prize. Instead, he turned and began to chat with the beaming Mrs. Yrujo, delighted to be liberated from the near clutches of the dour Merry.

Nancy guided Buster past the table into the smaller dining room on the left.

"You don't mind do you?" She whispered pertly. "We try to be democratic but our instructions are to herd the belligerents and critics into the smaller room. I fear Mrs. Merry was too adroit."

Buster soon found himself seated at a round table with no position for a guest of honor. Directly across from him sat a scowling Minister Merry. As fate would have it, two places away on his right sat the equally displeased French Minister. A Senator and a strange female separated the two belligerents. Buster deduced that this was the closest a Frenchman and an Englishman had been in years without gunfire.

Nancy, who sat on Buster's left, making his evening, leaned over, brushed a pointed breast against his arm, and whispered:

"Have you noticed the English end every sentence with a question? I have been practicing for my conversation with Minister Merry."

The confidence, delivered in a sardonic tone, made Buster realize that pele mele had been stage managed.

"I say Mr. Minister, a pleasant day, what?" Nancy spoke directly to Merry.

Buster feared that the sour man would take offense at her tone, but he apparently found nothing wrong with it. Pleased to be addressed at last by someone who knew who he was, the Minister embarked on a lengthy discussion of the vagaries of Washington weather.

Later, when his turn came, Buster asked the Minister if he had yet found adequate housing. Washington's uncompleted state was a frequently discussed topic. Most Congressmen lived in crowded boarding houses, and the senior government officials had quickly occupied the few available homes.

"We have located an inadequate situation," Merry huffed, acknowledging Buster's presence for the first time. He was apparently offended by his youth and interpreted the seating order as a deliberate slight. "Mrs. Merry considers it a hovel."

Buster did not know what to respond to this remark, but Merry did not seem to notice his silence. Under the table, Nancy kicked his leg sharply with the toe of her shoe.

"Two hovels, in fact," Merry continued. He paused to sip the wine, swallowed, and frowned to express his disapproval. "French, I assume." He did not look to his left at Minister Pichon.

"What a delightful wine," Pichon exclaimed, filling the silence that followed Merry's remark. "I assume it must be from the case of choice burgundy I brought with my shipment from Paris. A gift from the First Consul."

"We have two small houses," Merry spoke, over-riding his diplomatic antagonist. In Merry's view, Pichon did not exist.

Buster for his part could not understand why Madison and Jefferson had included both ministers. If the affair was intended to honor the recently arrived and accepted Merry, why did Jefferson antagonize him by inviting the Frenchman? Jefferson might think he was demonstrating neutrality, but in Buster's opinion he was simply being naive and showing lack of consideration.

"We have connected the two to make them tenable, but the construction is almost too much to bear. And we have no well. Water is a major problem." Merry once started was hard to stop.

"And how do you find our food?" Nancy asked pertly as Merry paused to again sip the wine.

Her question caused Merry to choke. Buster wondered if the poor man's death at Jefferson's table would create a diplomatic incident. Fortunately, after much coughing and hacking and after turning bright red in the face, Merry regained control. He studied Nancy, apparently attempting to determine if her question had been serious or simply provocative. The English were not known for their taste in food.

"We have difficulty obtaining adequate provisions," Merry finally resumed his monologue. "Meat is mostly game, tough and sinewy, and vegetables almost impossible to find. But I assume you know that too, Miss Furman. I'm sure you look forward to returning to North Carolina."

Merry adroitly indicated that he remembered who the attractive young lady was and the identity of her father. Since most of Merry's contacts could be assumed to be in the Federalist camp, the effort surprised Buster.

"But the larger problem I find is that of etiquette," the Minister declared war without pausing for a response. "I am not quite sure whether its absence is caused by ignorance and awkwardness or by design."

At this point, Minister Merry paused. He glared around the table and made clear that he expected his views to be conveyed to President Jefferson. He was speaking specifically not generally. For the remainder of the meal, Minister Merry fiddled with his food in a glowering silence. The other guests respected his passion and restricted themselves to whispered conversations with immediate partners. Buster, excited by the occasional touch of a hand, the casual knock of a knee or the heavy brush of a breast, was hypnotized by Miss Furman. Later, he could not recall a single word he had said in response to the constant flow of questions. Despite the queries, Nancy acted as if she had known Buster all of his life.

When the meal ended, Minister Merry gruffly bid farewell to his dinner companions, retrieved Mrs. Merry, bowed curtly to the President and departed. He was soon followed by the French and Spanish ministers and their spouses. As soon as the door closed on the last foreign guest, a sudden hum of spontaneous conversation filled the room.

"What was that about?" Buster asked Nancy.

"Don't you know?" She asked brightly and rushed off to confer with Dolly who was sited near the door.

Buster surveyed the room, noticed that only Jeffersonian officeholders and Republican politicians remained, and decided that as the only member of the neutral opposition left standing, the time had come for him to depart. He shook hands briefly with Secretary Madison, feeling some of the antagonism that Minister Merry had undoubtedly sensed, addressed his social appreciation to his host and approached Dolly and Nancy at the door. He paused before Nancy.

"I hope I have an opportunity to see you again, Miss Furman," he said, and meant it.

"Do you?" She smiled noncommittally but squeezed his hand firmly for a little longer than necessary when he offered it. To Buster's surprise, she leaned over with eyes sparkling and whispered in his ear.

"Do you know what they call Minister Merry in London?" She asked.

"No," Buster answered loud enough for Dolly to hear. "What?"

"Tres Gai," the astounding girl answered her own question for the first time that evening. She nodded formally at Buster and turned her attention to Dolly.

"Thank you for coming, Mr. Satterfield," Dolly said, coolly studying Buster with her eyes while her broad smile conveyed enchantment.

As Buster made his way down the stairs, Dolly stared after him. She turned, smiled more sincerely at Nancy, nodded approval, and then turned to the next departing guest.

ALEXANDRIA

MAY 1807

Buster, ignoring the clatter of the printing press behind him, sat with his feet elevated, his left foot clamped tightly over his right ankle whose heel rested on the table corner, and stared at the wall. Several blank sheets of paper and his quill lay near the spot where his left hand rested with fingers absently tapping an unheard beat. Buster, at age thirty, was taking stock of his life.

The last four years had been moderately successful. He had acquired a wife, Nancy, and was waiting for the birth of his first child. The *Herald* had grown in circulation and influence, and Buster had served two successful tours in Virginia's legislature. He was widely regarded in Richmond as a political comer.

On the debit side, he suffered from a growing, gnawing disappointment with his life. Of late, he had become conscious of a depressing sense that he was merely repeating something that had happened before; he was becoming another James. Buster had always lived in his grandfather's long shadow, proud of the older Satterfield's service with General Washington. Buster knew that others described him as the very image of his grandfather, and there was nothing he could do about that. Buster as a young man had consciously tried to emulate James, but now he was concerned that he may have overdone it.

James, who prided himself on his scholarship, had attended William and Mary, and Buster, a generation's hop later, had followed. James had founded the *Herald*, and Buster had been delighted to replace his grandfather as proprietor, ignoring his father Jason's unstated but apparent desire that Buster join him and Skinny in managing his various business interests. Jason, who frequently complained he did not have time for the details, preferred the challenge of the next venture, but Buster had turned away from his father. With James' encouragement, Buster had dabbled in Alexandria politics and then with the formidable support of his own newspaper had served two terms in the state legislature in Richmond. The problem was that in politics as in life he did not know where he, Buster, not James nor Jason, stood.

Jason was a self-declared Federalist. James waffled, not quite able to digest many of Tom Jefferson's strange ideas, not a centrist and not a states rights advocate. Buster at first stood with his grandfather, but now, he was not sure. He believed less government is better; the national debt should be abolished, and the budget balanced; and he wanted the federal government to protect the security of the nation and guarantee that every citizen could earn a living and a businessman enjoy the profits he dared to acquire. Unfortunately, neither of the two parties, the Federalists and the Republicans, met his needs.

More personally, writing, editing and publishing the *Herald*, a small regional newspaper, no longer offered the challenge it once had. He had entered politics to broaden his horizons, but he had found that his craving for public recognition was not strong enough to make the personal compromises of principle that the profession demanded acceptable. His grandfather's world had changed. In James' youth, Williamsburg, then the capital of colonial Virginia, had been a place of conflict and challenge. The royal governor clashed with the Burgesses, and the issues were large. James' generation had their Revolution, and all Buster faced was a pale imitation. In a real sense, Jefferson's attempt to mount a second revolution had failed. He had cut expenses, shrunk the deficit, and projected a common style. Despite all of his pretensions and disclaimers, the power of the federal government had grown at the expense of the states. Richmond was a backwater, and Buster could not convince himself that the issues found there were worth the price. He had decided to not stand again for the legislature.

James understood. Jason was delighted, convinced that Buster was finally coming to his senses and would soon opt to join the family enterprise. Jason had already declared that he wished to be free to concentrate on shipbuilding.

Construction of Jefferson's gunboats, many of which were destined for the Chesapeake, and planning for more "Clippers" occupied his attention. Buster had not asked how Jason could build ineffective gunboats at the same time he railed at Jefferson for destroying the navy and endangering the nation's security. Buster had also not protested that managing a brewery and store and warehouse was not his dream.

Buster, the third generation, had grown up in his grandfather's shadow. Now, at thirty, he realized he wanted to be his own man, and he did not know how. He had obligations. He had a wife and an unborn son to support. Life at home was difficult. Nancy had had two quick miscarriages and now was struggling to preserve her third pregnancy. She spent most of her time in bed trying to give Buster the male child that the Satterfield elders and Buster so craved. In doing so, she had become a self-centered shrew. The bright, charming and beautiful girl he had married had become a housewife. Buster knew that girl still existed, would return when the current ordeal passed, but life was still difficult.

What to do? What to do? Buster's fingers tapped.

Buster realized he needed a friend to listen to his problems. His father had Skinny, and his grandfather had had Mason and Washington and many others. Buster had James, but he was growing older, less patient with Buster's problems.

At seventy-three, James had outlived his peers. News of John's death three months before had hit his grandfather hard. As long as his twin lived, James had felt he had someone to turn to, and now he was alone. It depressed Buster to hear his grandfather lament: "And now I will be the next to die." Whenever Vivian or Buster tried to abuse him of the idea by pointing to his still problem free health, James would reply:

"It's only right. I am now the oldest living Satterfield, and it's my turn."

Buster's thoughts depressed him. In an attempt to escape, he willed his hand to stop its frenetic tapping, rose, and walked to the door.

The two printers, each twenty years Buster's senior, paused to stare after him. His sullen tapping had been a distraction.

"Mister Buster is worrying himself sick," the taller confided to his companion.

"For what?" The second responded, glad that the morose proprietor had left. "If I had his problems, I would be a rich man. He should try being me."

Buster folded his hands behind him and paced down Royal Street. He needed a challenge, some excitement to lift his depression. He ignored the chirp of the birds, the bright May sunshine, the cheerful spring blossoms, and the restful, deep green, full leaves that surrounded him.

At the corner of Duke Street and Royal, he stepped onto the cobblestones without looking either direction. A clatter on his left broke his introspection at the very moment a solid blow knocked him forward to his knees. Buster tipped as his momentum catapulted him in a somersault over his right shoulder.

"Whoa. Whoa. Stop there," a high pitched voice halted the horse.

Buster shut his eyes and tested his body. He lay flat on his back. His left shoulder ached where the horse's body had struck him. His fingers worked. He wiggled his toes. His right ankle stung; Buster assumed he had turned it. His palms and his knees burned. He sat up, noticed the torn left leg of his trousers. He rubbed the dirt from his hands on the sides of his pants and reached down to touch his bare knee. It was bleeding from several scrapes but did not appear to be seriously damaged. In embarrassment he folded the torn cloth of his trousers over the knee and looked around to see if anyone had noticed. He knew immediately that it had been his fault. He had stepped in front of somebody's horse and had been appropriately punished for his inattention.

To his right, on the board walk that led past Market Square, an old lady watched. Beyond her, two young boys stared, open mouthed, at Buster. He looked left. A buggy drawn by a large and nervous horse had stopped. The horse worriedly studied Buster. The twist of the curious horse's head embarrassed him even more.

"Say fellow. You walked right in front of my horse," a high pitched voice squealed.

Buster looked at the buggy and saw an effeminate, young man about his own age. He had long sandy hair parted in the middle and folded back over protruding ears. His drawn face was marked by a long, thin nose and large eyes surmounted by high, arched eyebrows. The man's pale lips were pursed into a tense expression of feminine disapproval. He held a buggy whip in his right hand, defensively.

Buster recognized him immediately and was even more dismayed by his predicament. To have been careless and to have walked into a stranger's horse would have been discomfiting; the fact that the witness to his heedless behavior was John Randolph was too much to bear.

Buster, still sitting, now with his hands braced behind him, looked up at his victim.

"I say," Randolph removed his peaked hat and rubbed his brow. "Aren't you Mr. Satterfield?"

Buster nodded affirmatively. He could not bring himself to speak.

Randolph, "Johnny" as he was disparagingly called by his colleagues in the House of Representatives, dropped his whip and reins and leaped gracefully to the cobblestones.

"This is indeed a coincidence," Randolph spoke in the high pitched voice. "What a break. I intended to look you up not run over you."

Buster, despite his consternation, had to laugh at the man's sincerity. He did not seem to realize how incongruous his words sounded. Buster wiped his hands together, felt the sting and stickiness from his scratches, and then pushed the palms along his trouser legs. The rip had rendered them irreparable anyway. A little blood would make no more difference.

Randolph leaned over and studied Buster's face.

"I see no major damage, Mr. Satterfield," he declared politely before hopping back and offering his hand.

Seeing no alternative, Buster let the man assist him to his feet. To tell the truth, Buster did most of the work by pushing with his left hand and turning as he rose. Randolph passively clutched Buster's right hand but did not seem to exercise any pulling muscle.

"I do believe we are relatives," Randolph said, turning his grasp of Buster's right hand into a placid handshake. "Of a distant sort."

Before responding, Buster again brushed his trousers and attempted to turn the torn flap over his right knee inwards to conceal the flesh. He glanced at Randolph's immaculate but sober black suit with wide lapels.

"My Aunt Vivian is a Randolph," Buster said.

"Of course. Married to James. We are all so proud of James and Mr. Washington," Randolph trilled.

Buster, despite his condition, was entranced by Randolph's voice. Buster had never heard the man speak, but he was reputed to be the finest if most vitupera- tive orator in the House of Representatives. A leader of the House during Jefferson's first administration at the age of twenty-eight, Randolph, an ardent Republican, had emotionally turned on his President. Now, suffering in the shad- ows of failed leadership, "Johnny" led a group of dissidents who styled them- selves "Old Republicans." They professed to carry the standard of republicanism that they alleged Jefferson had discarded. Randolph was reputed to have been the victim of a vicious childhood disease that had rendered him smooth faced, impotent, and very, very feminine. His attacks on his enemies, however, were so unrestrained and replete with barnyard terms that they earned him no sympathy. Of late, Randolph and his Old Republicans had emerged as supporters of a disgruntled James Monroe who reputedly was considering a challenge to Jefferson's chosen successor, James Madison. Buster, still unable to conceal his doubts about the man he called "the Mouse," suspected he and Randolph had more in common than Vivian's distant bloodlines.

"May I do something to help recompense the damage I have caused?"

"The pleasure would be mine," Buster replied. He was intrigued by the fact that Randolph claimed to have been seeking him.

Buster suggested that they meet in ten minutes at Gadsby's, explaining he wished first to return home to wash his hands and change his trousers. Buster did not want to risk further damage to his pride by appearing in public in his present condition. Randolph agreed, mounted his buggy and guided his horse towards the popular ordinary at the corner of North Royal Street and Cameron. The building, which formerly housed a series of taverns known variously as the Bunch of Grapes, The Fountain, the City Tavern, the City Hotel, was now simply called Gadsby's after John Gadsby who leased it in 1795. Gadsby had installed the lavish decorations and furniture that made the ordinary one of the most popular spots in the Federal District. It was particularly regarded as a site for discreet political consultations.

When Buster entered his town house, he heard female voices echoing down the stairs from the bedroom. He looked at his hands and pants with disgust, then he decided to brave the challenge. He was glad that Nancy had visitors. He paused at the top of the steps and listened. He heard the reassuring sound of Lily's, his mother's, husky voice and Vivian's quick laugh. Both were obviously trying to cheer his wife.

"My, God, what happened to you?" Nancy saw him first.

"I ran over a horse," Buster said glibly as he extracted a fresh pair of pants from his closet.

"Did you damage him?" Vivian asked.

"No, seriously," Nancy persisted. "What happened?"

"Still the questions," Buster tried to deflect her. He referred to a standing family joke, Buster's persistent accusation that his wife lived by asking questions.

"Buster," his mother interceded firmly.

Buster recognized the tone. Whenever Lily wanted a straight answer, she used a prim, hectoring intonation. Since she normally was easy going, Buster had learned very early in life to heed the command.

"Aww, it's nothing. I stepped off Royal Street without looking and a buggy came up Cameron and the horse bumped me. It was my fault. I tore my pants," he dispiritedly flapped the torn material.

"Your good ones?" Nancy asked, not sure whether to be upset or not.

Given her emotional condition, Buster knew that he would have faced a tearful remonstrance if his mother and grandmother had not been present.

"No dear. These old checkered ones that I never liked."

"The ones I gave you for your birthday? My first present to you?"

"Oh Christ," Buster blurted.

"Buster," Lily remonstrated.

"I surrender. I'm outnumbered," Buster capitulated. "I'm devastated. I deliberately tore my favorite pants."

"Whose buggy?" Vivian interceded with a question Buster could answer.

"Johnny Randolph, your relative, I assume," Buster said.

"Johnny Randolph of Bizarre?" Vivian mused, citing the odd name her distant relative had given to his southern Virginia plantation. Vivian did not know what connection her father's family had to John Randolph but did know that most of the Virginia Randolph's were related somehow. "I think he is a fifth cousin or some such thing. Not of the kissing variety."

Buster laughed at his grandmother's ambiguity.

"He might kiss, but I'm not sure what or whom," Buster cracked.

All three Satterfield women laughed. John Randolph's odd mannerisms were well known.

"I promised to meet him for tea at Gadsby's," Buster volunteered as he backed out of the room carrying his fresh trousers.

"Be careful," Vivian laughed.

Buster, not sure whether she referred to another horse or to her cousin, hastily departed while he was ahead. Vivian as usual improved his disposition by her very presence.

When Buster arrived at Gadsby's, he noticed the large stage coach parked in the cobblestoned courtyard and detoured to the second of the two entrances—Gadsby's consisted of two interconnected buildings—and entered stepping on the very spot where George Washington was reputed to have left his boot imprint on the day he accepted his commission as commander of the Virginia Regiment prior to the French and Indian War. Buster assumed that Randolph, an experienced resident of the Federal District, would knowingly seek respite from the stage passengers in one of Gadsby's smaller salons. He guessed correctly and found Randolph seated alone on a leather chair in a corner where he could see the street from a narrow window.

Randolph rose, greeted Buster, and guided him into an identical chair adjacent to the window. Both men sat with their backs to the wall with a clear view of the room door and the access hallway. Buster assumed that Randolph intended this to be a private discussion.

"I have taken the liberty to order tea," Randolph said as a servant backed into the room carrying a silver tray encumbered with an enormous, ornate silver tea pot, a matching cream pitcher and a lidded sugar bowl. Two fine china cups nestled in their saucers delicately rattled as the man maneuvered the tray through the narrow doorway.

"Excuse me sirs," the stately white-haired African apologized for his presence.

"Ceylonese will do, I hope. I prefer Lapsong Souchong but I am informed that Gadsby's has none," Randolph spoke prissily.

"Sorry sir," the African's deep voice resonated, making Randolph's high pitched whine sound even more feminine.

"No problem," Buster contributed, completely indifferent to tea of any provenance.

"I will pour it myself," Randolph dismissed the servant. "And shut the door when you leave. I want some privacy."

"Yes sir," the servant backed from the room, carefully shutting the door as instructed.

Randolph lifted the lid of the pot and stared inside. He leaned over and sniffed.

"This will do," he said and pored both cups full.

He handed one to Buster, careful not to allow the brimming cup to overflow.

"Sugar? Milk?" He asked.

"No thank you," Buster replied, unable to see how he could add either without risking a flood.

"Good," Randolph approved, giving an importance to Buster's decision that it did not deserve.

"Tell me, cousin. Where did you get a name like Buster? I have often wondered."

"I believe it is from my Randolph side," Buster replied quickly, without thinking. "So my grandmother Vivian tells me."

Buster's glib answer disconcerted Randolph who coughed daintily into the handkerchief that he carried concealed in the sleeve of his ruffled shirt.

"Yes, well, to business."

Buster wondered what business Randolph had with him.

"I must confess I am very dissatisfied with our President. He is betraying the principles of his very own republicanism."

Johnny's words did not shock Buster. It was common knowledge that Randolph had broken with the leader of his party and now led a small faction in Congress devoted to what he described as "True Republicanism." Nancy's father, Senator Rodney Furman, frequently denounced Randolph as a party traitor intent on bringing the opposition back into power. Randolph's arrogance and willful tongue combined with his fiery and capricious temperament to create many enemies. Jefferson had been quoted as saying that he wished he had a party leader who promoted unity rather than the opposite. The final wedge between the two men developed following Jefferson's attempt to work out a face saving compromise in the Yazoo controversy, a contretemps that resulted from extravagant land speculation by corrupt Georgia legislators. Jefferson, recognizing that honest small investors would be hurt if the corrupt speculators were dealt with harshly, worked out a compromise that gave the legislators modest rewards but saved the innocent from financial devastation. Sensing political blood, Randolph had jumped in with both feet by announcing that "No True Republican" could support the compromise.

"I am most surprised by Mr. Jefferson's and Mr. Madison's bestial behavior. They have first destroyed this country's ability to defend itself, and now they are patiently permitting their French friends and the English to humiliate us."

Buster recognized that Randolph referred to Napoleon's infamous Berlin Decree which declared a blockade of English ports and forbade the landing of English products in French ports. The English had quickly reacted in kind and American trade with Europe was halted. The dismal portent for New England's manufacturing and shipping interests and the agricultural products of the southern states was obvious.

"And now, he has treated his good friend Mr. Monroe so badly."

"I'm sorry. I have not heard about his treatment of Mr. Monroe." Buster spoke honestly. Jefferson, Madison and Monroe were considered Virginia's power triad who, working together, planned to succeed to the presidency seriatim, giving Virginia twenty-four years of dominance in the White House. Any serious disagreement among them would break the chain and offer serious political portents.

"Yes. Well, I have been in direct correspondence with Mr. Monroe, and I assure you he is very displeased, indeed."

"I understand that Mr. Monroe and his colleague Mr. Pinckney should be pleased. They recently submitted to the President a treaty that they have negotiated with the English."

"Yes, and, if I may speak confidentially, Mr. Monroe is in for a shock. Mr. Monroe's words have not reached Washington, yet Mr. Jefferson and Mr. Madison have decided to reject them."

"How can they do that if they have not read the treaty?" Buster noted that Randolph had not paused to obtain his assurance that he would keep their conversation confidential. He was interested, however, because he believed Madison was perfectly competent to engage in such subterfuge if it would be personally rewarding.

"The English Minister unwisely passed his own copy which arrived by a fast English courier ship. The English are already placing caveats on a treaty draft they had accepted from Mr. Monroe and Mr. Pinckney. I understand a message has been sent informing the Ministers that the President has rejected the treaty and their efforts have been for naught."

"Are you sure?"

"Of course."

"May I print this story?"

"Certainly, cousin. That is why I am telling it to you. But of course, do not mention my name."

Buster studied Randolph and wondered what his game was. Revenge against Jefferson and Madison was obvious, but what else?

"You say you are in correspondence with Mr. Monroe. What will his reaction be when he learns his friends have rejected his treaty?"

"He will be devastated. He will of course recognize that Madison has undercut him with the President."

"Why did they reject the treaty?"

"I don't know for sure. Something about the terms being too favorable to the English. Also," Randolph paused and smiled thinly at Buster, bending his wrist in a gesture to emphasize his point. "No mention was made of impressment."

"But that should have been a major issue addressed by the treaty."

"Who knows what Mr. Monroe's private instructions from Secretary of State Madison were. I cannot believe Mr. Monroe would have set such an important issue aside on his own authority."

"And what will happen when Mr. Monroe learns of his betrayal?"

"He will come home in disgrace."

"And what will his two closest friends, Jefferson and Madison, say?"

"After Madison is elected President, they will cry crocodile tears and offer poor Monroe a sinecure. Governor of Louisiana or some such demeaning thing. This to a man who expected to become President."

Buster assumed there were nuggets of truth buried in Randolph's words. The man of course had his own political agenda, but his story tracked with Busters' suspicions. Madison and Monroe had been long time collaborators with Jefferson, one in the Senate and one in the House. They had been the political workers on whose shoulders Jefferson stood as he played the statesman whose head inhaled a stratosphere unsullied by political machination and intrigue. James and Buster had long suspected that Madison and Monroe were simply Jefferson's catspaws.

"And what do you advise him?"

"Now that is the nub of the question," Randolph smiled.

Buster silently waited for Randolph to respond.

"The why I am here, cousin. My visit of course is not purely familial. But first, you must answer a question from me."

"And that is?"

"What are your views about all this?"

Buster was stunned into silence. He did not know what to say. He was not sure what his views were.

"And why should my views matter?" Buster asked, stalling for time.

"Again, I will speak frankly. Can I rely on your discretion?"

This time Randolph waited for Buster's response.

"I will in print not quote you without your permission."

"Very well. People do say some of the most outlandish things about me. They even allege a razor has never touched my smooth cheeks." Randolph paused and watched for Buster's reaction.

Buster decided to ignore the provocation. He steadily returned Randolph's cool gaze.

"You have made a favorable impression upon some of my true Republican colleagues in Richmond. I personally read the *Herald*, every issue. Sometimes, I think you lean too far backwards trying to be fair and objective, but you read our President and Secretary of State correctly. Your father is a loyal patriot, even if his views are distorted by Federalism; at least he is wise enough to prepare for war, not the opposite like Mr. Madison and Mr. Jefferson; and James, of course, is a hero."

"So much for my family," Buster interjected. "What are your plans?"

"Fairly said," Randolph did not take umbrage. "I am encouraging Mr. Monroe to fight back, to restore his good name by contesting Mr. Madison for the Presidency."

"In 1808?"

"In 1808."

"But if he swallows his pride, he can wait, be Secretary of State to President Madison, then have his turn at the first office in eight years."

"Why wait? So many things can happen, and, besides, friends have betrayed him. That is the worst treachery of all."

"Has Mr. Monroe decided?"

"We shall see."

Buster did not know what else to say. He still did not know why Randolph had approached him.

"And of course there is you," Randolph continued. "Mr. Monroe will need friends. And helpers. Would you manage his interests in Northern Virginia?"

"And if I did. What about the *Herald*?"

"It would of course support Mr. Monroe and denounce Mr. Madison and Mr. Jefferson."

"I am not a member of a political party. I'm neither a Republican nor a Federalist."

"And you need not be. You can be an independent who supports Mr. Monroe."

Buster studied Randolph. He did not trust the man and did not like him, but he was offering Buster a way out of his personal dilemma. If Monroe should become President, he would provide Buster with entre to political power at the nation's center if that were something he wanted. On the other hand, if he should actively support Monroe and his political faction, his family life would go to hell. Senator Furman, his father-in-law, a loyal Jeffersonian, would not understand, and Nancy would be furious. Buster decided that Randolph as a prospective collaborator was no more appealing than Madison.

"I do not personally know Mr. Monroe. I cannot support publicly someone I have not met and have not given my trust." Buster heard the stilted tone of his words but Randolph apparently chose to ignore it.

"That's fair. I ask nothing more now than you talk with Mr. Monroe."

"And I can report the substance of our conversation to my readership?"

"Without mentioning my name."

"Agreed."

Randolph sipped from his cup of lukewarm tea and smiled. He raised his cup as if offering a toast.

"An interesting morning," he said, then sipped a second time.

NORFOLK, VIRGINIA

JUNE 22-23, 1807

At nine in the morning of June 22nd, Jason's West Indies schooner the "Sad Sally" rounded the point and entered Hampton Roads, the water junction where the James River merged with the Chesapeake Bay. Captain Moses Wallace stood on the "Sally's" quarterdeck and studied Lynnhaven Bay on his right. First Mate Toddy Satterfield stood at the Captain's elbow and watched the cautious old seaman's lined face as he studied the array of sails that dotted the horizon.

"Something's up," Captain Wallace muttered to himself. "There's usually a Brit man-of-war lurking in the area, but that's a flotilla."

Captain Wallace handed the glass to his mate who was on his final cruise aboard the "Sally." The trim schooner, named for Jason's aunt, James' sister, was a frequent visitor to Norfolk, a regular stop on its Alexandria to the West Indies sugar run. The "Sally" was a good sailer, not as fast as the larger "Clipper," but it usually made its southern run without incident. Lately, however, the presence of English ships had become more worrisome, and Captain Wallace was not one to take chances. Despite the fact that the frequency with which British men-of-war stopped American merchantmen searching for deserters had increased, Norfolk and other American ports on President Jefferson's explicit orders continued to respect international custom and as a neutral allow all belligerents free access to its harbors for reprovisioning and repair.

"I see a frigate, at least fifty guns, and three war sloops." Toddy, who had spent the last three years aboard the "Sally" learning his chosen profession from the reliable Captain Wallace, still liked to check his seamanship and knowledge of ships against his master.

"Yep, and they're up to no good. There must be a Frenchie in the waters hereabouts."

French warships, like the English, sought sanctuary in American ports. The vastly greater numbers of English men-of-war made this a dangerous practice, but ships operating so far from their homeports had to take on water and food for their crews. As a consequence, both nations engaged in a dangerous game of cat and mouse. Wallace assumed the English ships anticipated an early enemy sailing and in their eagerness had penetrated American waters. Usually, they waited on the high seas for their prey to surface.

"Do you think they'll stop us?"

Toddy was not worried. None of Jason's schooners had been stopped yet. The common assumption was that the small crews, no more than fifteen to twenty men, uninteresting cargo, grain on the out voyage and sugar and molasses on the in, did not make them worth the effort. The nimble, fast sailing schooners usually disappeared over the horizon as soon as another sail was sighted, and to catch them the slower English ships had to box the traders into elaborate traps, and they weren't considered important enough to bother.

"Some say that Bonaparte and Tsar Alexander are about to make peace and that will mean the Frenchies will be free to turn their armies on the English. The worry has the English fleet on edge. More of their seamen are deserting, and they are working harder to get them back."

"But we don't have any deserters on board 'Sally,'" Toddy persisted.

Jason, determined to minimize any potential losses, had conscientiously insisted that his schooners employ only native American seamen no matter how experienced and available the English deserters might be. His captains were under specific orders not to supplement their crews in foreign ports with English volunteers.

"Won't keep them from stopping us," Wallace said, reaching for the glass when he noticed the English frigate come about. "You're drifting," he called to the helmsman. "Keep her tight, and we'll show the Englishers "Sally's" heels."

The "Sally," despite her heavy load of wheat sacks, had her sails full and quickly left the English squadron behind. Toddy was delighted. He looked forward to an extra night in Norfolk; Captain Wallace cautiously wanted to wait for the English to clear the area, and Toddy anxiously anticipated spending the time exchanging stories with his cousin J.J.

The "Sally" had anchored off Yorktown the previous evening, and Toddy had sent a message to J.J., who still attended the College in Williamsburg, announcing that the "Sally" would spend the night in Norfolk and inviting his cousin to meet with him if he could. The two had grown to be like brothers during their two years together in Alexandria at the academy, and it had been three years since they parted. Toddy's future seemed set; Jason had promised him that after this last cruise on the "Sally" he would be promoted to first officer on the "Clipper." Toddy knew that with war now imminent, Jason planned to build at least two more clippers. Toddy hoped that if he performed successfully as first officer he would obtain command of one of the new ships. J.J.'s plans appeared less certain. Vivian had confided that in his recent letters J.J. had appeared "down," disappointed with his life at the College and uncertain about his future. Toddy wanted to meet his cousin and cheer him if he could.

The "Sally" cleared Hampton and turned on a southwesterly tack towards Norfolk.

"Sail ho," the forward lookout called, breaking into Toddy's thoughts.

"Another frigate," Captain Wallace said, peering at the approaching vessel through his glass. "Outward bound from Norfolk. Flying the Stars and Stripes."

Toddy's heart beat a little faster with pride. Sighting an American frigate was rare. Thomas Jefferson had retired all but three, and these for reasons of economy spent little time at sea.

"Which ship is she? Can you make her out?" Toddy glanced from the approaching frigate to his captain then back again. His eyesight was much sharper than Captain Wallace's and he wished he would share his glass.

"Can't tell at this angle." Captain Wallace, almost as if he had read Toddy's thoughts, turned and handed him the glass. "Here, you give 'er a try."

During their first year together on the "Sally," Wallace had kept his distance from the novice seaman. Toddy had assumed that coolness resulted from his being a relative of the owner who had first promised command of the "Clipper" then withdrawn it. Toddy, despite his favored position, had accepted his role as an ordinary seaman and had worked hard. A quick learner, he had soon earned the respect of the other crewmembers. Eventually, he had worked his way up to assistant helmsman and had demonstrated he was a "natural seaman," one who intuitively responded to the demands of current and wind. Captain Wallace had gradually accepted Toddy's presence on his bridge and soon did what he could to enhance the young man's seamanship. A year ago Wallace had appointed Toddy first mate, a surprise given his age and limited time at sea. Captain Wallace had grown to consider Toddy a protege; his relationship to the owner was almost forgotten. Toddy was not sure how his mentor would react when he learned that Toddy was being promoted to the "Clipper," but he hoped the older man would be pleased for him.

"I can make her out. She's the 'Chesapeake.'"

Toddy's announcement was not a surprise to either of them. Both knew the "Chesapeake" had been anchored off Norfolk, but the old sailor's rules did not countenance opinion or guessing. He insisted that at sea only confirmed facts be considered.

Toddy waved to the "Chesapeake's" quarterdeck as they passed, and one of the watch officers returned the gesture.

"How many crew would "Chesapeake" carry?" Toddy asked.

"A frigate will carry four hundred men," Captain Wallace answered.

The "Sally" made Norfolk about one in the afternoon. To Toddy's surprise, the harbor was full, an indication that something was afoot.

"We better touch base with the harbor master first thing and find out why those ships are not about their business," Captain Wallace said.

Wallace went below while Toddy maneuvered the "Sally" to an anchorage some distance from the customs officers. They had nothing to hide because their cargo was of American origin and destined for a foreign port; there simply was

no room closer in. Wallace, who disliked dealing with people, delegated responsibility for negotiating with local officialdom to Toddy. He quickly donned a
clean shirt and trousers and with two crewmen as rowers took the "Sally's" long
boat to the closest pier.

Just as they were docking, several muffled claps of what Toddy took to be
thunder echoed from the east. Toddy turned in the direction of Lynnhaven Bay
and saw flashes of light. He looked in puzzlement at the two seamen.

"That's not thunder, that's cannon fire," the younger opined.

A series of repeated claps followed.

"Those Englishers must be testing their cannon," the older seaman said
authoritatively.

Toddy nodded, glanced apprehensively eastward one more time, then
climbed ashore.

At the customs shed several of his questions were answered. The English
squadron had been lying offshore for over a week hoping to trap two French
armed vessels that had been in Hampton for repairs. While waiting, H.M.S
"Melampus" had come ashore for water. To prevent desertion, the crew had been
confined on board ship, and only the "Melampus's" captain's barge had been put
into the water. Several English seamen seized their opportunity, commandeered
the barge and fled ashore defiantly dodging English gunfire. Nearby American
seamen added to the confusion by cheering the escaping deserters. Later, irate
English officers had demanded the return of their sailors, but the Americans had
first stalled then replied that they had been unable to find the deserters.
Subsequently, three of the deserters had enlisted as crew on board the American
frigate "Chesapeake," apparently in the belief that such service gave them sanctuary. International law and custom dictated that men-of-war were immune to
search and seizure. On the other hand, merchant ships were fair game. Since
most American ships had British seamen among their crews, the vessels that
Toddy had observed lining the harbor were those who were waiting for the
English warships to clear the coast before sailing.

Captain Wallace had authorized Toddy to spend the night on shore after he
had completed his duty call at customs. Captain Wallace fondly recalled J.J. from
his one journey on the "Clipper" when J.J. had braved seasickness and performed
exemplarily aloft as lookout. To Toddy's knowledge, J.J. had never ventured to
sea again.

Since neither Toddy nor J.J. knew Norfolk well—it was virtually a new town
as the old Norfolk had been burned to the ground by the old colonial governor
during the Revolution—Toddy had suggested in his note that they meet at the
customs shed. Not sure that J.J. would have the time to travel to Norfolk, and not
certain that his note had reached J.J. at the College, Toddy paused when he exited the customs and appraised the area. He noticed a shabbily dressed stranger
with a full black beard and shaggy shoulder length hair lounging under the
waterfront's single, struggling tree. Toddy ignored the man and looked for an
ordinary. The solitary tavern located across the street hardly looked appropriate

for gentlemen. Through the open door Toddy could see and hear drunken seamen singing and shouting. While he watched, a burly barkeep propelled a flailing drunk through the doorway. The drunk staggered and fell headfirst into the gutter, his head dangerously close to a steaming pile of horse manure. Toddy waited for the prone man to roll into the dung when he tried to regain his feet, but he lay where he fell, motionless. A scraggly woman with no teeth rushed from the dark interior of the bar, approached the prone man and stopped. She glanced in each direction of the street, noted Toddy standing near the customs shed, cackled and bent over and quickly searched the seaman's pockets. Satisfied, she spun and hurried back into the bar clutching whatever she had taken from the prone drunk.

Toddy decided to walk south into town, hoping to find a more appropriate place to wait for J.J. Toddy ignored the shabby, bearded man under the tree as he passed him.

"Not going to give me the shoulder, are ye mate?" A familiar voice said.

Still walking, Toddy turned towards the speaker. As a defensive measure, he thrust his right hand into his trouser pocket to protect his cash.

"Don't recognize your own kin, huh?" The bearded man challenged, then laughed uproariously.

"J.J.," Toddy shouted and rushed towards the bearded man who jumped to his feet and embraced him.

"Afraid I'm after your cash?" J.J. laughed.

"J.J.," Toddy repeated, relieved. "This isn't the most attractive environment."

The two cousins chatted as they walked.

"I've got us a room at the Wild Boar," J.J. said.

"The Pig? Like at home?"

"The very same. Perfect for wastrels but with a little more class than your harbourfront emporium." .

In the distance, the steady boom of canon fire repeated itself. This time the noise continued for several minutes before subsiding into silence.

"You know what that is?" Toddy asked.

"Cannon fire. I understand an English squadron is along the coast."

"We passed it this morning,," Toddy said. "A frigate, at least fifty guns, and several war sloops."

"What are they up to?"

"Waiting for a couple of Frenchies, I hear."

"Sounds like they found them."

The Wild Boar, unlike the waterfront tavern, was empty when the two cousins entered. They selected a table in the corner and waited for a barmaid to appear.

"Will you have an ale?" J.J. asked, not sure if his cousin had acquired the taste.

"Chilled?" Toddy asked, referring to Jason's specialty.

J.J laughed. "This is sailor heaven not an AleRoom. How many does Jason have now?"

"Only three AleRooms and one brewery, but he supplies every ordinary and inn on the Virginia shore with brew and ice. A competitor has opened a brewery in Georgetown."

"I hope he has fire insurance," J.J. laughed, remembering the night they had burned Brown's Brewery. "Jason's not a man to suffer competition."

The barmaid finally appeared, took their orders with a contemptuous dismissal of the seaman and the shabby, shaggy bearded man, delivered the ales, and then disappeared again.

After exchanging the usual pleasantries, bringing each other up to date on family developments, births and deaths, achievements and failures, Toddy enthusiastically described his future.

"And Jason has promised to make me first officer of the 'Clipper,'" he enthused. "Can you imagine that? Remember how green we were on that first cruise? I've learned I was right. The sea is the life for me. No more staring at a stinking horse's backside in a dusty field." Realizing that he was dominating the conversation, Toddy then asked what the future held for J.J.

His cousin hesitated before responding, drawing lines from the circles left by the foaming mugs on the tabletop. Toddy tried to read J.J.'s expression, but the beard concealed his features. Toddy could see the brilliant emerald of J.J.'s eyes, but the flash of enthusiasm was not present.

"William and Mary has not been the challenge I anticipated," J.J. confessed. His voice sounded disinterested. Toddy discreetly waited for J.J. to continue.

"Williamsburg's not as james remembered it. Since the capital moved to Richmond, the town has died. William and Mary is Williamsburg's only attraction, and it is nothing more than an academy filled with irresponsible kids taught by four disinterested professors."

"But you will be finishing soon," Toddy tried to add a tinge of optimism.

"Maybe. I was so far behind the others that it's taking me an extra year to graduate, and I've had to find a job to pay my way. I couldn't spend any more of Eli's money," J.J. referred to his father. "And Grandpa John's death didn't help."

"What do you do?"

"I'm a stable boy. I take care of the College's stables."

The thought seemed to depress his cousin, so Toddy tried to change the subject.

"And girls?" Toddy had already met a young lady in Alexandria and was making plans.

"None. I spend most of my time at the books. The College's all male, and none of the town girls will have anything to do with the students."

"Well, in another month it will all be over. Then what?"

"If I pass my examinations I'll be free. All depends on them."

"I'm sure you will knock them."

"I'm not."

J.J. seemed disinterested. "Why not ask Jason to let you come to sea with me?" Toddy tried to sound enthusiastic.

"The sea's not for me. I get too sick."

"What then? Teaching? Law? Medicine?"

"None of that interests me."

"What about the mountains? Farming?"

"No."

Toddy could think of nothing left for J.J. to pursue. He had ruled out the professions.

"There's one thing." J.J. paused, as if hesitant to elaborate. "The army." When he uttered the word "army," J.J. smiled for the first time.

"The army?" The idea surprised Toddy. Nobody considered the army for a career. Jefferson had reduced the professional officer corps to a handful who spent their time fighting Indians in the west.

"I've decided that I want to build things."

"But what has that to do with the army?"

"Have you heard of West Point?"

"The fort on the Hudson that Benedict Arnold tried to betray to the English?"

"Yes. "

"I've heard all about that from Gramps."

"Well," J.J. said. "I am going to continue family tradition in my way. I am going to West Point, the scene of one of James' successes, or near failures as he tells it."

"What will you build there?"

"I see I need to educate you," J.J. joked, then regretted his offhand comment when he saw the dismay on Toddy's face. He had not realized that his cousin was sensitive to the fact that he had gone on to college and Toddy had not.

"I mean," J.J. spoke quickly. "The military academy."

Noting the confusion on Toddy's face, J.J. explained.

"As an opponent of a standing army, Jefferson opposed the creation of a military academy when he was Washington's Secretary of State. As one of his last acts of office, presumably to taunt Jefferson, John Adams proposed that Congress create a military academy. Eventually, Jefferson's Congress approved a much-scaled downed version that met the President's reservations. Given his propensity for dallying with science, Jefferson thought the creation of a school for engineers a worthwhile endeavor. It 's now in existence, headed by a nephew of Benjamin Franklin, a family connection that presumably makes him a scientist."

"Sounds interesting."

"It's not a big deal, only twenty students, but I've applied."

"Do you have a chance?"

"I doubt many others are interested."

"You might have to trim that," Toddy referred to his cousin's overflowing beard.

J.J. laughed and fluffed his unruly mane.

The boys, now young men, spent the evening reliving old times. As the employed family member, Toddy insisted on paying their bills, and J.J. deferred, promising to carry the weight next time. In the morning they parted, J.J. for Williamsburg and Toddy for the customs house. He felt guilty for being away from the "Sally" overnight and suffered from a slight hangover.

He found the customs house in a complete state of chaos. Ship captains and naval officers mixed with the customs officials, turning the normally placid harbor center into bedlam. Toddy cornered a young naval lieutenant and asked him what had caused the excitement.

"Haven't you heard?"

Toddy, befuddled, shook his head negatively.

"The English attacked the 'Chesapeake' yesterday."

Toddy immediately recognized the name of the American frigate that he had so proudly watched as they passed in Hampton Road.

"Why?"

The lieutenant patiently explained.

"The 'Leopard,'" which Toddy immediately assumed to be the fifty gun English frigate they had seen in Lynnhaven Bay, "hailed the 'Chesapeake' when she exited the roads. The 'Chesapeake' stopped and accepted a British party who carried orders from Admiral Berkeley in Halifax. Berkeley commands the British North American Fleet," the lieutenant explained when he noted Toddy's blank expression. "They claimed that the 'Chesapeake' carried many British deserters in its crew and directed any British captain who met the American ship to stop it, show the order, and demand that she be inspected for deserters."

"But they can't do that," Toddy protested. "Not search an American man-of-war. That violates our sovereignty."

"And in American waters, too," the lieutenant added heatedly. "Captain Barron, who commands the 'Chesapeake,' refused. He denied that any British deserters were on board his ship."

"Good for him," Toddy said.

"Maybe," the lieutenant said cryptically. "The English party returned to its ship, which then fired a warning shot over the 'Chesapeake's' bow. This was followed immediately by a heavy barrage which took the unprepared 'Chesapeake' by surprise. The 'Chesapeake' suffered mortal damage, and many seamen were killed and wounded. Captain Barron, following this treacherous attack, lowered his flags and the British boarding party returned. They arrogantly declared the 'Chesapeake' a prize of war, searched the ship and took off four crew members."

The lieutenant paused for Toddy to express his indignation and then whispered: "I understand three were Americans and one, only one, was an English deserter. The 'Chesapeake' then returned to port with three feet of water in her hold and masts and sails severely damaged. A dispatch has been sent to Washington, and all say this means war. Poor Captain Barron. He lost his ship without firing a gun."

"And the English squadron?" Toddy asked, wondering what all this would mean for the "Sally."

"They remain in Lynnhaven Bay, defiantly anchored in American waters."

"And what are we going to do about it?" Toddy was prepared to fight.

"What can we do? Send President Jefferson's harbor boats after them like flies against an elephant?"

Toddy thanked the lieutenant then circulated through the room and listened to the heated conversations. The universal opinion of the mariners was that the United States had no option but to go to war. The English needed to be taught a lesson. After about an hour, Toddy recognized that he would learn no more than the lieutenant had already told him. He then hurried back to the pier and hired a boat to take him out to the "Sally."

There, he found that the news had already reached the crew.

"When do we go to war, Toddy?" One of his mates called.

Toddy shrugged, indicating all was beyond him. He hurried to the quarter-deck where he found Captain Wallace pacing.

"What should we do?" The Captain asked, dispensing with the usual pleasantries.

Toddy did not know and said so.

"We can't sit in Norfolk forever," Wallace expostulated. "Jason expects us to deliver this wheat to Martinique and to be back with a load of sugar in four weeks. The dratted English could sit in the bay for months."

"They stopped the 'Chesapeake' because they had information she had deserters aboard, but they haven't touched a merchantman for weeks," Toddy began thinking aloud. Sometimes he found that conversation helped lead the cautious Wallace into making decisions. Toddy recognized that left to his own devices, Captain Wallace would dither.

"So they say," Wallace countered. "But that doesn't mean they will not tomorrow."

"And we don't have any deserters on board. Jason always opposed that."

"I know. Does that mean they won't blow us out of the water?"

"What would Jason do?" Toddy voiced the one question that could force Wallace to make a decision.

"What would he do? Why he would sail right under their bows," the exasperated Captain almost shouted.

"Then, that's what we should do. The British are waiting to see how we respond, and they know it will take days for word to reach Washington and for them to react. They'll let us go and wait for Jefferson's response to the 'Chesapeake.'"

Captain Wallace glared at Toddy and resumed his pacing. Toddy's brash suggestion made sense, but it was still a risk.

The next morning before dawn the watch shook Toddy awake in the crew's cabin.

"The Captain's decided. We sail immediately," he said in a loud voice that immediately halted the snoring chorus.

"All hands to your duty stations," Toddy called while running towards the hatchway carrying his boots.

He found Captain Wallace standing by the helm on the quarterdeck. He hopped up and down putting on his boots while the captain talked.

"The wind's fresh, the tide's ebbing and the sky's overcast. If we can get to windward, we can be on the ocean before the English can catch us."

"Aye, Aye, Captain." Toddy wanted to escape Norfolk and said nothing that might dissuade the captain from his course. He knew Wallace had paced until late in the night wrestling with his decision.

"It's what Jason would do, remember that," Captain Wallace admonished.

Toddy wondered if Wallace was afraid of losing his command again because Jason thought him too cautious.

"Do you agree?" Captain Wallace demanded.

"Aye, sir," Toddy tried to sound nautical.

"They might not be able to catch us, but they sure will be able to delay us with their cannon," Wallace said.

"Yes, sir."

"And you still think we should sail?"

"Yes, sir, definitely. "

"Then, let's be at it."

Toddy was impressed. He had always respected Captain Wallace's seamanship but had doubted his courage. Today, he was proud of his captain.

Within minutes the schooner's sails were aloft and they were underway. Captain Wallace, having made his decision, did not pause to give the crew time to have breakfast. Toddy noticed that all moved with alacrity; he assumed that most were like himself, too afraid to complain of hunger.

The tide was running and the easterly wind let "Sally" tack as she wished. The weather conditions were ideal for the quick sailing schooner.

Captain Wallace set a course that took "Sally" close to Hampton on the north side of the Roads. This let her tack across the running Chesapeake towards Cape Charles keeping them as far to the north of the English Squadron in Lynnhaven Bay as possible.

"They won't be able to tell if we plan to turn north into the Bay and stay in American waters or if we're heading for the Atlantic," Toddy observed.

"Exactly," Captain Wallace smiled for the first time that morning.

As soon as they cleared Hampton Roads and entered the Bay, a lookout on the English frigate in Lynnhaven Bay spotted them. Within minutes signal flags were flying on the mast of the man-of-war.

"They want us to stop," Toddy said. He had spent many hours at sea studying the accepted international signal system.

"Ignore them," Captain Wallace ordered.

The "Sally" continued its flying journey under full sail as the "Leopard" communicated with its squadron schooners and sloops with signals Toddy could not read. Two of the schooners raised their sails and turned in pursuit.

"The "Leopard" knows she doesn't stand a chance of catching us, so she's sending her schooners."

"They don't either," Captain Wallace smiled, growing more confident with each passing minute.

They had a good mile lead on the first schooner.

"And we're out of cannon range," Captain Wallace lowered his glass. "Good work lads," he called to his crew who anxiously watched the English squadron on their stern.

"Bring her about," Wallace ordered.

Toddy noted they had reached a point east of Cape Charles where a turn to the south-southeast would take them into the Atlantic Ocean at the maximum distance from the anchored frigate.

"They caught the 'Chesapeake' unawares but they won't catch "Sad Sally," the helmsman gloated.

Toddy hoped he was right. He could not understand why the two English schooners were still pursuing when it was clear that the "Sally" was free.

He watched as the southern tip of Cape Charles passed their stern rail.

"Sails on the port bow," the forward lookout shouted.

Toddy, who had been watching the pursuing schooners, turned to the port and felt an immediate falling sensation in his stomach.

An armed schooner and a war sloop with English flags flying emerged from behind the southernmost tip of eastern Maryland. One glance was enough to determine they had the proper angle to cut them off. The English squadron had carefully led them into the trap. The war sloop, which was several hundred yards in front of the schooner, fired a warning shot. It splashed a good fifty yards ahead of "Sally" and to her starboard. They had the range.

"We've had it," an ashen-faced Captain Wallace muttered. He turned to Toddy.

"First mate, lower the sails and strike the flag."

With those words, Captain Wallace, recognizing he had lost his command, turned and sought solitary refuge in his cabin.

"Lower the sails and strike the colors," Toddy shouted, mouthing the saddest words he had every spoken.

CHESAPEAKE BAY AND ALEXANDRIA, VIRGINIA

JUNE 1807

Toddy turned the "Sad Sally" and her furled sails into the wind and waited for their pursuer to approach. At about one hundred yards distance, the English schooner duplicated the "Sally's" maneuver, pivoted, and lowered a long boat for her boarding party. The schooner was close enough for Toddy to read her name, the "Belona." The English carefully kept their starboard guns manned and pointed menacingly at the "Sally." Both ships bounced in the rough sea, and the long boat had difficulty approaching the "Sally." The delay gave Toddy time to wonder about the origin of the odd name, "Belona."

Finally, a red-faced English junior lieutenant, who Toddy judged to be about his own age, and four armed crewmen boarded the "Sally." The lieutenant pushed past the staring American sailors and made his way to the quarterdeck where Toddy waited.

"Lieutenant Wythe of H.M.S "Belona," the bearded officer announced and flipped his hand past his forelock in what Toddy interpreted was an insolent form of salute.

Toddy, irritated by the man's presence as well as his surly demeanor, replied with a sullen stare.

"And you are the captain?" The officer demanded.

"The captain is in his cabin," Toddy replied, trying to match the man's tone. Toddy considered him an intruder, not a guest.

"Fetch him," the lieutenant ordered.

Toddy insolently stared at the English officer, and neither neither moved nor replied.

The ruddy-faced officer flushed a deep red. He was conscious of the fact that the American crewmen and his own boarding party were watching.

"Did you hear me?" He demanded.

Toddy took his time replying.

"And who are you to give me orders?" Toddy asked. "This is an American vessel in American territorial waters. You have no authority here."

The lieutenant drew his saber from its sheath and raised it. His boarding party, reacting to the tension, turned their weapons on the "Sally's" crew.

Toddy did not know what to do next. The "Sally" did not carry any armament, only a few pistols and cutlasses stored in a chest in the captain's cabin. Toddy was fully aware of the fate of the "Chesapeake" and realized that the English cannons could easily sink the "Sally," sending ship, cargo and crew to the deep. Before either Toddy or the Englishman could take the next irrevocable step, Captain Wallace emerged from the hatchway. Captain Wallace, dressed in his best uniform, walked calmly with all the dignity he could muster to the quarterdeck. Toddy was proud of him.

"My name is Wallace, and I am captain of this vessel," he declared coldly.

"Lieutenant Wythe of His Royal Majesty's warship 'Belona,'" the red faced lieutenant replied as he carefully returned his saber to its sheath.

"And what are you doing on the 'Sally?'" Captain Wallace demanded.

"Captain, we have reason to believe that English deserters are on board your ship. Please summon your crew to muster."

"On what authority?"

"See those cannons?" Lieutenant Wythe demanded. "If you do not muster your crew this minute for inspection, I will return to my ship and sink this scow forthwith."

Captain Wallace studied the English officer. After the confrontation between the "Leopard" and the "Chesapeake," a warship, Wallace did not doubt his word. He turned slowly towards his gathered crew and spoke calmly:

"Muster on the fan deck."

Captain Wallace brushed past the waiting lieutenant and, followed by Toddy, proceeded aft.

"Keep her in the wind," Wallace ordered the helmsman, indicating he should remain at his wheel.

Lieutenant Wythe glared at the helmsman, uncertain whether to leave him at his post or to order him aft. Finally, he recognized the necessity of manning the wheel. He was fully conscious that the American captain had appeared to take control.

"Form a line," Wythe ordered when all were standing in the stern. "Shoot the first man who disobeys," he instructed his boarding party who nervously watched the Americans.

"What's your name?" He demanded of the first American, a short, middle aged man.

"Adams, sir. "

"Where are you from?"

"Baltimore, sir."

"And your family?"

"Baltimore, sir."

"Can you prove it?"

"Ask me anything about Baltimore. I can answer it."

The answer momentarily stopped the lieutenant. He knew nothing about Baltimore.

"That proves nothing. Show me your papers."

"I have no papers."

Wythe studied the man.

"Empty your pockets."

"I have nothing in them, sir," Adams replied. He pulled his pockets inside out to prove his word.

"Hmm," Wythe seemed unsure what to do next. He had not expected the seaman to carry papers or to be able to prove his nationality. Wythe had to rely on his wits to unmask the English deserters. The problem was not a simple one because Englishmen and most Americans talked alike and looked the same.

Adams trembled as he waited for the Englishman's next move. He knew his life depended on the next few seconds. Finally, Wythe decided.

"Stand over there," he ordered, indicating a spot near the rail away from the line of Americans.

Adams did not know whether he had been freed or condemned.

Wythe approached the next man and repeated the process. Toddy, standing at Captain Wallace's side, knew that all the crew were bonafide Americans. He hoped that fear did not provoke any of them into giving suspicious answers. While they waited, Wythe interrogated each man in turn. Eventually, all were standing next to Adams. Only Toddy and Captain Wallace remained. The red faced Englishman without a single English deserter to show for his efforts turned to Captain Wallace with a frown on his face.

"You, sir," he sneered at Wallace, "are obviously an American. No self respecting English officer would command a vessel such as this."

Toddy smiled to himself. The "Sally" was a trim schooner that could easily leave the "Belona" in her wake. The Englishman had failed in his mission and would return to his captain empty handed.

Wythe turned quickly and caught Toddy with a smile on his face. The Englishman's sneer made Toddy regret his mistake.

"And you, sir. What's your name?"

"Satterfield," Toddy replied.

"Really? Satterfield. Are you telling the truth?"

"I was born Satterfield, and I stand here Satterfield," Toddy said defiantly.

"An English name," Wythe challenged.

"An American, I am proud to say."

"And I say English. What ship are you from?" Wythe asked his question quickly, hoping to catch Toddy off guard.

"The 'Sally.' As fine a ship as ever sailed the ocean."

The "Sally's" crew mumbled agreement, irritating the already discomfited Wythe.

"Quiet there," one of the boarding party threatened with his musket.

"Where were you born? Lancashire?"

"Loudoun."

"London?" Wythe smiled.

"No. Loudoun. In the Short Hills."

Lieutenant Wythe turned to his party.

"Bosun. This Satterfield is a deserter from London. Take him."

Two burly boarders stepped forward and grabbed Toddy by the arms. Before he could react, they had hurled him over the stern into the waiting long boat.

"Stay there!" Captain Wallace shouted. "That man is an American. His relative owns this ship."

"A likely story," Wythe laughed and drew his cutlass and pointed it at Captain Wallace. "Don't move captain, or I will run you through."

The Englishman leaped over the stern into his boat. His four boarders carefully followed. Captain Wallace and his crew watched helplessly as the English craft turned and made its way back to the "Belona."

"Not to worry son," Captain Wallace called to the struggling Toddy. "We'll straighten this out."

"Watch and you'll learn how we handle deserters," Wythe called back. He turned and struck Toddy viciously on the side of the head with the flat of his cutlass blade.

Toddy fell silently to the deck, and the Englishman laughed as he slid his cutlass into its sheath.

As soon as the long boat reached its ship, Toddy was shoved aboard and hustled out of sight. The English hoisted the boat aboard, raised their sails and turned towards Lynnhaven Bay. Signal flags fluttered as the "Belona" communicated with its squadron.

A dumbfounded Captain Wallace turned from the rail and faced his crew. He did not know what to say. Even worse, he did not know what to do. He pivoted slowly, silently, and returned to the quarterdeck.

"Hoist the sails and get underway away from these devils," he ordered.

"What course captain?" The wide-eyed helmsman asked as the captain's orders echoed through the silent ship.

Captain Wallace stared at the waiting seaman. He did not know what to say. He had a full hold of wheat consigned to the West Indies. He had just lost the owner's kin. He asked himself which direction Jason would take, south to the destination or north, back to Alexandria with the cargo still on board and his mate a prisoner of the English. Captain Wallace walked to the rail. Over his head the sails flapped as the helmsman held "Sally" to the wind waiting for orders. The forlorn officer watched as the "Belona" raced towards the English frigate.

"Good luck, son," Captain Wallace repeated himself. He knew that life for a normal seaman on board an English man-of-war was hell. That was why so many deserted. He could imagine the punishment that a deserter faced, even an alleged deserter.

"Take her into the Bay and back to Alexandria," Captain Wallace said deject-edly. He walked slowly into his cabin and was not seen again by the crew until the "Sally" docked in Alexandria at the pier opposite Jason's office.

"Christ, what's she doing back?" Skinny blurted.

Skinny had been standing at the window watching the shipwrights lay the keel for "Clipper II." Jason had finally decided war was imminent and had ordered the construction of the "Clipper's" sister ship. The "Clipper" had not been seen for months in Alexandria. Only Skinny and Jason knew that she had been sent to the West Indies. There, she had abandoned her ill-fitting career as a fast cargo hauler; now, she had been launched on the mission for which she had been intended, privateering. Operating out of Martinique, the "Clipper" with her new captain and crew preyed on English merchantmen. The French authorities happily supplied the American vessel with letters of marque and reprisal. Jason would have been happier if his dream had operated under its true colors, but the French flag would have to do until Jefferson learned that his policy of diplomacy and economic pressure was fated to fail. Then, "Clipper" could hoist the Stars and Stripes and seize French and English shipping.

"Who's back?" Jason demanded irritably. He hated it when Skinny talked so vaguely that you did not know what he was discussing.

Skinny rubbed his stump and studied the "Sally." She was supposed to be in the West Indies. He knew she could not have completed her voyage yet. Neither Captain Wallace nor Toddy was on the quarterdeck. One of the older seamen was conning the vessel. Skinny's stump itched, a sure omen of trouble.

He could see no sign of damage, and the "Sally" was heavy in the water. She still had a full load of cargo. Skinny knew it was not possible that she had returned with the wheat, but he could not imagine where she had offloaded and acquired a return cargo so quickly.

"They couldn't have gotten much farther than Norfolk," Skinny observed, ignoring Jason's question.

"Norfolk? The 'Sally?'" Jason asked.

Jason exchanged a worried glance with Skinny and rushed to the window. News of the "Chesapeake's" encounter with the "Leonard" had reached Alexandria. Yesterday's *Herald* had been filled with accounts of the treacherous English attack on the American warship. First reports had indicated that four of the "Chesapeake's" crew had been killed and some twenty seriously wounded.

"Wallace would not have let the "Sally" get involved with the English squadron," Jason declared as he pushed next to Skinny at the window.

"There's Wallace now," Skinny declared.

Skinny and Jason watched as Captain Wallace crossed the deck with a heavy tread.

"Something's happened," Skinny said.

Jason returned to his desk and waited. His ship appeared sound, and her captain was coming to report. He would wait for the bad news, confident it would be something he could handle easily.

Skinny remained at the window and watched as Captain Wallace plodded across the pier. Something was troubling the man; something had happened that he did not want to report. The "Sally's" crew was also behaving strangely. They were silently lashing their vessel to the dock. The usual ebullience that accompanied a homecoming was missing. Skinny returned to his desk and waited, wondering what and how much this latest adventure would cost him. Life with Jason was not boring.

James saw the unanticipated return of the "Sally" from his porch.

"The "Sally's" back," James called to Vivian who joined him.

"It's too soon, isn't it?" She asked.

Both had been worried about young Toddy from the moment they had heard of the "Chesapeake Affair." Buster had used the words "Chesapeake Affair" in his first headlines, and the sobriquet had stuck. Now, whenever anyone referred to the invidious English attack, they called it the "Chesapeake Affair."

James nodded.

"I didn't hear of any other ships being attacked. Did you?" She asked.

"No," James replied. The "Sally" appeared sound. He worried that Captain Wallace had lost his nerve and had been afraid to challenge the English squadron. Jason would be furious if he had, but James was concerned that an American captain would not stand up to the English. Weakness invited contempt, and that inspired abuse.

James and Vivian watched as Captain Wallace trudged across Union Street and entered Jason's office.

"I don't see Toddy," Vivian said. Usually Toddy commanded the quarterdeck when the "Sally" docked.

James patiently waited and again pondered the odd name Jason had given his schooner. "The Sad Sally." James wondered why he had called his beautiful ship "Sad." He had assumed it had been because his sister had lost two of her children at birth. James hoped that some strange premonition had not given Jason an unconscious insight into the future.

"Captain Wallace. What are you doing here?" Jason spoke as soon as the wan Wallace entered his office. He had intended to wait quietly for the man to report his story, but his patience had cracked.

"Mr. Satterfield, Jason, I... ." Wallace hesitated before continuing. "I... . lost him."

Skinny, whose desk was situated near the door, smelled the fumes first. The man had been drinking.

Wallace, without bidding, dropped heavily in the chair situated along the far wall where it was placed so the occupant could talk to both Skinny and Jason. Wallace clutched the sides of the chair and clenched his hands until the veins popped. He took a deep breath and tried to speak.

"Lost who?" Jason blurted. "Just tell me. Get a hold of yourself."

Skinny reached into his desk drawer and extracted a bottle of rum that he kept there for emergencies. Without looking at Jason for permission, he poured a small glass full and handed it to Wallace. The Captain gratefully took it, raised it to his lips and emptied it. He wiped his mouth with the back of his hand and, fortified, looked again at Jason.

"I lost Toddy," he gasped.

Jason shrank back into his chair and stared. His lips tightened, and his green eyes flared. They locked on Wallace who shrank under their intensity. Jason waited. Skinny caught his breath. Toddy was a Satterfield family favorite.

"The English caught us coming out of the Roads. Toddy and I decided to continue to the Indies and outrun them. Some were frightened by the attack on the "Chesapeake," but we thought we could outrun them. We were too, but they caught us in a box."

Jason's continued silence made Wallace even more nervous. Skinny retrieved the glass and refilled it. He started to offer it again to the distraught Wallace, but one glance from Jason's blazing eyes stayed him. He drank it himself instead.

Wallace, once started, blurted out the entire story describing the English lieutenant, his arrogant interrogation of the crew and his seizure of Toddy.

"Impressed," Skinny declared. "Life will be hell, but he's alive. We'll get him back." He spoke with more confidence that he felt. Impressed seamen rarely returned; they disappeared into the bowels of the English navy and their far-flung empire.

"If they don't string him from the yardarms," Wallace mumbled.

All three men knew that the English frequently hung deserters as an example to the others.

"Thank you Captain Wallace," Jason spoke quietly, trying to calm the unsettled man. "You did all you could. It's not your fault."

"I didn't know whether to go on to the Indies or come back and report. I hated returning with the wheat."

"You did right, Captain," Jason said.

Jason glanced at Skinny, and the look told Skinny that the Captain had commanded his last Satterfield ship.

"I must tell the family before the crew spreads the word," Jason rose.

"Captain Wallace," Skinny addressed the pale man. "Let's you and I visit the Pig and make plans."

Jason nodded his appreciation to his friend for taking responsibility for Wallace.

"Here comes Jason," James reported needlessly to Vivian who sat at his side. "Something has happened to Toddy," she declared presciently.

James noted his son's measured gait and tense face. The green Satterfield eyes blazed with contained anger.

"It's Toddy," Jason said as soon as he mounted the porch. "The English have impressed him."

Jason remained standing as he repeated Wallace's story. When he finished, Jason studied his father and asked:

"What should we do?" James was the family's most experienced English fighter.

Vivian and Jason waited patiently while James thought. Finally, he spoke.

"First things first. We must inform his father," James referred to his dead brother Will's son Eric who lived at the family homestead in the Short Hills. We must tell Buster. He can orchestrate the public protest through the *Herald*. Somebody can talk with Jefferson and Madison and the English Minister, and we must get information on that frigate, the "Leopard."

"Right," Vivian agreed. "We stand a better chance of getting him back with public pressure." Both she and James remembered the time she had joined the raid to recover James when he had been captured in New York and was going to be hung as an American spy.

"We don't stand a chance of attacking an English man-of-war and getting him off alive," James studied his son. He knew that action would be Jason's first reaction. "But if we know where he is, we can make enough racket to make sure he's fairly treated...and released." James spoke with more confidence than he felt. He wished that his brother John were alive to take charge.

"There's no question of his being a deserter," Vivian opined. "Therefore, if we can keep the English from hanging him to hide their mistakes, we will be able to get him back through Jefferson's diplomatic pressure."

"The 'Chesapeake Affair' will help," James continued, suppressing the intense sadness that the thought of his brother had produced. "Everyone's calling for war. Now in Toddy's case we have clear proof he is not a deserter. The English will want to show their good will by releasing him."

"If they don't kill him first." Jason studied his parents. He had informed them before acting because he wanted to save them the grief of learning of the fate of one of their favorite relatives by chance. He belatedly recognized that he should have known they would take charge.

"I'll talk with Buster," James said, rising.

"And so will I," Vivian said.

"What should I do first?" Jason asked, surrendering.

"Have Skinny talk with the crew and get every detail," James ordered.

"And then you saddle up and get to the Short Hills and inform Eric and the family. When you get back, we'll talk about getting the word to J.J. in Williamsburg. He should be of help," Vivian said.

"And I will have them take the cargo off the 'Sally,'" James added. "We'll want her to sail immediately to track that English frigate, 'The Leopard.'"

"Do you think they'll transfer him to the frigate, not keep him on the schooner?" Vivian asked.

"Certainly," James replied, remembering his cell room on Admiral Howe's flagship. "They'll want to make an example of him, punish him first."

"How?" Jason asked.

"Cat-o-nine tails and then the brig," James said grimly. "That means the 'Leopard.'"

Vivian nodded agreement.

"I wish the 'Clipper' were here. She could sail rings around the frigate."

"Not to worry. The "Sally" can keep up with a frigate, even with the cannon."

Jason looked questioningly at his father.

"Have Skinny select the crew, put four nine pounders with powder, balls, water and provisions and all that on her. She should sail tomorrow," James said.

"She'll be ready by the time I get back," Jason said, declaring his intention to captain the "Sally."

"Right," Vivian said. "The "Leopard" won't be sailing for Halifax for several days. It will take that long for the English to react to Jefferson's pressure over the 'Chesapeake.' Then, they will want to get her to Halifax out of our reach."

"They'll probably send her back to England from Halifax," James said.

"Maybe," Vivian said as she and James stepped from the porch.

"I'll catch Skinny at the Pig, give him his instructions, and then get out to the Short Hills," Jason called.

"Tell Skinny to report to us after he gets started, either at the *Herald* or here," James ordered.

"We have some writing to do," Vivian agreed.

"And when you get back, see us before you go sailing off," James ordered.

Jason watched as the old couple hurried down Union Street. He was surprised to see his father, who usually slouched as he moped along, walking briskly with a spring in his step.

ABOARD THE "LEOPARD"

JUNE 1807

Toddy lay silently and pondered his alternatives. His head throbbed from the blow delivered by the English officer, but he was conscious. He was unshackled, but the officer sat in the stern with one foot planted on Toddy's back. Toddy considered leaping overboard before they reached the English schooner, but his common sense told him this would accomplish nothing. They would either shoot him in the water for attempting to escape or retrieve him and beat him again. He decided that if he remained passive they would treat him less harshly and maybe give him the opportunity to persuade the schooner's captain that he was American.

The rowers on the port side boarded their oars, carelessly dropping them on top of the prone Toddy. The blade of one hit him squarely on the back of his head. The blow hurt, and Toddy fought back the urge to complain.

"One deserter, captain," the lieutenant called.

Toddy looked up and saw an older officer peering at him from the rail of the schooner.

"Doesn't look like much. Quickly, get him back on board. "Leopard" is signaling for an immediate Captain's assembly."

"On your feet, Satterfield," the lieutenant kicked Toddy viciously in the ribs. "Or you'll feel more than the side of my blade."

Hands grabbed Toddy by the arms, and he found himself forced to his feet in the unstable long boat.

"Be alert, there," the captain shouted as the long boat bounced sharply against the schooner's hull. "I'll have you eating Mrs. Murray's porridge if you mark the 'Belona.'"

Toddy recognized the threat. Deserters told the story of being forced to eat Mrs. Murray's porridge. Sailors were bent over the barrel of a ship's cannon, lashed down and whipped unconscious with the cat. Somehow the scene evoked the image of a tar eating slop from a bowl like a cat and gave rise to the threat.

Within minutes, the long boat was hoisted aboard the schooner and secured in place on the unsteady deck.

"Bring her about and make a course for 'Leopard,'" a firm voice ordered.

"What shall I do with this devil?" The lieutenant asked.

"Shackle him to the aft rail," the captain ordered. "We'll deal with him later."

Two burly seamen shoved Toddy aft and within minutes he found himself chained to the stern rail.

"You be facin' the cat soon, mate," one of the seamen muttered.

Toddy sensed a glimmer of compassion.

"What'll happen to me?"

"Same as begits all ye unfortunates unlucky to be caught."

The seaman did not explain, and Toddy did not ask. Seamen rushed about raising the sails. A few cast pitying glances in Toddy's direction, but most scurried about their tasks, ignoring his presence. The sails filled as the schooner turned and ran before the wind towards Lynnhaven Bay and its rendezvous with the frigate. Toddy peered over the stern at the "Sally." He felt hollowness in his stomach when he saw his ship's sails unfurl. The "Sally" turned into a port tack and raced away in the opposite direction, abandoning Toddy to his fate.

The schooner captain ignored him, giving Toddy no opportunity to plead his case, to point out the grievous mistake that had been made. He sank to the deck and braced his back against the stern rail. His hands were lashed behind him, and the chain held him tight. He tried to force himself not to worry, to watch the schooner's officers and crew, searching for positive signs.

Within half an hour, the "Belona" approached "Leopard." Toddy viewed the immense frigate with despair and a growing fear that he would never see his family, Alexandria, America again. Gone was his freedom, his chance for command. In their place he faced a life of drudgery and abuse in the bowels of the English navy. Once Albion had you in her clutches, Toddy had heard, you were never free again. He knew that as a deserter he would face maltreatment even worse than that afforded a regular seaman.

"The Commodore orders that the deserter be brought on board," an authoritative voice ordered over a voice trumpet, calling from the frigate's bow rail.

"Good," the hostile lieutenant who had boarded "Sally" said as he approached Toddy. "Get him aboard 'Leopard,'" he gruffly ordered the two burly seamen who now stood nearby.

"What's going to happen to me?" Toddy asked plaintively.

"Sorry mate," the seaman who had shown a spark of kindness replied softly, speaking so the officer could not hear. "The bastards have four others from the "Chesapeake" on board "Leopard." You'll be lumped with them, I fear."

"What does that mean?"

"A taste of the cat, the brig, and a sea voyage to Old Bailey."

"Prison?"

The tar looked back to the lieutenant who had returned to the quarterdeck to talk with the schooner's captain. The seaman nodded his head in reply to Toddy's question and then whispered a warning.

"Watch out for that one," he indicated the lieutenant.

"He's one of "Leopard's" officers, and a real mean one at that."

Before Toddy could ask another question, the other seaman succeeded in loosening the chains and jerked him to his feet. His hands were still bound behind him.

"Hurry him along," the lieutenant shouted.

"He wants to display his prize," the seaman muttered.

As soon as Toddy's feet hit the frigate's deck, the lieutenant gave him a vicious shove. Toddy stumbled forward and fell, hitting his head on one of the mainsail capstans. He felt blood spurt from a gash on his right temple. He blinked trying to keep it out of his eye. He could not wipe it because his hands were still tied tightly behind him.

"Take him to the brig," the lieutenant ordered.

Once again coarse hands pulled him to his feet.

"This way, mate," a tar said, not unkindly, as he and another seaman lifted Toddy to his feet.

"Poor bastard. Caught ye, did they?"

Toddy obediently tried to keep his feet and do what he was told. He was dragged forward along the main deck then shoved down a narrow passageway leading to the bowels of the ship. Several times they passed hurrying crewmen. Toddy was conscious of the blank stares as the seamen watched his descent. When they finally reached what Toddy assumed to be the cable room in the ship's bow—he could hear the swells smashing into the ship's hull far over his head— one of the seamen grabbed him to keep him from staggering into a thick door that blocked the passageway. The second seaman placed his mouth near a small, barred opening, no more than six inches square, and shouted.

"Gorse! Open up! We have another."

Toddy heard the ring of keys as they rattled against each other. Someone shoved a key into a lock on the other side of the door, turned it three times, and then pulled the door open. Inside was the largest, dirtiest man Toddy had ever seen.

Black broken teeth protruded from the front of his wide mouth. He smiled cruelly at Toddy. Without a word, he reached out, grabbed Toddy by the hair and pulled him through the partly opened door. With a minimum of effort he slung Toddy forward, crashing him to the floor. The giant shoved the door shut, rattled his keys, and turned the lock three times.

"Good luck, mate," one of the sailors called through the grate.

Toddy listened as their heels clacked on the floor as they retraced the passageway.

The huge man laughed, grabbed Toddy by one of his still bound arms and effortlessly pulled him to his feet. He dragged Toddy several feet down the unlighted corridor, paused, unlocked a solid door and shoved Toddy inside. Toddy lay on the floor where he fell. The room was pitch dark. The giant leaned over and swatted Toddy on the side of the head with his open palm. Toddy's head snapped left, hit the hard wall, and he fell unconscious.

Later—Toddy did not know whether minutes or hours had passed—he awoke in blackness. His head ached all over. He raised his hands to touch it, to assess the damage. He had to clench and unclench his hands; the rope had cut off the circulation, and he could not feel his fingers. Gradually, movement restored his sense of touch. He carefully felt the caked blood on the side of his head. The bleeding mercifully had stopped. He touched the back and the sides above his ears. It took him several minutes to decide the damage was minimal. He pivoted his head on his neck, and sharp daggers of pain forced him to stop. He felt the coarse deck underneath him, but he could see nothing. He blinked his eyes, but only blackness remained. He did not know if he were blind or simply without light. He remembered James' stories of his imprisonment on Admiral Howe's flagship. The thought gave him hope. James had survived; so could he.

Toddy pushed himself into a seated position with his back against the wall. He turned and his foot banged hard against the opposite wall. He was unable to extend his leg. His cell was no more than three feet wide. He forced himself erect with the two walls to his sides. He reached in front of himself and took one step. His extended fingers rubbed against the curved wall of the hull. He turned, took two steps and felt the door. His cubicle was no more than three foot wide and five foot long.

Toddy shuddered and wondered how long a man could survive in such a space in the darkness. He did not have room for even the slightest exercise. Within days he would be a blind, crippled wreck. Toddy willed himself to fight the panic. He lowered himself to the floor and leaned his back against the door, relaxing when he extended his legs. He listened. Silence. He could not sense movement. The ship was at anchor.

Hours later, Toddy heard a scrape in the corridor outside the thick door. A small vein of dim light appeared under the door. Toddy knew hours had passed, but he did not know how many. He listened carefully, but he could not hear a sound. The door was too thick. He slid across his cell and turned with his back to the hull and face towards the door. He waited and waited.

Just as he was about to give up hope—he did not know what he waited for, the sound of a voice, any voice—the door was shoved open. The bulk of the giant sailor with the rotted teeth filled the doorway. The light of a distant candle flickered behind him. Toddy imagined he could smell the man's rancid breath. The silent man leaned over and dropped two objects to the floor. He backed out of the room and closed the door. Toddy studied the crack of light until it disappeared, and he was back in blackness.

Toddy crept forward, feeling cautiously. He assumed the tinny sound he had heard was the clatter made when the giant dropped his meal to the floor. His fingers found a damp spot. He carefully explored the area and discovered a battered tin cup on its side. The man had deliberately spilled his water. Toddy, remembering he had heard two sounds, spread his fingers and searched further. He encountered a thick, sticky mass. His mean gruel contaminated a five-inch area. Toddy retreated to the hull where he resumed his former position. Hunger pangs gnawed at his stomach. He remembered waking that morning and rushing with the crew topside without pausing for his morning biscuit. It seemed so long ago, but only a few hours had passed.

Later, the giant returned. He gave Toddy a slop bucket partly filled with salt-water. He ordered him to clean up his mess and to prepare for the night. Toddy assumed he was to scrub his cell then use the bucket for his bodily functions.

The next day—at least Toddy assumed it to be the next day—his door opened, and remained opened. The giant directed Toddy to get his slop bucket and to follow him. To Toddy's surprise, the jailer led him down the dim corridor, leaving unlocked doors open behind him, then up through narrow passageways to the lower deck. Seamen stepped back whenever they encountered the plodding giant and stared with pity at Toddy. It was then that Toddy realized he was being used as an example of what would happen to the others if they attempted to desert.

Toddy dumped the bucket on command at the stern, then lowered it with a rope to the ocean to refill it. He thought about leaping overboard but rejected the idea, knowing it would be suicide. He followed the giant that one passing seaman respectfully called Gorse back to his cell. As Gorse watched, Toddy scrubbed. When he finally had his torture box spotless, he turned to face the silent man. Gorse indicated he should leave the slop bucket and follow him again. This time Gorse turned right, walked to the end of the corridor, and unlocked another door. He indicated for Toddy to enter, and he did. Gorse slammed the door shut behind him.

"Welcome mate," a cheerful voice greeted him.

Toddy studied the dimly lighted room. The speaker, a small, thin man, about ten years older than Toddy, lay on a dirty mat on the cell's far wall. He wore a dirty striped shirt. Three others sullenly watched Toddy from their mats. A scant three feet was available in the center of the room.

"A deserter?" The man who had spoken first asked.

"I'm an American," Toddy said defiantly.

"Don't blame me, mate," the man said. "Call me Jenk, short for Jenkins."

Toddy noticed the man's cockney accent.

"A deserter?" Toddy asked.

The man nodded proudly. "From His Majesty's sloop, the inglorious 'Halifax.'"

"And you gentlemen?" Toddy asked the others.

He received no reply. They sullenly ignored him.

"They be Americans, like yourself," Jenkins laughed.

Toddy later learned that all four men had been taken from the "Chesapeake" and charged with being English deserters. Only Jenkins admitted that the accusation was true. He had fled from the "Halifax" during a water visit to Norfolk. He had immediately enlisted on the "Chesapeake." During a chance meeting on the Virginia waterfront, he had encountered two of his former officers. Pleasantly drunk at the time and accompanied by mates, Jenkins had unwisely but rudely insulted his former tormentors. They had complained to the English squadron commander, and it had been Jenkins' defiance that had led to the Admiral's orders, which precipitated the "Chesapeake Affair." The other three, also had been seamen on the "Chesapeake." Unlike Jenkins, they persisted in their claim of American citizenship, though Jenkins frankly confided that while currently Americans they had previously served on English ships. They were his mates.

Toddy immediately perceived why the English did not believe his denials. He spent three days in the locker with the four other "deserters." His first night in the dark room had been standard procedure. Jenkins explained that Gorse introduced every new guest to his jail with a night in the closet, a not unsubtle warning of what would follow if the prisoner did not behave himself. Toddy took the message seriously.

Three days after Toddy joined his cellmates, "Leopard" raised anchor and set to sea.

Jenk asked Gorse their destination, and the giant replied with one word: "Halifax."

Although Toddy and the others would have liked to know more, Jenk advised them not to bother asking Gorse.

"He knows no more," Jenk explained.

The days were long; the food terrible, and except for Jenk, the company miserable.

"Don't worry," the friendly Jenk advised. "It'll be worse."

He was right. On the third day at sea, at high noon, Gorse with a smile opened the door and beckoned for Jenk to follow him.

"This be it," Jenk told the others with a flash of fear in his dull brown eyes. "Be brave," he said softly.

He obediently followed Gorse who locked the door behind him.

One hour later, Gorse returned without Jenk. He pointed at another of Toddy's cellmates. Gorse locked the door behind him, and the two disappeared down the hallway. The exercise was repeated two more times until Toddy was alone. Then, his turn came. He obediently followed Gorse's broad back and jangling keys. Toddy struggled to keep his lips from trembling. He feared he was about to join his fellow "deserters" and dangle from a yardarm on a rope.

Again, the sailors they passed in the passageways stared with concern. Several muttered words of encouragement.

When they emerged in the bright sunlight on the fan deck, Toddy turned and stared at the masts. The sails were full, the canvas taut. To Toddy's relief, not one body swayed in the fresh wind. Sailors lined each side of the deck. Most were sour faced and watched Gorse and Toddy with disapproval. A few, however, appeared to be enjoying themselves. They were laughing and pointing at Toddy, enjoying jests at his cost.

"Next time, mate, don't be caught," one called.

Gorse led the way to the stern. There, Gorse stepped back leaving, Toddy alone.

"Thirty strokes," a stern faced officer wearing a clean blue and white uniform with full epaulets ordered.

Toddy assumed he was the ship's captain. Several officers, including the sneering lieutenant, flanked him.

Two seamen grabbed Toddy by the arms and rushed him to a twenty-four pounder, the last in a long row of large cannon lined with their muzzles facing closed firing holes. The two men halted before the cannon and ordered Toddy to remove his blouse. Toddy saw pools of blood and pieces of flesh decorating the barrel and the immediate deck.

To his right a muscular bosun stood wiping his cat with a bloody cloth. Toddy recognized the striped shirt that Jenk had worn. The cat's leather wrapped handle was about a foot long, the leather stained with brown smears. The bosun carefully rubbed each of the nine leather throngs with the striped rag, pausing to clean each of the nine knots in each leather string. He hesitated and gave particular attention to the leather sinker at the end of each throng.

"All right bosun. Get on with it," the captain ordered.

The bosun nodded to the seamen who bent Toddy over the unforgiving iron of the cannon. They expertly lashed his hands and feet tightly. Toddy could not move. While he was testing the ropes on his wrists, he heard a grunt followed by a whistling sound.

The muscular bosun expertly brought the nine knotted throngs evenly across Toddy's back. The lead sinkers smashed against the cannon, and Toddy screamed in agony. His back was aflame. He had never suffered such pain.

Without pause, The bosun struck a second and a third and a fourth time. Toddy's mind had rebelled at his sudden first scream, embarrassed at the unmanliness of it all, but Toddy could not help himself. Each time the cat's nine tails bit deeper. Toddy's flesh and blood mixed with the gruel of the four men who had preceded him. Toddy prayed for unconsciousness, but none came. The bosun was an expert. At fifteen, his strokes were as even as they had been at one. The bosun, who had nothing against his victims, merely did his job.

At twenty, the pain lessened as Toddy's body tried to defend itself with numbness, but by then his mind was screaming with his voice. Twenty-five, and the cat continued its even beat. At thirty, Toddy's mind surrendered, and he collapsed into unconsciousness. A hiss swept through the assembled ranks as each seaman involuntarily exhaled a deep sigh of relief.

"Very well, bosun," the captain spun on his heels and returned to the quarterdeck.

The bosun nodded at the two seamen who moved quickly to untie Toddy's limp body. The bosun stooped, retrieved Toddy's shirt, and used it to wipe his cat.

A whistle sounded.

"All hands to duty stations," a deep-throated mate relayed the captain's order from the bridge.

Most of the seamen frowned as they returned to their posts. They had witnessed four men receive thirty lashes, and the fourth, Jenkins, a defiant, repeat deserter, had suffered one hundred. The captain announced that when recovered he would be hung from the foremast yardarm as an example to his peers.

The two seamen carried Toddy's torn and bleeding body below.

An hour later Toddy awoke to the groans of his companions. He lay on his stomach in a taut hammock. His back was stiff, and he could not move. The pain was almost unbearable. The flames ate at him from neck to backside.

"I've seen worse," a voice spoke beside him.

Toddy realized that somebody was coating his back with a thick, greasy substance.

"Not to worry," the voice indifferently reassured him. "The bosun knows his job. One of the best with the cat I ever seen."

A sudden bolt of pain flashed through Toddy's body. The man's fingernail had caught in a flap of torn flesh.

The man flipped a piece of Toddy's skin that had caught in his long fingernail onto the floor, then resumed his coating.

"You'll be about in three days. Not as agile at first as before, but able to work the slop buckets. Maybe in a week you'll be back in the riggin' if the captain doesn't change his mind and string you lads besides Jenkins."

Toddy opened his eyes and fought the pain. He could not raise his neck but through his left eye he saw his four companions lying in a row. Their backs were coated with a black substance. Blood oozed through the grime and dripped to the floor. The battered Jenkins, three bodies over, groaned. His blood ran in small torrents.

"Not to worry mates," his parched voice cracked.

Three days later a mild mannered bosun appeared at the side of Toddy's hammock.

"All right, mate. On your feet, and she'll be right."

Toddy raised his head and studied his tormentor.

"Last in, first out," the man said.

Toddy did not regret the man's appearance. For three days he had suffered in the twenty-two inch space allotted to each seaman. Two days ago, a summer storm had struck, and the frigate had rolled and moaned. Each of the hammocks in the thirty-hammock row had swung with the ship's motion. Toddy's back, which had started to scab, stung and burned, but the brutal pain had subsided. Thirty hammocks swinging in motion had combined with the ship's twisting rolling to make Toddy seasick. Each turn had caused Toddy to retch painfully into the slop bucket that a thoughtful crewmate had placed underneath Toddy's perch, maybe out of compassion but probably in self-defense. The agony had led Toddy to resolve to raise his tortured body today, and the mate's appearance gave him additional motivation.

Toddy, still on his stomach, lowered his left leg to the floor and slid sideways. The bosun caught his arm and held it while Toddy righted himself. He felt the tear of the scabs on his flesh.

"She'll hurt at first, then you'll be right," the man promised. "I've felt the bite of the cat me-self."

Toddy and his three cellmates, now granted the liberty of the ship, devoted the ensuing days to emptying slop buckets and mopping heads, the meanest shipboard jobs that could be found.

Once an hour Lieutenant Wythe, the red faced officer who had impressed Toddy, found a reason to pass by and torment him. Wythe seemed to consider Toddy's rehabilitation a personal crusade. He took particular delight in the fact that Toddy appeared a stranger to English sea customs and to the layout of a battle frigate. Wythe, a cruel and sadistic man, was hated by the entire crew.

Jenkins, crippled by his one hundred strokes, continued to lie helplessly in his hammock. Toddy did what he could to alleviate the pain, but more than flesh seemed to have been broken. The ship's doctor never reappeared after that indifferent first day, and Jenkins drifted in a moaning semi-consciousness. Presumably, the ship's officers wanted the crew to witness what happened to deserters, particularly unrepentant, second time offenders.

While Toddy's back healed and he enjoyed the liberation from the brig, his depression continued. He dumped the slop buckets and wondered if he would ever get a chance to escape. The prospects did not appear good. The other crewmembers confided that "Leopard" was heading northward away from American waters. The confrontation with the "Chesapeake" had created some kind of diplomatic imbroglio. During the period Toddy had been confined in the ship's hold, the captain had received sealed orders from the English Minister in Washington. Normally, a naval squadron commander did not accept orders from diplomats, only from his fleet admiral and the War Office, but the orders from Washington which the captain did not share had contained a report of American reaction which indicated that the "Leopard" may have precipitated war. In order to personally defend himself with his superiors, the captain weighed anchor for Halifax.

This was bad news for Toddy. He had talked with the crew enough to learn that the frigate was virtually a prison ship. Only those crewmembers that the officers trusted were allowed ashore in the best of conditions. Toddy reasoned that once his back healed he might be able to leap from the frigate and swim to shore when the ship approached for reprovisioning or water, but Halifax presented a different story. In the British port, he would have no refuge. Shore patrols would simply sweep him up and return him to ship to face punishment as a second time deserter. Toddy had no wish to remain on board ship, but he certainly could not face one hundred lashes and near death like Jenkins.

As hopeless as Toddy felt the situation he faced was, he would have been noticeably cheered if he could have witnessed a sight that appeared over one hundred miles to "Leopard's" stern.

Jason, Skinny and J.J. stood on the quarterdeck of the "Sally." J.J., who the "Sally" had picked up in Yorktown, had just completed a twelve-hour, red-eyed watch in the crow's nest. He had reluctantly descended the quivering mast at dusk.

"Three days and not one sighting," he complained.

"Don't worry, lad. We know where she's heading."

J.J. nodded, but Jason's words did not raise his spirits. He could still picture the exuberant Toddy on the night they had spent together in Norfolk. Neither could have imagined that the next day Toddy would be captured and buried in the hold of an English ship. J.J. had returned to Williamsburg. Like the others, he had been incensed when he learned of the cowardly attack by "Leopard" on "Chesapeake," but he had no way of knowing that his cousin had been seized the next day. Four days later a courier delivered a letter from "Gramps" detailing the bad news. Two days after that he joined Jason and Skinny on "Sally" and sailed for Norfolk where they learned that "Leopard" and its squadron had upped anchor and departed Lynnhaven Bay, sailing northward. Jason immediately surmised that "Leopard" was fleeing for Halifax with its prisoners, fearful that its continued presence off the American shore would serve as a flaunting reminder that could provoke an excited populace to the brink of war.

The "Sally" was now in pursuit. Neither Jason nor Skinny nor J.J. dared voice the key question. What would they do if they found the "Leonard?" They did not know for sure that Toddy was on board the frigate, and even if he were, not one of the three could propose a plan for recovering him safely. For all they knew, he could already be hanging from a yardarm. The crew, many of whom had been on the "Sally" when Toddy had been taken, were all volunteers, tough and determined, but they were no match for a British squadron led by a fifty-five gun frigate. Their four nine pounders and arsenal of pistols and cutlasses were greatly overmatched.

All they could do was pursue the flying English squadron and pray for luck.

FEDERAL DISTRICT OF WASHINGTON

JULY 1807

"Mr. Satterfield," Secretary of State James Madison, the "Mouse," as Buster had pegged him, addressed Buster formally. "I fully understand your concern over your cousin, and I assure you the United States Government is doing everything in its power to rectify the unfortunate situation."

Buster listened impatiently to Madison's words and immediately concluded that the government would be of no assistance in obtaining Toddy's release.

"Impressment is a dreadful act," Madison continued, apparently assuming that by lecturing Buster, he could assuage the problem. "And the 'Chesapeake Affair' as you so aptly dubbed it marks a turning point. Although we are not going to give up our efforts, the English behavior makes it perfectly clear that diplomatic pressure will not be enough. I assure you that President Jefferson and myself are determined to make the English apologize and cease this dreadful violation of our sovereignty."

"I appreciate your determination, particularly in view of the reaction of the American people," Buster said wryly, referring to the popular demand for a declaration of war. "And I agree we must be insistent on the principle of our sovereignty, but I am more concerned about the fate of my cousin Toddy Satterfield."

"I share your reaction," Madison frowned, indicating he felt Buster was being unreasonable. Madison rose to his full five feet six inches, turned his back on Buster, and peered out the window at his splendid view of the Potomac.

Buster waited impatiently for Madison to continue.

"I assure you that we are doing everything possible," Madison said, turning back to face Buster.

"And that is?"

Madison glared at Buster's impertinence.

"It's not possible for me to share every government secret with you and your newspaper. Diplomacy to be effective must be conducted in private."

"Have you cited Toddy Satterfield by name in your discussions with the English government?"

Madison's pause told Buster that he had not.

"And if you haven't, will you?"

"Certainly. We will leave no stone unturned."

"And if diplomacy fails?"

"There are always economic sanctions. They are under active consideration."

Buster recognized it would be futile to point out that economic sanctions had been used before with no avail against a power that controlled the world's seas. Any ploy that hurt the American people more than the intended victim was doomed to failure. Buster also knew he was wasting his time. Madison could protest to the British Minister in Washington, instruct Monroe in London to issue a demarche, or send a protest to London directly from Washington. Any message sent either by the English Minister or Madison to London, whether to the English Government or Monroe, would require a minimum of four to six weeks. Their response, and one could predict the initial reaction would not be definitive, would consume another four to six weeks. By then, Toddy would be either dead or lost in the morass of the English Navy.

Buster also realized that Jefferson had reduced the army and navy to the point where threats were meaningless. The government could not defend American harbors, let alone speak of retribution. Buster decided his only hope would be to persuade Madison to deal directly with the English Minister in Washington and ask him to intervene directly with the English Admiral in Halifax, ordering him to rectify the grievous error by releasing Toddy forthwith.

"And you know, Mr. Satterfield, though it pains me to say it, there is another problem." Madison paused and watched Buster for a reaction.

"And that is?" Buster asked coldly.

"If I may speak frankly," Madison began and hesitated for effect before continuing. "My use of the name Satterfield with the English might be counterproductive."

"Why is that?" Buster glared at Madison, dropping any semblance of cordiality.

"It is no secret that your father operates privateers in the Indies. I have heard that your "Clipper" has taken many English prizes. They consider this illegal behavior that should be punished. I understand that at this very moment your father has additional privateers under construction in Alexandria. Who will be their prey but the English? Do you expect them to react kindly to the mention of the name Satterfield? By making an issue of Toddy's capture, you may provoke your relative's hanging as a pirate."

"Toddy is not a privateer. He was on an American commercial vessel in American territorial waters."

"I understand that, but the English may think we are splitting hairs. Does not the "Sally" belong to your father who is responsible for the privateering?"

Buster had to admit that Madison's point was well taken, but he sensed the man was not trying to be helpful. He was paying Buster and Jason back for their failure to support the Jefferson administration.

"I know nothing about my father's shipping business. I can assure you, however, whatever the case, that Toddy is an innocent victim and deserves the support of his government."

"And what do you expect us to do?"

"At the very least, you might register an official complaint with the English Minister in Washington. Do what you must over the 'Chesapeake Affair' but ask the Minister to intercede with his Admiral in Halifax on Toddy's behalf. Since the English pretend they only impress English deserters, point out that a clear mistake has been made in this case that they can rectify immediately."

"I shall do that," Madison said. "Do you have any views as an influential citizen on the 'Chesapeake Affair?"

Buster did not want to say anything that would lead Madison to renege on his commitment.

"If I were President Jefferson, I would do what my father is doing."

"And pray what is that? Engage in illegal activities?"

"No! Prepare for war because I assure you diplomatic pressure and economic sanctions failed before 1776 and will do so again."

This time Madison paused before responding.

"Strictly between us, as gentlemen, and not for your newspaper, I must confess that I agree most wholeheartedly with you. However, diplomacy and economic pressure must be exhausted first. The final decision is not mine, but I assure you considerable attention is being paid to our lack of military might. This is a subject for the Congress to redress."

Recognizing that further discussion would be counter-productive, Buster thanked Madison for his time and departed, unsure whether or not the man would live up to his promise to intercede with the English Minister.

Upon leaving the State Department offices, Buster rode directly to the Capitol hoping to find John Randolph. He had heard that Randolph was in town attempting to rally support for an effort to pressure Jefferson to recall the adjourned Congress for a special session to consider the "Chesapeake Affair."

Fortunately, he found Randolph at his boarding house not far from Capitol Hill. Unfortunately, Randolph's mood was not good.

"President Jefferson refuses to call the Congress into session," the prissy legislator declared without preamble. "He is afraid we might declare war. In that he may be right because we are not prepared for it. He claims the Executive is making every necessary preparation, and what could that be? Without Congress he cannot mobilize a more extensive army and navy."

"Mr. Randolph, I have just met with Mr. Madison," Buster interjected hoping to interrupt Randolph's speech and focus him on Toddy's problem.

"I hope you enjoyed yourself," Randolph laughed. "Nobody else does with our brave Secretary of State."

"I appealed on my cousin Toddy's behalf," Buster said.

"Ahh," Randolph became serious. "An unfortunate occurrence. Your relative has suffered the same fate as hundreds of other American seamen. What is his government doing for him?"

"Only talk, I'm afraid. Mr. Madison promised to present a demarche to the English Minister, asking him to intervene with the English Admiral."

"He should do this for every impressed American," Randolph asserted. "Is there anything I may do to help?"

Buster noted the clever gleam in Randolph's eyes. The politician had seen an opportunity. Buster, no novice, was prepared to bargain.

"Mr. Monroe in London may be able to assist."

"But of course. I will write a letter immediately. What should I say?"

Buster briefed Randolph of the details of Toddy's seizure. He stressed that Monroe's presentation should emphasize that the unfortunate situation gave the English the opportunity to demonstrate their good will. In the face of American protests over the "Chesapeake Affair," the English could admit a mistake was made in Toddy's case and release him.

"This generous act would demonstrate the English argument that they impress only English citizens," Buster said.

"And by doing so, they can show they are willing to rectify a mistake," Randolph concluded enthusiastically. "I will have a private letter on the next ship departing for England. Is there something I can do here? Talk with the President? Madison? The English Minister?"

"I think the English Minister would be useful."

"Excellent."

The two men discussed the approach in detail. Finally, Randolph concluded with a lament.

"If Congress were in session, I could give speeches."

Buster agreed.

"The President has informed me I am being counter productive in trying to force an immediate session of the Congress. He states that sufficient information is not at hand to permit informed legislative action. First, diplomatic negotiations must be completed before Congress can address the next steps. I, of course, do not agree. We may not be able to declare war, which the President wishes to avoid at this time, but we can assist in preparing for war."

"The President does not agree?"

"He does not. He confides that he soon will call for Congress to convene on October 26th. Meanwhile, he plans to return to Monticello for the summer months. Is that leadership in the time of crisis?"

"And Mr. Madison?"

"The same. Home for the bad months."

Randolph noted Buster's dismayed reaction.

"But don't worry," Randolph smiled. "Friends will help friends."

Randolph waited for Buster's nod of appreciation and was not disappointed. Buster prepared to leave.

"And another subject, Mr. Satterfield," Randolph delayed him with a limp hand on Buster's wrist.

"Have you been able to consider the subject of our last conversation?" Randolph asked, referring to his suggestion that Buster and the *Herald* consider supporting Monroe should he return home and contest Madison's bid to replace Jefferson as president.

Buster looked Randolph squarely in the eyes, attempting to convey his absolute sincerity.

"I have. I will."

"You will support Mr. Monroe's candidacy over Mr. Madison?"

"You have my firm commitment."

"Personally and in the *Herald*?"

"Yes."

"Will you contest a seat in the Congress for yourself as an Old Republican candidate?"

"No."

"Well, one can't have everything," Randolph smiled and offered his hand to cement the bargain.

"So," James summarized the situation. "The 'Revenge" sailed on July 17th for Europe with Randolph's letter for Monroe and Madison's demarche, whatever it may be."

James paused long enough for Buster to nod his head.

"And Randolph has talked with the English Minister. Are you sure of that? Can we trust Randolph?"

"He has his peculiarities," Vivian added before Buster could respond.

In the back of the shop, the printing press clattered. Buster's head ached from the noise and from his grandparents' persistence.

"I'm sure we can trust him," he finally answered. "He wants something in return."

"That you promised without consulting us," James accused. He had made no secret of his dissatisfaction with Buster's agreement to support Monroe.

"Oh, Gramps," Buster protested. "I had no choice. We must get Toddy back whatever the cost."

James glared. He had to agree, but he did not like it. To be placed in political partnership with an unpredictable rogue like Randolph was not something he could swallow lightly.

"At least he's a relative," Buster appealed to Vivian who responded with an enigmatically sweet smile but said nothing.

"Jason, J. J., Skinny and the 'Sally' are underway and searching," James continued his synopsis. "Presumably, the English Minister has sent his intervention to the Admiral in Halifax."

"I can't guarantee that," Buster said. "I can only hope he has."

"And the public is aroused," James said.

"Cruiky expects a large turnout for the parade this afternoon."

"Another wonderful bedfellow," James said.

Buster referred to Cruiky Cruikstaff, Richard Hodges' second at the almost forgotten duel. Cruiky had emerged as a tool of the Old Republicans on Alexandria's town council. John Randolph had directed him to support Buster's campaign on Toddy's behalf, and Cruiky had grudgingly responded. Neither Cruiky nor Buster to James' regret had made Hodges' death a public issue.

"Our President has taken the high ground," Vivian contributed.

"Reparation for the past and security for the future," James snorted.

"Be fair, James," Vivian admonished. "Tom Jefferson has demanded reparations for the damage inflicted on the 'Chesapeake,' the release of all five seamen including Toddy, and abolition of all impressment of Americans from American ships."

"And he has ignored the thousands of other Americans who have been illegally seized by the English," James snorted. "He's doing the minimum."

"He knows the English refuse to consider the issue of impressment," Buster said.

"James, Buster," Vivian settled the issue. "It does no good to argue among ourselves. We have done all humanly possible for Toddy. All we can do is wait."

"What approach has the best chance of success?" Buster asked.

"Jason," Vivian and James answered simultaneously.

Buster studied his grandparents, then all three laughed together for the first time since Toddy's seizure.

HALIFAX, NOVA SCOTIA

JULY 1807

J.J. stood in the bow of the "Sally" and peered futilely into the thick fog. A mist of light rain drizzled from the gray sky. J.J. was soaked but oblivious of his discomfort. He knew it was dawn, but the thick, gray black clouds concealed the searching sun. A strong easterly wind and a heavy surf propelled the "Sally" shoreward. Jason had furled "Sally's" sails, all but the partially reefed mainsail, and still the brisk wind propelled the ship forward at a dangerous clip. Only one member of the crew had ever visited Halifax, and he stood at J.J.'s side.

"I can't see shit," the man complained, unable to conceal his fear.

"We're near land," J.J. said. "I can hear the surf. Listen."

"I hear it," the man replied, the fright causing his voice to break.

The "Sally" was approaching the English port blind. Every man on board knew that a minor mishap in the fog would result in sudden capture. The English flag hung from "Sally's" mast, but in the fog it offered no protection. Jason's plan, the little he had shared, depended on the pennant's acceptance by the crews of the English men-of-war who were anchored somewhere ahead of them. Certainly, Jason had suggested, the confident English would be relaxed in their home port; none could expect an American schooner to be so foolish as to sail directly under their cannon. Jason did not know whether his cousin Toddy was in Halifax or not. The "Sally" had not sighted the "Leopard" and its squadron during the entire weeklong sail northward. All they had was Jason's certitude. He just knew the English had taken Toddy to Halifax. Now, he refused to delay a few hours and wait for the fog to lift.

"It'll be easier to sneak into port in the fog," Jason had said, ignoring the fact that no one on board "Sally" had the slightest idea where Halifax was.

"If we miss the shoals, we'll beach her on the shore rocks," the seaman complained softly. "And we'll be lucky to do that. Otherwise, we'll climb the stern of a man-o-war."

"We have to anchor," J.J. concluded. "A few more minutes and we'll be on the beach."

J.J. turned and hurried sternward towards the quarterdeck. There, he found Skinny standing anxiously behind the helmsman, waiting to promptly relay every order. As soon as J.J. appeared, Skinny nodded mutely towards the port rail where Jason leaned with elbows on the rail and his left ear turned towards the shore.

"We'll beach her in minutes," J.J. blurted.

"Bring her into the wind. Drop anchor," Jason ordered.

The helmsman did not wait for the order to be relayed. He immediately spun the wheel and brought "Sally's" bow to the windward. The mainsail flapped in protest, and several crewmen rushed forward to lower and furl the last piece of canvas. All but Jason and J.J. sighed with relief. Now, they anticipated, Jason would wait for the fog to lift. They could learn where they were and under the protection of the false pennant seek a safe anchorage. It was foolish to come this far.

"Lower the boat," Jason ordered.

J.J. and Skinny rushed to the "Sally's" waist to assist the crew. Neither intended to be left behind.

As soon as the longboat was in the water, Jason joined Skinny, J.J. and two crewmen.

"Shove off and take us to shore," Jason ordered the two rowers.

As soon as they were clear of the "Sally," the surf caught the boat and drove them beachward. It was all the two experienced rowers could do to keep the bow pointed toward the shore. Within minutes, the boat crunched into hard gravel. All jumped out into the knee-deep cold water and pulled the heavy boat's bow onto shore.

"Wait here," Jason ordered the two crewmen.

He turned and headed away from the water. On land, the fog was lighter; they could see maybe five steps in front of them. Jason, followed by J.J. and Skinny, scrambled over the boulders that faced their narrow strip of rocky beach. After a climb of about fifteen feet, the land leveled out, and they crossed a sandy dune covered with foot long, dried grasses.

"Which way now?" J.J. whispered to Skinny who answered with an unknowing shrug.

Suddenly, Jason halted and held up a hand signaling for silence. J.J.'s sharp ears detected a familiar sound, the crunch of wagon wheels on gravel. On their left a dim light appeared. It was nothing but a round, dull glow in the mist. As the three men watched, the glow steadily came closer, and the crunching grew louder. A horse snorted. Suddenly, a wagon appeared.

"Whoa," a voice called. "What be ye boys doing out here in this misery?"

"We're fisherman lost in the fog," Jason replied immediately. "We anchored off shore and came in with the long boat."

"Foolish business in these waters," the man declared.

"Why are you about yourself?" Jason asked.

"Tis my business. I've milk for the King's Navy," the man said.

"In Halifax?"

"Where else?"

"Will you give us a ride?"

"Can't walk five minutes?" The man asked.

"Not in this fog," Jason replied.

"It'll cost you," the farmer said suspiciously.

"How much?"

"A shilling?"

"Done," Jason said, knowing that he was being taken.

"Hop in, and mind the milk. Spill any and ye'll pay."

Jason, J.J. and Skinny climbed into the back of the wagon. The farmer chuckled and slapped the reins.

"How do you see in this stuff?" Jason asked, pretending to be friendly.

"Can't. But they knows the way so well they don't have to see," the farmer indicated his team.

J.J. wondered how they would ever find their long boat again.

"Any farmhouses nearabouts?" Jason asked. "I might have to find my way back."

"Them rocks you climbed over. They're right on the point. If you're anchored there, a few hundred yards to your right is the entrance to the bay. Lucky you stopped there. The bay's filled with ships. The Admiral's having a conference."

"What about?"

"Don't ask me. Ask the Admiral."

The wagon jounced along in silence until the farmer decided to say more.

"Hear tell there's been trouble to the south."

"Yanks?" Jason used the word that the English applied to all Americans.

"None but."

Jason shrugged and feigned disinterest.

By the time they reached town, the sun had risen in the east, suffusing the sky with a gray light. The rain had stopped, and the wind had thinned the fog enough for them to see the outlines of the town. As best as they could tell, the harbor was filled with masts. The streets, however, were deserted.

"Where you be going?"

"Breakfast, hot and cheap."

"Ye be wantin' the Goose."

"The Goose?"

"Yep. Not much, but the food's cheap."

As he listened, J.J. decided the last thing he wanted was to eat in a Halifax ordinary surrounded by English seamen. He looked at Skinny and could tell from his expression that he felt as J.J. did. However, Jason was the boss. J.J. wished his cousin were less impulsive. He suddenly realized that neither he nor

Skinny carried weapons. Jason had his long knife with the "J.S." carved in the handle in a sheath anchored in his belt in the small of his back where his long shirt concealed it but that was all. J.J. longed for his hunting rifle and wondered what the three of them could do even if "Leopard" and its squadron were in Halifax, and Toddy were on board. The English would not let the deserters ashore, not even in an English port, not for a very, very long time. J.J. visualized the three of them sneaking on board an English frigate, overpowering the crew, and freeing Toddy. The thought made him shake his head in dismay.

"Here she be," the farmer stopped the wagon and held out his hand.

Jason extracted a leather bag from his pocket and carefully selected a worn shilling. He parted with it reluctantly. The farmer laughed.

He slapped the reins and without another word departed into the grayness of the morning.

"What do we do now?" J.J. whispered.

"We have a fine breakfast," Jason answered.

"And find out if "Leopard" is in port," Skinny added.

"And then talk with a member of her crew," Jason explained his plan.

The idea was simple but difficult of fulfillment. They ate a heavy breakfast in the busy ordinary, but found it difficult to linger. Most of the other patrons were sullen seamen recovering from hangovers and disinterested in talk with three strangers. Finally, after three abortive attempts to start conversation, Jason led his two companions back into the street. The fog had lifted, and the summer sun, lacking the heat it carried to the south, tried to burn away the grayness. Jason sent Skinny back to the longboat with instructions to return to the "Sally," find an inconspicuous anchorage, and then to rejoin Jason and J.J. in the late afternoon at the Goose. Jason reasoned that if they had no luck obtaining the information they needed from shopkeepers, they might find some drinking seamen willing to chat about their ships at one of the harbor front taverns.

By the time they rejoined Skinny and two of the sailors who had been on "Sally" when boarded—according to Skinny he thought they might help identify a "Leopard " crewman—they had learned that "Leopard" indeed was in port. Unfortunately, it was not accessible. "Leopard" and its squadron was anchored in the outer harbor. It was reprovisioning and taking on water, but all was transported to the frigate from the docks by the ship's crew and boats. Strangers were not welcome. J.J. and Jason had watched the reprovisioning for as long as they could. They succeeded in identifying several crewmen from the "Leopard." When finally evening fell, Jason dispatched the two sailors to scout the town while he, Skinny and J.J. returned to the docks and waited for one of the "Leopard's" boats to deliver off duty sailors to shore. Just as they were about to give up in failure, a long boat filled with loudly talking seamen docked.

"Leopard's?" Skinny asked, and Jason nodded.

The three followed the jostling sailors to the nearest ordinary, which was already filled with noisy tars. Jason paused, took Skinny by the arm, and spoke to J.J.

"Let's not all three appear together. You go first J.J. See what you can learn. If you're not able to make friends, come out and one of us will try. We'll wait over there," he indicated a second crowded tavern.

J.J., who Jason selected for the task because he reasoned the young man's appearance would be more disarming, entered the crowded ordinary. He was accustomed to the Pig in Alexandria and the ordinaries in Williamsburg that catered to students, but he had never seen anything like the waterfront tavern. The tables were full and the area near the bar jammed with flushed and belligerent seamen. J.J. was shoved and challenged twice before he was able to acquire a foaming mug. Each time a drunken tar wanted to fight, but J.J. carefully backed away. Finally, he found a place at the far corner of the bar where he could stand with his back to the wall, lean his elbows on the bar and have only his left flank exposed to the jostling seamen. During his first mug of ale, three fights developed. Each was quickly resolved by the large bartender who kept a hefty, polished club under the oak bar. If he could reach the swearing brawlers from the safety of his protective wood barrier, he would deftly swat the belligerent beside the head and let him fall to the floor where he was quickly ignored. Eventually, the subdued drunk would arouse, look in confusion about, rub his sore head, conclude he had fallen accidentally, and return to the fray.

J.J. watched and listened with dismay to the mass confusion that bubbled about him. He learned nothing of "Leopard" and worried that he would not be able to escape from the bedlam unchallenged. J.J., a husky young man, was proud of his muscular frame and ability to defend himself, but his short observation had made him leery of the bartender's quick club. He had no interest in being bashed along side the head while thrashing another.

Suddenly, a giant of a man appeared beside him. Toddy sipped his ale and looked out of the corner of his eye at his new companion. He feared that any frank look would be misinterpreted, and he had no desire to test his strength against this hulking seaman. J.J. had heard a phrase to describe creatures like this one—"he was so large that he blocked out the light of day." The man leaned on the bar and grunted to indicate he wanted ale. The bartender, no midget himself, promptly responded. The giant folded an immense hand around the mug, lifted it to his thick lips and drank until the mug was empty. He smashed it back on the bar and grunted to indicate he wanted another.

"Sure, Gorse," the bartender quickly refilled the mug.

The huge creature wiped the semi-circle of foam from his upper lip. J.J. decided the man was not only the largest person he had ever seen but also the ugliest. Gorse appeared to sense J.J.'s scrutiny. He turned his massive head and studied J.J. with his globe-like eyes. He exhaled to indicate his disinterest in what he saw and returned to his ale. Again, he raised the mug to his lips, drained it and smashed it on the bar for more.

"Gorse's from 'Leopard,'" the bartender explained to J.J., nervously trying to make conversation to distract the giant.

J.J. did not know what to say, so he remained quiet and drained his mug in his own gesture of distraction.

"Gorse's the jailer," the bartender elaborated.

Gorse grunted disapproval, drank his ale, turned and pushed his way through the sailors who backed away as soon as they saw him coming.

J.J., relieved that the man had left, ordered another ale. The bartender promptly refilled J.J.'s glass.

"He didn't pay," J.J. observed.

"He never does. Would you try and make him?"

"No," J.J. said honestly.

Later, the bartender paused to chat with J.J. who unlike most of the patrons appeared friendly and unthreatening.

"Wow, the jailer, huh." J.J. said, a comment not a question.

"How would you like to be one of those five Americans from the 'Chesapeake' in his hands?" The bartender asked before responding to demands from the other end of the bar.

J.J. almost dropped his half-empty mug. He had his answer. Toddy was on board the "Leopard." He waited until the bartender approached, handed him a pound note, waved good-by and carefully picked his way through the mob of belligerents.

"Good work," Jason patted J.J. on the back when he had reported what he had learned.

"Christ," Skinny exclaimed. "Poor Toddy. I saw that monster. I'll fight the whole crew but not that guy."

Jason nodded grimly.

"Let's find the others and see if they have located any crewmen from the 'Leopard.' We have to talk with one of them, but not that monster."

To their disappointment, the two "Sally" crewmembers had had no success. They had found nobody who resembled the boarding party. Jason had not expected success; they had been looking for four men out of a crew of four hundred. The five men decided to return to the Goose and wait while Jason decided what to do next. Jason knew he had to locate a "Leopard" crewman they could interrogate and find out how Toddy was being treated and if there were any plans for bringing him ashore.

The night ended in disappointment. All five men spent the night at the Goose at Jason's expense.

The next morning Jason dispatched the two crewmen and Skinny on a mission about the town to identify a friendly seaman from the "Leopard" while he and J.J. went shopping. Jason required two hours to locate what he was looking for, a copy of Blackstone's "Commentaries." Jason paid a price that J.J. thought exorbitant and had the book wrapped in used brown paper and tied with string.

"What on earth do you need that for?" J.J. asked. Although he did not say it, he thought Jason had more important things to do than shop for a copy of an English book.

Jason only smiled in response.

"I must return to the Goose and study my purchase," Jason said.

"And I must search the town for a "Leopard" crew member," J.J. replied heatedly, making no effort to conceal his disapproval of Jason's behavior.

"Very well. If you see the others, tell them to join me at the Goose for dinner."

Jason returned to the Goose. When alone in his bare room, he unwrapped the book. He studied the worn cover, then grinned with pleasure. He took a stub of a pencil and a scrap of paper he had obtained from the ordinary proprietor and after much thought wrote a simple message.

"Tonight. Two Bells. Descend anchor cable."

After studying the message and deciding it was adequate, he opened Blackstone's Commentaries. He leafed through the pages, constantly studying his brief message. Eventually, he ended up with a series of three digit numbers. After double checking his numbers with different pages in the book, he set Blackstone aside. He copied the numbers on the sheet of used wrapping paper he had acquired from the storekeeper. They formed four lines across the page. He compared the lines with his original list. When satisfied that they were an accurate copy, he laid the paper face up on the table in front of him. He placed Blackstone in the center of the paper, then rewrapped the book and tied it with the string. He balled his original message and list of numbers and burned them in the fireplace. Then, he waited for J.J., Skinny and the crewmembers to join him for dinner.

Only J.J. and Skinny appeared; both were excited.

"While you were resting with your book," J.J. said accusingly, the boys found a friendly crewmember from the "Leopard."

"Where is he now?" Jason ignored J.J.'s tone. He understood the youth's agitation.

"At the ordinary near the pier," Skinny replied, carefully watching his friend. He knew Jason well enough to know that every action had meaning in a crisis.

"Good," Jason said and rose from the table where they were preparing to dine. "Don't order," he directed J.J.

In a few minutes Jason returned carrying the wrapped package.

"Take this, give it with this five pound note to the crewman, and tell him he shall have another after he has safely delivered it to Toddy."

"But why? What will he do with a book?" J.J. demanded.

"I'll tell you later. Just do as I ask. Tell the crewman the book is from Toddy's concerned family. It will give him something to pass his hours on board ship."

J.J. looked at Jason with skepticism in his eyes, but he took the book and did as he was ordered.

Within an hour, just as Jason and Skinny were finishing their meal, J.J. and the "Sally" crewmen appeared.

"It's done. We are to meet the sailor tonight and pay him his second five pound note," J.J. said.

"Good," Jason smiled graciously. "Now the three of you sit and have your meal. Skinny and I will keep you company."

That night the sailor from the "Leopard" returned and reported he had delivered the book to Toddy who had accepted it without comment. J.J. paid the man the second five pounds, and he departed happy.

"He probably threw the book away," one of the "Sally" crewmen observed sarcastically.

J.J. and his two companions finished their ales and were preparing to depart to report to Jason when one of the crewmen grabbed his companion by the arm.

"Don't look now, but I think a friend of ours just entered."

The two men kept their heads down and twisted with their backs to the door. Neither wanted to be identified in Halifax. Recognition could mean arrest and death.

"He's stopping at the bar," J.J. reported.

The two seamen turned.

"It's him," the second seaman confirmed.

"Who?" J.J., who had a frustrating day, demanded. He was irritated by Jason's refusal to explain his actions.

"The lieutenant who boarded us. The red-faced one who took Toddy."

"From the 'Leopard?'"

"The same."

"You two leave quickly now while his back is turned. Tell Jason. I will stay here and watch him. He won't recognize me."

The two men successfully departed without being seen. While J.J. watched, the red-faced lieutenant drank alone at the bar. He did not appear to have any friends. Two other officers entered the ordinary, saw the lieutenant at the bar, pointed and whispered, then deliberately sat at a table as far from the bar as they could.

Within twenty minutes Jason appeared. He joined J.J. at his table and signaled for a mug.

"Is he still here?" Jason asked.

"The red-faced lieutenant at the bar."

As Jason watched, the man rudely slammed his empty mug on the bar and demanded another.

"What shall we do?"

"Wait.

"For what?"

"Be patient J.J. We will wait until he leaves then go with him."

The minutes dragged past. After several mugs, the lieutenant became intoxicated and began to harass the middle-aged barmaid. At first, he simply patted her backside as she stood next to him at the bar relaying her orders. She countered by moving away from the lieutenant. Once, when he grabbed her by the arm as she passed and said something to her, she slapped him. After an initial flash of anger, the lieutenant laughed and ordered another mug.

"What are we going to do?" J.J. asked.

"Be patient," Jason replied.

Finally, the lieutenant carefully counted out some coins, threw them on the bar and departed.

"Now," Jason said. "You return to the Goose and tell the others to be ready to return to the "'Sally."

"But," J.J. began to protest but noted the flash of Jason's clear green eyes. They reminded him of the night in Brown's Brewery.

"Right," J.J. agreed and watched as Jason hurried from the room.

Jason summoned the barmaid and settled their bill. He then walked slowly out of the ordinary, deliberately concealing his nervousness.

The night was overcast and a fresh wind blew in from the harbor. Overhead, a dim half moon could be seen through the scurrying clouds.

"Watch it mate," two drunk sailors crowded past.

"The streets of Halifax were filled with drunken sailors and their hired women. J.J. looked in both directions, but Jason and the English lieutenant had vanished. He turned and did what he was told. He hurried back to the Goose to alert Skinny and the two crewmen.

Jason followed the staggering English lieutenant in the direction of the harbor. He knew he had to act before the man reached the pier. Just as the lieutenant lurched past a dark alley, Jason jostled him from the side.

"Hey, watch it, sailor," the lieutenant said threateningly.

Jason stepped close, smiling, and reached his left hand across his body, caught the lieutenant by the arm and turned him toward the alley. The officer pulled his arm to free it then froze when he felt the sharp jab of the long knife that Jason held in his right hand penetrate his side. Jason shoved hard enough to make his point then spoke.

"Easy mate. I just want a little talk. Walk down that alley."

The lieutenant, still feeling the courage of the alcohol, started to pull away. Jason held him firmly and shoved the knife a little harder. Pain shot along the Lieutenant's left side.

"Not feeling well? I'll help you." Jason spoke loudly and turned for the benefit of two drunken sailors who had paused to watch.

"Me mate had a little too much," he smiled, "but he'll be right."

The two sailors nodded and continued their boisterous stagger down the street.

"Move," Jason ordered and twisted the blade.

"Take my money," the lieutenant pleaded.

"Keep your money mate. I only want a few words."

The lieutenant responded to Jason's pressure and moved into the alley. It led between two dark buildings and emerged on a bluff overlooking the harbor.

"Here," Jason shoved the man roughly in front of him.

They descended the sharp slope to the water's edge. A boulder shielded the spot from the busy pier no more than forty yards away. Jason withdrew the knife from the man's side, spun him around and caught the point of the blade under his chin. He pushed upward, penetrating the skin. Blood flowed in a small stream onto the officer's dirty shirtfront.

"Name?" Jason demanded.

"Wythe, for God's sake. Take my money and let me go." The man's neck bent back trying to escape the knife's pressure.

"Rank?"

"Lieutenant."

"Ship?"

"'Leopard.' What does it matter? What do you want with me?"

"Position?"

"Command the boarding party."

"You take the deserters?"

"Yes."

"The 'Chesapeake?'"

"Yes. So what?"

Jason held the man's shirt front and shoved the knife deeper. The man desperately clutched Jason's knife hand.

"Let go," Jason warned and twisted the knife.

The man groaned with pain and held his hands away.

"Put them behind you," Jason ordered. "The more trouble you are, the longer this will take."

"What do you want?" The man pleaded.

"And the 'Sally?'" Jason asked.

"Yes. "

"You boarded her?"

"Yes. "

"Well, Lieutenant Wythe," Jason said. "There is just one thing I want you to know."

Jason paused and waited for his words to register.

"What's that, man?"

"Lieutenant Wythe. My name is Satterfield."

Jason watched as the recognition clouded Wythe's eyes. Satisfied the man knew who he was, Jason withdrew the knife from Wythe's neck with a flip that severed a jugular vein, stepped back, then plunged the knife deep under the breastbone into the heart. Wythe collapsed to the ground. Jason carefully wiped the knife with the initials "J.S." on the handle on the dead man's back. He lifted the back of his shirt and slipped the knife back into its sheath. It was the third time Jason had killed with the knife, and he had to treat it carefully. Although a present from his father, it was still one of James' prize possessions. He considered it a family heirloom that Jason one day would have to pass on to Buster or maybe Buster's son.

Jason reached down and ripped one gold epaulet from the lieutenant's blue uniform jacket.

HALIFAX, NOVA SCOTIA

JULY 1807

The half moon peeked through the sullen sky, providing barely enough illumination for J.J. in the bow of the long boat to make out the form of the anchored frigate. Despite their rag wrappings, the oarlocks shrieked an occasional protest that J.J. hoped was drowned by the crash of the folding whitecaps as they prepared to assault the nearby beach.

"Five minutes," Jason in the stern whispered.

"Jason says five minutes," one of the two men who sat at the oars repeated for J.J.'s benefit. "Stay alert."

"Board your oars," Jason ordered.

The two rowers immediately pivoted the blades of the oars into the boat. One inadvertently nicked the side, and J.J. winced at the sound. He knew that at night the slightest noise carried like the sound of a loose, windblown shutter in an empty house. He squinted, hoping the effort would improve his night vision, and studied "Leopard's" stern. As pleased as he was with Jason's stratagem which he had revealed when all were back on board "Sally," J.J. could not be sure that Toddy would remember James' tales about the codes he had used to communicate with agents in occupied New York City during the Revolution. If Toddy did recall the exciting stories, he would know that the three digit groups of numbers that Jason had written on the inside of the worn wrapping paper was a simple code. Jason had used Blackstone's "Commentaries" because that was the book James had employed, hoping the title would jog Toddy's memory if the seaman had delivered the "present" as he said he did. The numbers were keyed to the Blackstone text. In each three-digit group, the first number referred to page, the second to line on that page and the third to a word in the line. According to James, his agents had been briefed to use the first letter of the identified words. When all of the letters thus selected were put together, the agent had his message. Jason assumed Toddy would remember the code because two generations of

Satterfield children had gleefully communicated with each other using James' wartime cryptography.

If Toddy had received the book and had found the list of numbers on the wrapping paper and if he had remembered the code, he would descend the "Leopard's" anchor chain in three minutes. This also assumed that Toddy could slip from the crew quarters, bypass the ship's in-port watch, and climb down the cable chain without detection. J.J. worried that all these variables made Toddy's escape a very chancy endeavor. Knowing the English would allow Toddy only this one chance—if something went wrong he would be returned to Gorse's clutches—J.J. worried.

Jason's timing had been phenomenal. He had guided the longboat from the anchored "Sally" and had arrived at the frigate with only minutes to spare. Jason had stressed that every second they lingered near the "Leopard" greatly increased their chances of discovery. If that happened, the English would have four more Americans to hang from the yardarms.

The incoming waves forced the longboat dangerously close to the frigate. J.J. recognized that if Toddy did not soon appear they would have to put the oars back in the water and depart.

"He didn't get the message," one of the rowers whispered.

J.J. looked back at Jason who ignored the man. Jason's eyes studied the ship's looming bow, and J.J. grasped the sides of the long boat and stared into the gloom trying to locate a moving shadow.

"Put the oars back in the water and keep us near the chain, silently," Jason ordered.

The long boat had drifted some twenty yards from the angled chain.

J.J. had been about to surrender hope when he saw a shadow slip over the bow and appear to grasp the chain. It did not move. J.J. wondered if his eyes had played a trick upon him, flashing a false image on his straining vision. A sound made J.J. catch his breath. He heard two voices. Then, presumably part of the night watch, two men paused near the bow. J.J. could see their heads over the bowrail, but he could not hear what they said. J.J. willed that they be only two sailors passing the weary hours of a long night; in port, even on a man-of-war, they would be inattentive. J.J. looked at Jason and pointed upward. Jason nodded and grasped the knee of the nearest rower. He silently indicated the man should hold the oar in the water, motionless. If one blade should catch an errant tip of a whitecap, the noise would attract the attention of the watch. Minutes passed. J.J. again was about to give up hope. The long boat continued to drift, and J.J. knew they could not risk another approach.

Suddenly, the men in the bow turned and slowly made their way aft. Unbelievably, the shadow on the anchor chain began to descend. J.J. tried to imagine what Toddy must be thinking: excited to be so close to freedom; hurting from harsh treatment; placing his faith in his family rescuers, assuming they would be waiting at the point where the chain entered the water. He would not be able to climb back up the chain. If the long boat were not there, Toddy would plan to slip into the water, swim to shore and somehow make his way a thousand miles through the southern wilderness to freedom.

"Take us to the chain," Jason ordered, "quietly."

J.J. leaned forward in the bow, ready to grasp his cousin. He tilted his neck back and saw Toddy's form. J.J. caught the chain and held the long boat from scraping. Toddy's descending foot slipped on J.J.'s hand. J.J. reached up with his free hand and grabbed the back of Toddy's shirt. Toddy winced in pain.

"I've got him," J.J. whispered, then pulled backwards.

Toddy released his hold on the chain and fell into the boat landing on J.J. who in turn tumbled against the backs of the rowers who immediately began pushing the longboat stern first with the tide and surf away from the frigate. J.J., Toddy and Jason stared at the receding bow of the frigate, waiting for the watch to appear and give the alarm, alerted by the sound of J.J and Toddy falling backward.

Seconds passed; the tide and the oars pushed the longboat into the gloom.

"We've made it," J.J. whispered, exultantly hugging Toddy who lay on top of him on the deck of the boat.

Again, Toddy winced.

"Thank God," Toddy groaned and pulled himself erect, turning to sit in the bow and face J.J. and Jason.

"Thanks, Jason," Toddy sighed.

J.J. touched his cousin again as he sat beside him on the seat.

"Don't celebrate now," Jason cautioned, fighting a smile. "We're a long way from being out of this yet."

Fifteen minutes later they were on board "Sally."

"We must sail immediately," Jason said, whispering commands to the waiting crew who had joyously welcomed Toddy back.

"They will discover I am gone at first light," Toddy said. "The bastards hung Jenkins," Toddy blurted. "He was one of the crewmen from the 'Chesapeake.' They hung him from the yardarm just before we docked. All the crews on the other ships cheered."

"Let's give the bastards something to remember us by," Jason said impulsively.

His words sent a shiver up J.J.'s spine.

"Skinny," Jason ordered. "You get the ship underway and sail directly under the bow of the 'Leopard.' J.J. come with me. Toddy wait here." Jason, like the others, had noted Toddy's bent back.

Jason grabbed two crewmen and pulled them with him as he rushed forward.

"Hurry," he ordered. "Roll these two starboard cannon and put them in their places on the port side."

"They'll put the "Sally" out of balance," a sailor warned. "We'll lean to water. Open the ports and the sea'll sink us."

"Do as I say," Jason ordered.

J.J., the two crewman and Toddy, who had ignored Jason's instructions, hastily removed the pins locking the two starboard nine pounders in place and rolled them to the port to join the other two cannons. Jason sent other crewmen below to fetch powder and four balls.

"Lock them in place and load them. Don't open the ports and don't fire until I give the order."

Jason rushed back to the quarterdeck and relieved Skinny at the helm.

"Skinny, go forward. When I give the order, open the ports and fire as we pass 'Leopard.' We'll only have one pass then we'll have to run for it."

Skinny was glad to be relieved of the wheel. The weight of the cannon unbalanced the ship and made handling difficult.

"Give me a hand," Jason ordered the helmsman.

Together, the two men struggled to hold the bucking ship.

"All sails aloft," Jason ordered.

He looked up and saw Skinny still standing on the quarterdeck.

"Forward!" Jason ordered.

"Jason," Skinny pleaded. "When I open the ports, the sea will flood in and capsize us. It's not worth it."

"Go," Jason insisted.

In the distance, the form of the frigate materialized. Jason turned the wheel and prepared to pass "Leopard" moving as fast as the "Sally" could sail heading from the harbor towards the sea. Despite the tack into the northeasterly wind, the weight of the cannon tipped the "Sally" inward toward the frigate.

"This lean will force the muzzles downward," Skinny tried one last time, staring first at Jason and then at the approaching ship.

"Damn it, Skinny, that's the point. Take the wheel or the guns," Jason shouted.

Skinny finally realized Jason's intent. The cant of the ship would ensure that the cannon balls would strike "Leopard" below waterline. Four large holes and she would sink immediately, blocking a good portion of the channel and impeding pursuit.

Skinny had difficulty racing along the tilted deck. When he finally reached midship, he found J.J., Toddy and two crewmen standing beside the cannon holding lighted fuses. Four other crewmen waited obediently beside the ports. Skinny stared at the frigate as the "Sally" rapidly approached.

"Ship ahoy," a member of the watch had finally spotted the careening schooner. "Bear off," the sailor shouted, not realizing the "Sally's" intent, assuming drunken seamen were cavorting.

The stern of the anchored ship passed in a blur.

"Now," Jason shouted.

The four crewmen whipped open the ports.

"Fire!" Skinny shouted, almost hysterical.

J.J., Toddy and the two crewmen stuck the fuses to the touchholes. All four cannon roared. The combined impact of the recoiling cannon forced the "Sally" off course. Jason and the helmsman fought the wheel trying to control the racing schooner. Water raced in the ports. Skinny turned, looked to Jason for instructions, then back at the rushing water. "Sally" tilted precariously.

"Quick," Skinny shouted. "Dump the cannon overboard."

J.J., Toddy and the crewmen responded immediately. The cannon after their recoil had rolled back to their ports. One by one, eight men grabbed each cannon by the base and tipped it overboard. After the last fell, "Sally" righted herself. Water flowed from the flush deck back out the open ports. J.J. and Toddy, exhausted by the effort, collapsed against the wall of the inner cabin. The sailors rushed to their workstations, and Skinny hurried to the quarterdeck.

Jason stepped back from the wheel and turned the ship over to the helmsman.

"Sail her due east," he ordered.

The man looked southward towards New England with longing eyes.

"They'll expect us to turn due south as soon as we clear the harbor. That's where the pursuit will go. Take us due east," Jason repeated.

Jason and Skinny stared to their stern. There, a pleasant sight met their eyes. "Leopard" was canted to starboard and the deck met the waiting waves. Sailors were leaping overboard and already small boats from other ships were gathering the swimming men. Confusion reigned. By the time "Sally" had disappeared into the blackness, not a sail had been raised.

"They'll never find us," Skinny exulted.

FEDERAL DISTRICT OF WASHINGTON

DECEMBER 1807

Buster sat at his working table and with disgust reread for the third time has latest attempt to write an amusing, satirical essay describing life in Alexandria at the end of the year, 1807. He candidly admitted to imitating Washington Irving's delightful Salmagundi stories, which were published in New York. No matter how hard he tried, Buster could not approximate the man's light touch. Buster decided that his quill was made to transcribe weightier, political thoughts. Life in the Federal District focused on politics. There were many humorous facets to political life, but one could not describe them without creating lifelong enemies.

Despite the fact that the door, which connected the newspaper office with his town house, was closed, Buster could hear the stalwart protests of his son, Scottie. For an infant approaching his sixth week on earth, Scottie had the strongest sense of self-importance and the most intrusive voice Buster had ever encountered in a child. From that momentous day when he entered the world on November 13th, 1807, Scottie had dominated the Buster Satterfield household. Scottie had commenced crying the moment the doctor delivered his life giving slap, and he had not stopped. Buster had already forgotten what it was like to have an uninterrupted night's sleep.

Buster had welcomed the birth for many reasons, the most important because he had assumed that liberation from pregnancy would free Nancy to become the carefree spirit he had married.

Nancy's health had recovered, but the birth had done nothing for her disposition. Nancy acted as if Buster were responsible for all the ills of the world, most particularly hers. She claimed the Furmans as far back as history registered had never had a child like Scot Andrew Satterfield. His disposition, according to Nancy's frequently stated thesis, was directly attributable to his Satterfield genes. Buster had tried to dispute this point, first on his own, then by appealing to James and Vivian. His grandmother, unexplainably, agreed with Nancy, rigidly proclaiming that the far-flung Randolph family tree had never produced anything to equal the new frog voiced grandson. James, who Buster normally could rely on for support, remained inexcusably detached. The usually placid James had been excited by Scottie's appearance, but, after three visits, had abruptly limited his appearances at the town house to once or twice a week and then at meal times when Scot, otherwise occupied, could be expected to be his most peaceful, which was not saying much.

Nancy, when she was not blaming her first child's personality on Buster's genes, occasionally admitted the abnormality might have something to do with her selection of a doctor. Doctor Parke, a young man who specialized in child-birth, professed to follow the procedures of Doctor Samuel Bard as prescribed in his popular book on midwifery.

Scot was a healthy, alert child in possession of all of his extremities and fac-ulties. The problem, in Buster's opinion, stemmed from his son's apparent inter-est in everything going on about him and frustration in not being able to partici-pate fully at his tender age. Consequently, he demanded with his loud voice those attentions that were not volunteered.

Buster studied the wall that separated his office from his home and wondered if the time had not come to build a new structure for the *Herald*, one several blocks removed from his home. Either that, he reasoned, or he might offer Nancy a newer and grander mansion, something more appropriate to her status as a Senator's daughter, again, some distance from the newspaper.

He had to do something. Even the clatter of the printing press did not drown out the child's constant complaining.

Buster tossed his attempt to imitate Washington Irving aside and reread his end of year edition of the *Herald*. It was filled with news of James Monroe's December 13th return from London. Unlike the Republican newspapers such as the National *Intelligencer*, which printed Madison's thesis: Monroe returns in dis-grace, the *Herald* treated the event like the Second Coming. It sickened Buster to have to compromise his objectivity in this way, but he had to fulfill his commit-ment to John Randolph. Buster had saved a measure of self respect by not writ-ing the fawning articles himself or declaring Monroe to be the *Herald*'s candidate, but he had opened his newspaper's columns to any pro-Monroe writer who wanted his praise published. Buster was certain that Randolph had noticed this subterfuge on his part, but he had not protested. Presumably, he had been too occupied with Monroe's recent descent on Washington, a scant ten days after his return to the United States from his post in London.

Buster had never personally met "his candidate," but he had researched his life. Monroe, at forty-nine, was younger than the other two members of the Virginia triumvirate. Madison was seven years older and Jefferson fifteen, but Monroe was junior in years only. Unlike Jefferson who shunned military service during the Revolution, Monroe had enlisted in the Third Virginia Regiment and had served with distinction as a combat officer rising to the rank of captain. After being wounded in the shoulder, he had performed as an aide to Lord Sterling. He had even been present when Major James Wilkinson of General Horatio Gates' staff confided the letter from General Thomas Conway that led to disclosure of the infamous Conway Cabal against George Washington, an event that had caused James considerable difficulty.

After the war, Monroe had led the Senate while Madison dominated the House of Representatives and Jefferson served as Secretary of State. Prominent in Virginian politics, Monroe was elected Governor on four occasions. Washington appointed him as Minister to France, and Jefferson named him Minister to London, his most recent position. Monroe in Buster's mind was a man of stature, not a simple tool of John Randolph and the Old Republicans.

The link with Randolph, however, is what gave Buster heartburn. Buster again, as he had many times before, paused to regret his arrangement with the volatile, quixotic member of the House of Representatives. Without the onus of that desperate bargain made to save Toddy, Buster's support of Monroe could be justified on many counts. Even James thought highly of the man, but discoloring it all was the political compromise. If he were not forced to view the occasion through that embarrassing prism, Buster would be looking forward to his year end dinner at one o'clock with Randolph and Monroe at Gadsby's. At the least, whatever the meeting might cost him in political terms, Buster anticipated he would develop material for an interesting report for the *Herald*. He had already heard that Monroe was infuriated by his treatment since his return from England by his two closest friends, Jefferson and Madison. Buster's readership would be titillated by any insight into the intimate dispute that he could garner.

Buster's contemplation was suddenly interrupted by the opening of the connecting door between the newspaper office and the family town house. Buster looked up and discovered Nancy beaming one of her most glorious smiles at him. In the background, young Scottie wailed.

"Hear him, dear?" Nancy asked. "Your son and heir is proclaiming his presence."

"As usual," Buster said, rising to greet his wife. "What have we done to ourselves?" Buster gave voice to a thought that was constantly with him.

"Oh, don't worry, dear. Scot's a trial, but Doctor Parke assures me that he will grow out of it. He's troubled by colic or some such thing."

"It's not me that I worry about," Buster replied. "It's you. Us. He's such a strain. When he's not crying, he's demanding attention somehow. We never have any time together."

Nancy shut the door behind her, muting somewhat Scot's laments. Buster moved forward and embraced his wife.

"He is a trial," Nancy laughed. "Doctor Parke has recommended a new prescription."

"Do you think we should inflict another medication upon him? Won't it have a long term effect?"

"I agree," Nancy replied seriously as she stepped back from Buster. "This one is different. Dr. Parke called it a spirit bath."

"A spirit bath? What's that?"

"We soak him in a mixture of warm water and whiskey. Dr. Parke says it has a calming effect."

"I'm sure it does," Buster laughed. "The fumes make him drunk. We could get the same effect without the bother of a bath if we add whiskey to his milk."

"You may be right, but I'm ready to try anything." The smile left Nancy's face.

"You look dressed for town," Buster observed, trying to change the subject.

"Yes," Nancy's face brightened. "I have to get away. Your mother with cotton stuffed in her ears is watching Scottie. Even the Africans need relief from his tyranny."

"I'll be here until one when I have my meeting with Monroe and Randolph. I'll check on Lily and Scot before I go, so you take as long as you like."

"I thought I would visit Daddy. "

"He doesn't come by as much as he once did."

"I wonder why?" Nancy laughed and almost cried at the same time.

Buster walked Nancy to the door and helped her climb into the buggy that the young African boy on loan from Eastwind drove.

"Mornin' Mr. Satterfield," the young man said.

"Morning Amos. Drive carefully," Buster admonished. "Will you take the ferry or the long bridge?" Buster referred to the newly completed bridge connecting Virginia to the Federal District where Senator Furman lived.

"The bridge," Nancy replied. "It's so much easier."

"Be careful," Buster repeated. He still got queasy crossing the long and swaying structure.

"I'll see you this afternoon."

"Let's take a long walk," Buster suggested. "Alone."

"We'll see how Scot is behaving," Nancy half agreed.

"We know how he'll be behaving," Buster replied.

Buster stood on the porch and watched as the buggy carrying his wife departed sedately. After it had turned the corner, Buster returned to his worktable. He looked at the door to his house, thought about visiting his mother, heard Scot's muted squalls, and changed his mind.

At five minutes to one, Buster, wrapped in a heavy cape, stepped off his porch and walked towards Gadsby's. The sun, surprisingly strong for the last day of December, cast its warming rays earthward. Buster walked briskly, speaking to occasional acquaintances. The streets of Alexandria were filled with residents enjoying their temporary respite from winter. Only the brisk river breeze that cut across the north/south streets reminded them of what was yet to come. Buster, who actually liked cold weather, looked forward to January and February, the most likely months to bring snow. Buster privately thought that those days when a heavy wet snow draped the rooftops and trees and ground were among nature's most glorious offerings. He did not confide this belief often, particularly not when Nancy was around, because his North Carolina reared bride despised cold weather. She was one of those persons who needed bright sunrays to enhance her spirit. Buster had laughed when Nancy had first confessed this thought, but he had discreetly watched his wife's behavior and had learned that on gray days she was depressed and moody and on bright, sunny days cheerful and effervescent.

Gadsby's was crowded when Buster entered. A polite African dressed in red and white wool took his cloak and hat when he entered.

"Mr. Monroe and Mr. Randolph be waitin' in de main room," the man confided.

Buster nodded and wondered if everyone in Alexandria knew his business. Politics seemed to attract public attention, and Gadsby's was the place in the Federal District where most political deals were negotiated. Still, Buster did not consider himself a politician; he was an independent newspaperman who occasionally dabbled in politics. Every time that he did he felt a little sullied, as if he had compromised another principle. He suspected that today would be one of those times.

"Mr. Satterfield," John Randolph's high, squeaky voice greeted Buster as he approached.

Randolph, a tall but emaciated man, rose and offered his long bony fingers. Buster instinctively grasped the man's hand and squeezed in self-defense. Randolph winced, and Buster released the damp hand quickly.

"And this is Mr. Monroe. I don't believe you have met."

Buster turned and found himself facing a middle-aged man of about his own height. Buster was impressed. Compared to the Mouse, Secretary of State Madison, James Monroe was handsome. He had clear hazel eyes, a pronounced masculine nose, a firm chin with a deep cleft. He wore his hair clipped shorter than fashion demanded and combed it straight back. The hair's natural brown had faded and was tinted by unpowdered white; the short length made Monroe appear much younger than his forty-nine years. The contrast with Madison encouraged Buster. Madison was a short old man whose naturally suspicious expression conveyed cunning and deceit; Monroe radiated masculine strength and good will.

"Mr. Satterfield. I have heard much about you," Monroe's voice was firm and deep. His tone assured sincerity.

"Mr. Monroe. Welcome home," Buster replied, trying to match Monroe with an inflection of warmth and good will.

The three men sat at the same time, each carefully projecting the right amount of deference to the others. Randolph, obviously in an enthused state, opened the conversation by summarizing his impression of Monroe's reception on his first visit to the capital after his extensive overseas service.

"Mr. Monroe's sincere friends have greeted him with enthusiasm, but as for certain others, who should remain nameless, little can be said."

Monroe listened to Randolph's words with an impassive face. Buster had the impression that he was embarrassed by the personal remarks but tolerated them coming from the well meaning but idiosyncratic Randolph.

"Mr. Monroe, I want to thank you for your kind efforts on behalf of my kin during his time of impressment," Buster said sincerely when Randolph finally paused, giving Buster his first opportunity to speak directly.

"I thank you, but I must apologize for not doing more. Distance and elapsed time rendered my efforts futile. Fortunately, your father taught the stubborn English a lesson."

"Yes, but your efforts were sincere and appreciated," Buster persisted. He admired Monroe's tact, recognizing that Jason's adventures in Halifax which were so enthusiastically greeted by the family and his fellow citizens must have created many problems for the American Minister at the Court of Saint James.

"As soon as I received Mr. Randolph's letter outlining Toddy's situation, I immediately protested to the Prime Minister and demanded his release. The Prime Minister was embarrassed to learn what his navy had done. I am sure that we would have obtained Toddy's release if your father had not already rescued him. An act that I, an old military man, commend."

"I wish the same could be said for the President and the Secretary," Randolph interjected. "Can you believe that Secretary Madison never mentioned your cousin's impressment? And instructions for a demarche concerning the 'Chesapeake Affair' arrived in London on the very same ship that delivered my letter."

Randolph's words surprised Buster, and he did not conceal his reaction. He recalled his meeting with Madison and the Mouse's promise to intervene on Toddy's behalf.

"I must say," Toddy replied. "That does surprise me. Secretary Madison promised me personally that he would submit a demarche on Toddy's behalf."

Buster turned from Randolph to study Monroe and was surprised by the concerned expression he found on the man's handsome face.

"I must humbly ask" Monroe began slowly, "that you not mention that disclosure in your newspaper. It's a private confidence."

"But it would be most useful for the public to know about Madison's dishonesty and deviousness," Randolph protested, his voice rising shrilly.

"As an appointee of the administration, theoretically under Mr. Madison's supervision, I cannot violate any confidences. It would be most unprofessional."

"But it would be politically useful," Randolph protested.

"Mr. Randolph, please excuse me, but I must make one thing perfectly clear. I have agreed to allow my name to be placed as a candidate for the nomination of the Republican Party for President of the United States, but I will not violate my personal integrity to achieve that high office."

Dismay clouded Randolph's face, but before he could protest, Monroe turned to Buster.

"Mr. Satterfield. I understand the purpose of this meeting is to discuss your support for my nomination. I assume that I have your assurance that everything we discuss here will remain in confidence and will not be printed in the *Herald*."

"That is understood," Buster agreed. "However, I reserve my rights as guaranteed under the First Amendment of the Constitution to report the facts as I learn them independent of this conversation."

"I respect that," Monroe replied with a disarming smile. "I would not want the situation otherwise."

"I do not understand, James," Randolph protested, "how you can so calmly accept the treatment accorded you by Jefferson and Madison, your former friends."

"Friends can have honest disagreements, Mr. Randolph. I am disappointed in President Jefferson and most particularly in Secretary Madison, but I still consider them friends. We have simply encountered a cool period in our relationships."

"This man is too noble," Randolph turned to Buster.

Buster recognized that Randolph was continuing the disagreement by deflecting it in flattering terms.

"May I ask how you were treated?" Buster asked Monroe.

"It's a fair question," Monroe replied. "Were I in your position I too would expect an answer. I will speak candidly for your information only. Agreed?"

"Agreed," Buster answered.

"When I returned a short three weeks ago, I did so with a strong sense of betrayal. I was shocked when President Jefferson on Secretary of State Madison's recommendation refused to sign the treaty I had labored so long to attain. He did so before he actually received the copy I had sent along with my elaborations. This I found personally insulting. From that point onward, my position in London was undermined. My English counterparts recognized that I did not speak with the authority of Washington. Then, Madison appointed a special negotiator 'to assist me' as he said. I could not believe that my two closest friends in the world treated me thusly, and they did so with an implicit accusation, that I had failed to include the issue of impressment in the treaty. I assure you, given your personal concern about the subject, that impressment was not included only because the English adamantly refused to consider the subject. They would not bend. If I had persisted, there would have been no treaty."

"And the President and the Secretary knew this?" Buster asked.

"Most certainly," Monroe replied, staring directly into Buster's eyes. "I proceeded as I did with their full authority."

"Jefferson's and Madison's?" Buster asked.

Monroe paused before answering.

"To be precise, I communicated via the Secretary to the President. Only the Secretary wrote back to me, transmitting my instructions. I had to assume he spoke for the President. In my mind both spoke through Madison's pen. On an issue of this importance, Madison could not issue directions other than at Jefferson's order. Our President does like to work through others. It keeps his hands clean. I know this from long personal experience."

"Then, what happened?" Buster could not believe he was being informed of the most intimate details of the relationship between a President and a trusted friend and subordinate.

"Impressment was transformed from being an issue between the English and the Americans to one of critical political importance within the United States. The 'Chesapeake Affair' made impressment a question of war. The President and the Secretary of State, political creatures that they are, as I and Mr. Randolph are, recognized they had to cauterize the problem. They placed the blame for failure to address the issue of impressment solely on me. I am the scapegoat."

"Don't you feel ill treated?"

"I do, and that is why I permit my name to be placed in nomination against Mr. Madison. It is a matter of pride and principle. This is not the first time I've contested an election with Mr. Madison. Did you know that?"

Monroe's statements surprised Buster.

"No sir. I had assumed you, the President, and Mr. Madison had always been close friends, a triumvirate."

Monroe smiled.

"When I returned from the war, Mr. Jefferson was Governor of Virginia. I knew him only casually, but being without a profession and interested in politics I consulted him. He advised that I study law. I returned to William and Mary and under his counsel read the law. When the capital moved from Williamsburg to Richmond in 1790, I asked Mr. Jefferson what I should do. He, having taken an interest in me as he has many young men, advised me to move to Richmond and continue my study of law under him preparatory to a political career. I did so. I subsequently served in the House of Delegates and then the Senate of the United States. Mr. Jefferson has long been my mentor."

"And Mr. Madison?"

"He has always been closer to Mr. Jefferson than I. Nearer in age, they have constantly worked together. Mr. Jefferson is the thinker, and Mr. Madison his implementer. It was so twenty years ago, and it is true today."

"And you were subordinate to Mr. Madison in Mr. Jefferson's eyes?"

"At the beginning. Over the years, as I aged and grew more experienced, I became a co-equal, Mr. Jefferson, of course, always being a little more equal."

"Then, Mr. Jefferson did not rank Mr. Madison higher than yourself?"

"Not as friends. Not as political comrades, but," Monroe paused, aware of the intimacies he was revealing. "But," he continued finally, "Mr. Jefferson and Mr. Madison have always been closer in one respect. Both hold more universal interests than I, in science, nature, farming, philosophy. They frequently correspond and discuss these subjects. My interest is more focused. I do not have the breadth of genius possessed by my two friends. I am a political animal, and our relationships have been bound by personal respect and politics."

"I understand your disappointment," Buster sympathized. "And now I must ask a final question."

"How have they treated me following their betrayal and my return?" Monroe anticipated the question.

Buster nodded.

"Very well. I will not discuss this subject again, but I will tell you. They have received me as a friend. They have entertained me, and they have discussed many subjects, but they have not asked me about our relations with England, a matter to which I have devoted my every waking hour over the past few years, and they have avoided discussing politics, the basis of our decades long relationships."

"And why is this?"

"I am convinced I have been selected to shoulder the blame for past mistakes and that I am being shelved to ensure Mr. Madison's election as President Jefferson's successor. They may fear what I know and what I am capable of doing. They have offered me insulting sinecures, such as Governor of Louisiana, and I have rejected them. I am not without my principles. I am not without other friends."

Buster, who was totally persuaded of Monroe's sincerity, had one more question.

"You did not tell me when you last competed with Mr. Madison for an elective post?"

"In 1788 in my youthful naivete—I was about the same age you are now—I campaigned against Mr. Madison for a seat in the Congress, and I lost."

"I hope you do not lose a second time," Buster spoke sincerely.

"Will you assist Mr. Monroe?" Randolph asked.

"To the best of my ability."

"Will the *Herald* endorse him?"

"The *Herald* and myself personally."

"I must admit that I have been worried about your behavior of late," Randolph said in a voice devoid of emotion.

"I have allowed supporters to write favorable articles."

"But you have not personally, and neither has your paper endorsed Mr. Monroe," Randolph said.

"After this conversation, Mr. Monroe has my fullest trust and support."

"May I consider you a personal friend?" Monroe reentered the conversation.

"I would be honored."

"Done, friend," Monroe smiled and offered his hand.

Unlike Randolph's weak grasp, Monroe's hand was firm and strong.

"You recognize, of course, that I cannot actively campaign on my own behalf and cannot attack Mr. Jefferson and Mr. Madison, not personally, and not for their policies?"

"I do and would not expect you to do otherwise."

"Because they remain friends despite the fact I anticipate Mr. Madison and myself, as competitors, may encounter a cool period."

Buster recognized that it was the second time Monroe had used the phrase "cool period."

"Then, I hope I'm able to fill in a small part of that void," Buster said and meant it.

"And, I, for my part, would prefer that Mr. Monroe would be more active on his and the country's behalf, but I understand his position," Randolph said. "However, Mr. Satterfield, I do not feel that way about yourself. Will you personally accept a role as an active participant in the political arena?"

"I will campaign for a seat in the House of Delegates," Buster referred to the Burgesses by their new name. "The subject has been mentioned to me before, so I hope I am not being presumptive."

"Welcome to the challenging world of politics," Randolph said, offering his own limp hand for commitment. "I will alert Mr. Cruikstaff to support you."

Buster hesitated. Thomas Cruikstaff had been the second at the duel with Hodges and had been a thorn in Jason's side on the Alexandria town council. Buster recognized that Cruiky was the enthusiastic leader of the local Old Republicans and harbored political ambitions of his own.

"I understand that you and Mr. Cruikstaff have had your differences, not all of which were political, but don't let that worry you. Such disagreements are matters of the past. Politics do make strange bedfellows, not all of whom are welcome all the time. Agreed?"

"Agreed." Buster spoke honestly.

During the remainder of the dinner, Randolph gushed politics, Monroe urbanely discussed world issues, and Buster privately wondered how he was going to inform Nancy, Jason, James and Vivian about this conversation. All four were political animals with strongly held views.

RICHMOND, VIRGINIA

1808/1809

In January, the Republican dispute between James Monroe and James Madison came to a boil. The Madisonites in Congress attempted to quickly cool the contest by scheduling a Republican Party caucus for January 23rd. The leaders reasoned that if they nominated James Madison as the party candidate they could forestall any action in the key state of Virginia by Monroe supporters. When the caucus met in Washington, the congressional leaders quickly demonstrated who was in control; a prearranged motion dispensed with the need to place the names of the various candidates on a ballot; instead, the caucus moved immediately to the balloting without prior nomination. It was no surprise when the party machine produced eighty-three votes for James Madison against three for Monroe and three for George Clinton of New York. The national leadership thereby ordained James Madison as the Republican Party's candidate to succeed President Jefferson.

Anticipating this development, John Randolph and the Clinton supporters had boycotted the caucus. At Randolph's urging a caucus of Virginian members of the Republican Party scheduled a meeting in Richmond to consider the state's position on the nominations. The reason the party's national leadership had tried to preempt this action with their Washington congressional caucus was in Virginia the party was evenly split between the Monroe and Madison supporters, and nobody could predict the outcome of a caucus.

Buster was caught up in this maelstrom. Since the Richmond party caucus was scheduled for January 21st, the day before the national meeting, he had to choose between the two. The Richmond meeting had been set for January 28th, but when Randolph learned of congressional plans, he had moved his Virginia caucus ahead by seven days to thwart the national leadership's machinations. Buster, because of his commitment of support to Monroe, traveled to Richmond despite the fact he was not a member of the House of Delegates, yet. Since it all was pure politics, minor details like holding office mattered little; Buster attended the Richmond caucus as a voting participant simply because Randolph decreed that he should.

Once involved, Buster had little time to contemplate the wisdom of his actions. Madison's supporters tried to create the impression that their candidate had national support and that Virginia would be left behind as the only state not adhering to the leadership's selection. This was an effective argument in the sense it placed the Virginia Party in the potential position of opposing the candidacy of a native Virginian selected by his predecessor, also a son of Virginia.

When Monroe's supporters held firm, Madison's advocates tried to outmaneuver them. They scheduled a Virginia Republican Party caucus to be held at Bell's Tavern on January 21st. Not to be outdone, Randolph orchestrated a meeting of Old Republican Party supporters of Monroe at the Capitol at the same time. Buster, somewhat amused by all of the machinations, loyally attended the second caucus and voted extemporaneously for James Monroe. At the Bell Tavern one hundred and twenty-four party regulars voted for James Madison. At the Capitol building, where caucuses normally were held, Monroe was nominated by a vote of fifty-seven to ten. An unanticipated outcome of the Old Republican caucus was the selection of Buster as the rump faction's candidate for Congress from Northern Virginia. Buster had pointed out that Alexandria was officially a part of the Federal District and he was thus disqualified to be a candidate, but Randolph's supporters countered by stating that he could qualify by declaring that Eastwind in Fairfax counted as his permanent place of residence. Such legal distinctions were not considered a problem at the time.

The Republican Party in Virginia thus ended up with two candidates for President, James Monroe and James Madison, while the national Republican Party had but one, James Madison. Nobody was confused; all understood the situation. During the subsequent campaign, Monroe adopted the position that the voters had the right to chose between himself and Madison. Jefferson piously regretted the contest between his two dear friends. Jefferson privately corresponded with Monroe and succeeded in keeping their friendship afloat. Monroe and Madison ceased to speak to each other. During the early campaign in Virginia, the supporters of the two candidates concentrated on peripheral issues. Monroe's writers attacked the caucuses. In August Madison enthusiasts criticized Monroe for violating his instructions and accepting humiliating treaty conditions that had to be rejected by Secretary of State Madison. This led Monroe to respond with the allegation that Madison's deplorable handling of foreign affairs had influenced him to contest Madison's candidacy for President. Monroe's supporters described him as the best man to lead the country, the one most experienced in the problems of the day. They stressed that Monroe was not committed either to the embargo or to war. They did not say how he would solve the problems.

In Alexandria Buster adopted the "best man for the job" issue. This in his opinion was James Monroe. When the Monroe campaign shifted to foreign affairs, Buster avoided this sensitive dispute between Madison and Monroe, believing that the United States should present a bipartisan face to the world at large, and concentrated his criticisms of the administration on national defense. As Buster visited the backcountry of Fairfax to introduce himself, he found himself unable to balance the demands of politicking and publishing a newspaper. To his surprise, Nancy, not James and Vivian, stepped in to fill the gap.

In November, James Monroe lost an election campaign to the diminutive Madison, this time decisively. Nationally, Monroe failed to garner a single electoral vote; in Virginia, Madison overwhelmed Monroe, 14,665 votes to 3,408. Madison soundly trounced the Federalist candidate, Charles Cotesworth Pinckney whose support was largely limited to New England and some back counties in North Carolina, Maryland and Delaware. Immediately following the election the Madison supporters in Virginia turned on the Old Republicans with vengeance in mind. They deprived Monroe supporters of their seats on the Governor's Council and purged the party. Buster, a surprise victor in Northern Virginia by a mere one hundred and three votes, was one of the few Monroe supporters to emerge unscathed. Buster attributed his polling success to one simple fact: Federalists, recalling James' unselfish service during the Revolution and still supportive of Jason for his unstinting devotion to Federalist causes, voted in large numbers for the Satterfield name despite the fact that Buster stood on the Old Republican ticket. His selection of issues had also helped; the Federalists believed in a strong military and were attracted by Buster's calls for strengthening both the army and navy.

Buster's immediate family presented a supportive, single face to the voters. Inside family councils, they were anything but united; only determined support for Buster personally held them together. His father, Jason, remained a Federalist to the core; neither Madison nor Monroe could carry Jason's candle. James, a genuine uncommitted at heart, vocally supported Buster's candidate Monroe. Vivian, still incensed by Madison's duplicity at the time of Toddy's impressment, actively supported Monroe, writing highly laudatory articles on Monroe for the *Herald* at the same time she created vicious personal attacks on Madison's integrity. The family surprise, however, was Nancy. As Buster's wife, she was expected to be one hundred percent loyal. In fact, following the lead of her Senator father, Nancy emerged as a Republican Party stalwart. James Madison was her man.   Fortunately, for family peace, Nancy's work at the *Herald* obediently adhered to the family guidelines: unswerving support to Buster and Monroe.

On the day after the election returns were in, the family met at James and Vivian's riverfront home to decide what to do about the *Herald*. Buster's election as Congressman meant that he would have to withdraw as editor/publisher; he simply would not be able to perform both jobs. No one in the family wanted to let the *Herald* die. Neither James nor Vivian could shoulder the burden, and Jason refused. James suggested they offer the job to Skinny, recalling that during the Revolution Skinny had successfully managed the newspaper for the family. Jason refused to let Skinny go; he needed him to oversee the brewery, warehouse and store while Jason concentrated on his first love, building ships. The family conference lapsed into silence, considering the ramifications of closing the *Herald*.

"I'll do it," Nancy pertly volunteered.

All, including Buster, stared at her in surprise. Nancy had adequately filled in while Buster campaigned, but all had considered this a short-term solution. Nancy still had a full time job as Scottie's mother.

"I think that is a wonderful idea," Vivian immediately agreed, affirming the idea before Buster could dissent.

"So do I," James concurred.

"Then it's settled," Jason stated with relief.

"But... ." Buster began.

"I can handle it," Nancy declared. "I will insist on having full authority."

"Of course," Vivian agreed. "That's the only way." Vivian studied the others, recalling the times she had substituted at the paper. It had been frustrating trying always to serve as James' alter ego.

Buster who had no other solution was dismayed but kept his silence. He knew that his wife, despite her charm, could be headstrong when it came to politics. Always her father's daughter, she had been immersed in politics since the day she could talk. Buster did not want the *Herald* to fold, and he preferred that his wife remain at home with Scottie, but he saw he had no choice.

"Very well, Mrs. Satterfield. The *Herald* is yours. Change the masthead." Buster capitulated gracefully.

The next day, at John Randolph's suggestion, Buster crossed the Potomac on the new bridge and visited the Capitol for the first time as a Congressman elect. John Randolph, the only surviving Virginia old Republican, conducted the tour and introduced Buster to the clerks and the few Congressmen present. The old Congress had already adjourned.

"Representing a district so close to the Capitol gives you a decided advantage," Randolph declared. "You can work while the others are home consulting their districts."

Buster decided that the time had come for him to gradually disassociate himself from his political mentor. John Randolph, once a power in Congress, had over time allowed his idiosyncratic behavior to discredit him. He had been replaced several years earlier as the floor leader. He still displayed flashes of his oratorical brilliance, but his bitter and biting tongue wounded as many as it persuaded. Buster did not want to make Randolph an enemy, but he intended to be his own man, and national defense would be his issue. He had already decided to make a demand for an enlarged navy the cornerstone of his first speech. He knew enough about politics and tradition that he would not stand up on the first day of the new Congress and ask to be heard; he would bide his time and strike when the opportunity presented. He also recognized that the victorious Republican Party would not treat him kindly; he like Randolph and other Monroe supporters could expect to be treated like outcasts.

Buster returned home late that first day filled with plans and looking forward to sharing them with Nancy. He had to visit Albemarle and work out a new strategy with James Monroe, who anticipated that despite his competing candidacy that he would be offered a position in the new administration, maybe Secretary of State. Buster knew that Monroe had offered to return to London to help with the new negotiations.

When Buster entered the town house, he was greeted by Scottie's loud howls. Now, one year old and somewhat mobile—he was a crawler of the first order—Scottie roamed the first floor of the Satterfield home at will. He greeted his father at the door and was rewarded with an enthusiastic hug. Nellie, Scottie's black nanny, stood several feet away and watched with wide eyes. Nellie spent her days following Scottie on his non-stop inspection of the house.

"Where's Mrs. Satterfield?" Buster asked, handing the now frowning Scottie to Nellie.

Buster shook his hand to indicate that Scottie was wet and needed to be changed.

"She be dere," Nellie replied, inclining her head in the direction of the newspaper office. "Been dere all day."

Nellie took the now screaming Scottie who had expected more from his father and headed towards the back of the house. Buster approached the door that led to his old office with a slight trepidation. What had once been his castle now belonged to Nancy, and he was not yet accustomed to the idea. He wondered if he should knock before entering because Nancy did not like to be disturbed when writing. Buster knew she would be busy preparing the text for tomorrow's edition of the *Herald*, her first as publisher.

Buster recalled that Nancy had never knocked. At times he had wished she had, but he had recognized that as his wife it was her prerogative to move through the connecting door at will. Buster decided to establish the same precedent.

Nancy looked up as Buster entered. She sat at Buster's old table. He studied it fondly. What had once been covered with Buster's comfortable litter was now arranged in neat piles. The recently polished tabletop gleamed through the orderly stacks. Buster glanced to the back of the room and saw the two freedmen, once his employees, quietly setting type. Buster thought they looked at him strangely. He smiled, and they nodded back. Somehow, the old familiarity was lacking. Buster felt like an intruder.

"Hello dear," Nancy greeted him. "Give me ten minutes to finish this article, then I'll join you."

Buster recognized he had been dismissed. He studied his old realm, realized it was no longer his, and quietly retreated back to his townhouse, to Buster and his torment.

"Please see if you can calm that child," Nancy called as Buster closed the door. "He has been rampaging all day."

As promised, Nancy joined him in ten minutes.

"Will you have to work tonight?" Buster asked, recalling the times he had to return to the shop after a light supper to finish an article for the next day's edition.

"No dear," Nancy smiled sweetly. "My time is yours."

"You know tomorrow is Tuesday?"

"Yes dear, I know."

"And your first edition is due." Buster had expected Nancy to work late tonight but not to forget when the paper had to be published.

"The men are setting the last article now," Nancy smiled. "You will hear the press shortly."

Buster stared at his wife, unable to hide his disbelief.

"Four pages?"

"Four pages. A complete issue," Nancy replied.

"You write faster than I do," Buster said.

" I know."

"I must travel to Albemarle and confer with Mr. Monroe," Buster decided to break his news suddenly. After he spoke, he paused, wondering if he should admonish his wife not to print that disclosure. He realized for the first time that having an independent wife in the newspaper business would present problems for a politician. Buster always looked forward to sharing his views and experiences with his wife; now, he wondered if that pleasure would be circumscribed.

"Daddy wishes you would distance yourself from Mr. Monroe. He says that if you do he might be able to reestablish you in the party in a year or two, after you pay your penance."

Buster did not like to be told what daddy thought. He had his own plans, and they did not include breaking with James Monroe who he respected.

"Was your father here today?"

"No I saw him in Washington."

"You were in the city?"

"Yes."

"Shopping?"

"Working on a story," Nancy replied. "I stopped by the President's House and met with Mr. Madison and President Jefferson."

"My enemies?" Buster asked, flabbergasted.

"You're going to have to restore your objectivity," Nancy said sweetly. "Politicians must work with everybody."

The next day Buster acquired a small office. He recognized that others had larger and much grander offices, but he appreciated that as a newcomer he did not rate the perquisites the older members had earned. The diminutive office, no larger than Scottie's nursery, did worry him. A chance meeting with Representative Wilson Cary Nicholas did. Nicholas and Senator William Branch Giles were now two important members of Congress. They were President Elect James Madison's men who had managed his Virginia campaign. As a consequence, they were fully aware of Buster's support for Monroe and friendship with the discredited John Randolph. Nicholas had bluntly made it clear that the Republican Party leadership did not consider Buster one of their own. They did not need his vote; he could expect no favors, only the worst committee assignments and no helpful consultations with the White House. Buster had not realized what his classification as an Old Republican meant. He was to every intent and purpose an independent with no party structure and no helpful colleagues to rely on, except for John Randolph. Buster wondered if he should consider allying himself with the Federalists; they after all had helped elect him, but he could not bring himself to do so. He disagreed with too much that they represented. They were the party of John Adams and New England, the dead Alexander Hamilton, his New Yorkers, the rich bankers, and all that.

Buster crossed the long bridge that night less apprehensive of the swaying; he was too preoccupied with his position in Congress. He looked forward to discussing his problems with Nancy and getting her advice; she had learned politics at her father's knee and had sound judgment.

Buster tied his horse at the stanchion in front of his house and eagerly mounted the stairs to the porch. He had his hand on the front door latch and was preparing to enter when he heard Scottie's loud wail. Buster paused then decided to enter the newspaper office instead, confident that Nancy would be there. He would greet his son later.

When Buster entered, he found Nancy sitting at her desk. Several small stacks of the *Herald* set on the floor near the door, waiting to be delivered. Buster nodded at the two freedmen, his old friends and colleagues, and again noted their apprehensive demeanor. They acknowledged his presence and nervously returned to cleaning the ink from the now silent press. Buster knew the pattern by heart. First they would clean the ink cylinder and rolls, then the typeface before breaking the print blocks and returning the type to the individual slots, alphabetically.

Nancy, who was reading a copy of the first issue of her paper, looked up when Buster entered.

"Welcome home from the fray, darling," she bubbled.

Buster remembered how it had felt to examine his first edition of the paper after James had turned management over to him. He decided to set his personal problems aside and help Nancy celebrate the occasion.

"Your first edition," he smiled. "May I read a copy?"

"Yes dear. I saved the very first one off the press for you. To treasure."

Nancy picked up a copy from the table in front of her and handed it to Buster. She placed it on the table and turned it to face him; Buster waited, prepared to professionally appraise it.

The first thing he saw shocked him. In big black print, much larger and bolder than anything he had ever seen before, the headline blared:

"UNDER NEW MANAGEMENT: *HERALD* PROCLAIMS INDEPENDENCE

"Responding to the demands of her readership, Mrs. Nancy Furman Satterfield, Publisher of the *Herald*, today announced the newspaper's renunciation of its most recent editorial policy of partisanship and its return to true and unbiased objectivity."

Buster could not believe what he read.

"This is a joke. Tell me it is," Buster pleaded.

"Do you like it? It catches your attention, doesn't it?"

"How could you do this?" Buster asked.

"Honey, it's just business. It has nothing to do with you. I wanted to shake up this stodgy old paper."

"It wasn't stodgy," Buster protested. "It was me."

"I know, dear," Nancy said, rising. "Bring your present and we will go home and greet Scottie. I can tell from the racket that he has been anxiously awaiting your arrival."

"But look at the other stories," Buster pointed at a front page article that announced:

"President Elect Madison Discloses to *Herald* Intent to Build Frigates, Increase Size of Army and Navy, Regardless of Budget Impact!"

"How can he do that?" Buster sputtered. "That was to be my first speech. And all those headlines. You will offend our readers."

"I don't think so dear," Nancy said. "We had to print an extra five hundred copies for the Federal District. Didn't you see them?"

Buster had seen nothing in the Federal District. He had been too absorbed in his own thoughts to register what was happening about him.

"But this supports Madison," Buster protested.

"No it doesn't, dear. If you read further, you will see that I quote your friend Mr. Randolph and others, carefully giving both sides their due."

Buster did not know what to say. He looked at the freedmen, his friends, and they nodded, unable to conceal their smiles. Nancy took Buster's arm and led him towards the connecting door. As they approached, he paused, realizing he had left his copy of the paper on the table, and returned to collect it.

"I must read the *Herald* to discover what else I've missed today."

Nancy kissed him on the cheek, grasped his free arm and led him into the house.

"Now tell me dear," she said. "How was your day at the Capitol?"

Buster carefully closed the connecting door. Scottie propelled himself forward on hands and knees to greet them, and Nellie watched with wide eyes. Buster briefly ignored his son who immediately tried to climb up his father's pants legs.

"Make me one promise," he asked, facing Nancy.

"Yes, dear."

"Anything that we discuss in this house on this side of the door is not to appear in print."

"Agreed," Nancy said.

She leaned over, picked up a smiling Scottie, squeezed him affectionately, and handed him to his father.

"Now discuss your day with your son, and I will check in the kitchen to see what is being prepared for supper."

"But I wanted to talk with you," Buster lamented.

"After I check on the food and you welcome your son," Nancy said.

Buster, holding Scottie who began pulling on his nose and hair, one hand each, stared after his wife. He remembered his own preoccupation after a day at the newspaper and surrendered.

In response to his growing need to discuss the future with his new friend James Monroe, Buster in early February, 1809, decided to risk the threat of a mid-winter snow storm and set out for "Highlands," Monroe's Albemarle home. The air was cold, a good ten degrees below freezing, and the wind chilled Buster to the bones. His horse responded to the challenge and reacted to the cold by maintaining a fast gait as he picked his way through the hardened ridges and ice covered puddles.

Monroe, alerted by a household servant, met Buster at the door. Having expected to find a man of Monroe's stature living in a plantation house of the same standard as Monticello or Mount Vernon, Buster found Monroe's Piedmont home little larger than an expanded settler's cabin. It had the same sloped roof and only two chimneys. Buster had heard of Monroe's financial difficulties; he had even had to sell furniture to his friends Madison and Jefferson to pay for his expenses while preparing for his trip to France as Jefferson's Minister Extraordinaire.

"Welcome, Buster," Monroe greeted his young friend warmly. "Welcome to the healthy air of the Piedmont."

"I wasn't sure where to find you, James," Buster replied, relieved to have located Monroe. "I heard you had purchased a home in Richmond."

"Yes, that's true," Monroe guided Buster to a seat near the blazing fire. He took Buster's coat and hat and handed them to a shabbily dressed house servant. "I still have my money problems and find that I must sacrifice my life as a gentleman farmer," he smiled at his words and pointed at his humble furnishings, "and must try to recoup my fortune by practicing law in Richmond."

"While staying close to politics," Buster said hopefully.

"First let me warm you with a cup of tea, and then we can talk about the depressing subject you mentioned."

Monroe left the room and gave instructions to the servant, ordering tea and asking that Buster's horse be led to the stable and welcomed properly.

"As you can see," Monroe continued apologetically when he returned, "I have not prospered in government service. Like others, I fear I am land poor. I have my investments in Loudoun County, your grandfather's homeland, and in the west, but my creditors beckon."

"Times will change, James," Buster tried to reassure his friend who sounded depressed.

Buster had journeyed to have his own sagging spirits raised and instead found himself trying to cheer Monroe.

"Above all, hang on to the land in Loudoun. You will need it. "

Monroe smiled. He watched as the servant poured the tea then departed.

"I wish I could be as optimistic," Monroe said. "It's been a difficult winter."

"Have you talked with Jefferson or Madison?" Buster asked.

"I see Tom when he visits Monticello, but Mr. Madison and I are not speaking."

"Has President Jefferson hinted at the possibility of an appointment?"

"Nothing."

"Who would make a better Secretary of State than a man who has been Minister in both England and France?"

Monroe dejectedly shook his head. "My withdrawal from public life has become permanent."

"I doubt that," Buster said. "You have too many friends to allow that to happen."

"Not as many as one might hope," Monroe countered. "My vocation is now the law, making money for my family, and improving my neglected land. I'm interested in experimenting with clover and plaster of Paris as some of your constituents in Fairfax and Loudoun have tried."

"Have many friends visited you?"

"My closest adviser these days is my son-in-law."

Buster remembered George Hay from his days in Richmond. Hay, some twenty years older than Monroe's daughter Eliza, was a successful lawyer who had long been prominent in Republican politics.

"How is Mr. Randolph?" Monroe asked.

"That is one of the subjects I wished to discuss with you," Buster replied.

Monroe politely waited for Buster to continue.

"I fear our dear friend is becoming more eccentric than ever. The setback suffered during the recent election has made him quite frantic."

"I suggest, Buster, that you consider distancing yourself from poor John if you can without compromising your principles."

"That thought has also crossed my mind."

"I've been considering a reconciliation with my party," Monroe confided, watching Buster's reaction closely.

"I think that would be best," Buster said. "The Old Republican faction is dead."

"I never wanted to do anything to damage my party," Monroe continued. "I ran as a Republican not in opposition. I tried not to criticize the Administration in a harmful way."

"That was apparent to all, James." Buster used the older man's name naturally.

"How do you recommend I repair my ties?"

Buster thought carefully before replying. "I suggest you correspond with reliable friends still influential in the party, such as John Taylor of Caroline."

"An excellent idea," Monroe agreed, making a note to himself on a sheet of paper that rested on a nearby side table. "And yourself?"

"I thought I might do likewise, though it's difficult with John Randolph lurking nearby."

"You must do what your conscience requires," Monroe said. "And what issues do you plan to address."

"National defense," Buster answered. "The condition of the army and navy is deplorable. War looms."

"That it does. I sense Mr. Madison also has plans. Maybe, maybe this is an area where you can find common purpose."

"I hadn't thought of that."

"And your newspaper?"

"Is under new management. It's already seeking a common ground."

"I've noticed that," Monroe laughed. "I hadn't realized it was part of your master plan."

"It wasn't," Buster said ruefully. "I'm now following the lead of my political master."

Buster stayed in Albemarle for two days. He enjoyed Monroe's company and all the talk was not politics. When he left, Buster did so with a good feeling that he had helped his friend as much as had been encouraged himself.

FEDERAL DISTRICT OF WASHINGTON

1811/1812

In March 1811, Buster's two-year long winter of frustration and ignobility ended. His first term in Congress had been a miserable one. John Randolph, angered by Buster's attempt to be his own man, shunned him. The stalwarts of the Republican Party, offended by Buster's truant support for Monroe over the victorious Madison, ignored him despite his advocacy of a stronger military in much the same terms proposed by the new President.

James Madison as Jefferson's Secretary of State for eight years had loyally implemented his President's program: abolish the national debt by cutting expenses, especially those planning for war. Consequently, the army and navy had been reduced to harbor defenders and Indian fighters. Jefferson expected to solve his problems with England and France with diplomacy and economic sanctions. By the time Madison replaced his friend and master, events had proven these policies threadbare, and Madison began his turn as President with a call to prepare for war. Madison's policy evolution brought him to the point where Buster had started. Buster, despite sharing a common program with the President, in March, 1811, could not decide whether Madison, now free to be his own political master, had shed some of the tatters of Jefferson's more radical and misguided philosophy, or whether Madison, an astute political animal, had simply adapted to the demands of the time.

Certainly, Madison could not ignore the fact that diplomacy and economic sanctions had failed to impress the French and English who continued to harass American shipping and violate the country's sovereignty at will. New England was aroused; the sanctions had damaged American commerce and industry far more than they had persuaded the hostile powers to desist. In the recent congressional by-elections, a new breed of legislator was sent to Washington: the War Hawks. Included among the returning Republican Party hacks was a small group of energetic young men who styled themselves "New" Republicans. Not troubled by a simple matter of nomenclature, Buster easily shifted from the Old Republicans of John Randolph to the New Republicans. Buster in his way had merely attempted to protest against the failing policies of philosophically blinded Jefferson and Madison, and the new crop of realistic legislators provided him with natural allies.

Henry Clay, John Calhoun, Richard Johnson, Jonathan Roberts, Peter Porter and Langdon Cheves arrived to give the Congress the finest crop of able young leaders that it had seen in years. The mavericks elected Henry Clay Speaker, and a new, electric wave of energy coursed through the stodgy legislature. At the time, the Congress physically consisted of two halls with the connecting chamber yet to be constructed. The roof of the newly completed House of Representatives leaked, but the new boys did not seem to mind. Speaker Clay symbolically decreed the changed order by banishing John Randolph's dog from the chamber; in the past such an action would have produced a tantrum; as one wag noted, no one before had dared turn the dogs out.

At the other end of Pennsylvania Avenue, a new spirit developed. James Madison's first cabinet had been described by friends as "mediocre." Madison had attempted to repay his many political debts and had surrounded himself with hacks; sectional balance and political necessity combined with an attempt to use the reward of high office to heal party wounds occasioned by the Old Republican revolt led by Randolph produced the worst cabinet in the short history of the country.

Madison would have preferred to have James Monroe at his right hand as Secretary of State, but political expediency and hard feelings prevented this appointment. Madison had thought about Jefferson's Secretary of the Treasury, the able Albert Gallatin of Pennsylvania, as his second choice, but Gallatin had too many political enemies. Finally, Madison had settled on Robert Smith, the brother of the influential Senator from Maryland, Samuel Smith, who had decided that if he could not be Secretary of State his brother should be. Madison knew Robert Smith too well; the amiable, lazy mediocrity had been Jefferson's Secretary of the Navy; recognizing that he would have to do all the work, continue to be his own Secretary of State, Madison compromised on Smith. Two years later, he regretted his decision and finally fired Smith, opening the way for the man who should have been appointed in the first place, James Monroe.

Monroe, following his own counsel, confirmed by Buster, had worked for two years to overcome his heresy and return from the political wilderness. He had written to John Taylor of Caroline and had consulted with his old mentor, now elder statesman, Thomas Jefferson. At his neighbor's suggestion he sold his house in Richmond, a symbolic act designed to signal his distancing himself from the Old Republicans who still dominated the State House. In October 1809 Monroe attended a banquet in Richmond honoring Thomas Jefferson, his first public appearance with one of the other members of the Virginia triumvirate since the election.

The public demonstration of fealty prompted President Madison to ask Jefferson to sound out his old friend Monroe to find out if he would consider a public office such as Governor of Louisiana or a high position in the army. Monroe replied he would take no office that required him to report to a man other than the President. In May 1810 Monroe visited Washington for the first time in two years in order to "settle diplomatic accounts." He met directly with President Madison, and, as he later recounted to Buster, he had been well received. This encouraged Monroe to further cleanse himself by running for Virginia public office. From this decision, events had moved quickly. First, he was elected to the House of Delegates; a short time later, on January 16, 1811, he was elected Governor with the full support of the Republican Party. Three months later, on March 20, 1811, President Madison offered James Monroe the post of Secretary of State, completely restoring the party maverick to grace.

The appointment of his friend Monroe as Secretary of State, the election of the War Hawks, and Madison's change of policy towards the national defense made Buster a happy man. At home the connecting door to the newspaper now remained open. Buster and Nancy were finally in full political agreement. The bone of contention had been removed. The *Herald* again supported Buster's political views. Scottie, age four, had changed. An active and alert child, he no longer had to scream for attention. He frequently busied himself at his own miniature desk in the newspaper shop and had his own toy press, created by the two freedmen. Nancy had hired two apprentice newsmen to assist her and had more time to devote to editorial tasks and her son.

James and Vivian had aged, but both retained their health. Jason and Skinny continued to expand their growing enterprises; Jason had "Clipper III" and "Clipper IV" under construction. The smell of war was in the air, and, anticipating that the day when Madison's government would issue letters of marque and reprisal authorizing American privateers to prey on French and English shipping, Jason was determined to be ready with the fastest predators afloat. In the interim, "Clipper I" and "Clipper II" worked the West Indies; "Clipper I" sailed out of Martinique and harassed the English merchantmen, and "Clipper II" used Barbados as it home port while preying on French shipping.

Toddy, fully recovered from his Halifax experience, had served his learning tour on board "Clipper I" and had replaced the captain when the latter transferred to "Clipper II." Jason would have given Toddy the new ship but reasoned that discretion required Toddy to sail from French waters against English commerce. He reasoned that the English in Barbados, where he based "Clipper II," might take umbrage at Toddy's presence.

J.J. had completed his two years at West Point and was now a freshly minted engineer lieutenant in the United States Army. His specialty was the construction of harbor defenses. This greatly pleased his cousin Buster. The one bill that Buster had drafted and seen passed into law during his first term in the House authorized thirty thousand dollars to be used to improve the defenses of the ports of New York, Baltimore and New Orleans. Politics prevented the Republican dominated Congress from approving expenditures to protect the port of Boston in Federalist Party controlled New England. J.J. now labored for the Port of New York.

On April 1st, 1811, an exuberant Buster, after enduring the first of a long line of April fool pranks by an irrepressible Scottie, bid his family good day, rode through the Virginia countryside where he observed the greening of the grass and the budding of trees and bushes, crossed the long bridge and hurried to his new office. As the newly appointed Chairman of the House of Representative's War Committee, Buster had to prepare for his first meeting with William Eustis, Madison's Secretary of War. Buster knew the session would be tedious and did not look forward to working with the New England physician who had been selected as a political compromise. Eustis, a two term Congressman and a loyal Republican, was the son-in-law of an influential New Hampshire Republican, John Langdon. Eustis with no military qualifications was amiable enough, but he was simply not a man who could prepare his country for war.

Thoughts of Eustis took the edge off Buster's anticipation for the day. The War Hawks had revitalized Congress, but Madison's cabinet remained an impediment. Henry Clay had appointed men under forty to chair every important committee, deliberately trying to match interests with assignments. Buster who had no military experience but who had made a name for himself during his first term, was one example. Buster assumed the fact that he came from a defense minded family had helped. James had distinguished himself during the Revolution, J.J. served in the Army, and Jason was one of the country's foremost ship builders. Jason's views on the need for a strong navy were well known.

The first item on Buster's agenda was a call on Secretary of State James Monroe at his new office. This was the visit responsible for Buster's good mood. He sincerely believed that the country stood to gain with the hard working and clear-minded Monroe at the Mouse's elbow. Buster still privately referred to Madison as the Mouse. He could not disassociate the distasteful image of the frowning, diminutive Madison the day he promised to assist Toddy from his mind's picture of the new President.

At fifteen minutes until ten, Buster needlessly informed his clerk where he would be, and departed. The man smiled after his departing Congressman; Buster after two years in Congress still behaved as if he ran a one person office; the clerk after all kept track of his appointments and knew where Buster was at every moment in case the Speaker, the Secretary or another important man summoned. The President still coldly ignored Buster, but the clerk was confident that James Monroe's arrival and Buster's new position as committee chairman would soon change that.

The air was warm, and Buster took off his overcoat and laid it across the saddle. He debated whether to walk or not, but he decided he had not left himself enough time to ensure that he was not late for this his first official call on Secretary Monroe. They had already consulted several times privately as they made political plans, but this was Buster's first formal visit to the Secretary in his new office.

Buster looked around him in disgust as he followed Pennsylvania Avenue. Thomas Jefferson's poplars had taken hold, but the roadway was still rough and unpaved. Several times his horse had to detour around the pigs scavenging in the garbage that Washington's residents unceremoniously dumped in the streets. Numerous boarding houses had sprung up around the Capitol hill, but Pennsylvania Avenue remained wild and unsettled. Public buildings to house the government's several departments were under construction; none were imposing enough to impress Buster who thought the nation deserved better in its capital. After twenty years, George Washington himself would have expected more. The city was still a frontier village when compared with Boston, New York or Philadelphia.

Buster hitched his horse to one of the several posts that had been positioning in front of the building that the State and War Departments shared. Monroe and his wife occupied an unimpressive house on F Street within walking distance of the office. Buster knew that Monroe had heard the snide comments about his choice of residences, but the unassuming Secretary ignored them, confiding that his financial situation was still precarious, particularly since his brother was proving to be a problem with his extravagances. Monroe, Virginian gentleman that he was, continued to cover his younger brother's expenses.

"Buster," James Monroe welcomed Buster. He rose and met Buster halfway across the large office.

Buster stepped past the clerk who had escorted him into the Secretary's presence as soon as Buster appeared. Buster assumed that word of his close relationship with the new Secretary had already spread. In the past, Madison's clerk had kept him waiting a full half-hour or longer.

"Mr. Secretary," Buster smiled, genuinely pleased to see his friend. "This office, and another nearby, fit you." Buster referred to the room occupied by Madison in the President's House.

"James, will do, old friend," Monroe said. He grasped Buster's right hand firmly and clasped Buster's arm with his free hand, using his politician's skills to emphasize warmth.

Monroe followed Buster to the window and stood beside him as Buster appreciated the splendid view of the Potomac.

"One day," Buster exclaimed, revealing his good cheer. "One day this city will be magnificent."

"But it's not there yet," Monroe agreed. "We must see what we can do to hurry that day along."

Monroe remained standing until Buster took a chair facing his friend's desk. Neither man stood on formality. Monroe poured Buster a cup of tea from a silver pitcher that waited on his desk. He slid the tea across to Buster and looked up.

"James I... ." Buster began but was halted by the Secretary with a cautionary wave of his hand.

As Buster watched, Monroe walked around his desk and across the large room. He softly closed the door and returned to his chair facing Buster.

"My clerks are all anxious. They fear the new broom, and they gossip horribly," Monroe explained his action. "Now we can talk freely."

"How do you find the President?" Buster asked, genuinely concerned. He had feared that Madison's appointment of Monroe to the Secretary of State position was another political maneuver designed to give the political Machiavelli a scapegoat if needed.

"I'll speak frankly Buster. He's still the old friend I once knew. He recognizes the problems we face and that he needs help. His cabinet is a disgrace."

"The selections were his," Buster replied, not so willing to be forgiving as his friend. Buster shook his head in disapproval. "The times do not permit such a luxury. Can he rise above politics?" Buster's doubt was evident in his tone.

"I think so," Monroe answered. "I've known Mr. Madison a very long time. We have worked closely together on Mr. Jefferson's agenda."

"But can he work on one of his own?"

"I think so. That's why I'm here."

Buster realized that Monroe's appointment was a partial answer to his questions, his doubt.

"Neither you nor I, friend, would be sitting here today if Mr. Madison were not prepared to do what is necessary."

"Has the President discussed defense and war with you?" Buster had heard rumors that the President had designated Monroe to serve as his conduit to the Congress, charged with preparing the nation for war.

"The President recognizes that past policies have failed. He has entrusted me with 'putting the nation in armor' as he so aptly phrases it."

"That pleases me. And the Secretary of War? I must meet with Secretary Eustis later in the day."

"Secretary Eustis is a gentleman, but he is not equipped to prepare our nation's military. He still lives Mr. Jefferson's dream."

"That cheap gunboats can defend our harbors and a citizen militia will fight our wars?"

"Yes, unfortunately."

"Then changes must be made."

"The President realizes this. He hopes to work with the new leaders of Congress and bring the party and the nation around to the realization that war is imminent. You recognize of course that the President endorsed your elevation to your current chairmanship?"

Buster let the surprise show. He had thought his appointment had been made by the new Speaker's decision to cast seniority aside when he made his selections.

"No. I did not. I would not anticipate that Mr. Madison would accept me in a position of responsibility. Our relationship, as you know well, has not been amiable."

"Mr. Clay is still a member of the Republican Party whose leader is the President. The Speaker informed the President of his intentions."

"He did not object?"

"He heartily endorsed the choice. The President is now determined to place strong and able men in positions of trust."

"I wonder how the President will react when the Congress passes a bill calling for the addition of 10,000 regulars to the Army?"

"He will approve," Monroe responded without hesitation.

"And the authorization of 50,000 volunteers if necessary?"

"If that's enough."

"And the building of naval ships and the arming of merchant vessels?"

"That too."

"And the negative impact on the budget?"

James Monroe rose and began to pace.

"War is at hand. We must prepare the nation. We have no choice."

"Thank God," Buster declared. "A new day has arisen. And what has brought about this change in Mr. Madison?"

"The President is not an unintelligent man. He has the finest mind, next to that of Mr. Jefferson, that I have encountered. He's a political animal who for his entire career has implemented the wishes of his master. This was by choice. Times have now changed. Mr. Madison is President and must make the decisions. I assure you they will be the right ones."

"I understand your loyalty, James," Buster spoke frankly as a friend. "And I pray that you are correct."

"I am."

Not long after this conversation, Congress adjourned. Buster's initial enthusiasm was dampened by conversations with fellow Republicans who held a hundred and eight to thirty-six majority in the House. Most supported his proposals for enhancing the army, but many of the straight line Republicans, still unwilling to abandon Jeffersonian principles, opposed the expenditures required to expand the navy by ten frigates and an equal number of men-of-war.

In May 1811, an incident happened in the lower Chesapeake, which fortunately did not involve a Satterfield ship. British warships responding to the re-imposition of the on again off again non-intercourse act reappeared and began to stop American ships headed for France. Angered by the increase in the numbers of Americans impressed by English warships, President Madison ordered the U.S.S. "President" under Commodore John Rodgers to halt the English violations of American sovereignty. The "President" had encountered at the entrance to Chesapeake Bay a British warship, which the Commodore took to be a like sized warship the "Guerriere." When the English ship did not respond to the American signals, Commodore Rodgers gave the order to open fire despite the impending nightfall. Within fifteen minutes the English ship capitulated. Commodore Rodgers was dismayed to learn that he had captured the much smaller "Little Belt," a corvette.

In the diplomatic furor that followed, each government supported its captain. The American public was delighted; finally revenge for the "Chesapeake Affair" had been extracted. Madison, on behalf of the nation, applauded Commodore Rodgers and his crew.

In June, a new English Minister arrived, Sir Augustus John Foster. He carried letters that declared that reparations for the "Chesapeake" would be withheld until the "Little Belt" incident was resolved to English satisfaction.

In November the War Hawk Congress convened, determined to prepare the country for war. President Madison, following an agenda prepared by Buster and Monroe, recommended enlarging the army, building ships for the navy, stockpiling military equipment and completing and enlarging the military academy at West Point. The Congress finally approved the enhancement of the army but failed by a close vote in the House of 62 to 59 to approve the recommendations for the navy. A few of the western War Hawks who looked to the army to defend their citizens against the English-inspired Indian raids voted to divert the available resources from the navy.

Jason was incensed, but Buster, now the politician, recognized that the vote had been close, and he had only to swing three War Hawks to support the navy to achieve his, Jason's, and the President's objective.

In February 1812, James Monroe, over Buster's dissenting advice, acceded to a Madison demand. Monroe unwisely paid a self-described French Count fifty thousand dollars for documents that allegedly proved that the English Governor of Canada was engaged in a conspiracy with Federalist New England leaders opposed to their government's war plans to split New England off from the Union. The sensational documents turned out to be letters drafted by the Count himself. They revealed no names of the alleged American conspirators. When it was finally learned that the Count was a notorious French con artist, the President and Secretary of State were sorely embarrassed.

More importantly, in Buster's opinion, the rejection of his proposals for the navy placed the United States in a difficult position. With a navy one-sixth the size of the English North American fleet, with few experienced officers and men and an incompetent Secretary of Navy with marginal seafare experience, the United States was dangerously vulnerable. Despite this weakness, relations between the United States and England had deteriorated to the point that the President recommended to Congress that it declare war before adjourning in March. The session dragged on as this momentous issue was discussed, and Speaker Clay maneuvered to thwart the planned adjournment. Congress could not decide whether to declare war on both the French and English, the English alone, or the French. War fever so engulfed the country that few paused to consider the country's unpreparedness for battle. The politicians, like Tolstoy's sheep, led by following in front of the public's whim.

On June 1st, a clerk read President Madison's war message to a joint session. The President cited the old charges of impressment, seizure of commerce, violation of sovereignty and pretended blockades.

Following the reading, the House and Senate returned to their respective quarters to contemplate war. An alarmed British Minister received offers to buy his fine stable; clearly many anticipated his early departure. On June 4, 1812, the House voted 79 to 49 for war. The Senate dillied and dallied. On June 17, the Senators finally joined their House colleagues with a 19 to 13 vote for war.

The President signed the declaration. The United States and England were in a state of war.

FEDERAL DISTRICT OF WASHINGTON
AND THE CHESAPEAKE

AUGUST 1814

On the morning of August 18th, 1814, at exactly eleven o'clock, Jason burst into Buster's office in the Federal District without pausing to greet his son's clerk. After several minutes of excited, one-sided conversation, Jason erupted.

"Damn it Buster. What good is it having a son who's Chairman of the House War Committee and a friend of the President and the Secretary of State if you can't tell me what's going on?"

Jason was thoroughly and angrily frustrated.

Buster stared at Jason. He, like his father, was disconcerted by the news his father had just delivered.

"I'm sorry, dad, but I don't know anything about it. If the President and the Secretary knew anything, they would have told me."

"How can the country be invaded without the President knowing? What are we paying you people for?" Jason had a boatyard and ships on the high seas to worry about.

Jason was so angry that Buster would have risked laughing if the situation were not so serious. Buster had been busy at his desk reading the latest reports from the War Department when Jason pushed past an anxious clerk and burst unannounced into Buster's office. Jason reported that the "Clipper I" with Toddy in command had just docked in Alexandria. Toddy, returning to his homeport for provisioning after a successful forty days at sea, had encountered a large English convoy of at least fifty ships sailing on a direct line for the Chesapeake. A frigate and a schooner had tried to intercept the "Clipper I," but the swift ship had quickly left them in its wake.

"Toddy says they are entering the Chesapeake," Jason repeated for the third time. His words were more of an accusation than a report, as if Buster were personally responsible.

Buster recalled the debate that had disrupted the Cabinet last spring when British ships began raiding southern shores. Secretary of State Monroe had insisted then that the activity was a prelude to a move on Washington, but Secretary of War Armstrong had discounted the view as alarmist, opining that the English were only harassing the Bay area. Armstrong had insisted that the militia was adequate to cope with the threat, and President Madison agreed with him. Monroe then tabled concern about the government's lack of intelligence on British plans and movements and suggested that a warning system be established along the Chesapeake. Armstrong's negative reaction overrode him. Defense was a matter for the War department to address not the Secretary of State.

Buster had not known what to think. He believed that his friend Monroe was not completely objective on the subject of Armstrong. The two men had been bitter rivals since the day in February 1813, that Armstrong had joined the cabinet, replacing the hapless Eustis. All had recognized Madison's need to find a Secretary of War capable of managing the country's military effort. The war in Canada was not going well. Armstrong had been a major in George Washington's army, an aide to General Horatio Gates. A New Yorker married to a sister of Robert Livingston, he had served as a Minister to France. At the time of his appointment, Armstrong had been a militia brigadier general in charge of the City of New York's defenses. He was not, therefore, without a military background, and his appointment was politically wise, a sop to New York.

Unfortunately, Armstrong was an abrasive man with a sharp tongue who not only aspired to the presidency but also detested James Monroe. Armstrong shared his in-law's, the Livingston family's, resentment against the Secretary of State which dated back to the days when Livingston and Monroe shared negotiating responsibilities in France and contested the credit for managing the Louisiana Purchase.

"I must report immediately to the Secretary of State," Buster said, rising from behind his desk to face his father.

"Did Toddy have any more information than what you told me?"

"Only that fifty English warships have entered the Bay," Jason repeated. "They are not coming our way for tea." Jason pounded his son's desk with his clenched fist. "You can tell your friends that I want to know what they are going to do about it."

Buster nodded as he circled the desk and headed for the door. He understood what troubled his father. Nothing stood between Alexandria and the British fleet. They could sail directly up the Potomac, and Jason's shipyard would be one of their primary targets.

"Do you have any ships in the Potomac other than "Clipper I?"

"Two schooners."

"I'll keep you informed."

Buster knew as well as his father that his ships had no place to go. If the English sailed up the Potomac to Alexandria, Jason's ships could retreat upstream a few miles as far as the great falls, then they were trapped.

When he arrived at the State Department, Buster found Secretary Monroe busy at his desk. He quickly related Jason's alarming news and together the two men rushed to the President's House where they briefed a shocked President Madison.

"I fear you may have been correct, James," Madison referred to his Secretary of State's earlier concerns about a British move against Washington.

Monroe studied his friend with barely concealed irritation. He had been so concerned about Armstrong's dilatory conduct as Secretary of War that he had written a letter to the President recommending that Armstrong be fired. Instead, the President had ordered the Secretary of War to remain in Washington and to cease playing general in the northern campaigns where he had succeeded in antagonizing most of his generals who resented Armstrong's interference. A month ago, on July 2nd, the President had reacted to Monroe's concerns by creating a new military district encompassing the Chesapeake Bay and the Potomac and had appointed William Winder, a Maryland lawyer, to command it. Winder, the brother of the Governor of Maryland, was commissioned a brigadier general and ordered to provide for the defense of the capital. Although a political general, Winder had a military background; he had been captured and exchanged following the battle in the north at Stoney Creek.

General Winder had immediately buried himself under an avalanche of paper intended to establish his new command. In Monroe's opinion, Winder was a paperwork general and not a very good one at that. In normal times, he would have been perfect for Washington, but he was not the man to defend the capital against an invading force. Winder had ordered the nearby states to hold ten thousand militiamen in readiness to come to Washington's defense.

Secretary of War Armstrong, still skeptical that Washington was an objective, busied himself with everything but the defense of the capital. Although over 100,000 militiamen were carried on the rolls of nearby states, Armstrong's deliberate procrastination delayed their mobilization.

Jason and Toddy's news caught the American military in a state of complete and inexcusable unpreparedness.

"We must immediately alert General Winder and Secretary Armstrong," Madison reacted, dispatching a clerk to find both men.

While they waited for the two men to appear, the President, the Secretary of State, and Buster anxiously discussed what need be done. Finally, after an hour, Monroe in an extreme state of frustration declared:

"Mr. President we cannot wait. We must find out what is happening."

"What do you recommend?" The President asked.

"With your permission, Buster and I will ride south and scout the lower bay."

The President studied his Secretary of State. He knew the suggestion was not as ridiculous as it sounded. Monroe had had considerable experience as a military officer during the Revolution. In fact, Monroe had spent as much time leading troops in combat as any of today's generals. Still, Madison hesitated. He could imagine what the Federalist press would have to say when they learned the Secretary of State at the moment of crisis rode off to scout the enemy.

"If the English are landing," Monroe continued, "you have no need for a Secretary of State. Diplomatic negotiations are at an end. We have nothing left to do but fight."

"Very well," Madison agreed. "We need reliable information."

Monroe and Buster rushed out the door of the President's House and encountered General Winder and Secretary of War Armstrong. Buster impatiently recounted the story of the English fleet for the third time. Armstrong smiled and again doubted that the English would be so foolish as to attack Washington.

"At the very most, Baltimore will be their target," Armstrong sneered.

Winder, however, reacted with near panic.

"I must summon the militia," he said as he turned to his horse.

Monroe seized his arm.

"First, consult with the President. Buster and I will ride south and collect the needed intelligence."

Armstrong laughed, and Monroe glared.

"I will assign my escort to ride with you," General Winder referred to the four cavalrymen who waited in front of the President's house.

"Very well," Monroe agreed.

"Shall we take time to change into our riding clothes?" Buster asked. He looked down at his black suit and patent leather shoes.

"No time for you to return to Alexandria," Monroe replied instantly. "We will stop at my house. I will have something to fit you."

Buster agreed. The two men retrieved their mounts from the State Department and rode quickly to Monroe's modest F Street home. Within minutes, Monroe had briefed his wife, and he and Buster had dressed more comfortably. Monroe's worn shirt and trousers fit Buster adequately, but the riding boots were a little too large. The two men joined the cavalrymen and then hurried south on the Bladensburg Road.

The ill prepared scouting party rode hard, but it required the better part of two days for them to cover the fifty miles to the small town of Benedict on the Patuxent River. Several delays were necessitated by the need to find replacement horses, which panicked farmers, were reluctant to surrender. Fortunately, Monroe had been wise enough to bring along a sizable pouch containing expense money. From this sum he paid three times what each replacement horse was worth, but he reasoned the crisis demanded it.

While Buster, Monroe and their escort hurried southwards, the fifty-one ship English fleet separated. Captain Sir Peter Parker in his frigate "Menelaus," accompanied by two schooners, set sail up the Chesapeake heading towards a point north of Baltimore where he could disrupt communications between Washington and Philadelphia and New York. Simultaneously, Captain James Alexander Gordon in the frigate "Seahorse," accompanied by the frigate "Euryalus," a rocket ship, four bomb ships and a dispatch schooner set sail for the

Potomac River; their mission was to create a diversion by menacing Alexandria and the Federal District from the river. The main fleet element entered the Patuxent River with the town of Benedict as its destination. On board the flagship "Tonnant" were Admiral Sir Alexander Cochrane, the commander-in-chief, Rear Admiral George Cockburn, the local English expert who had commanded raiding forces harassing the Chesapeake for the past year, and Major General Robert Ross, the commander of three regiments of infantry, marines and seamen, 3,000 men in all, who would mount the march on Washington.

On August 16th, Rear Admiral George Cockburn, the "Scourge of the Chesapeake" in "Albion" had rallied with the fleet commanded by Admiral Sir Alexander Cochrane who ruled the South Atlantic from his headquarters in Bermuda. On board were General Robert Ross and his men from the Fourth, Forty-fourth and Eighty-fifth Regiments. Battle hardened by Wellington's campaign in Spain, the regiments and their commander were well tested. Their orders were to create a diversion on the coasts of the United States to relieve pressure on Canada. The fiery raider Cockburn had other plans. He had already sent a message to Dolly Madison threatening one day soon to bow in her parlor.

Admiral George Cockburn, who had obtained flag rank at forty, was already a legend. He was not the youngest naval officer to make admiral at forty; Lord Nelson had done so at thirty-eight, but Cockburn, the son of a distinguished Member of Parliament, was true navy. At the age of ten he went to sea as a "captain's servant." By age fourteen, he was a fledgling officer on a war sloop. At age twenty, he made lieutenant and two years later obtained command of a fourteen-gun sloop as a post captain. His heroics earned him the prestige of becoming a protege of Lord Nelson. In 1803 he commanded the ship that carried Minister Merry to Norfolk and his Washington mission where he fell victim to Jefferson's pele mele. Cockburn and his vessel had continued on to New York where the captain became involved in a bitter dispute with local authorities over eight of Cockburn's seamen who had seized the opportunity to desert. Cockburn had taken the insult personally. In 1813 Cockburn was assigned to command a squadron whose orders were to carry the war to America. Cockburn in his flagship "Marlborough" had stationed himself off Lynnhaven Bay and had made life difficult for sailing vessels and the towns of the Chesapeake. His experiences prior to Admiral Cochrane's arrival led him to conclude that an attack on Washington was feasible. He was determined to seize the American capital and teach the upstarts a real lesson.

At their first meeting on "Tonnant" on the sixteenth, the commander-in-chief had been reluctant. His orders were to harass the Americans but not to engage in extended operations some distance from the coast. His force, originally planned for 13,000, had been drastically reduced to 3,000, and Admiral Cochrane was determined not to over-commit himself. General Ross, who was to command on shore, was a disciplined leader who always commanded from the front. Despite their cautious preconceptions, both Admiral Cochrane and General Ross were overwhelmed by Admiral Cockburn's fire and enthusiasm. He had successfully punished the American shores for the past year.

"Very well, Admiral," Admiral Cochrane conceded. "I will defer to your expertise and General Ross' authority." The commander-in-chief had the responsibility of deciding where to land the army, but General Ross had tactical control once ashore.

Cockburn studied his commander-in-chief, knowing he had carried the day. Cochrane with his white hair, round face, over-sized eyes, fiery red complexion, double chins and portly body looked as if he had been stuffed into his uniform. Cochrane had been an able commander in his day, but the soft life of Bermuda and age had dulled his fighting edge. Cochrane no longer had the spirit to overwhelm determined and successful subordinates, particularly well connected ones like Cockburn.

Cockburn turned to General Ross. Ross, ten years younger and forty pounds lighter, still was a battle minded general. Accustomed to the movements of large armies on the battlefields of Europe, the game of strike and burn was new to Ross, but Cockburn was a seasoned master. Earlier in the day Cockburn had taken Ross ashore to introduce him to the terrain and let him see for himself how easily his troops would be able to traverse it against minimal odds. Ross had not been able to believe they had been able to scout the terrain without challenge. He was worried because his men would be forced to fight without cavalry and artillery. They had been assembled as a raiding force not an army preparing to march on the enemy's capital.

The risk of overextending this small force with minimum firepower too far from its base, the fleet, worried him, but he had had to accept the enthusiastic Cockburn's assurances that Washington lay only fifty undefended miles inland. Ross, though more cautious, wanted a sensational victory as much as the younger Cockburn, and the lure of Washington was irresistible. Both men speculated that the capture of the American capital would so demoralize the Americans that they would capitulate. Napoleon had surrendered in the spring and now the Americans certainly recognized that the English now had the world's mightiest force to turn upon them.

"General Ross. Your views?" Admiral Cochrane interrupted Ross' musings.

"I agree with Admiral Cockburn. We can take Washington."

Admiral Cochrane studied his fellow commanders. He knew he was soft, but he was not yet senile. He was determined to make clear where responsibility for this risky decision rested.

"You are prepared to take your troops over fifty miles of enemy terrain without cavalry or artillery, overcome superior forces, capture the American capital, then relinquish it?"

All three knew that their force was not strong enough to hold Washington if the Americans chose to retreat then fight back.

"Yes sir." Ross was determined not to be intimidated by the older man.

"My spies tell me that Washington will be defended only by untested militia who have yet to be mobilized and armed," Cockburn intervened, determined not to let Ross back down.

"Your spies. Can they be trusted?" Cochrane asked, scrubbing his brow with a piece of cotton. He sat in his great cabin dressed as a commander-in-chief should, in his heavy wool uniform. Despite the ocean breeze coming through the open porthole, Cochrane was convinced that the temperature off the American coast was hotter than that in Bermuda.

"Many of the plantation owners along the Chesapeake were loyalists during the Revolution and were badly treated by the patriots. They still consider England home."

"And if their information is correct, that we face only unprepared and untrained militia, can your troops march fifty miles in this abominable heat? And then back, under hostile fire?" Cochrane, who remembered Concord, turned to Ross. "You have neither horses nor wagons."

"We will carry what we can, confiscate what we need, and live off the countryside," Cockburn interjected.

"Then, we shall proceed," Cochrane decided. "But with one proviso. If we encounter firm resistance, we withdraw. Our orders are clear on that."

"Lieutenant James Scott, my aide, will maintain constant communications between us," Cockburn offered, determined to keep any orders to retreat under his control. Cockburn intended to take Washington whatever the cost.

"Very well," Admiral Cochrane grumbled. "Good luck. When do you plan to disembark?"

"At dawn," Cockburn said.

Ross nodded agreement. The prize tempted his pride as a Wellington general.

The night of August 18th, Admiral Cochrane as Commander-in-Chief issued his final orders directing his forces "to destroy and lay waste such towns and districts upon the coast as may be found assailable."

Secretary of State James Monroe, Buster, and their scout squad of guards halted on a low hill about one quarter of a mile from Benedict and the western bank of the Patuxent River. With the setting sun behind them, they stared at a fearsome sight.

The river was filled with English ships of war at anchor. Small boats of every description, barges and pinnaces and cutters, hurried in streams from the waiting ships, conveying brightly dressed troops to shore. Already units had formed as rallying points, and columns of smoke rose as cooks prepared to feed the red clad soldiers who milled about like ants.

"I count twenty-three square riggers," Monroe spoke softly.

He did not fear being overheard. The English sentries patrolled their outposts some distance away. Having encountered not a single musket shot in resistance, they paced as securely as if they were in Westminster Square. The people of Benedict had either fled their town, or they perspired in their homes behind closed doors. In the distance, a few civilians could be seen talking with English officers.

"I wonder what they are saying?" Buster spoke aloud but was addressing himself.

He and Monroe, like the soldiers who had accompanied them, were staring at the debarking troops with awe.

"This is more than a raid," Monroe observed professionally. "Twenty-three ships and I estimate at least a regiment if not more."

"It looks like they be forming near three headquarters," the sergeant who commanded their guards observed.

"I think you're right, sergeant. Would you say three regiments, or brigades or what?" Monroe asked.

"Too soon to say, sir," the sergeant replied. "We could try to move closer and identify their insignia."

"Not worth the risk. How many would you estimate?"

The sergeant, Monroe and Buster tried to count the milling troops.

"Maybe a thousand," Buster guessed, "but it's difficult to tell with the boats unloading more all the time."

"If they form in columns, we could count better," the sergeant observed.

"If they form in columns, they are marching somewhere. What do you say is their objective, Buster?" Monroe asked.

"Washington or Baltimore, they're about the same distance."

"If you were the commander, Cockburn, I'm sure, where would you go?"

"The Federal District," Buster replied without a pause.

"To what end?"

"If it's Cockburn, it will be to burn the town. He'll know the President and the Congress will flee before he can arrive."

"Agreed. It's Washington," Monroe declared.

"Should we ride to warn the President?" Buster asked.

"No," Monroe decided quickly. "We must find out for certain what their plans are."

"I wish I knew what they are discussing," Buster again studied the cluster of civilians conferring with the English. They appeared to be gesturing towards their town.

"Loyalist and friends of John Bull," Monroe hypothesized. "This area is loaded with them. The redbacks will find many willing collaborators."

While Buster continued to watch the landing boats and milling troops, Monroe scribbled a short message on a piece of paper he took from his saddlebags. He turned to the sergeant.

"Have your most reliable man take this to President Madison at the President's House."

"Yes, sir," the sergeant saluted the Secretary of State and hurried back to where his three troopers waited.

Monroe turned back to Buster.

"That will tell the President what we know. I urged him to summon the militia to Washington and dig their fortifications forthwith. We will delay here until we can learn which direction the troops take and in what numbers. I have seen no sign of cavalry or artillery. Without cavalry they cannot scout or pursue us, and without artillery they will not be able to overcome our fortifications. There's hope, if we are ready."

"Do you think I could pass as a loyalist?" Buster asked.

Monroe studied his friend and then the English troops. He immediately perceived what Buster planned.

"It's not worth the risk," he said. At the very same time, he realized that they needed to know the English objective.

"I can do it," Buster said. Buster studied the clothes that Monroe had loaned him. They were ill fitting and shabby.

"You look the part," Monroe laughed.

"I'll wait until tomorrow morning. They'll be nervous tonight, their first ashore."

Monroe and Buster watched the boats land and discharge troops until night fell, and they could see no more. Then, they retreated to the forest at the base of their little hill, cared for their horses, and shared the scraps of food that they carried in their saddlebags.

In Washington chaos reigned. Citizens packed their bags and loaded their wagons with valuables. Some with their families and what possessions they could carry retreated northward towards Frederick, and other streamed across the Chain Bridge and the Long Bridge to sanctuary with friends in Virginia. Most movement came from the ranks of the citizenry. The army was nowhere to be seen. On Madison's instructions General Winder sent riders to Virginia, Maryland, Pennsylvania and northward calling for the immediate mobilization and dispatch of the militia to defend Washington. Three regiments stationed in Baltimore were ordered to the Federal District. Captain Barney's flotilla retreated up the Patuxent. President Madison sent orders that Barney was to be prepared to scuttle his small force, blocking English access to the upper reaches of the river, and to bring his seamen, experienced with cannon, to Washington to aid in the defense. General Winder was suddenly overwhelmed with administrative problems; he needed weapons and ammunition and tents and provisions for his soon to arrive militia. The paperwork confined Wilder to his office for two days, so long that subordinates began to plead for someone to lead them.

Secretary of War John Armstrong watched the clamor with cynical detachment. He refused to believe that the English intended to march on Washington, and to anyone who asked he replied that Baltimore is their destination. He firmly believed that the efforts to defend Washington were wasted; as a consequence, he stood aside and shirked his duties.

At the President's House, an elderly and not very well James Madison performed the job of his Secretary of War and General Winder. He worried about troop dispositions. Brigadier General Van Ness, the commander of the militia of the Federal District and Winder's second in command, appeared in a state of distress. He reported that General Winder was so preoccupied with the paper work he did not have time to deal with the confused, unarmed but arriving militia. Van Ness asked to be appointed commander vice the ineffective Winder. The harassed President told Van Ness he was out of order and instructed his Secretary of War to find another job for Van Ness. Out of the President's hearing, the inscrutable Armstrong told Van Ness he was not needed. Van Ness resigned on the spot from the militia and set about on his own to organize a civilian defense force.

A group of citizens, concerned about the confusion that they saw about them, held a public meeting and decided to build fortifications at their own expense at Bladensburg at a key junction of the coastal roads. The harassed Winder accepted the offer.

In government offices worried clerks on their own authority packed vital documents. Secretary of War Armstrong observed a senior clerk hastily packing the Declaration of Independence. Armstrong did not interfere but observed that he thought it was all wasted effort because he did not think the British had any intention of marching on Washington.

Dolly Madison at the President's house, a witness to the confusion that had stricken the government, made her own decision to save her valuables. While her husband, the President, attempted to rally his government, the jolly Dolly and her servants packed.

THE PATUXENT AND THE FEDERAL DISTRICT

AUGUST 1814

Throughout the night, the small craft scurried between the men-of-war and the shore, ferrying troops. By mid morning Brigadier General Ross' three regiments were ashore. He paused several hours to rest the late arrivals and to give them time to acquire their land legs. After noon on Saturday, August 20th, the general gave the order and his regiments in three columns began their march. The road from Benedict took them a short distance inland then turned north towards Nottingham about twenty miles upstream. Admiral Cockburn tried to parallel the march with his small flotilla of tenders and armed boats filled with marines experienced in riverine raiding.

About ten o'clock, Monroe, Buster and the three escorts withdrew from their hill and raced through the countryside to a point not far from the junction where the Nottingham road turned northward to parallel the Patuxent River in the direction of Baltimore and Washington. The road was empty, and nearby farmhouses deserted. The farm families who lived close to the anticipated route of march had received the word and had sought sanctuary with friends and relatives elsewhere.

About one mile from the junction, Buster found a farm that suited his purposes. While Monroe and the escort waited, Buster circled the vacated farmhouse. Buster halted, knocked on the door, and called loudly to announce his presence. Receiving no response, he pushed on the closed door and entered. Dirty dishes, apparently left behind from a day old dinner, littered the table. Buster counted four places. He assumed the farm had been occupied by a couple and two children who had fled in haste. He closed the door carefully behind him and circled the house to inspect the barn that stood behind the house. It too was empty, but Buster found a large scythe leaning against the wall inside the door. Buster picked up the scythe and returned to his horse. Taking the reins in one hand and carrying the scythe in the other, Buster led his mount to the road where he rejoined Monroe and their escort.

"The family has fled; this looks like a perfect place for me to meet our visitors," Buster tried to sound offhanded when he spoke to Monroe.

"Are you sure you want to go through with this?" Monroe asked, concern in his voice.

"We have to learn their destination," Buster emphasized the obvious.

"Very well, then," Monroe said, rising in his stirrups and studying the countryside. "Give us your horse, and we will take cover in the woods over there."

Monroe pointed at a thickly forested area about a quarter of a mile across a brown hay field behind the barn.

"And I will help Mr. Farmer with his harvest," Buster indicated a partially cut field of wheat that stretched from the road towards the forest north of the farmhouse.

"Be careful," Monroe cautioned. "We'll wait in the woods until you join us. Don't stare at the troops. Try to ignore them. Be a simple farmer worried only about your crop. We'll count their numbers from the forest."

Buster nodded, handed the reins to Monroe, and grasped the scythe in both hands.

"Do you know how to use that?" Monroe, an experienced gentleman farmer, asked.

"I spent a summer in the Short Hills. I learned more about harvesting than I ever wanted to know."

"Very well," Monroe said, as he directed his horse towards the forest behind the barn.

Two of the escorts, stern faced, kneed their mounts and followed. The sergeant paused long enough to ask Buster if he wished the trooper to take his place.

"I've harvested many a bushel of wheat in my day," the sergeant volunteered.

"No thank you, sergeant," Buster replied. "This is my idea."

Buster watched as the sergeant followed Monroe and the other two soldiers around the barn. As soon as they had disappeared around the side, Buster turned and walked towards the wheat field. Although not an expert, he recognized that the farmer had a rich crop. The tall golden spikes reached to his knees. He picked one stalk and paused to rub the full head in his palms. Hard kernels fell to the ground. Buster assumed the farmer must have been brokenhearted when forced to abandon his next winter's bread at its peak moment. Buster vowed to do what he could to assist the absent farmer's harvest while he used the field to explain his presence.

The farmer had spent the previous morning cutting his grain. Thick swatches lay in rows where they had dropped before the scythe's wide blade. He had cut about one third of his field before quitting for dinner. Then, word of the debarking English must have arrived, and the family had fled in panic. Buster decided to work the edge of the field as far from the road as he could get. He assumed that a frightened farmer, concerned for his crop, would keep as much distance between himself and the marching columns as he could.

Buster began swinging the scythe. It required thirty minutes before he acquired a comfortable motion. After about an hour, he paused. The noonday sun was hot; his back and arm muscles ached, and blisters had begun to form on his hands. He had not thought of that. If a suspicious soldier studied his hands, he would find the tender skin of a city dweller. Buster studied the backs of his hands and was pleased to note that they were properly tanned. He buttoned the sleeves of his ill fitting shirt around his wrists and hoped the soldiers would assume he was merely protecting his arms from the sticky wheat chaff.

Buster wiped the sweat from his forehead and cheeks, streaking the tanned skin with dirt. He looked down the road and saw nothing. He listened and heard only the farm birds. Finally, he lay down the scythe, returned to the farmhouse where he lifted a bucket of cold water from the shallow well, doused himself thoroughly, then returned to the wheat field. After another hour, his muscles screamed, and his hands burned, but he continued to swing the scythe. Buster took time to envy Monroe and the soldiers waiting comfortably in the shady woods. The sun increased in intensity, and Buster could see heat swirls rising from the ground. At about three o'clock, Buster decided he could labor no more. He rested the scythe blade on the ground, leaned against the long handle, and considered another trip to the farmhouse. Pangs of hunger replaced the nervous twitching of his stomach. Before he could decide, a distant rumble caught his attention. His initial reaction was thunder or gunfire, then he caught the rhythmic beat of marching drums.

Buster looked back at the forest where Monroe waited, seeking reassurance, got none, then turned towards the road. He stood at the farthest point in the field from the hard, dusty track. The beat grew louder, and soon Buster was able to discern the slap of marching feet. In the distance a flash of color caught his attention. As soon as the lead elements of the first column came into view, Buster turned his back to them and began to stroke the wheat with his scythe. His tension fed his motion, and the wheat fell in swatches.

The marching troops were almost abreast of him, some fifty yards away, when Buster allowed himself to look up. He stopped stroking, leaned on his tool, and watched. The marching soldiers were impressive in their heavy red and white wool uniforms. Each carried a large knapsack on his back and a long rifle on his shoulder. Their faces were beet red; they were suffering from the heat worse than Buster. As he watched, an officer, wearing a saber and gold epaulets, issued a command. A sergeant turned and barked an order. The drums stopped, and the column halted. The sergeant shouted again, and the soldiers dropped to the ground on each side of the road. The lucky ones found protection from the punishing Chesapeake sun in the shade of the trees. The officer again spoke to the sergeant and pointed in Buster's direction.

Buster wondered if he should run. Four of the soldiers rushed across the wheat field towards him, and he knew it was too late. He belatedly recognized that their long rifles would have stopped him in any case.

The four soldiers circled Buster and lowered their rifles so that the muzzles pointed at the pit of his stomach.

"A hot day, mister," the sergeant said, ignoring the incongruity of his friendly words and the aimed rifles.

Buster nodded and continued to lean on his scythe.

"A fine crop," the sergeant said, breaking off a stalk and rubbing the kernels much as Buster had when he arrived in the field.

"It will give you much flour," the sergeant said as he indifferently dropped the grain to the ground. "For your family or the market?"

"Family," Buster grunted, speaking for the first time.

"In the house?"

"Visitin'"

"Not because of us?"

Buster nodded sourly.

"But you couldn't leave your grain?"

"It's time to cut," Buster said stubbornly, hot and tired and feeling his role.

The sergeant studied Buster, then made up his mind.

"Where's your well?" He asked.

"House." Buster replied.

"Show me," the sergeant ordered.

Buster, silently, turned and grasped the handle of the scythe, a farmer preparing to carry it with him, unwilling to leave his valuable tool in the field where others might take it.

"Leave it," the sergeant ordered.

Buster gently placed the scythe on the ground. The sergeant and the three soldiers followed as he led them through the field to the house.

"There," Buster pointed at the well.

"Poisoned?" The sergeant asked suspiciously.

Buster went to the well, lowered the bucket, then drank deeply from it, carelessly spilling the water on his shirt, which was already soaked with sweat.

The sergeant nodded to one of the soldiers who hurried to the well. The sergeant sent the other two to inspect the house and barn.

"Empty, sergeant," they called back quickly.

The sergeant waved to the officer who spoke to another sergeant who called to the resting column. Suddenly, masses of soldiers streamed to the well. Buster stepped back and sought refuge on the rickety porch of the house. He sat on the edge and watched. Soon, the officer who he had seen in the distance approached.

"Lived here long?" The officer asked, apparently trying to make small talk.

"A mite," Buster replied, reasoning that the less he said the better.

"Ever been to Nottingham?"

"Once."

"How far?"

"Don't know."

"Guess."

"Fifteen, sixteen miles."

"And then to Marlboro?"

"Yep. "

"How far?"

"Don't know."

"Don't know much, do you?" The officer sneered. Thinking better of it, he tried to speak more kindly. "Don't be worried. The General has issued strict orders that we are not to touch civilian property. We're not going to burn your house or harm you."

Buster tried to look as if the words reassured him.

"What's your name?"

Buster in his inexperience had not expected such a question.

"Cruiky" he replied using the first name that popped into his mind.

"Well Farmer Cruiky," the officer began again. "We are not going to harm you, but Admiral Cockburn's a different story. You've heard of Admiral Cockburn?"

Buster had heard of the "Scourge of the Chesapeake." He nodded affirmatively.

"How far to Marlboro from Nottingham?"

"Ten miles, I hear," Buster stammered. "Don't know for sure. Never been there."

"And from Marlboro to where the road splits, one for Baltimore and one for Washington?"

Buster did not reply, and the officer glared.

"How far from Marlboro to Washington?"

"Don't know."

The officer turned to his sergeant who took a step towards Buster.

"A day," Buster blurted. "The way you're travelin'."

"Thank you Farmer Cruiky," the officer turned, walked a few steps, then spun back to face Buster.

"Where are your horses?"

"Only have two," Buster gulped. "Wife and the young'uns have the team and the wagon."

"Where?"

"Visitin'."

The officer frowned, obviously weary of the conversation.

"Sergeant," he ordered. "Form the column."

The sergeant turned, shouted his commands, and the grumbling troops reformed their column of twos. The drums began their beat, the sergeants barked, and the march recommenced.

Buster returned to his field, retrieved his scythe and resumed his cutting, ignoring the passing column. He cut steadily, and the long red line took two hours to pass. As soon as the rear guard disappeared in the distance, he walked to the well, drank deeply for his thirst and in case somebody was watching, considerately returned the scythe to the barn, and then hurried across the dried hay field. As soon as he entered the forest, Monroe and the three troopers joined him.

"You look awful," Monroe laughed.

"I feel awful," Buster replied, displaying his blistered hands. He stretched his aching muscles then spoke.

"Washington," he declared. "They wanted to know how far from Marlboro to Washington."

"Just as I thought," Monroe sighed. "We counted three regiments, some five thousand soldiers."

"And Admiral Cockburn is somewhere about."

"Probably on the river with his gunboats as artillery,"

Monroe took a piece of paper from his saddlebags, quickly wrote a report, folded it, and handed it to the sergeant.

"For the President?" The sergeant asked.

"Yes. Take it yourself and describe for him what you've seen. Tell him Mr. Satterfield and myself are heading for Marlboro."

"Do you think they will take the crossroad that leads from north of Nottingham to Wood Yard?" The sergeant asked. "It's much shorter than going through Marlboro."

Both Monroe and the sergeant studied Buster.

"He didn't ask, and I didn't volunteer," Buster replied. After a few seconds of thought he continued. "But I would not be surprised that they learn of the cut off. The officer knew what he was doing."

"Then tell the President we are going to Wood Yard," Monroe decided quickly.

"Yes, sir. "

The sergeant saluted and rode off in the direction of the farm.

Monroe and Buster watched as the sergeant crossed the road and disappeared into the woods to the west.

"The sergeant has a good idea," Monroe agreed. "He's circling the column to the west and then he will head north to Wood Yard and Old Fields. We'll do the same."

Concerned about the heat, General Ross moved slowly, pausing frequently to rest his heavily burdened troops who suffered in the intense August temperatures. The first night Ross stopped after covering only six miles. Monroe and Buster on horseback had no difficulty circling the panting soldiers. A thunderstorm, typical of the area, struck at midnight on Saturday, soaking the exposed Englishmen. At dawn on Sunday, August 21st they resumed their trek.

Early that morning, Monroe and Buster reached Nottingham. They alerted the local militia and encouraged the residents to move their valuables. That done, they hurried onward to Wood Yard where General Winder had established his headquarters a little over half way between Benedict and the Federal District. Here, Winder had two thousand troops and twelve six pounders. Monroe and

Buster reported their observations to the American commander. He was alarmed to learn that the English marched at least 5,000 troops, greatly outnumbering his first defensive outpost. Winder had some 3,000 troops including the Maryland regiments deployed to Bladensburg where they labored on fortifications, and he realized he had unwisely split his army, but he had had no choice; he had not known which road the English would take.

At five in the afternoon on August twenty-first, the skirmishers of Ross' advance guard reached the outskirts of Nottingham. The Maryland militia had wisely withdrawn. Many of the residents, alerted by Monroe and Buster, had fled. Those that remained huddled in their homes. A few staunch loyalists welcomed the arriving English as liberators and answered their many questions while directing them to shelter and provisions.

The next morning General Ross' column continued northward towards Marlboro. During the day, Monday, August 22nd, Admiral Cockburn reported. After having parted with the General on the night of August 20th, Cockburn's flotilla had followed the Patuxent attempting to roughly keep pace with the marching troops so as to provide cannon support if needed. The gunboats had encountered no opposition until they reached Pigs Point just south of Marlboro where they found a small American flotilla, which had been reported to be commanded by Captain Barney, an America seaman of no small reputation. Cockburn had landed his marines to circle the blockade by land then proceeded forward with his gunboats. He discovered that Barney had scuttled his boats and blocked further passage. Cockburn left Captain Robyns in command of his craft and proceeded with his marines and armed seamen to Marlboro, some thirty miles from his destination of Washington.

Ross and Cockburn missed the road to Wood Yard, where Winder worried and waited, and proceeded along the main road to Marlboro. As soon as his scouts reported this development, Winder retired to Old Field, a point equidistant from Washington and Bladensburg. From here, as soon as the English committed themselves irrevocably—they could march north from Marlboro to Baltimore or turn northeast as Monroe and Buster had predicted they would towards Bladensburg and Washington—he could either rush to Bladensburg to reunite his army or back to Washington to defend the city. In any case, he allowed the English to proceed unimpeded.

In Washington on August 22nd, the sergeant delivered Monroe and Buster's report to President Madison. The President gave it more credence than General Winder had. He ordered the militia units that had arrived from Virginia and Maryland to march to Bladensburg to meet the enemy. He passed the word that important government documents and records should be moved. In the afternoon, after having decided to bolster troop morale with his presence, he gave final instructions to the busy Dolly and departed to join General Winder at Old Fields.

Unaware of the President's plans and discouraged by the disorganization they found at Winder's headquarters, Buster and Monroe on fresh horses departed for Bladensburg where they found General Tobias Stansbury who had arrived late on the night of the twenty-second with 3,500 troops. Monroe, Buster and Stansbury waited for Winder to join them and reunite his army in the brink of time before the advancing English force.

President Madison, his Attorney General and his Secretary of Navy spent the night with General Winder at Old Fields. In the morning, Tuesday, the twenty-third, the President reviewed the troops, ate dinner then hurried with his entourage back to Washington. Without their knowledge, General Ross' army had passed within three miles of their camp.

As the morning unfolded without the appearance of Winder and his army at Bladensburg, Monroe, Buster and General Stansbury worried. Rumors that Winder had been captured circulated, adding to the unease.

They need not have worried about Winder, for after the President's departure General Winder, assuming the British were moving towards the Navy bridge by-passing Bladensburg, had ordered his army to withdraw from Old Fields to the city to defend the Federal District.

General Winder hastened to Washington on the President's heels on the night of the twenty-third without informing his units at Bladensburg of his intentions.

At the President's House a group of Virginia militia officers appealed for arms for their units. They had previously requested weapons from Secretary of War Armstrong, but, believing they were not necessary for the defense of Washington because he still insisted the English were moving on Baltimore, he had refused to issue them. President Madison sent instructions to Armstrong to arm the Virginians. At nine PM a weary and confused General Winder surprised the President who had assumed his General was at Bladensburg confronting the enemy. Monroe had sent word that an attack was imminent. The President ordered the exhausted and uncomprehending Winder back to the Navy Yard to rest; Winder was limping from an injury suffered when he fell off his horse; rushing to and fro, he had exhausted three mounts during the day.

The next morning, August 24th, Winder sent a message to the President requesting an urgent meeting at his headquarters at the Navy Yard. Monroe and Buster also attended. They had no sooner arrived than Madison dispatched them back to Bladensburg to help position the defense, which anticipated immediate attack. Secretary Armstrong and an aide arrived late, greatly irritating the exasperated President. Armstrong opined that the militia would have no chance to defeat regular troops then remained silent. Madison in anger ordered Armstrong to Bladensburg to assist General Winder in defending the city. The President dispatched General Winder to lead his troops to Bladensburg and reunite his army. President Madison, carrying a pair of dueling pistols and accompanied by aides, hurried along behind. It took an hour to reach their destination.

The President, riding hard, passed the weary militia and entered the center of Bladensburg, halting at a bridge. A single sentry, surprised by the President's sudden appearance, warned that they were about to be encircled by the enemy, and the aging President led his weary group back within American lines.

On a nearby hill they found General Winder, Secretary of State Monroe, Buster and Secretary of War Armstrong. A still angry Madison asked Armstrong if he had advised General Winder, and Armstrong replied he had not but would do so if ordered; the President instructed him to do so. Gunfire made conversation difficult; finally, the President directed the cabinet members to return with him to Washington and to leave the fighting to the soldiers.

The British, facing numbers twice that of their own, attacked in waves. The battle, which began at one, was over by four. The concentrated English firing and the frightening roar of the ineffective Congreve rockets terrified the undisciplined American troops. The American line collapsed into Winder's advancing militia rushing to help.

General Winder, dismayed by the chaos, ordered a general retreat in the hopes of regrouping his forces for a defense closer to Washington. Commodore Barney and his seamen provided a covering fire that held the English at bay long enough for the panic that was later described as the "Bladensburg Races" to ensue.

The running militia overtook the President and his Cabinet on the road to Washington.

After arrival at the President's House, it did not take long for President Madison to decide that defense of the city was hopeless. He ordered General Winder to regroup his forces at the Montgomery Court House and to make his plans for a counter attack there. Finally, President Madison departed for Virginia to join with his wife who had fled hours earlier accompanied by a wagon load of White House treasures including a portrait of George Washington that had been wrenched from the wall.

Everything had proceeded smoothly for General Ross and Admiral Cockburn. As they marched towards Bladensburg on August 23rd, Admiral Cockburn felt compelled to honor his commitment to their Commander-in-Chief, Admiral Cochrane, to send his aide Lieutenant Scott back to Benedict to inform the Admiral of their progress to date and plans for attack. He did so, waiting until what he thought was the last minute, but the Admiral responded promptly. On the morning of August 24th, just as dawn was breaking, an exhausted Lieutenant Scott appeared with an order: the force was to return immediately to Benedict and re-embark. The Admiral had gotten cold feet. Cockburn, too close to turn back, discussed the matter with General Ross; both men acknowledged the implications of disregarding a direct order, but they agreed they could not turn back with their target a short sixteen miles away. At Admiral Cockburn's urging, General Ross gave the fateful order to attack. Tactical decisions on land were his.

Buster whose role had been reduced to that of observer parted from Monroe as soon as they had reached the District and galloped for Alexandria to alert his family. He threaded his way across the long bridge, which was packed with fleeing refugees and their possessions. On the Virginia shore he turned south and rushed to Jason's office. With apprehension, remembering his unfulfilled promise to keep his father informed, Buster mounted the stairs. He burst into his father's office and caught Jason in mid sentence.

"And here is the inconsiderate and unappreciative son," Jason continued, turning from Skinny to his son.

"I'm sorry dad. I didn't keep my promise."

"I know that," Jason laughed sourly.

"I was with Secretary Monroe scouting the English."

"I know that, too. Couldn't you two important leaders have found a better way to organize our defense than ride around spying on the English like a couple of privates?"

"We had no choice. Everything was in chaos."

"And the entire country knows that too."

"The British are entering Washington as we speak, and a flotilla is coming up the Potomac to attack Alexandria. Fort Washington will not be able to hold them."

"Even Skinny knows that. What other invaluable information did you acquire?" Jason shook his head in disgust.

"What are you doing about your ships? The 'Clipper?'" Buster knew how much it would pain his father to lose the "Clipper."

"The only thing we can do," Jason replied. "Toddy has taken the 'Clipper I' and the two schooners and sailed them upriver as close to the falls as he can get them. I told him to anchor them close to shore, tie lines for balance and face all of his cannon to the river. If the English try to take them, they'll pay a price. Skinny and I plan to join Toddy at the last minute, and we will fight them till they die."

Buster recognized his father had no choice. The British flotilla blocked his path to the Bay, and the Anacostia River was not navigable for the ocean sailing ships.

"They'll take Alexandria and burn the shipyard if not the town. Cockburn is a savage."

"Your friend Cruiky and his pals are preparing to surrender Alexandria," Jason said in disgust. "Not a fighter among them. The town has voted to surrender."

Buster walked to the window and looked down on the shipyard. Workers were rushing about loading tools and supplies on wagons.

"I'm moving as much as possible. The British will take all the naval stores they can lay their hands on."

"What about the two ships in the slips?" Buster referred to the keels of the two vessels that were under construction.

"There's nothing we can do. I can't even sink them."

"Dad, I'm sorry. There's nothing I could have told you if I had stayed here that you haven't already learned."

"I know, son," Jason agreed. "I was just venting my frustration. It's that fool Jefferson and his friend Madison's fault. Jefferson and his silly gunboats. The frigates just flick them away like gnats."

"I agree," Buster said. "I tried my best."

"I know you did son. Have you seen Nancy?"

"No. I must get home now."

"She's at the paper. She and Vivian are rushing to keep these fools informed." Jason's words halted Buster.

"And Gramps?"

"He's at home. He's not feeling well."

"I've got to see him too," Buster called as he rushed for the stairs.

Buster had worried about visiting his father but confronting his wife troubled him more. He had thoughtlessly rushed out of town without informing her of his plans. At a time of crisis, he had abandoned his family without a word.

Buster remounted his horse and galloped through the crowd to the newspaper office. The door was wide open, and he rushed in. Nancy and Vivian and the two reporters sat around Buster's old worktable writing furiously. Scottie sat at his little table in the corner scribbling his own report. The printing press clanked. One of the freedmen was setting type and the other feeding paper into the machine.

"Daddy," Scot called, spotting Buster first.

"Hello darling," Nancy smiled without pausing with her report.

"The British are coming, dear," Vivian's eyes sparkled as she spoke.

"I'm so sorry, Nancy. I rushed off and left you and Scottie to worry. I was thoughtless."

"I know dear. President Madison was kind enough to inform me. He gave me the first news of the English landing, and we got out an extra."

"We mentioned you and Secretary Monroe kindly," Vivian interjected. "Brave scouts, stalking the dreadful English."

"But I should have told you," Buster persisted. He knew he would not get off this easy. "There was no time."

"That's all right dear," Nancy smiled. "We can discuss it another time. We're really very busy now."

Buster stood dumbfounded, watching his wife and grandmother putting out his newspaper.

"Go change your clothes and get back to your Mr. Monroe. I'm sure there is much you have to do."

Instead of doing what he was told, Buster pulled a chair to the table and sat next to his wife and began writing furiously.

"What is that?" Nancy asked.

"The story of the Bladensburg Races," Buster replied.

AUGUST 24/27, 1814

WASHINGTON IN FLAMES

Buster completed his story on the "Bladensburg Races," slid it across the table to Nancy, rose, and with his son, Scottie, in tow headed for the connecting door.

"Wait dear," Nancy called.

Buster paused and did what he was told.

"This is excellent," Nancy declared after reading the first paragraph.

Then, to Buster's dismay, she picked up a pencil and began editing his copy as she read. Buster was proud of his clear, legible prose and could not stand and watch his wife correct it. When he had been editor, she had had nothing but praise for his stories, and now she was editing his best first hand account ever.

"I'll wash, change clothes, then I have to get back to Washington," he announced.

"Be careful dear," Nancy said, distracted as she read. "And do come back quickly when you get another story like this one. The readers will like it."

"The English are coming up the river and will arrive in Washington momentarily," Buster declared. "I doubt you will have another edition."

"People always want to know what's going on," Nancy responded.

"Cruiky is going to surrender Alexandria," Vivian announced, repeating the subject of the headline story she was writing.

"And the militia is preparing to destroy the long bridge on this end so the English cannot cross from Washington," Nancy added.

"What?" Buster asked, shocked.

"Yes," Nancy affirmed. "So you had better hurry if you are returning to the city."

"You may have to take the ferry back," Vivian added.

Buster was amazed. The two women, his wife and grandmother, were so engrossed with getting out the *Herald* that they did not comprehend what the arrival of English troops meant. Buster understood. If he had not witnessed the marching English troops and the terrible devastation at Bladensburg, he might have reacted as they were, writing as if they were describing a big game, but the Congreve rockets flashing overhead, and Captain Barney's roaring artillery, and the bloodshed and sheer panic were impossible to describe. He felt a terrible responsibility for what was happening. He recalled how blithely he had voted to declare war while knowing full well that the country was totally unprepared. He could now understand James' incomprehensive disbelief as he had watched the drama unfold. Buster was now determined to make up for his naivete.

Scottie accompanied his father and watched as he shaved, bathed quickly from a porcelain wash pot, and dressed. He threw James Monroe's grimy clothes into a corner wondering if he would have a chance to return them to his friend.

At the door, Buster paused to embrace and kiss his son and to promise to return soon to tell him about the war. Buster led the horse he had been riding—he did not recall where he had acquired the sad creature—to the barn, turned him over to the African who worked in the yard, saddled one of his own horses, and set out for the great falls where Toddy had anchored Jason's ships.

After the thunderous three-hour battle at Bladensburg and the mad flight of the American militia, General Ross and Admiral Cockburn paused and gave their men a chance to rest and regroup before continuing the some ten miles to Washington. The delay also gave the fleeing Americans a chance to clear the area. General Ross aptly perceived that a too aggressive pursuit might provoke a defensive response; he gave the panic a chance to spread.

As his officers reported, General Ross had been able to gauge the intensity of the battle. Captain Barney and his seamen had effectively managed their cannons and had been responsible for the most damage the Americans had inflicted. General Ross' statistics indicated his troops had suffered almost two hundred casualties, sixty-four of whom were dead. He estimated the American losses were three times higher. He knew he had been lucky. If the American defense had been properly organized, the superior numbers supported by artillery would have defeated his small army. General Ross was thankful that Admiral Cockburn's estimate of the American militia's fighting prowess had been accurate.

At six in the evening, General Ross ordered his troops to reform for the march on Washington. He could have rested overnight at Bladensburg, but he agreed with Admiral Cockburn's conclusion that they should continue the action, take Washington, while the American troops were in a disorderly retreat and the English professionals high on victory.

General Ross and Admiral Cockburn were in the van when the English forward elements approached the American Capitol.

When Buster reached the great falls about five o'clock in the afternoon, he found Jason's ships anchored in a semicircle some distance from shore. He obtained a ride to "Clipper I" in one of the longboats that shuttled from ship to shore ferrying ammunition and balls. He found Toddy on the quarterdeck anxiously gazing down river.

After greeting his cousin, Buster described the action at Bladensburg and the confusion in Washington and Alexandria.

"There's still no sign of the English on the river," Buster said when he noted Toddy's anxious looks to the south.

"Your father wanted me to anchor close to the shore, but this is the best I could do," Toddy glanced towards the Virginia shoreline some fifty yards away. "The river's too shallow. The "Clipper's" aground here."

"Your threat will come from the frigates," Buster opined. "The English have no artillery, and our militia plans on destroying the bridge."

"How much time do we have?"

"I don't know," Buster replied honestly. "Their army is approaching Washington, I'm sure, but I don't know where their ships are."

"Do you think they will come this far upriver?"

"You're a better judge of that than I. Is the channel deep enough for their ships?"

"That depends on what they send. Sea going vessels can reach Georgetown," Toddy indicated the sister port to Alexandria located on the Maryland shore about a quarter of a mile from where they were anchored. "I'm not sure their frigates can come this far north, but certainly their schooners can. We could have a chance against schooners trying to maneuver in the narrow channel. At least I tried to set up my field of fire to catch them as they come around that bend." Toddy pointed down river.

"What we need is information," Buster opined, anxious to find out what was happening in Washington.

"I'm almost organized here," Toddy volunteered.

"Jason said he and Skinny would join you here when the British appear off Alexandria."

"And you're sure there are no English ships in sight?"

"None when I left Alexandria a half an hour ago."

"Then let's cross to Washington," Toddy said. "I must find out what kind of ships the English have in the river."

The two Satterfields commandeered one of the "Clipper's" long boats and had the rowers take them to the Georgetown shore. They left the boat and two men there with instructions to wait for their return. They captured two loose horses they found wandering in the confused melee in central Georgetown and galloped against the tide of fleeing citizens and militia towards the President's House. Buster wanted to meet with the President and Secretary Monroe and learn the latest.

"You're headin' in the wrong direction," several of the militia warned them.

"The English are in the town."

The two cousins rushed along Jefferson's road, one of his few positive contributions to the national city, arriving at the President's House about dusk. They tied their horses in front and rushed in through the open door. Inside, they found one servant absently staring at the table in the formal dining room.

The table was set for a formal dinner. Plates and silver were in place; wine cooled in ice on a serving table and linen was distributed.

"Da President plans to entertain some of da cabinet and officers," the servant explained, having recognized Buster.

In the kitchen they found legs of lamb and shanks of beef turning on spits. Pots and pans filled with food set waiting on the grates. Buster grabbed a long loaf of fresh baked bread, broke it in half and handed a share to Toddy. He had not paused to realize he was famished.

"I be watchin' da meat," the bewildered African explained.

"Where is Mr. Madison?" Buster asked kindly.

"He be gone and Miss Dolly too."

"Do you know where?"

"Miss Dolly left with Massa Freeman, da butler, and da wagons. Den da President done come, looked around, den went to da ferry. Whar dey is or wen dey come I don' know."

Chewing on their bread, Buster and Toddy strolled through the downstairs rooms. Everywhere was evidence of a hasty departure. Dolly's infamous yellow damask covered furniture remained, but the rooms showed signs of panic. Drawers were open, and linens draped over the side. In the large oval room they surprised two militiamen, looting. Buster hollered, and the two men fled through an open door. Buster tripped over some wood. He looked down and saw the discarded frame from George Washington's portrait. It appeared as if the frame had been broken when pried from the wall. The picture had been taken, but the frame discarded.

A sudden explosion shocked both Toddy and Buster.

"That's powder not cannon fire," Toddy observed professionally.

They rushed to the porch and saw flames reaching skyward.

"Somebody's set the navy yard on fire," Buster opined.

"The English must be close."

The two cousins rushed back to their horses but found them gone.

"Let's go up Pennsylvania Avenue towards the Capitol," Buster suggested.

"Carefully," Toddy agreed. "We don't want to be shot by a frightened militiaman or the English."

Pennsylvania Avenue was deserted. The few houses were dark with doors and shutters closed. They passed the French Ambassador's house and saw a man standing on the porch. He waved.

"That's Monsieur Serurier," Buster said as he waved back.

In the distance the flames at the Navy Yard burned high into the sky.

"The naval stores must be burning," Toddy said, pointing at the columns of black, acrid smoke coiling into the darkness. The sun had set, and twilight had descended on the city. They noted the open doors of the abandoned government buildings.

As they approached a point midway between the President's House and the Capitol, several men came running out of the gloom towards them.

"The English are at the Capitol," one of them warned.

Toddy and Buster paused and studied each other.

General Ross had stopped his horse in front of the Capitol and turned to study the American parliament building when several musket shots rang out. His horse tumbled to the ground throwing Ross to the side. Admiral Cockburn dismounted and rushed to the General's aid.

"I'm all right," General Ross said, rising to his feet and ineffectively attempting to brush the dust from his dirty uniform.

The general's horse lay dead several feet away.

"Clear that building and burn it," Cockburn shouted to several English soldiers who were milling nearby, unsure what to do. They had been instructed not to harm private structures until fired upon from them.

The soldiers rushed into the house on the square found that whoever had fired the shots had fled, then set it on fire. Soon the Capitol was bathed in the eerie light of the reflected flames. Troops of the Third Regiment deployed in a line in front of the odd structure—two ornate wings with a temporary structure connecting them. On the order of Lieutenant Evans, they fired warning shots into the structures and then advanced slowly. Once inside, they found the buildings empty. The troops rushed about collecting chairs, tables, papers, books, anything they thought would burn, and stacked them against the walls.

Admiral Cockburn and General Ross strolled through the buildings as the soldiers hurried about their duty, shouting and laughing as they worked. Admiral Cockburn retrieved a document, "An Account of the Receipts and Expenditures of the United States for the Year 1810," which he took as a souvenir. The two commanders chatted as they waited for the soldiers to light their fires. Once satisfied the building was burning well, they retreated outside. Admiral Cockburn mounted his horse, and General Ross acquired a replacement from his aide who had commandeered it from another officer.

They looked about them. Encountering minimum resistance, the English soldiers were fanning out through the rough city. Occasional shots rang out as the soldiers encountered deserters and looters. A few houses erupted into flames, victims of reprisals by angry Englishmen. As the two commanders watched, flames began to consume deserted government buildings.

"I do believe the Americans have presented us a gift," Admiral Cockburn smiled broadly, the flames casting shadows across his handsome face.

The two men, preceded by several lines of troops and surrounded by guards, made their way down the now illuminated Pennsylvania Avenue. Behind them, flames crept up the walls of the Capitol.

"Shall we pay our respects to Jemmie and Dolly?" Cockburn asked, using his favorite word for disparaging the American President.

From where Toddy and Buster stood, the dispersing troops appeared to be shadows darting to and fro as the fires behind them backlighted their dashing figures. They too heard the random shots.

"We best get out of here," Toddy warned.

Without answering, Buster pivoted and ran with Toddy at his heels back down Pennsylvania Avenue towards the President's House.

When they reached the French Minister's residence which was clearly marked by a large flag, Buster stopped to catch his breath.

"You go back to Georgetown and your ships," he gasped. "I'm staying here." He pointed at the French Minister's house. "I want to see for myself what the English do."

Toddy paused to argue.

"The English don't have enough troops to hold the city. This is a raid," Buster explained. "I want to be able to report to the President with accuracy what they have done."

"You won't be able to see much from there," Toddy protested. "And they may not respect the Frenchman's flag. I assure you, you don't want to be an English prisoner." Toddy could almost feel the heat of the flames on his scarred back.

"No. You go," Buster shoved his cousin. "I know what I'm doing."

A shot rang out nearby, and Toddy turned and ran along the road to Georgetown.

Flames leaped skyward from the Capitol and four nearby buildings where congressional papers had been stored.

Cockburn and Ross dismounted in front of the President's House and entered. If he could have, Cockburn would have rode his horse through the front door. Inside, they found the building deserted. Cockburn chuckled with glee when he found the formal dining room with the set table and cooling wine. They toured the kitchen, the oval room, and the other reception areas before mounting the stairs to the second floor. There, they studied the open drawers and abandoned personal possessions of the Madisons. Half-packed boxes and traveling cases littered the rooms.

"I do believe Jemmie and Dolly departed in a hurry," Cockburn observed.

Cockburn reached into a packing case and extracted a snow white dress shirt with ruffles and an embroidered front. To Ross' amazement, Cockburn quickly took off his dirty jacket and soiled shirt and donned James Madison's formal shirt. It fit snugly but buttoned. Several of his companions followed the Admiral's example. With this one exception, the Admiral forbade looting and placed guards on the doors. He and Ross returned to the formal dining room where the two commanders laughingly gathered, surrounded by staff officers. Cockburn seated them at the table then formally poured the wine.

"To Jemmie," Cockburn stood at the head of the table and raised his glass in toast to the absent President.

His guests raised their glasses and repeated the phrase: "To Jemmie."

The officers seized plates and followed their commanders into the kitchen where they filled them with crudely cut slices of lamb and beef. They returned to the dining room and quickly ate. When finished, Cockburn took one quick, final tour of the downstairs, lifted a pillow from the seat of a side chair in the main sitting room, and declared:

"So I can place my bottom where the lovely Dolly has placed hers. To remind me of her bountiful presence."

He laughed uproariously then stamped to the front door with his arm across General Ross' shoulders and the pillow under his opposite elbow.

As they exited the door, Admiral Cockburn looked inquiringly at General Ross who nodded.

"Burn it," Cockburn ordered, then walked briskly to his horse without looking back.

Once he was mounted, a civilian approached.

"I am Minister Serurier. I represent the people of France, and our countries are not at war."

Admiral Cockburn, in a congenial mood, nodded and raised his hat in a mocking gesture of respect.

"Admiral Cockburn of His Majesty's Navy. And this is General Ross." Cockburn waved deferentially toward his companion. "How may we serve you?"

"Please spare our house. It is the property of the people of France." Serurier pointed to the building marked with a large French flag.

"But of course, sir," Cockburn replied sarcastically. "Our troops have orders to spare private dwellings. We certainly have no wish to offend the French people."

Cockburn turned and ordered that a guard be posted to protect the French Minister's house.

"And now, sir," Cockburn excused himself from the fawning Frenchman. "We have duty to perform."

During the night, the excited English troops torched the public buildings. Many were ignited under the personal direction of Cockburn and Ross. In addition to the White House and the Capitol, the Treasury, War Office, National Archives including a splendid and irreplaceable library accumulated to assist Congress' efforts, barracks, stores, powder magazines and several private homes fell to the flames. Only the Patent Office where a clerk persuaded the English soldiers that the papers were the private papers of individual American citizens was saved. Admiral Cockburn took particular pleasure in supervising the destruction of the offices of the *National Intelligencer*, the subsidized outlet of Jefferson, Madison and the Republican Party, which had denigrated him as the "Scourge of the Chesapeake." Cockburn watched as troops dumped trays filled with lead type into the street and stamped on it.

"Make sure you get all the 'C's,'" Cockburn called with a laugh. "So they can't abuse me any more."

At the long bridge over the Potomac, troops set fire to the nearest spans while across the river in Virginia the militia was doing the same thing to prevent the English from attacking their shore.

At midnight a violent seasonal thunderstorm struck and dampened some of the flames, but the drenched English soldiers enthusiastically worked through the night. Many had found abandoned stocks of wine and rum that they cheerfully shared with their friends. Despite the hilarity, the troops spared the citizens they encountered and their private homes, only a few of which were accidentally ignited by nearby fires.

During the night, Buster huddled miserably in the French Minister's home. He took notes and listened to the rumors, but he could see little.

At the great falls, Toddy waited as he watched the fires burning in the distance.

In Alexandria, Jason fumed as he plotted with Skinny, determined to do what he could to subvert the city council that under Cruiky's leadership had decided to save the city. The town fathers pleaded with the militia to leave their town and let them meet with the approaching English ships in order to work out an amnesty, giving the English what they wanted in return for a promise to spare Alexandria. Jason encouraged the militia to fight, but he sensed a waning spirit, particularly as the flames rose over Washington across the river. The militia officers themselves were confused, unable to decide whether to prepare their defense against the approaching ships or to anticipate an attack from the army across the Potomac. Late at night, most Alexandrians, thankful that they lived in Virginia and not in Washington or Georgetown, went to bed anxious about what the next day would bring.

Admiral Cockburn rose at dawn the next day, somehow acquired a wide, white mare, and rode conspicuously down the center of Pennsylvania Avenue to satisfy himself that the destruction was sufficient. He passed the President's House, nodded at the smoldering ruins, and surveyed the other government buildings. Where necessary, he directed troops in their efforts. At the Navy Yard, he found a rope walk filled with hemp and tar and offered advice which soon sent a towering pillar of billowing black smoke skyward. At mid morning he returned to Dr. Ewell's house near the Capitol where he and Ross had established a temporary headquarters. There, Cockburn found an anxious Ross preparing to withdraw.

A powder magazine was discovered at a point near the Eastern Branch. Ordered to destroy the powder, English soldiers enterprisingly dumped the kegs down a deep well. Unknown to them, the powder soon rose in a stack above water level. Somehow, an unfortunate accident ignited the exposed powder—none lived to explain how it happened—and the powder exploded, killing twelve English soldiers and injuring thirty others.

About noon a sudden tornado struck the town, uprooting trees and tearing roofs off the buildings that were not burning. The storm quickly subsided, and Ross and Cockburn met at Ewell's to assess their actions. During the day, Ross had met with obsequious delegations from Georgetown and Alexandria who had pleaded that their towns be spared. Having no intention of diverting his forces or assuming the delay that such attacks would require, Ross had been noncommittal. Convinced that they had destroyed all of the city's public buildings and pleased with their success, they decided to withdraw.

They declared a public curfew for civilians; no one but authorized personnel was to be permitted on the streets after eight P.M. In order to cover their retreat, they waited until sunset. Their troops lighted campfires and tried to give the impression they were settling for the night. They did not want to face an aroused countryside and suffer the ignominy that their predecessors had during a raid on Concord during the Revolution. Both commanders wanted an orderly and disciplined withdrawal. They had heard rumors that the Americans were reforming nearby and planning for a counter-attack.

At nine P.M., the three columns formed, and the silent soldiers, carrying as many wounded as they could, set out for Bladensburg and Marlborough. At Bladensburg, they halted for an hour and waited for the stragglers to rally. Then, without further delay, they continued on to Marlborough. There, feeling more secure, they rested their exhausted troops for seven hours.

At Nottingham, Admiral Cockburn recovered his waiting tenders and boats and prepared a report for Admiral Cochrane. Cockburn and his marines and seamen then followed the Patuxent while Ross and his soldiers marched. On Monday, August 29th, the troops arrived at Benedict having victoriously completed their fifty-mile inland raid on the American capital. The exhausted troops rested on shore that night and boasted of their exploits; on August thirtieth they re-embarked on their ships and set sail.

WASHINGTON AND ALEXANDRIA

AUGUST 27/28, 1814

On Friday morning, August 27th, Buster woke in Minister Jean Mathhieu Serurier's house to silence punctuated only by the sound of chirping cardinals and finches. He listened for the noise of random gunfire but heard nothing. He hurriedly dressed and rushed downstairs. The front door was open, and he cautiously peered out. The Frenchman was standing on his porch studying the smoking remains of the President's House.

"I belief the English have lef'," The Frenchman said. "I listen, and I hear nothin' but birds."

As they watched, Buster heard doors and shutters opening as nearby residents cautiously probed the safety of their environment.

"Such destruction," the Frenchman shook his head. "The Emperor was never this bad."

"I'm going to check the Capitol," Buster said.

He shook hands with his host, thanked him for his gracious sanctuary and for ignoring the risk of being accused of concealing the enemy, and departed.

Other careful citizens were exploring Pennsylvania Avenue. Buster was appalled when he saw the damage that Admiral Cockburn had left behind. Every identifiable government building had been burned. Buster passed the wreckage of his rival, the National *Intelligencer*, and made a mental note to remind Nancy to print additional copies of the *Herald*. If she hurried her next edition, she could beat their Georgetown competitor. Newspapers nationwide would reprint her stories of the destruction of Washington. If she got her papers on the first stages, she would be read by the nation.

This realization prodded Buster to walk more quickly. He hurried up Pennsylvania Avenue to the Capitol. He surveyed the ruins and paused to talk with Doctor Ewell whose house had been appropriated by the British commanders. Ewell himself had been drafted into service as an intermediary between the

English and the townspeople. Thanks to his intervention, many local homes and boarding houses had been saved. Ewell quickly briefed Buster on what he had seen and heard. Buster continued on to the Navy Yard where he surveyed the devastation, some caused by the English and much by the yard commander trying to deny supplies to the invaders. On his return, Buster met Doctor Thornton who was caring for the seriously wounded the English had left behind, unable to transport them back to the ships. Dr. Thornton had promised Ross and Cockburn that the abandoned English soldiers would be fairly treated. Buster did not know if they would be or not.

Finally satisfied that he adequately understood what had happened to Washington, Buster appropriated a wandering horse and rode towards the bridge. There, he discovered that the bridge had been destroyed from both ends. Desperately, he looked around, wondering if he would have to ride all the way to the chain bridge to cross the Potomac. He was about to turn northward when to his surprise he saw the ferry crossing from the Virginia side. It had one passenger. When the ferry landed, Buster recognized Cruiky who was serving as Alexandria's intermediary.

"You're too late, Cruiky," Buster called, relishing the flash of disappointment that crossed Cruikstaff's face.

Buster realized that Jason would draw considerable satisfaction from Buster's description of that look.

"What do you mean?"

"The English army's gone. Check for yourself. They sneaked away in the darkness last night."

The ferryman cheered and asked excited questions as Buster led his horse aboard. Buster imagined he could see the man mentally counting the money his ferry would earn as he took the place of the destroyed bridge.

"He says the English ships are still coming up the river to destroy Alexandria, and he's working to save it," the ferryman blurted, pointing at Cruiky.

Buster turned to speak to Cruiky but was treated to the sight of his back as he galloped away.

"Don't want to say anything for the newspaper, Cruiky?" Buster called, unable to keep his satisfaction out of his voice.

Alexandria's emissary ignored him.

When Buster reached the Virginia shore, he rode hard for Alexandria. Back at the newspaper, he rushed in and found James, Vivian, Nancy and Jason sitting around the worktable drinking tea. The two freedmen and Scottie were doing likewise in the back of the room.

"Buster," Nancy shouted, relief on her face, as she hurried to embrace him. "We were so worried. Toddy told us you stayed behind, then we heard the explosions, the noise and saw all the flame and smoke"

"I'm all right," Buster reassured the assembled Satterfields. "I spent the time safely with the French Minister. This morning I toured the city. If we hurry, we can get out an edition, put it on the stages, and the *Herald* will be the first to tell the country what happened here."

As Buster hurriedly related everything he had seen and heard, Vivian, Nancy and James took notes. When he finished, James took command.

"I will write about the army, Cockburn and Ross and their sneaky departure. Who wants to report the fires and the destruction?"

"I will," Vivian volunteered.

"And I will describe the people, Ewell, the French Minister, Doctor Thornton, the prisoners, what happened at the *Intelligencer*, particularly that, and the explosion at the Navy Yard and the burning of the bridge," Nancy decided.

The two freedmen prepared their press.

"Son, let's leave the staff to their work and you and I step outside," Jason said, taking Buster's arm and leading him towards the door. "And don't forget the English ships coming our way, and Madison and Dolly and Monroe and the rest of the government spread all over the county," Jason called back to remind his family of the other stories.

"Maybe I should help," Buster paused at the door.

"They can handle it. You've done your job, so far," Jason said, pulling Buster on to the porch.

"I saw Cruiky this morning," Buster reported, anticipating his father's concern.

Buster related the incident at the ferry.

"There's a frigate and two schooners sailing this way," Jason said, shaking his head. "The town council is trying to mediate. They want Cruiky to offer the English anything they want if they don't burn the town."

"The militia?"

"They pulled out last night."

"That's for the best," Buster observed. "Since their army has withdrawn, maybe the squadron will turn around and leave us alone."

"And maybe not. Those ships will want their share of the glory. After coming all this way, they may not want to let the army take all the credit."

"They're probably Cockburn's sailors," Buster agreed. "They'll know how to pillage and burn."

"We had a couple of incidents last night," Jason said.

Buster waited for his father to explain.

"Some of the rowdies at the Pig got drunk and decided the town should fight the English. A couple of citizens tried to persuade them otherwise; a fight developed, and two were killed, one rowdy and one citizen. The militia took the ring leaders with them."

"What do you think we should do?"

"Since the army's gone, Cruiky's right. We should talk with the English and try to persuade them to leave. It goes against the grain paying the damned English not to attack us. That's what we fought the Revolution for."

"What about Toddy and the "Clipper?""

"They'll be all right if the English stop here. If not, we'll fight them. I'll not let them take my ships. We'll sink them first."

"When will they get here?"

"Probably tomorrow, if the latest fisherman to arrive from the Bay can be believed."

Buster realized that his problems were not over.

"What should I do?"

"I suggest you find Madison and your friend Monroe and tell them what happened in Washington and what might develop here. Tell them to keep the militia out of Alexandria and let us handle it. We don't need the treatment that their ineptitude caused in Washington."

After talking with his father, Buster again changed his clothes while chatting with his goggle eyed son, spoke briefly with his wife, saddled a fresh horse and set off in search of President Madison. Jason had heard he had spent the night at the home of Reverend John Maffitt some five miles from Wiley's Tavern near Great Falls. When he arrived at Maffitt's, Buster learned that Madison had indeed slept there but had departed in search of his wife Dolly. Buster dutifully followed Madison to Falls Church then onward to Rokeby only a mile from the Maffitt's where apparently Dolly had spent the night. Unfortunately for Buster, Dolly, pursued by her husband, had moved on to Wiley's at Great Falls. At dusk the tired, elderly Madison who had spent most of the past three days in the saddle rushing from Washington to Bladensburg and back and then to Virginia was reunited with his wife. Two hours later, Buster, in darkness, also arrived.

He reported to Madison his account of the destruction of Washington and the English departure. He also related the threat to Alexandria and Jason's appeal that Madison restrain the militia who might irresponsibly provoke the English into reprisals. Madison agreed and dispatched the necessary orders. Dolly and her party spent the night at Wiley's.

At midnight, President Madison, Buster and several companions departed Wiley's for Conn's ferry above Great Falls. Buster would have preferred to stay at Wiley's and wait for morning, but the President insisted he had to regain command of his government and army. At Conn's ferry, the tired party found the river raging from the recent storms and were forced to wait, wet and weary, for dawn when the ferryman finally agreed to test the angry current. After reaching the Maryland shore, Madison began his search for General Winder. When they finally reached the Montgomery Court House, the President was dismayed to learn that the elusive Winder who often mistook frantic rushing about for action had departed hours earlier for Baltimore to prepare the city to repel an anticipated English attack. Secretary of State Monroe who had joined with Winder before Madison's belated arrival had traveled to Baltimore with Winder. Madison at least found this small piece of news encouraging.

Unwilling to give up his quest to regain command of his government, Madison and his party, including Buster, rode an additional ten miles to the home of Henrietta Bentley. A helpful Quaker, she prepared beds in her parlor for the exhausted party. Madison by this time had spent more than eighteen hours in the saddle. Buster had the terrible feeling that he was repeating the hectic events that preceded the battle at Bladensburg, following the government as it rushed frantically from one place to another, accomplishing nothing.

The next day, Madison dispatched riders to find Secretary of War Armstrong, Secretary of State Monroe, and Secretary of the Treasury George Campbell, instructing them to meet him in Washington. Madison, Buster and their party then departed Mrs. Bentley's and headed for Washington. Madison was distressed by what he found but insisted on inspecting his city immediately.

Buster, who still doubted the Mouse's capacity for leadership, was impressed by the old man's stamina and determination to perform his job. While they were touring the city and listening to complaining citizens, they heard a large explosion in the distance. Buster immediately feared the English squadron had arrived and was attacking Alexandria. Later, he learned he was only half-right. The English squadron had arrived as he had anticipated, but the explosion had been set by the commander of Fort Washington, a small gun position overlooking the Potomac whose mission was to defend the capital from attack by river. The fort commander had evacuated the fort and exploded his powder without firing a shot after the English squadron's appearance.

While Buster accompanied Madison on his tour of Washington, Alexandria negotiated with Captain James Alexander Gordon. Cruiky, hat in hand and accompanied by two quaking fellow members of the council, sailed out to the English frigate which had anchored off Alexandria and had begun to menace the city with its guns. Skinny and Jason watched the event from their office, and James and Vivian viewed from their porch. James had difficulty keeping up with the kaleidoscopic change of events of the past week.

After considerable negotiation and several hours of fawning, Cruiky returned to shore.

Captain Gordon was delighted with the report he had heard of Admiral Cockburn's successes. He was sure that he would receive credit for having created a successful diversion, his main tactical task, but he was disappointed at his late arrival. The various storms and subsequent raging current had delayed his transit of the unfamiliar waters. He was determined, therefore, to extract his own modest victory. He had been tempted to turn his guns on the city and punish it as Cockburn had the capital, but he exercised restraint when Cruiky's delegation promised considerable spoils in return for the sparing of the city.

Captain Gordon's small flotilla anchored off Alexandria overnight, continuing to menace the city with its guns. The Captain smiled with anticipation as his sailors in longboats and city citizens in a variety of craft streamed between the city docks and his ships. In the end Alexandria paid as ransom over one hundred tons of tobacco, flour, naval stores and merchandise that had filled the holds of the merchant ships in its harbor and the floors of its many warehouses. In addition Captain Gordon confiscated twenty-one schooners and cutters that took his fancy and were needed to transport his spoils. As a punishment, Gordon's men also scuttled several of the larger ships whose owners had not emptied the holds with the alacrity that the English commander felt the situation deserved.

Jason, who had saved most of his goods and his three ships including "Clipper I," relaxed after he learned from Cruiky that the English had agreed to take their booty and depart as soon as it was loaded. Jason realized that if he had not moved his beloved "Clipper" and his three schooners to the great falls that he would have lost them. Now, he was in a position to move his goods back to town and transport them and any others that survived the English plunder at exaggerated prices. He knew exactly who he would charge the most.

In Washington Secretary of State Monroe arrived in time to participate in a discussion between the President and an agitated Doctor Thornton who claimed to represent the citizens of Washington. Worried about the presence of the English ships across the river in Alexandria, the stressed citizens wanted to send a private delegation to the English to negotiate the capitulation of the city without further needless damage. Madison instantly refused. When Doctor Thornton persisted, Madison turned to Monroe, who he had placed in charge of the future defense of the city, and asked what he would do if a delegation attempted to approach the English ships.

"If any delegation attempts to move towards the English," Monroe replied dispassionately. "It will be repelled by bayonet."

President Madison turned to Thornton.

"I believe you have your answer, Doctor," Madison said, dismissing the intermediary.

On the afternoon of Monday, August 29th, the always-belated Secretary of War Armstrong appeared. By that time the army and militia officers who blamed the Secretary for their recent defeats because of his failure to take any actions to prepare for the defense of Washington had made clear their unwillingness to further serve under him. They went so far as to threaten to tear up any orders Armstrong issued. President Madison responded by sending the Secretary on a lengthy vacation to visit his family in New York. Monroe later confided to Buster that Madison had hesitated to dismiss Armstrong outright for fear of causing political damage in the north. One week later, a disgruntled Armstrong who had delayed following the President's orders to take a vacation and had waited in Baltimore where war preparations were under way, submitted his resignation. Armstrong later publicly criticized the President for his conduct and blamed Monroe for the sacking of Washington because he had undermined Armstrong's position in the War Department.

After considerable discussion, Admiral Cochrane accepted Admiral Cockburn's recommendation that the fleet follow up its Washington success by attacking Baltimore. Unfortunately for the English, the eighteen day delay before the decision to attack was made gave a more determined American command the opportunity to prepare for the anticipated assault. Monroe, as acting Secretary of War, made the necessary decisions. J.J. among others was one of the engineers detailed to Baltimore to assist in constructing the needed fortifications. The British attacked; Francis Scott Key wrote his "Star Spangled Banner," and the English were repulsed.

In the aftermath, the Satterfield family continued to thrive. Jason prospered; Toddy sailed "Clipper IV" to the East Indies fulfilling his dream; J.J, stayed in the army; Buster moved from the House to the Senate during President Monroe's first term; Vivian and James ultimately succumbed to the ravages of time; and Scottie... .

Of Scottie, we shall hear more.